DEATH ON THE ICE

A NOVEL

ROBERT RYAN

headline
review

Copyright © 2009 Robert Ryan

The right of Robert Ryan to be identified as the Author of
the Work has been asserted by him in accordance with the
Copyright, Designs and Patents Act 1988.

First published in 2009 by HEADLINE REVIEW
An imprint of HEADLINE PUBLISHING GROUP

First published in paperback in 2009 by HEADLINE REVIEW
An imprint of HEADLINE PUBLISHING GROUP

Cataloguing in Publication Data is available from the British Library

ISBN 978 0 7553 4722 3 (B Format)
ISBN 978 0 7553 5653 9 (A Format)

Typeset in Janson Text by Palimpsest Book Production Limited,
Grangemouth, Stirlingshire

Printed and bound in Great Britain by
Clays Ltd, St lves plc

Headline's policy is to use papers that are natural, renewable and
recyclable products and made from wood grown in sustainable forests.
The logging and manufacturing processes are expected to conform
to the environmental regulations of the country of origin.

HEADLINE PUBLISHING GROUP
An Hachette UK Company
338 Euston Road
London NW1 3BH

www.headline.co.uk
www.hachette.co.uk

For Jonathan Futrell

'What lots and lots I could tell you of this journey. How much better it has been than lounging in too great comfort at home . . . But what a price to pay!'

Robert Falcon Scott, 1912

The majority of temperatures are given in degrees Fahrenheit (except where noted) as used by Scott. In his journals, RFS talked about 'degrees of frost'; this is how many degrees below freezing (32F) the temperature had fallen. So 52 degrees of frost is -20F. Distances are normally measured in geographical or nautical miles, which are 1.15 statute (land) miles.

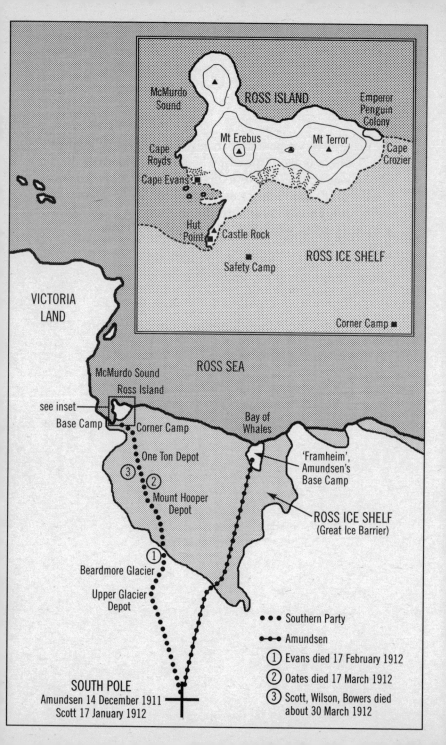

McMurdo Sound

ROSS ISLAND

Emperor Penguin Colony

Mt Erebus

Mt Terror

Cape Royds

Cape Crozier

Cape Evans

Hut Point

Castle Rock

ROSS ICE SHELF

Safety Camp

Corner Camp

VICTORIA LAND

ROSS SEA

McMurdo Sound

Ross Island

see inset

Base Camp

Corner Camp

Bay of Whales

One Ton Depot

③

②

'Framheim', Amundsen's Base Camp

Mount Hooper Depot

ROSS ICE SHELF (Great Ice Barrier)

①

Beardmore Glacier

Upper Glacier Depot

••• Southern Party

•••• Amundsen

① Evans died 17 February 1912

② Oates died 17 March 1912

③ Scott, Wilson, Bowers died about 30 March 1912

SOUTH POLE
Amundsen 14 December 1911
Scott 17 January 1912

Prologue

'*Many a man's reputation would not know his character if they met on the street*'

Elbert Hubbard (1856–1915)

The Western Front, 1917

Lieutenant Teddy Grant saw the woman arrive at the Bellecamp airstrip from the corner of his eye, just as Doyle, his air mechanic, spun the prop. She was stepping out of a staff car that had pulled up next to the farmhouse, lowering herself delicately on to a hastily laid platform of duckboards. A visit by a female who wasn't a nurse to a Royal Flying Corps frontline squadron was rare. Judging by her flamboyant hat, this one was certainly no Florence Nightingale. But Grant quickly dismissed her from his mind. His old friend Soldier used to say: 'They drive all rational thought from your head, replacing it with feathers and ribbons.' When you were charged with shooting down enemy balloons, feathers and ribbons were the last thing you needed fogging your concentration.

The engine caught on Doyle's second attempt. They exchanged thumbs up. Grant was always slightly surprised to see that the Irishman still had all his digits after the hazardous manual start. The mechanic ducked under the wing and yanked the chocks from Grant's wheels, then danced away as the plane immediately began to roll forward.

As usual, the Sopwith bucked, pulled and grumbled as Grant fought with it to keep the taxi line. The Camel was well christened. Like its namesake, it could be capricious and took careful handling. Front heavy, it would bury its nose into the field given the slightest provocation. When the first of the models had arrived a few months previously, they had bent propellers at a prodigious rate. Subsequently, the squadron lost pilots and machines as the airmen struggled to master the snub-faced scout's many idiosyncrasies.

In time, though, Grant had discovered it shared other characteristics with the ship of the desert: it was tough, fast and, if treated right, might just keep its master alive.

He used the blip switch to kill the ignition and slowed the plane to let his wingman, Jeremy Thompson, slip into the forward position. The Yorkshireman raised a gloved hand in thanks.

The strike planners at Wing had specified a pair of veterans were to take out the German 'sausages'. The squadron commander had a choice of two out of two: Thompson and Grant were the only flyers left worthy of the term.

The sun was barely clearing the spindly treetops and had not yet burned off the tendrils of mist, which lay over the whitened grass of the airfield like ribbons of chiffon. The night had brought the first hard frost of the season. The chilled air blasting into his Vaseline-smeared cheeks from the prop wash drove the blood from his face, leaving him waxen.

The cold didn't bother him too much, though. Although he wasn't as impervious to fifty-knot blasts of icy wind as his old colleague Birdie Bowers, Grant didn't suffer unduly from the temperatures found in this part of Europe. He told the other pilots that this was because of the Ontario winters of his childhood, even though Grant had never actually been to Ontario.

The leading Sopwith swung on to the strip. The note of Thompson's Clerget-Bentley engine changed, becoming angrier. Habit made Grant listen for the stutter of an incorrectly set fuel mixture, but there was none. Thompson accelerated along the strip, the plane bouncing over the frost-hardened soil. The ruts reminded Grant of miniature sastrugi, the wind-formed frozen waves on the Antarctic ice cap that confounded dogs, horses and men alike. Thompson's Sopwith lifted smoothly from the earth and banked left, slow and stately, the nose rising as it did so.

Grant followed him on to the ad hoc runway and carefully checked his own fuel mixture and choke. The Camel had a lethal trick it liked to play if the settings weren't to its liking: a stall at fifty or sixty feet after take-off. It had cost more than a few newcomers their lives.

Grant adjusted his goggles and slipped the trailing end of his leather helmet's strap into his mouth, an improvised bite-strap to protect his tongue and teeth from the chattering caused by the furrows in the soil. He turned on the engine once more, feeling the torque twist and snatch at the airframe. With nothing to hold it back, the Sopwith lurched forward and the world blurred as the trees rushed towards him. He pulled back the stick, corrected the inevitable yaw, and followed Thompson skywards, relishing the smoothness after the juddering progress over the field.

The propeller bit confidently into the dense morning air, dragging the plane higher. Grant passed through a hundred feet and listened to the whine of an engine perfectly on song. He sat back to enjoy a few moments of satisfaction.

That morning's sortie was an Army Artillery Coordination mission. Most flights involved offering protection for the slow FE2b photographic planes, which were highly vulnerable to the German scouts. This strike was to take down the tethered inflatables – the sausages – that were spotting Allied movements and calling the Hun artillery down on the infantry's heads.

The kite balloons were fifteen miles to the east, according to the intelligence report. For the first few minutes the Sopwiths passed over deceptively normal French arable countryside. There were cows and sheep and even farmers driving teams of horses; old men who stopped and watched the biplanes climbing. One of them waved. It was hard to believe there was a three-year-old war being waged just over the horizon.

Soon buildings that had lost their roof tiles came into view. Further on, they were mostly reduced to charred skeletons. Some had been re-walled and re-roofed with olive-coloured canvas sheeting, suggesting that they had been resurrected as billets. The woodlands and fields became scarred by bonks, circular blast marks, like an outbreak of smallpox across the land. The first field hospitals appeared, doing their usual brisk business. Nearby were the clearing stations, the repositories of the dead. They, too, were rarely idle. Adjacent to them were mounds of turned earth, like a poorly planned allotment: the careless, makeshift cemeteries of the front.

As the scouts passed through at three thousand feet, they flew over artillery installations and columns of shuffling men, moving to or from the front line. The closely packed bodies made them appear as a continuous dark snake slithering along the poplar-lined roads. They halted or moved aside only for the muscular Suffolk Punches dragging munitions drays overloaded with shells, or the ambulances ferrying the dead and wounded.

Then, directly ahead, Grant saw the familiar corridor of brown muck. It was a three-mile-wide blemish, where the earth was churned by shellfire, scored by deep trenches and sutured together with rusting wire. As he approached, ponds of grey-green water winked prettily in the sun, although Grant knew they were, in reality, pits of slime filled with decomposing bodies. For a number of years his vision of hell had consisted of traversing a crevasse-filled glacier with a blizzard of ice crystals blasting into his face, while trying to drag a two-hundred-pound sledge through thick snow that clogged the runners and fouled his skis. Better a week in those conditions, he now thought, than a single day in the trenches.

There was little movement from either side in the conflict. No puffs of artillery or columns of dirt thrown up by detonations. No senseless charges at chattering machine guns or rolling fogs of yellow gas, ready to turn a Tommy's lungs to foam and blacken his eyes to coal. No man's land was devoid of anything living. It was one of those days when the two sides took stock, like battered prizefighters in their respective corners.

Carefully, Grant scanned the junction of ruined earth and pristine sky. Two specks registered on his retina and he ran a glove over his goggles' lenses to ensure they weren't oil spots.

To his left, he saw Thompson wag his wings. He'd also caught sight of the observation balloons hoisted up above the German lines, floating about half a mile apart. That was unusually close, but it made for an easy division of duty. With a dip of his port wing, Thompson indicated he would take the one on the left. Grant raised a fist in agreement. They were travelling at over a hundred miles an hour now, and still climbing. They would swoop down on the two balloons and blow them out of the sky.

He stared down at the trenches below, imagining the faces staring back. Where was the Archie? On his most recent runs he'd been peppered by anti-aircraft fire. Now, not so much as a single flaming onion streaked up towards them. Nor were there any protective scouts, no sign of a Halberstadt or an Albatross in the cloudless sky.

Count your blessings, he reminded himself.

As they came closer Grant could make out the sausages' suspended gondolas. Ground crews often panicked and began to wind the balloon down as soon as an Allied plane appeared. Or the observers jumped, putting faith in their parachutes opening before they crashed to earth, swallowed by mud in a tangle of broken limbs and silken cords. Or the balloon crew fired on the approaching scouts with their new lightweight machine guns.

None of this happened. The inflatables floated, as vulnerable as the unsuspecting Weddell seals laid out on the ice around their water holes had been.

The two Sopwiths separated, fanning out to their respective targets, and Grant armed the twin Vickers, his feeling of disquiet growing. The balloon was beginning to fill his vision now. He could make out individual ripples in the skin, see the steel tethering cable, slack in the still morning air, the smaller telephone wire that sat next to it, and pick out the crew in their gondola. A crew who weren't, he registered, moving. Where was the usual funk at the appearance of the 'Soppies'?

He checked his rear once more, and then looked across at Thompson. His wingman had taken the Camel's nose down and had begun firing. His glowing tracers punctured the envelope at the midline, the shape already collapsing in on itself, pulsing like a jellyfish. Thompson was going to Stoke the Briar. This was a stunt that involved flying through the flames of the falling balloon, much as you might quickly put a hand through a candle flame. Except your hand wasn't filled with volatile petrol.

Grant was at perfect range for his first shots now, but he yanked the little plane left instead. A growing feeling of dread was making him hold his fire. The same unease that had once stayed his step on a snow bridge that had collapsed seconds later, that had made him bury himself in ice moments before the burning pumice from an eruption by Mt Erebus had fallen around him. He had no explanation for it, but he had learned to trust the sensation of foreboding.

You'd better be right, Trigger, he told himself.

The flash of the explosion from within Thompson's balloon dimmed the weak sun. A rolling sphere of black smoke and red flame reached out and engulfed the Sopwith. Even at that distance, Grant felt the blast buffet his airframe. The metal-tipped ends of his propeller sparked as it ploughed through a hail of debris. His left goggle lens cracked. Blood spattered on to the other, which smeared as he tried to clear it.

Thompson's plane was momentarily lost to the detonation's cloud, before it punched out from the other side trailing white vapour, its doped canvas already aflame. The pilot was slumped back, head facing to the heavens. Grant pulled on the stick, which took him above the remnants of the sausage, and watched as the front end of the stricken Camel burst apart, spewing a darker, oil-filled smoke, diving like a comet towards the German lines.

He scanned the immediate area for enemy planes. At any moment, he anticipated the impact of bullets from a hostile, but there was nothing. Just empty sky, soiled by the oily column that marked Thompson's crash site.

Grant mouthed the Prayer for a Drowned Sailor – there was none he knew for downed airmen, not yet – and turned the plane for home, trying to piece together what had happened. He listened carefully to the engine note, alert for any damage caused by the flying metal.

The temptation was to drop down and run low for safety, but he knew that would be a mistake. At low altitudes the Sopwith could not use its one major advantage, its manoeuvrability, the devastating fast turn to the right, the effortless loops it could perform. The Camel needed elbow room to be at its best. So he climbed, his head twisting back and forth, anticipating the growing dots of marauding planes bearing down on him. Behind him, the sky was still smudged with smoke, but there were no enemy scouts to be seen. He stood the plane on its wingtip and checked beneath him. Nothing, apart from a few puffs of ineffective anti-aircraft fire.

The blighted earth of the front lines quickly gave way to the golds and yellows of an unmolested autumnal countryside bathed in strengthening sunlight. He allowed himself to breathe more easily. Ahead was a flight of SE5s, four abreast, friendly shapes which would watch his back.

Beyond them was the Bellecamp airfield, the welcoming cruciform shape etched on to the farmland. For Grant, spotting it was always like the sensation of finding a depot flag in a blizzard or the first sighting of a mountain hut at twilight, after a long day's skiing. He let the nose drop and flipped off the engine to lose airspeed. The last thing he wanted to do was come in too fast now. Not with what he knew.

Once the Camel was parked, he left it to Doyle to assess any damage and crossed to the old stable block. He reported his suspicions about the balloons to Captain Dawson, the branch intelligence officer, who, once he had logged the details, told him that the squadron commander had requested to see him as soon as he returned.

'Me?'

'You. Major Gregory was most insistent. And you have a visitor. A female visitor. Best tidy yourself up a little. And, you know, sorry about Thomo.'

Grant didn't answer, merely nodded. It happened far too often for Dawson to have genuine emotion about the loss. Within hours, Thompson's belongings would be packed away and a replacement shipped in from the flying school at St Omer to take his billet.

'No empty places at breakfast' was the rule. In two days, Thompson would be just another fading face, his features already blurred in his old comrades' minds, his name mentioned once or twice and then nevermore. *San Fairy Ann*, as they said: it didn't matter. Thompson wouldn't have expected anything else, because he was once the green replacement for a long-forgotten flyer.

The squadron commander's office had once been the living room of the fortified farmhouse, the centrepiece of the estate they had requisitioned to create the airstrip. It was still furnished with heavy pine dressers, tables and chairs, although these had been pushed aside to make way for Major Gregory's own desk, made of fine polished cherry wood, which had been shipped over from the family seat in England. The S.C. was sitting behind it now and facing him, in a brocaded armchair, was the woman Grant had spotted emerging from the car just as he took off for the balloon sortie. She had removed her hat and coat to reveal a deep maroon velvet dress, with ivory buttons. The neck was a little too scooped for daywear, Grant noticed.

It was when he drew his eyes up from the pale skin of her throat that he felt a shock of recognition. He made an effort to keep his composure.

'Lady Scott, may I introduce Lieutenant Grant.'

'You know, I am not really supposed to be addressed as Lady Scott,' she scolded him lightly. 'I was given the status of a widow of a Knight Commander of the Order of Bath, but not the title.'

'Nonsense,' huffed the major. 'As far as the world is concerned, you are Lady Scott.'

She smiled and nodded, obviously not too distressed.

Grant swept off his cap as she rose to her feet. Kathleen Scott was as striking and imperious as ever and, judging by the S.C.'s flushed face, just as bewitching. His superior officer no doubt thought Grant's shock was simply fluster at being introduced to such a handsome woman.

'I am very pleased to meet you, lieutenant. I hear you are giving the Albatrosses a run for their money.'

The voice was lower in tone than he recalled, but still had a rich timbre that seemed on the verge of breaking into laughter. 'I'm trying, ma'am. How do you do?'

They shook hands. He waited for some sign that she knew his real identity, but there was none. Perhaps she didn't recall. After all, he had last seen her seven years ago, in New Zealand, when she had only had eyes for her husband and once more, fleetingly, under very different circumstances, two years later. And he was thinner, more lined than the gauche lad she had met back then and his hair was peppered with premature grey. Even his younger self might have trouble placing this gaunt flyer. She held his gaze and said: 'Well, lieutenant. And you? You're hurt?'

He reached up and touched his forehead. Grant had only had time to perform a perfunctory dusting down, which had mainly consisted of wiping the protective Vaseline layer from his face. The minor wound, a gouge created when something sharp had nicked him above his left eyebrow, was untreated. He didn't answer Lady Scott directly but turned to Gregory.

'We lost Thompson, sir. A new trick. The sausages were filled with high explosive and metal. Nails and the like. Either the balloons or the basket or mannequins in it, I'm not certain. But when it detonates, you fly into the shrapnel and the engine sucks in the metal.'

'How dreadful.' It was Lady Scott who spoke, sitting once more.

'And the pilot doesn't stand a chance. Thompson must have been cut to ribbons.' He pointed to his own brow, leaving them to imagine the effect of a thousand more bolts and washers. 'We'll have to outlaw Stoking the Briar.'

'You've told Dawson?'

'Sir.'

Gregory was silent for a time. Perhaps he was thinking about Thompson. But then he said: 'There are new Uncle Charlies from Wing for you, Grant.' The fledgling RFC had adopted the phrase from the army to mean any fresh set of orders. Quite who Uncle Charlie was or had been, nobody was entirely sure. 'Russia.'

'Russia?' Grant knew that the country was in the midst of upheaval, but not that the British had any role to play there.

'Yes. I imagine the Brass think you Canadians know a thing or two about the cold.'

Kathleen Scott laughed and Grant caught a twinkle in her eye. Of course he knew all about cold. But would she appreciate that?

'There'll be promotion. But I hate to lose you. Especially with Thompson gone.' He was quiet for a while longer and Grant knew he was already formulating the letter he would have to write to the grieving parents. As an eyewitness and friend, Grant would, of course, write his own account and tribute. 'But first, Lady Scott would like to interview you.'

'To do what, sir?' The S.C. repeated the gist of the sentence. An interview. Well, he was an Ace, he supposed, and had been recommended for the Military Cross, but Grant felt himself squirm at the thought of promulgating his lies in print. His flimsy story would fall apart. He'd have to admit who he was. And, besides, it was always unfair to single out any one pilot as somehow special, he felt. They all did their part. It had been the same with the expedition; the damned press was always looking for heroes within the group to promote. They had all been heroes for just being there.

'Interview me?'

'For *The Graphic*,' she said. 'An issue on how the colonies continue to support us during the fighting in Europe.'

'But I don't think that's entirely appropriate.'

'Nonsense. Females drive some of the ambulances these days, why should they not be journalists?' said Gregory, misunderstanding his objection. 'Lady Scott is taking you into town for a bit of peace and quiet.'

'I have a car waiting,' she explained. 'With a chauffeur, in case you are worried about a woman's driving skills. Shall we?'

While Grant was struggling for a reply, Lady Scott fetched her hat and coat and slid her arm through his, almost frog-marching him out of the office. Grant glanced over his shoulder at the major, hoping for a reprieve. Gregory simply winked and signalled for him to go. Then Lady Scott whispered something in his ear that made him hurry along. 'For goodness' sake, come along, Trigger, time is pressing.'

Trigger. So she knew exactly who he was.

They had just stepped from the farmhouse when the German scout appeared. It was a venerable monoplane Fokker, the one with the noisy Oberusel power plant, but it approached low and downwind, ensuring the sound of its engine only became apparent as it burst over the trees. The instant he recognised it as a hostile, Grant leaned against Lady Scott, pushing her into the doorframe. He should have buried his head to protect his face, but he was unable to take his eyes off the intruder. It came in level and the pair of dark objects hurled from the observer's position fell directly towards the centre of the field. As soon as the deadly cargo was unloaded, the engine note sharpened and the Fokker banked away, flashing the twin black crosses on its underside like an obscene gesture.

One bounce, thought Grant, watching the payload spin through the air. Two bounces. Must be on a timer, rather than an impact fuse.

Now he turned away and hunched his body over hers, tensed for the blast. Three.

Four bounces. Then silence. He risked a glance. The bombs had rolled to a halt.

For what seemed the slowest of minutes, nobody moved. Eventually, several air mechanics and riggers appeared from behind their cover, looking around sheepishly. Willis, the chief rigger, strode over to where the German device had come to rest. Gingerly, he kicked at it, alert for traps, before he hoisted the object up in the air.

'Boots!' Willis yelled.

There was some relieved laughter, but also much muttering. Grant felt a flash of anger at the insult, but suppressed it. The Germans would be hoping a bunch of reckless hotheads would take off in pursuit of the Fokker, wounded pride blurring their reactions. In their haste, the English pilots might not even notice the red triplanes awaiting them, hidden by the sun.

'Can I breathe now?'

Grant realised he had pressed his entire weight on Lady Scott. 'Sorry.'

'I think you ought to apologise to my hat.' She pressed it back into shape and placed it on her head. Grant helped her slip into her coat. She glared at the sky. There was no trace of fear when she spoke, simply irritation. 'Really, what was all that about?'

'The boots? That's just to let us know the Germans think we'd be more suited to the infantry.'

The only place in the heavily garrisoned town to have coffee and a chat without rough-cut customers offending a lady's sensibilities was the Hôtel Gascon. The establishment still clung to some kind of pre-war grandeur, despite having lost a wing to one of the Germans' rail-mounted artillery pieces. Breakfast was just finishing as they entered, but, after a word with the manager, Lady Scott secured the re-opening of the dining room for pastries and hot drinks. They had the place completely to themselves; the pale, under-fed waitress was too irritated by the extension to the serving hours to hover once the order was taken.

'You look well, Lady Scott,' he said.

'You look thin, tired and a little dirty.' There was sympathy in her voice.

'Not for the first time.' Robert Falcon Scott had always complained he didn't wash enough. Grant had countered that the English habit of bringing their 'civilised' bathroom habits with them wherever they went was ridiculous.

'You fly a Sopwith,' she said. 'A fine little scout, I hear.'

'Do you know aircraft?'

She looked cross. 'I flew with Mr Sopwith. In a dual-control plane. It was 1911, while Con was . . . there was a fuss from the family, Con's, I mean. They thought I shouldn't get noticed while he was away. Do you know, I think I was the second Englishwoman to fly?'

'No, but I can believe it. I'm just surprised you let someone beat you to it.'

'It's a family trait.'

If that was a joke, he didn't think it amusing. It wasn't done to jest about Amundsen's primacy at the Pole. 'How did you find me?'

She waved a hand as if it were nothing. 'I have friends in high places.'

'You always did, Lady Scott. You always did.' Like her husband, she could turn on blazing charm when required. Tales of men who had been ensnared by her were legion. It was unlikely that without her tireless campaigning and courting of crusty old admirals her husband would have been given that second, fateful crack at the Pole. It would be nothing for her to find the whereabouts of a Canadian airman. 'How is the boy?'

'Doodles is well, thank you. Peter. I must stop using that name. Too old for it now. Peter has given up wanting to be a drummer, thank goodness. Wants to command a Dreadnought now.'

'He must miss his father.'

'We all miss Con,' she said, once again using the diminutive derived from Falcon, Scott's middle name. There was a defensive note in her voice. There had been some mutterings at the way she continued her career as a sculptor – and her partygoing – after her husband's loss. But Grant knew she had never been the kind of woman to be imprisoned in widow's weeds for very long.

'You aren't taking notes, Lady Scott.'

'I'm not here to interview you, Mr Gran,' she said, using his real name for the first time. 'Not in that way. I'm here to ask a favour. Before they send you to Russia.'

He didn't like the sound of that. What kind of favour could he possibly offer? Nevertheless, he said: 'If I can help, Lady Scott.'

'Call me Kathleen, please.' She smiled and he remembered the power it could yield. Kathleen Scott was one of those women who often looked plain, especially in photographs, but to whom animation lent a whole new dimension. Her mischievous eyes, extravagant hair, dimpled grin and husky voice had certainly led those old admirals by the nose. You had to be on your guard.

Hot chocolate and pastries arrived and he waited till the sullen waitress had departed before speaking. 'So, Kathleen. How can I help?'

'I have written a book. Well, partly written. About my husband.' He made to speak and she raised her hand to silence him. 'I know.

15

Everybody who ever met him has written a memoir. I hear Cherry is working on his, now he is recovered.' She was referring to young Cherry-Garrard, another member of Scott's *Terra Nova* expedition and universally popular. A terrible melancholy and debilitating colitis had subsequently afflicted him. He would be writing his account hoping to exorcise some of those demons, but Grant doubted he would succeed. Cherry blamed himself for Scott's death, despite all the evidence to the contrary. 'But there is not one that gives the views of my husband.'

'His diaries.' A hastily edited version of his journals had been put out after his death.

'They do not tell the whole story.'

'No?'

'Diaries are written in haste, with slights and wounds still fresh. And mistakes and affronts still rankling.'

He had heard there were some personal slights by Scott taken out of the journals before publication; he wondered if any of them had concerned him. Unlikely. The British weren't so worried about saving the feelings of a mere Norwegian. Tryggve Gran sipped his hot chocolate. Teddy Grant had disappeared for the moment, side-lined as the Norwegian was forced to revisit his past. To a man, every surviving member of Scott's party had volunteered for the war upon their return. However, because his country was neutral, Gran had not been allowed to join the RFC. Quickly reborn as a thinly disguised Canadian, he was eagerly accepted because ready-trained pilots were a rarity. Teddy Grant was the pilot, but Tryggve Gran had been a polar explorer, a member of the most famous expedition ever undertaken at the bottom of the planet. Moreover, he was one of the team who had discovered that lonely, dispiriting tent, where men had endured suffering beyond belief and confronted death with a bravery the living could only envy.

He found himself gripping the cup, letting the warmth seep through the china into his hands. The old scar on his leg began to throb, as if scurvy was setting in. His chest ached, remembering the sharp, rasping pain of lungs sucking in super-cooled air. The memory of needle-sharp blasts of ice crystals caused his face to tingle. He swore the tips of his fingers were struck numb. Shackleton had been right. It never goes away, Gran thought, from the softest glow of deep-blue twilight to the ammoniac stench of the penguin rookery, there was always an echo of the South with you. You could leave that desert of ice, but it would never leave you.

She was waiting for him to comment and he picked up the thread. 'I feel the immediacy of diaries makes them a more valuable document than mere hindsight,' he offered. 'There is a tendency to fix things at a later date, to self-aggrandise. Even your husband—'

Her eyes widened in anticipation of the criticism.

What was it the English said? Mustn't speak ill of the dead.

'Go on.'

He did. 'I have read *The Voyage of the* Discovery.' This was Scott's account of his first Antarctic expedition. 'And I have spoken to Shackleton about it. He was adamant that it was a heavily revised version of the truth. He feels it maligns him.'

She didn't seem surprised. 'That's a very worn gramophone record. You've seen him, then?'

'Shackle? Yes. Earlier this year, before he went to South America.' He shook his head at the thought of the exhausted explorer, who was being wheeled around by the War Office to recount the tale of his hideous journey by rowing boat to seek relief for his men, stranded when the ice took their ship. It was a stirring cocktail of courage and self-sacrifice, and it usually did the trick for the troops' morale. Such was its immediacy, few in the audience would reflect on one salient fact that certainly did not apply to the generals of the Western Front: Shackleton never lost a man. 'He was drinking too much.' Gran had a sudden urge to order a brandy, which he ignored. They all drank too much these days.

'There you have it,' she said, as if that could account for all the bitterness Shackleton still displayed towards Scott. 'It was probably the alcohol talking.'

Gran didn't want to pursue the subject any further. Both Shackleton and Scott were, each in their own way, heroic and pig headed. He had found their falling-out ridiculous, each scarred by mostly imaginary wounds they refused to stitch. 'I don't understand what you want from me, of all people.'

'I want you to read the book. To tell me it is fair. To suggest changes. And to write an introduction—'

'But I was only one of many. There are others, there are Englishmen—'

She dismissed his protestations with a long sigh. 'All of whom have enough axes to grind to fell a forest. You know that. Or they are writing their own book with an eye on royalties. But here you are, fighting for our country. One day people will know about your efforts, about who Teddy Grant really is, about how he fought our war.' As if to punctuate her remark, there was the distant crump of a shell. A standing wave formed briefly in his hot chocolate. 'You are as much a hero as any of them.'

Gran shook his head at this.

'Yes you are.'

'I went South because I love to ski and thought I could convey that. On the way back from the Pole, I met a pilot who told me about the magic of flying, so I went to the Bleriot school and I learned to fly. And I made a promise to Soldier about what I would do if war came. I'm keeping my promise. Does all that make me a hero?'

'Where and how you opt to do what you love makes you a hero. You could choose to fly anywhere. At home, for the Germans. But, no. You are flying for England.' She frowned and leaned forward and for the first time he could see that her skin, beneath the fine powder around her eyes, was no longer young. 'And you are a Norwegian, Scott's Norwegian. That makes you dispassionate. I would like you to do this for me, for Con. For the Boy. And Soldier and Wilson. And Amundsen, if you like. You know I have no animosity towards him.' That was news to Gran. He recalled she'd agreed with the late Sir Clements Markham of the Royal Geographical Society, who had called the first man to the South Pole a liar and a cheat and, in private, much worse. 'Or any of your countrymen.'

'Really?'

She gave a small, knowing smile. Gran wondered if it was an oblique acknowledgement of the rumours about her involvement with Professor Fridtjof Nansen, one of his country's greatest explorers and the man who had introduced a young dreamer called Tryggve Gran to Captain Scott. 'And you can write what you like.'

'Because you can always change it.'

'You have my word I will change nothing without checking with you first.'

Gran experienced a small flash of apprehension. Like all flyers on the Western Front, he rarely made plans beyond the next twenty-four hours. It seemed too much like tempting fate. 'If I'm still around to be checked with. You know the average life of a pilot these days? It's measured in hours. I'm overdue my turn.'

Kathleen reached over and took his hands in hers. He felt a small charge throughout his body, as if he had been plugged into one of those electrotherapy machines that had been all the fashion before the war. A fresh warmth spread over his chest. It was surprisingly pleasant. 'That's new pilots. Not grizzled old polar men. Nobody clings to life like they do.'

This was certainly true, even if he didn't quite deserve to be described as grizzled or old just yet. 'And if I say no? What happens then?'

This was no idle question. He doubted Kathleen Scott was a woman who took rejection well. A quiet word from her could expose his subterfuge and have 'Teddy Grant' ousted from the RFC. 'I'll be disappointed.' She squeezed his fingers and let go. 'But that's all, Trigger.'

'Trigger' was what the English always made of Tryggve. 'I'd need to read what you have written.'

He saw the flash of victory in her eyes. He had rolled over too easily. 'Of course you will. And we should talk money for your efforts—'

This was going far too fast for Gran's liking. 'Later. I haven't said yes, yet. Because if you're looking for a mindless eulogy for the Owner, you've come to the wrong place.' He laughed at the phrase that had come to him unbidden. 'The Owner' had been the expedition nickname for Scott, one that hinted at his proprietary attitude to all Antarctic exploration. Although it was often used in the Navy as a substitute for 'skipper', it had always been more appropriate than most names for Scott. 'It's not the Norwegian way.'

Another shell landed, nearer this time, and he felt the wooden frame of the old hotel vibrate. A thin stream of dust rained from the cornice on to the next table. The war, it reminded him, was still out there.

'You think I don't know who Con was and what he was? But I can't sit by while others tear their own little strips off the story, like self-serving wolves. When this war is over, I want the truth out there.'

'It has be Oates's story as well. And Wilson's. And there's Bowers and Taff Evans. They are writing poor Taff out of it, you know.'

She ignored this remark. 'And yours and Cherry's and the rest. I know.'

'And there is someone hanging over even that second trip.'

'Shackleton.' Lady Scott exhaled loudly, as if this were an irritation. 'I suppose you would say none of it makes sense without him.'

'I was thinking of Teddy Evans.'

'The Lion of Dover?' She smirked slightly at the unlikely epithet for Scott's number one. Teddy Evans had been in command of HMS *Broke* when it encountered a large marauding force of German warships, intent on shelling Dover. Along with HMS *Swift*, the *Broke* sank two and rammed another, causing the surviving vessels to flee and offering Evans a second taste of glory. 'Possibly. But Shackleton more so.'

The whole story was a spidery tissue of interconnecting strands, like the complex filaments of ice webs that formed on *Terra Nova*'s rigging as they edged south. But Lady Scott was right, Shackle was a major component.

Gran finished his hot chocolate and took a bite of a delicate almond croissant. Perhaps he could risk a coffee before returning to the airfield. He felt in need of warmth. The heat from her touch had faded fast, like a parting kiss, and his core felt as if he'd been sipping iced water. 'I shall read it and let you know my decision. That is the best I can promise. Where can I contact you?'

She extracted a card from her purse and slid it over the table. 'Paris. I am supposed to be sculpting a head of Pétain. But so far I have seen more of his hands.' She wrinkled her nose to express her displeasure. 'You can always leave a message. Thank you, Trigger.'

'I haven't said yes, yet,' he repeated.

Her expression told him that she was confident he would. Then her eyes dropped. 'I have never, ever, asked this before of anyone.' She looked up and he felt pinned by the gaze. 'I always stopped them when they tried to tell me. It seemed morbid. Gratuitous. Somehow prurient, even for me. But I think I am ready now. Finally.'

He could guess what she was about to request. 'But Atch—'

'Dr Atkinson wanted very much to spare my feelings. He spoke only in general terms.'

Gran swallowed hard. 'You want to know what he looked like when we found him?'

It didn't take much to summon up the image of that forlorn tent, all but submerged by the winter blizzards. Then came the scramble though the two-metre-high snow wall, digging to reach the inside, some insane hope of life within driving them on. The panicked ripping of the seams . . .

'Yes. I want to know.'

. . . the sight of the bodies, three of them, mummified by months on the ice.

The kiss Tom Crean had planted on Scott's forehead.

'I saw no sign of scurvy.' There had been rumours that it was disease that had killed them. Atkinson, the surgeon, had told them the bodies bore no such signs. Instinctively, Gran added the other rider they had rehearsed, lest blame be heaped on the expedition's organisation. 'It was not starvation. Exposure.'

'That's not what I meant,' she replied. Lady Scott was well aware

21

that the official line was exposure, even though the party had run out of food and fuel. 'What did Con look like?'

He could still see the ruined face, chewed by a whole winter season of frosts. 'He was at peace.'

Lady Scott pursed her lips, irritated at the platitude. 'I loved him, Trigger. My soul shrivelled to the size of a walnut when he died. Only now, thanks to Peter, is it healing. I loved him and knew him. He wouldn't want you to say that unless it was true.'

Gran stared down at his drink. 'He was in the middle of the three when we entered the tent.'

'His face?'

Yellow. Glassy. Savaged by frostbite. The three gouged purple pits glistening on his cheeks, excavated down to the bone. 'He was covered in a layer of frost, ghostly white.' Ghastly would have been nearer the mark. 'The breath does that. At extreme cold. Forms a rime in the tent. As Atch doubtless said, I think he was the last to go. I have often thought of him, alone, waiting for his time to come.'

She gave a small sob, a sound so alien coming from her, it made his own eyes fill. Gran reverted to what he had told the *New York Times* reporter. 'He looked as if he might soon awaken from a sound sleep. I often saw a similar look on his face in the mornings, when he was of a most cheerful disposition.'

'Was he always of a cheerful disposition in the mornings?' she asked slyly.

Gran was well aware she knew the answer to that. 'He was holding . . .' He busied himself with the sugar and managed to run a sleeve across his eyes. 'He was still holding his pencil. It seemed to me he had been writing in his diary. His last act. As if he had one final thought he wanted to put down . . . perhaps to you. I think to you.'

She sniffed. 'And the others?'

'The others were still deep inside their bags, they looked like they had simply drifted off to sleep. The Owner, as I say, was half out, sitting up, as if in the midst of that one last effort of writing.'

He didn't mention the snapping of Scott's fossilised limbs, his arms breaking like a tree branch, as they positioned the trio for their final rest, or the sickening click of his tinder-like fingers as they released the diary from his grip. 'The three were laid out, at rest. We removed the bamboo from the tent, collapsed it, and made the snow cairn. We sang "Onward Christian Soldiers".'

'I know.' She took out a large handkerchief and blew her nose. 'His favourite.'

Gran recalled the little semicircle of men, stifling their sobs. 'You know you can't hide crying on the ice. No matter how hard you try.'

'What do you mean?'

'Your tears. They steam as they come out into the cold air. We all had mist around our heads that day.'

She blew her nose again. 'I can imagine. And you were one of those who looked for Oates?'

'I was. No sign. Afterwards, back at the tent. We made a cross for the cairn from my skis and I took the Owner's skis and used them to get back to the hut. So at least something of him made it back.' She gave a small laugh at this; perhaps it had been a pathetic gesture. 'We did odd things. Cherry took a copy of Tennyson from the tent. He had lent it to Bill. Said he was going to send it to Oriana.'

'He's a sweet man. Too sensitive, I fear.'

'Tom Crean said, what an echo they'll leave on this world. He was right. An echo that has gone round the globe. You know the rest, I am sure. From Atch. And Cherry. Your husband and the others, they died doing something great. There's nothing else to add.'

'Nothing at all?'

'No,' he lied. 'Nothing.'

Teddy Grant was given permission by Major Gregory to forego the afternoon patrol and settled down in his bunk with the pages Lady Scott had given him. The typed manuscript had a title, *A Price to Pay*, and it was already heavily corrected. His batman brought him over-sweetened tea in a tin mug and a plate of biscuits, and he began to read, wondering why he was quite so nervous.

Because, he eventually assumed, Teddy Grant lived in the moment, because his life depended on it. Scout pilots were not philosophisers or daydreamers. He didn't have time to think back, like Tryggve Gran, over days so cold you felt as if your spine could crack, of the crushing claustrophobia of a blizzard-lashed tent or snowed-in hut, the relentless, infuriating snap of wind-blown canvas. Now he would have to take himself back five years or more.

When he bit into the homemade biscuit he gagged. For a moment the consistency reminded him of pemmican, the high-energy dried meat-and-fat ration every polar explorer was forced to take. Gran chewed hard, letting the biscuit's sweetness blanket the slimy echo of hoosh, the stew the British had made from the pemmican, biscuit, bacon and whatever else was to hand.

He knew within thirty minutes that Kathleen Scott had been telling the truth about her insistence on veracity. The work, apart from the verbatim extracts of the Scotts' letters to each other, was measured and even detached in places, not unlike Amundsen's rather workaday account of his race South.

Gran skipped forward to the events he had actually witnessed, and found himself impressed, albeit critical of some of the stilted words she had put into people's mouths towards the end. Men simply didn't talk like that on the ice. You had no breath for long speeches. There were hours with no communication at all, as each became lost in the painful rhythm of man-hauling. And there were technical problems, too, with statute and nautical miles being used inter-changeably, as well as confusion over degrees Fahrenheit and Centigrade. There was no mention of the Winter Journey, the insane mission to obtain penguin embryos. And there was a spiritual element missing, a state of mind that only those who had been to the Big White could recognise: that when you stepped on to that ice, you somehow stepped out of time, into a different reality. Antarctica was ice, wind and rock, Oates used to say, and something else beyond man's comprehension. Gran had experienced strange things at the Pole, events and dreams he couldn't easily explain.

However, any flaws were easily corrected. But, to his relief, this was no hagiography, no love letter from a mourning wife.

A Price to Pay was a cold, unflinching look at events out on the bleak ice barrier – the best and worst place in the world – five years earlier.

From under the bed, Gran took his old leather satchel and extracted from it a sheaf of papers. His diaries and notes, some pages stained with blubber, others with tallow, preserved so that he could one day put the story down. A single sheaf fell out as he opened it, a piece of paper prematurely stiff and yellow, the writing fading. Once blue-black, it was now tobacco coloured. It was a letter from a long-dead friend. He retrieved it from the floor and placed it back in the pages of his diary.

Between them, perhaps he and Lady Scott really could cover the complete history of the expedition and the events leading up to it. If Gran had a reservation, it was this: perhaps the war-weary British public – and possibly even Scott's widow – simply wasn't ready for the true story of Scott of the Antarctic and what really happened out on the ice, eleven scant miles short of safety.

Part One

'This congress is of the opinion that the exploration of the Antarctic regions is the greatest piece of geographical exploration still to be undertaken'

Resolution of the Sixth International
Geographical Institute, London, 1895

One

London, 1900

The two men sharing the cramped office in Burlington House on Savile Row sat formal and straight backed, sizing each other up as they conversed. They were hemmed into one corner of the room by untidy piles of boxes and packing cases. There were samples of the chocolate Cadbury's would be providing, custard and baking powder from Alfred Bird and Sons, various recipes of high-fat pemmican, oil lamps of interesting design, candles, rolls of oilskin, britches and Burberry sledging suits. There was a great mound of finnesko, the fur boots the Esquimeaux used on the ice, along with bundles of the grass they stuffed in them for insulation. Next to them was a stack of the new double-compartment Nansen stoves shipped from Christiana. Elsewhere sat three different models of wooden sledges and a teetering pile of equipment catalogues, featuring everything from folding spoons to fur sleeping suits.

On the walls were two detailed maps of the Southern Hemisphere, with large lacunae where the most southerly continent should be. Dotted around the charts were images of whaling and sealing ships and the famous *Fram*, the polar exploration vessel of Fridtjof Nansen. Photographs of previous expeditions to both poles adorned the other spaces, men wrapped in so many clothes they lost any discernible human shape. Frequently they were posed before their tents or with their stranded ship as a backdrop. In the largest, a group of six with blackened faces, bandaged hands and raw, slightly haunted eyes were staring balefully at the camera. They looked shocked to find themselves there, on the ice, far from home.

There was even a husky pinned up, a grainy picture of a keen-looking animal on the snow, its harnesses laid out around it as if it were a canine maypole. The clutter, the hastily opened cartons and the carelessly displayed wall decorations lent the room a sense of fevered urgency.

'As you can see, Mr Shackleton,' said the older man. 'There is much to do.'

Each was dressed in his civilian best. Commander Scott noted approvingly that Lieutenant Shackleton's boots were as shiny as his own and his collar stiff and new. Shackleton at least buffed up well out of uniform, unlike some of his slovenly colleagues in the merchant service. Scott had already seen some howlers.

The commander picked up a piece of paper from his over-crowded desk and held up the report, which concentrated on Shackleton's service record with the Union Castle line. 'Armitage speaks highly of you. Which bodes well. He does not suffer fools.' Bert Armitage was Scott's newly appointed second-in-command, a good navigator, and a veteran of Arctic waters. He was also famously blunt in expressing his opinions.

Shackleton smiled. 'Well, that's good to know. That I'm not a fool. And to have it in writing. Grand.'

According to the dossier, the Anglo-Irishman had spent his form-ative years in England, so Scott was surprised by the thickness of his brogue. He wondered what they had made of that at Dulwich College. 'You realise, of course, that, although yourself and Armitage are merchant men, the enterprise, and the ship, will be run according to Royal Navy rules and regulations.'

'So I understand.'

'And you will have to sign an undertaking to that effect.'

'If required to do so, then of course I shall.' Shackleton leaned forward a little in his seat. Slightly shorter than Scott, but bulkier, he exuded an earthy physicality. He possessed sharp, steady blue eyes that made Scott think he would be difficult to unbalance or panic. He was also six years younger than the commander's thirty-two, although he did not act as if he were addressing an older man. Or, indeed, a superior officer. 'And I appreciate that you probably would have preferred a crew made up entirely from your service.'

Scott smiled at his perception. He was expedition leader because of the patronage of Sir Clements Markham, president of the Royal Geographical Society. He had championed Scott in the face of opposition from other factions in the Royal Society and the RGS, which were jointly behind this voyage to Antarctica. In the sub-sequent sparring for total control, Scott had been forced to yield some ground. The societies' scientists were no longer in charge of the expedition, but he had been restricted on how many RN personnel he could take. So he was obliged to turn to the merchant branch.

'There are good men in both services,' Scott said diplomatically. 'However, we must have but one code of discipline or the result will be confusion and anarchy.' He made a show of examining Armitage's report once more. 'Why do you want to go South?' Scott asked. 'Your record shows no predilection for cold climates.'

Nor yours, Shackleton thought, but didn't voice it. 'No, but I know square-rigged ships like the one you are having built. And there was the advertisement.'

'What advertisement?'

'In *The Times*.'

Scott tugged on his earlobe, as he often did when puzzled. 'You think the Royal Geographical Society advertised for expedition members in *The Times*?'

'Longstaff told me they did. Said I should get a move on if I wanted a place because so many would apply.' Llewellyn Longstaff was one of the expedition's more generous sponsors and had vigorously put Shackleton forward as a potential recruit. Scott could ill afford to cross anyone who was contributing to the expedition's meagre purse, which is why he had agreed to consider the Irishman. 'I have the wording still.'

Shackleton reached into his pocket, took out the handwritten note, and read it aloud: '"Men wanted for hazardous journey. Small wages. Bitter cold. Long months of winter. Constant danger. Safe return doubtful. Honour and recognition in case of success."'

Scott guffawed and clapped his hands together. 'Marvellous. But I think a little prank has been played on you, perhaps to hurry you along. There was no such notice placed.'

'Oh.' And then, Shackleton, too, chortled. 'Damn. It sounded right up my street. Apart from the low wages. A joke?'

'I fear so.'

'But it changes nothing.' He took Scott aback by leaping to his feet and jabbing at one of the charts. 'Even if that piece of fiction is Longstaff's idea of a jest, it surely holds true. Doesn't it?'

Scott fiddled with the unlit pipe on his desk. 'I suppose it does. It has a brutal honesty one has to admire.'

'Precisely. Pulls no punches. I like that. I can feel the tingle of anticipation already.' He swept his hand over the blank areas of the map. 'Terra Incognita. Constant danger. Not so worried about the honour and recognition at this moment, but I won't lie and say I haven't thought of the future. Of the privileges that accrue from belonging to a very exclusive club, for those who have been where no other man has trod. Cook, Ross, Perry, Franklin, Borchgrevink. And, now, Scott. And perhaps a footnote for Ernie Shackle. And a bit of cash.'

He finished off with a broad wink as he sat back down. Scott had to remind himself that they did things differently in the Merchant Navy. Scott was aware that those who risked the poles tended to do very well upon their return, but he would hesitate to proffer an urge for advancement – as opposed to pushing the boundaries of science and geography – as a reason for going South. Clearly, Ernest Shackleton had no such qualms.

'And you can be released from your duties with Union Castle? I intend to overwinter for at least one year down there.'

'Yes.'

'You know what that means? Overwintering.' Scott pronounced the word with all the gravitas he could muster.

Shackleton nodded. 'It means we should pack our best bed warmers.'

'I suggest you read the physicist Bernacchi's account of the *Southern Cross*'s Antarctic overwintering. It makes for uneasy reading.'

'How comes the ship?' asked Shackleton.

The expedition's vessel, a wooden coal-powered three-masted sailing ship, was being built in Dundee. Scott's reply was guarded. 'Well, I hear.'

'You hear? You've not seen it?'

Scott bristled a little at the implied criticism. 'My dear fellow, of course I've seen it. Just not recently. There is much to do here in London. Fundraising and the gathering of supplies. Planning an expedition such as this is like negotiating a series of increasingly tiresome locks, till, at last, you reach the open sea. Be assured, Reginald Skelton, my engineer, is keeping an eye on things. He was on the *Majestic* with me.' Scott said this as if it was all the recommendation a man needed. 'It is on schedule.'

'Which is?'

'She will be launched in February of next year. March at the very latest. You know, we might have unwelcome company going South?'

'So I hear.' The Scots, the French, the Swedes and particularly the Germans were putting together their own expeditions to Antarctica. The still-unfinished ship must sail for southern waters no later than August 1901, just over a year away, if the expedition was to take advantage of what passed for summer in the South. Shackleton indicated the happy husky on the wall. 'And you'll use dogs? I hear they are much in favour with the Americans and Norwegians. Although not with Markham. Is that true?'

'It is.' Scott leaned forward, as if Markham were next door, eavesdropping. 'No skis, no dogs, no primitive Eskimo ways, so Sir Clements advises.' The only truly noble way to achieve the poles, Markham counselled, was by man-hauling. It had a pure, heroic quality that appealed to him. There were acid tongues at the RS that claimed Markham simply liked the idea of young muscular bodies in harnesses. Scott thought such salacious tittle-tattle pure mischief making.

'However, we will take dogs,' Scott confirmed. 'I have corresponded with Nansen on the subject. He recommends Greenland

33

huskies, although Armitage has a promising contact in Siberia. But who knows what the ice will be like? Nansen himself admits dogs struggle on rough ice. We have to face the possibility that we will have to rely on our own resources.'

'Well, personally, there are none I trust as much, Commander Scott. When all else fails, you need to know you can rely on yourself. As for sitting down while dogs pull . . . well, as Sir Walter Scott said, "Too much rest is rust".'

Scott smiled at the familiar quotation. '"Ere long we will launch, a vessel as goodly strong and staunch as ever weathered a wintry sea",' he quoted. It was one of Markham's favourite verses.

'Longfellow,' Shackleton replied. 'Not always to my taste, but I applaud that sentiment. I'm sure she will be. And I'd be pleased to be on her.'

Scott stood and held out his hand. 'In which case, I think we should get along very well, Mr Shackleton. I would like to offer you a position as my third lieutenant. Subject to a medical.'

'You'll have no worries there.' The medical was another formality. Longstaff had let slip that the ship's naturalist and assistant doctor, Edward Wilson, had TB scars that should have disbarred him. The commander made sure it did not. And they'd find no such problems on the fit, young Irishman.

'I am sure that will be so.'

Shackleton had been warned that Scott was a cold, distant man, slow to show his emotions, but there seemed to be a smile of genuine warmth and pleasure on his face. It changed his rather ordinary features entirely, lending him a spark Shackleton had not previously detected.

Only as he gripped Scott's proffered hand did Shackleton feel the enormity of what he had accepted. Now he really did experience a lightning bolt of anticipation and excitement, leavened with a hint of apprehension. He was twenty-six years old and, for better or worse, he was going South, into the last great unknown, with the equally unknown, and untried, Scott.

Two

The Curragh, Co. Kildare, Ireland, 1900

Lawrence Oates loathed writing letters. It was worse than arithmetic and that was torture, almost as bad as Latin or Greek. Yet, he knew he must. His mother insisted.

Oates struggled with the grammar and spelling for ten minutes before he conceded defeat. 'McConnell!' he yelled.

His steward stuck his head around the door of the tiny quarters. 'Sir?'

'Want to earn yourself another sixpence?'

'Oh, aye, sir.'

'Come in, then.'

McConnell was a willowy man of thirty, a mere decade older than Oates, but already devoid of front teeth and much of his hair. He had left the employ of the Guinness brewery to find some adventuring. For the moment that consisted of putting the finest shine on his lieutenant's cavalry boots.

Oates slapped the coin on the table. 'Between us as always?'

'Oh, yes, sir. I'd rather fall on your sword than spread gossip.'

Oates laughed and swung his legs on to the rickety desk. He put his hands behind his head and leaned back in his chair. 'Go ahead, then.'

McConnell picked up the scrawled letter and began to read it, his mouth silently moving as he did so.

'I think it's *an* account, sir.'

'Pardon?'

'You've put "required to open *a* account". Should be *an*.'

'Change it, would you?'

McConnell picked up the pen, dipped it in the inkpot and added the letter. It wasn't hard to approximate the lieutenant's writing. He just had to pretend he was an eight year old again.

'And there is an apostrophe in Cox's.'

'Fine.'

McConnell spoke from the corner of his mouth, as if passing on a confidence or a racing tip. 'Some of the troopers were wondering if you would do them a service, sir.'

'Yes? Not write to their mothers, I hope?'

McConnell smiled. 'No, sir. They've got me for that if need be. There is a horse contest. On Saturday. A bit of a wager.'

'A wager? You know the colonel doesn't hold with such things.'

McConnell corrected another spelling mistake. 'That's why they didn't ask him, sir, and why they've asked you. They want you to hold the stake and officiate.'

'Who is it?'

'Troopers Regan and Lambton, sir.'

Oates thought for a moment. Personally, he saw no harm in competition between the men. It could only be good for the regiment and the troopers' riding ability. 'Very well. Get me the details. And tell them I'll take on the winner.'

McConnell's eyes lit up. 'Oh, well done, sir.'

'Read me the letter so far, can you?'

McConnell made a show of clearing his throat.

'"Dear Mother," – I've put a comma in there, sir, hope you don't mind.'

'No, punctuation was never my strong point. Carry on.'

'"Dear Mother",' McConnell continued, '"As part of my duties here I am required to open an account at Cox's, the regimental bankers. I need horses, boxing gloves and kit, new boots, and various parade requirements. If you could let me have a hundred and fifty pounds—"'

36

McConnell whistled at the amount.

'Do you know how much it costs to be an officer in the Inniskillings?' Oates asked.

'I do now, sir.'

Oates laughed. 'Don't be impertinent or I'll cut your wages.' Under new rules, a junior officer was not entitled to a batman; stewards, or 'Boots' as they were collectively known, had to come out of a lieutenant's own purse. 'Carry on.'

'"I should like to put it in as soon as possible as you have to pay for what you have ordered as soon as you have ordered it. I promise I shall live as cheaply as possible to the end of the year." That's it so far, sir.'

Oates had not been joshing with McConnell. Being an officer was, indeed, a constant stream of expenses, with no way he knew of turning off the tap. The mess kit, polo whites and everyday uniforms, plus the mess bills and McConnell's salary, had gobbled up most of his cash and now he needed two horses. The 6th Inniskillings might be the best heavy cavalry regiment in the army, but its officers had to bleed money to ensure they kept up appearances. Much as he despised himself for having to beg from his mother, she had ensured there was no other way he could function. Whenever he objected, she either feigned an attack of the vapours or threatened him, and the family, with disgrace.

'Titus!' Lieutenant George Culshaw, of the Sheffield Steel Culshaws, burst into his billet. He was the one who had nick-named Oates after the infamous Reformation cleric. 'Titus, we have orders.'

Oates swung his feet off the desk and snatched the letter back. 'And Boots,' he said, 'if I catch you reading my mail again, I'll fine you more than a tanner.'

'Sir. Very sorry, sir. Didn't mean nothing by it.'

'Get out.'

Oates scooped up the sixpence and made sure McConnell caught the fast wink before he pocketed it. He might make it a shilling this time. Boots saw the worst side of officers as it was:

drunk, disorderly, nursing a life-threatening hangover or even wrestling with one venereal disease or other they were too shamed to go to the MO with. The best Boots had the discretion of a priest. Better McConnell knew about his difficulties with writing than a man like Culshaw, who, in his cups, might tell the whole mess.

Once McConnell had left, Oates looked at the tall, blond lad with his extravagant moustaches.

'Orders,' he repeated.

'It's the army, Culshaw. There are always bloody orders.'

'Not like these.' The moustaches shivered with excitement. 'We are listed for South Africa. Under Captain Anstice. With fifty troopers.'

Oates stood quickly, almost spilling his inkpot. He replaced its cap. 'When?'

'Two weeks. On the *Idaho*.'

He hadn't heard of it. Some rust-bucket troop ship, no doubt. It would be very different from those trips on Union Castle with his parents, shipped south for the good of his weak lungs. Still, even if it wouldn't be First Class, it was adventure. 'I'll be right with you, Culshaw. Wait there.'

'Who you writing to?'

'Carrie. My mother.'

'You call her Carrie?'

'Carrie. Caroline. Mother. Mummy. Mama. I call her a lot of things.' Some he daren't repeat. 'If it gets the job done.'

'You short of cash again?'

'Culshaw, I'm always short of cash.'

'I thought you inherited when your father died.'

'I did. Gestingthorpe is technically all mine. It's just the money my father put a fence round.'

'I wonder why.'

'So I would call my mother Carrie, I suppose.'

'So there would be some left when you reach twenty-one, more like. Want to borrow some?'

'A few pounds, perhaps, till Mother replies. Look, let me finish it off.' He sat down once more and hastily polished off the letter, ignoring his slapdash spelling.

'Missed you at the races the other day,' Culshaw said.

'Had things to do.'

'On a Saturday?'

Oates did not want to let on what he had really been doing, tramping from one depressing establishment to another, wasting his time with his futile questions. 'Yes, on a Saturday. Was thinking of buying a boat.'

'Do you sail?'

'I'll have to if I buy a boat, won't I? But it might have to wait till after South Africa, I suppose. Now be quiet for a second.'

He scribbled some more:

Tremendous news, however. We are to go to South Africa to take on the Boers at last. Shall write again soon. Also need dark grey hunting frock coat, a pot hat and decent butcher boots – not my old ones, they wear them with soft legs and black tops here – and perhaps a saddle from Parkers in St Martin's Lane. Please send the money.

Yours affectionately,

L.E.G. Oates

Then he scribbled 'Laurie' underneath.

He blotted the ink, folded the single piece of paper and popped it into an envelope and let out a sigh of relief. One day he would find a way of being free of his mother's influence and his youthful misdemeanours would not be used as a rod to beat him into submission and penury.

'So, Culshaw. War, is it?'

'War it is.'

Oates stood and checked himself in the mirror. He was reasonably pleased with what he saw. He might not be quite the postcard cavalry officer that Culshaw was – he was clean shaven, for a start – but he was a good half inch taller and his eyes were clear and bright. Culshaw's were bagged and bloodshot, showing the strain of too many hours in the mess or at Lady Dora's house in town. Oates was bursting with vigour in comparison, and he didn't have to feign the enthusiasm in his voice. 'Well, about bloody time, is all I can say.'

Three

Discovery at Sea, 1901

It didn't take long for Robert Scott to appreciate that the new ship was not without its problems. She was called *Discovery*, a name chosen by Sir Clements Markham. The vessel had been delivered on time, but was cursed by shoddy workmanship. Scott had also discovered that she was too small. The ship's company of forty-seven – including five scientists – might have been comfortable, had not so much equipment been required. As it was, she felt over-stuffed and overmanned. Which made for short tempers.

There was worse than a few squabbles and the skipper's sharp tongue, however. The ship leaked. Not a little, but prodigiously. Because of the hull's complex, multi-layered structure, the source of the tons of seawater washing around its innards proved maddeningly elusive. Re-caulking had not solved the problem. The bilge pump could barely cope. Furthermore, she was a greedy beast. The engines consumed coal as if it were plankton being fed to a great whale.

Scott stood on the open bridge. They were two days out of Funchal, steaming south, and he knew his timetable was crumbling, even though he was still so very far from the ice. It was certainly partly *Discovery*'s fault. The ship pitched and rolled in the deep ocean swell, all wasted motion. The large overhanging bow, designed to crack polar ice, and the bulbous stern gave her excessive buoyancy. As they had found in the Bay of Biscay, a following sea could lift and turn her like a stray cork. Learning to keep her safe and stable would require a strong nerve and plenty of practice.

He could sense the strain of the engines through his feet, a rough vibration, like a horse tiring, its breathing becoming ragged. Smoke streamed from the funnel, thick and gritty, as if the fuel was only half burned. She needed much more efficient engines. The current ones had cost ten thousand pounds. He couldn't help but feel they had been nutmegged.

It was at moments like this that Scott could sense the brown fog of melancholy rolling through his brain. He could fight it off, with an effort of will, but it left him tired and short tempered. Yet he could not let the men see what a struggle it was for him to remain organised and steadfast. They simply assumed he was a martinet.

He examined the sky between the rigging and masts. It was a rich blue, dappled with feathery dabs of white cloud and the cruciforms of the curious petrels still following them. Despite the rather unpredictable swell, it was good sailing weather; the canvas was filled, giving some assistance to those feeble engines. But it wouldn't last.

At the end of his watch in the crow's nest, Armitage had pointed to a dark streak in the West, a strip of charcoal scribbled over the sky. He had warned that it could be something building and indeed, it had grown blacker in the past hour. If not that storm, then some other would catch them. How would the ship respond?

'Skipper.'

Scott started, plucked from his reverie when Shackleton stepped up on to the bridge, his face pearled with spray. Fully aware of his captain's habit of daydreaming, Shackleton wiped his eyes clear and waited while Scott composed himself. He handed Scott the coal consumption figures he had been asked to fetch from Skelton, the engineer. Scott groaned. They were worse than he thought.

'Thank you.'

Shackleton stepped forward, keeping his voice low. 'Sir, you know the men were expecting a briefing at Madeira.'

'Were they?' Scott screwed up the paper into a ball. 'What gave them that impression?'

'There was a rumour.'

'If only we could use rumour to feed the engines.' He held up the crumpled consumption figures. 'I think we need to address this first.'

'How? We can hardly re-coal in the Southern Ocean. What do you propose?'

Scott tutted. No RN officer under his command would make so bold as to ask such a question. 'Will you watch your tongue, Mr Shackleton. You aren't with Union Castle now. All in good time. All in good time.'

The *Discovery* gave a lurch as an oblique roller sideswiped her. Scamp, Scott's Aberdeen terrier, lost her footing and there was the sound of claws scrabbling on wood as she slid into Scott's ankles. He scooped the animal up and stroked its wiry muzzle. The dog whimpered appreciatively. 'So tell the galley to break out some of the lamb we loaded at Funchal for this evening. And the claret.'

'Aye.' Shackleton looked puzzled, and for once Scott shared his thoughts with him, throwing him a painter to be going on with.

'The gist of it is, bad news is best taken on a full stomach, Mr Shackleton.'

'Bad news?'

'I'm curtailing the scientific programme. We're not calling at Australia either. It's Lyttleton to check for the source of the leak and then straight down to Antarctica.' Shackleton's jaw worked, but Scott raised a hand to stop him speaking. He didn't care for Mr Shackleton's thoughts on the matter. 'If you'll excuse me.'

Before the dinner, Scott had one important task to perform in the wardroom and he left the bridge and headed straight there, with Scamp scuttling after him.

All on board shared the same food – a little touch of the Merchant Navy – but the ratings had their own, less well-appointed mess, minus the linen and silver and with beer and rum instead of wine

43

and port. If the ship was not perfect, at least the cosy wardroom, lined with cabins for the officers and gentlemen, was well up to snuff in all but dimensions, which were parsimonious. However, its burnished wood panels, ornate brass lamps, fine, solid furniture, French Salamander stove, mahogany dining table and brace of attentive stewards made for a most harmonious atmosphere. At least, till he broke the news to the scientists that he was cutting short their trawls and readings en route. Still, the real work was to be done in Antarctica. The best of them – Dr Edward Wilson, the zoologist, and Vere Hodgson, the marine biologist – would understand that and appreciate the crisis brought on by coal consumption. The others could go and hang.

Scott carefully took down the picture of Sir Clements Markham. It was time to break those particular ties. Sir Clements had achieved much, by a mix of guile, bullying and special pleading, but the old man's shadow must not loom over the ice. For better or worse, it was Scott's show now.

Four

South Africa, 1901

A sour mood permeated the first camp the Inniskillings made in South Africa. Oates's exhilaration at arriving in Cape Town with his troopers had been tempered by three things. One was the realisation that Captain Anstice, although a well-turned-out officer who looked magnificent on his horse, was a dithering fool when it came to command. The troopers, Oates felt sure, could sense his prevarication. The man had a whim of iron. Second, he was shocked by just how awry the South African campaign was going, with the Boers penetrating well into Cape Province itself. The third was the biggest blow, however. News arrived that Queen Victoria had died. An age was over. None of them had known any other monarch. He was sure the King was a good man, but it was difficult to see how anyone could replace the powerful symbolism of Victoria. It felt as though the whole Empire had shaken, a tremor of unease passing through a quarter of the globe. With the war progressing badly, it seemed as if everything that was certain in life was being called into question.

Culshaw had dared to voice what they all thought: could this be the end of England?

Oates was not the only one to blink away the tears when the passing was announced and there were many, many toasts that night. Then news came through that they were to entrain and move east, away from Cape Town to Aberdeen, and join with Colonel Herbert to take on a commando of Boers headed by Willem Fouche. Perhaps, Oates thought, they could honour their dead queen by bashing these guerrillas and ending the war.

'Shouldn't take long,' Anstice had decreed. 'After all, what use are mere farmers – Dutch farmers at that – against the Inniskillings?'

Oates, maudlin and in his cups after one brandy too many, thought that remained to be seen.

The column came under attack thirty miles short of Aberdeen, two days after leaving the railhead. It was late afternoon and the fierce heat of the day was only just abating. Not a cloud had troubled the sun for their march, yet at night they suffered tropical downpours that left them cold and shivering in their blankets. It was as if the southern African climate were a Boer supporter too.

Over the day, the procession of men, horses and carts had grown ragged, and although Oates and Culshaw made sure their own portion of the expeditionary force remained tight, they could do little about the other three hundred men who made up the mission to chase the Boers out of Aberdeen. Occasionally, Oates left his own troopers to try to ascertain why there were vulnerable stragglers. As often as not he was told to get back to his own business by a crotchety senior officer.

Disquiet had been gnawing at him for weeks. He was pleased to be at war at last – what man wouldn't be? – but this army was not the one of his imagination. As he had told his mother, there was much that was disappointing, from the quality of leadership to the paucity of some vital equipment and supplies. On the positive side, he had two good horses, especially Sausage, the charger he was riding that day, and one of his brace of servants was his old Boots, McConnell, who had managed to find passage.

Those little fillips aside, though, he had to admit that what he had seen of the British army so far was disenchanting to someone brought up on tales of the Peninsular wars. How did this ill-disciplined, ill-equipped mob defeat Napoleon? And the drabness of the new khaki uniform certainly diminished the army's impact.

It seemed the War Office wanted to make the men invisible. The latest ruling was to stop shining buttons, as they attracted snipers. What rot, Oates thought. Soldiers attracted snipers, not their fastenings.

They were moving through semi-arid scrub, low sandy hills covered mostly with thorns of one description or another – every plant seemed to come bristling with them – when Oates heard the first shots.

He whirled his charger around, and glimpsed four or five black wraith-like shapes cresting one of the low rises to the south. Captain Anstice signalled for Oates to stay put and spurred his horse forward, no doubt to consult Colonel Herbert, who was at the van of the column.

There came a series of distant cracks and he saw two or three muzzle flashes come from the raiders. Oates realised the men were firing from the saddle, like accomplished cavalrymen. Mere farmers, Anstice had said. These men didn't ride or shoot like farmers.

The air around him whistled and snapped. Another five men, blurred, darting figures, had appeared from beneath a bluff. Return fire had started from the British column, but it was like trying to hit fast-moving crows. And too many British soldiers had, like Oates, Martini-Henry carbines, rather than the more effective Lee Enfields.

Fresh firing erupted from the far side of the line and then from the vanguard. In a flash of clarity, Oates visualised the column as the enemy saw them: overstretched, underdefended and plodding along a valley floor, hemmed in by a series of hills and ranges.

Oates extracted the carbine from Sausage's flank and levered a round into the chamber.

'Dismount!' he shouted, sliding off his own horse.

Culshaw took up the call. 'Troopers dismount and suppress fire!' Individually, the carbine was a feeble weapon, but en masse it could be effective, just as long as the enemy was foolish enough to approach within its limited range.

Anstice returned at the double, his horse kicking up a plume of sandy dust. The captain began yelling at Oates and the Inniskillings.

He, apparently, didn't want them off their horses. They were to mount a counter attack.

'That's just what they want, sir,' Oates protested. 'A fight on their terms, in their country.'

Anstice, who had had trouble with Oates before, turned quite puce with anger and was about to lambaste his lieutenant when his two front teeth and top lip disappeared in a conical splash of crimson. His eyes went wide with shock, before his head dropped forward to show the entry wound. He slumped in the saddle and slid, almost gently, to the ground, his holed topee still in place.

By the time Oates pulled his attention back from the fallen captain to the marauders, the Boers had gone, swallowed by the hills.

It was getting dark, they were still a good few hours from Aberdeen, and there was a guerrilla force in the unfamiliar country around them. They were exposed and vulnerable to more hit-and-run attacks. The same thoughts must have struck others, because he felt a ripple of apprehension run through the column.

He re-holstered the carbine and bent down, struggling with the weight of the dead Anstice, and was relieved when other hands came to his assistance. Together they heaved him on to the saddle and bound his limbs under the belly of his horse. Another British grave to be dug in Aberdeen. It was, Oates considered, unlikely to be the last.

Five

Discovery at Sea, 1901

Scott prowled the over-laden decks, humming a selection of hymns to block out the continuing bleating of terrified sheep and the aggressive yapping of the dogs, both of which they had picked up in New Zealand. As he walked by the huskies' kennels they snarled and bared their teeth.

'No respect for authority,' quipped Wilson, who was sitting on a stack of coal sacks, sketching the hounds. Scott stopped to admire his work. On most days, Bill Wilson was able to turn out exquisite watercolours of animals and scenery. His work on South Trinidad had been inspired and inspiring. The dogs, though, were eluding him, as the many corrections and erasings testified. They were foul-tempered animals, these Siberian huskies, liable to nip man or beast that came within range or, failing that, each other.

Nansen had told Scott dogs would be good company on the ice. It would be like being chained to a lunatic, Scott thought. He'd reluctantly left Scamp behind, because he was fairly certain the huskies, especially the truculent beast they called Wolf, would snap him in two at the first opportunity. Each of the dogs had been assigned a sailor to feed and exercise them. Wolf's handler had the teeth marks to prove he had been given the cur of the pack.

'I find petrels far easier,' said Wilson, by way of an excuse.

'If you can think of a way to get petrels to haul sleds, I'd happily send these back on the first relief boat.'

'Happy New Year, by the way, Con.'

'Happy New Year, Bill.' They had postponed celebrations of both Christmas and New Year in memory of Able Seaman Charles Bonner, who had fallen to his death from the rigging as they left port. Not an auspicious start. Drink was involved. Although he was in no way to blame, Scott had taken the loss badly.

'How do you feel?' Wilson asked.

'Better, thank you. I think leaving Lyttleton was good for me.' He had confided in Wilson about his 'brown moments', when a melancholy crept through him like a cold front advancing over the sea. He had been forced to fight off several attacks while they tarried in New Zealand, searching for the source of The Leak. 'No more cables from Markham or the Admiralty. No more going cap in hand to sponsors. No more dignitaries and their wives poking their noses into every corner of the ship. No more speeches, thank the Lord.'

'And no more Maoris,' Wilson added, displaying his own prejudice. 'And their bogus ceremonies. And the crew is set.'

'At last,' agreed Scott. Even before they lost the luckless Bonner, there had been some fierce drunkenness on shore, with Taff Evans making a disgrace of himself. The man didn't actually recall being britchless in the rigging and he was so hangdog apologetic, that Scott let him off with a warning. However, the captain tongue-lashed two able seamen for their dereliction of duty and terrorising of the town. One of them promptly deserted. Now, in that scoundrel's place, he had Tom Crean, another RN man and a real bonus. Strong and capable, with an unhurried manner and a slow, laconic Irish wit when he was of a mind to display it, he exuded a natural confidence. 'I wish I could have a whole crew of Creans,' he said out loud.

'I think—' Wilson stopped and went back to shading the teeth of Wolf.

'Go on, doctor.'

'One could tire of the navy's ways. If one weren't navy.'

'Have you been talking with Shackleton?'

'Only about Swinburne. No, because I am a civilian the men occasionally talk in front of me. Some of them expressed concern about the duty roster.' Scott doubted they had expressed 'concern'; they would have carped and cursed about his insistence on strict routine. 'And about why they haven't been given a clear idea of your plans. If you intend to overwinter *Discovery* or leave a shore party and return the ship to Lyttleton.'

Scott turned and looked out to sea, hoping to quell his irritation before he spoke again. The sky had become brighter as they moved south, yet paler; it was a very delicate blue now. The sea, after some fierce troughs that had tested the inclinometer and the ship's loading, had grown oily and sluggish around them, presaging the appearance of sea ice. The previous day the air temperature had dropped enough to encourage the formation of ice-webs on the rigging. He would have to watch that. Despite what Shackleton assured him were his best efforts, the holds refused to offer any more space for provisions, coal and kerosene, so the surplus had been lashed on deck with the prefabricated huts that would form their base on the ice. *Discovery* was top-heavy. She'd survived a couple of bad rolls and vast depressions the size of slate quarries in the sea, but ice accretion might just be enough to tip her over. And, although they had wasted all that precious time dry-docking, she still leaked.

As he stared at the ocean, a whale fluked in the distance, the black tail hovering in the air for a few seconds before smoothly sliding away. At night they heard the huge animals hissing and squeaking, a combination of other-worldly sounds that unnerved some of the men. A new century and the thought of sirens could still infect the hardiest of sailors.

Scott turned back to Wilson, prompting more barking from the infernal dogs and a terrified response from the tethered sheep. 'Every man on this ship is wondering how I will fare on the ice. Including you.' He raised a hand to quash an interruption. Wilson was the only person he would dare share these thoughts with. 'I don't blame them. I would too. What you don't want is a leader who vacillates. Nor do you want one who allows the men too much idle time. So my orders are direct and unmistakable. And they will know my intentions when I am ready to tell them.'

Wilson looked at him with a very direct gaze. 'You're a little scared, I think, Con.'

To Wilson's surprise, Scott found this most amusing. 'If I wasn't a little apprehensive, I'd be more than a little foolish, don't you think?'

'Berg!'

It was Able Seaman Dell up in the crow's nest, his deep, resonant voice carrying above the snarling dogs and the querulous sheep and the thump of the engines. 'Iceberg, starboard side!'

Scott's face broke into a smile as Wilson leapt to his feet and the dogs threw themselves against their chains in a frenzy. Ice. It had begun.

'There, I see it,' said Wilson.

'Mr Royds!' Scott yelled, his breath rolling out clouds into the chill air. When the junior officer appeared Scott shocked him by saying: 'New Year's Day and our first iceberg. Get the galley to make up a rum punch ration for all hands.'

It wasn't a huge berg, a tabular with steep sides and a flat top and less than fifty feet high. But it was impressive enough to get every man up top for a good look as they steamed past it at a safe distance. The surface was a hard, translucent white, stippled with patches of trapped air bubbles that sparkled in the sun. It looked like a giant slab of seaside rock with the colours bleached from it. But where it touched the sea, the orphaned berg created a halo of various blues: there were rings of cyan, cornflower, azure and indigo. Occasionally a glimpse of a lurking shadow below the waterline hinted at the submerged mass that formed the foundations.

Trailing behind it was a smaller lump of ice, like a calf following its mother, this one expertly sculptured by the sea, with an opalescent arch bored through its body. As Scott examined this second floater's almost transparent edges, feathered in places to blade-like sharpness, he realised this was no youngster, but an older berg, already shaped and eroded by wind and wave.

'I've never seen anything like it,' said Wilson to Scott as they stood at the rail. The doctor was already analysing how to catch the ever-shifting play of silvery light across ice and water on paper.

Armitage, the ice pilot, overheard him and stopped what he was doing. ''Tis nothing, doctor. This is just the beginning. That's only a growler. The *Southern Cross* saw bergs a hundred miles long.'

'Isn't that almost a country?' asked Wilson.

'Aye, Dr Wilson. A country that melts. You know we can use the bergs for fresh water? Salt leaches out of them after a while.'

Wilson had heard this before, but feigned surprise. 'Really?'

Scott peered at the horizon. He could see a strange lumines-cence on the underside of the clouds. They looked as if they had been painted with mother-of-pearl. 'What is that?' he asked himself.

'Ice blink,' said Armitage.

'Ice what?' Wilson asked, genuinely baffled this time.

Tom Crean, enjoying a pipe nearby, answered for him. 'Ice blink. The light bounces off sheet ice, reflecting on the sky.'

Armitage, the old Arctic hand, chipped in, his voice carrying an unwelcome undertow, hovering between respect and fear. 'It's not any old ice. It's the pack ice. And we'll be hitting it soon enough, gentlemen.'

Bill Wilson felt the conflicting pull of anticipation and fear.

'And then, skipper,' said Tom Crean, slapping the rail, 'we'll really find out just how proud the shipbuilders of Dundee have done you.'

Six

Aberdeen, South Africa, 1901

The town the Inniskillings woke up to was surprisingly modest. Aberdeen was once a neat collection of well-to-do clapperboard houses and less desirable wattle-and-spit dwellings with a ludicrously grand town hall and a church, which had lost its spire. On close inspection, most buildings showed signs of war damage: at least three bloody battles had been fought over the humble burg. It hardly seemed worth the loss of life.

The Boers had left the column unmolested during the final march, allowing a series of rain squalls to do the work of draining morale for them. The British had pitched camp to the south of Aberdeen, with a few lucky officers obtaining billets in the town. But there had been tents waiting for the troopers, well used but serviceable, if a bit frowsty inside with the sweat of other soldiers and a smattering of mildew from damp storage. Despite that, it had been better than the other nights on the trail.

It was barely dawn when a runner summoned Oates to see Colonel Herbert. He'd been dreaming of Gestingthorpe, his mother and sisters and their first nanny. It was a long hot summer, and they'd been playing with Arthur, the cook's boy, damming the river. He shook himself awake and climbed into his dust-stiffened uniform. Young Arthur was dead, he remembered, as his brain re-ordered itself. Kicked in the head by a horse. The memory made for a glum start to the day.

Herbert had taken over the town hall as his HQ and black servants were unloading a very well-stocked baggage wagon. Herbert was sitting on a folding chair in the soft morning sunshine, watching the proceeding, sipping coffee. 'Ah, Oates. Shame about Anstice.'

That was clearly as much of an obituary as the fallen officer was going to get. 'Sir.'

'I'm minded to send out three patrols, see if we can't flush out that band of Boers that attacked us and killed your captain.'

Flush out. Oates didn't like the sound of that. From what he had seen of the Boers, they wouldn't be flushed out very easily.

'I want the Inniskillings to take the dried river bed to the east. Major MacMunn has a map of the area. There is a small settlement eight miles away, two farms. Some of these fellas' – he pointed at the porters, already glistening with sweat under the strengthening sun – 'are adamant they harbour the Boers. Say a commando group calls there every week or two for supplies. Give them some robust questioning, would you?'

Robust. That was a fine English euphemism. Oates wondered when robust slipped into rough. Beating up the men? Threatening the wives? Burning the farmstead?

'Oates?'

He had drifted away for a second. 'Sir.'

'I want you to pick fifteen troopers and be ready to leave within the hour. Clear?'

'Fifteen?'

Herbert put his coffee down and brushed the froth from his moustache. 'Fifteen, yes. And best take a scout.' He had caught an unwelcome inflection in Oates's tone. 'What is it?'

'Just that with a smaller number, we might slip out of camp unnoticed.'

'Unnoticed by whom?'

'Well, the Boers are probably watching, if not for the actual columns, for the dust a sizeable force would kick up. The Boers, I noticed, were riding in groups of five or six.'

A puzzled look crossed Herbert's face. Oates was apparently

suggesting they copy *the enemy*. 'Fifteen men. One scout. An hour. Dismiss.'

It was amazing, thought Oates as they left Aberdeen, how the rains made precious little difference to the countryside. The soil just soaked up most of the water that fell during the night like an enormous blotter. The sun dealt with the rest. The only green was around the river bed, which at least still had a number of stagnant pools along the bottom. Here and there sheep grazed on the banks, but they were scraggy-looking specimens. It was a strange country, he mused, some of it ridiculously verdant, other parts parched to endless dust.

Ahead of Oates, his gaze constantly swivelling between the low-lying hills that rose away from the river valley, was Henry Carlton, a civilian scout. Behind Oates were the fifteen troopers he had chosen for the party, held together by Staff Corporal Docherty, a foul-mouthed but efficient NCO who had made sure the Inniskillings were the smartest of Herbert's contingent.

They were four miles out of town when they heard the distant pop-pops. They sounded feeble, but worryingly familiar. 'Is that gunfire?' he asked Docherty.

'It might be, sir. The other patrols perhaps?'

'Perhaps.' But they wouldn't have got much further out of town than Oates.

'They might be in difficulties,' Docherty said, echoing his thoughts.

'Get the men into the river bed, staff corporal.'

With a few terse commands and economical hand signals, Docherty herded the men towards the wide ditch. It was the signal for the Boers concealed on the hillside to their left to open fire.

The slap of bullets entering flesh was clearly audible. The scout and his horse were first to fall under the sustained volley. He was dead before the horse crumpled, crushing him under her flanks. Docherty's animal gave a huge shudder, managed a half-whinny and died on its feet. The staff corporal leapt off to avoid being pinned by the collapsing mass of dying horseflesh.

Oates managed to turn Sausage and swung a leg out of the saddle as they scrabbled down the three-foot bank to the river bed. He hit the earth hard, pulled the horse down and extracted the carbine from the saddle holster. Around him the troopers were following suit, yanking their horses on to the dried bed, clear of the bullets still whining overhead.

'Two men down plus the scout. Four horses dead.' It was Docherty. 'Where the fuck did they come from, sir?'

Oates ignored the rhetorical question. 'Check for wounded. Keep your head down.'

Docherty crawled along the gulley, examining each man in turn. Upon his return he said: 'McGrath had a nasty gash around the ear, bleeding like a stuck pig. If he's lucky it's missed anything vital and only got his brain.'

Oates smirked at this. 'Anyone else?'

'Saddler, shattered collarbone, I should say. Can't fire.'

'Get those two to leave their ammunition and follow the river bed back to town. Divide their rounds between the men. They'll only be a distraction.'

Despite himself, Docherty looked impressed. 'Sir.'

Oates risked a peek over the edge of the bank. Crouched Boers were moving down the hill. He shouldered the carbine and let off a quick burst of fire. The others joined in. The shots were woefully ineffective, the earth spitting clouds of grit where the bullets were falling short of the commandos, but it sent them scurrying for cover.

He slid back down. 'Staff corporal?'

'Sir?'

Why wasn't he frightened? His mouth was dry, but then, it was hot and he could feel sweat running down his neck. His heart was jerking about in his chest, but not from fear. His mind remained unclouded by panic. He had expected his guts to turn to liquid. They had done no such thing. Oates was quietly pleased with himself. 'They've got decent rifles. We'll have to aim higher with these old crocks and hope for the best. I want you to space the men out and get them firing to keep the Boers on the hill-side where they are. Two at a time, random pattern of firing.

Understand? Don't want the lads being shot like fairground ducks.'

'No, sir.' Docherty looked worried.

'Problem?'

'Good idea, sir. But the ammunition won't last all day if we do it continuously. And them cunts'll be on us in a flash if we run out of bullets. Pardon me.'

'We only have to last till relief comes,' Oates said. 'They'll have heard the firing. And when our chaps get back, they'll raise the alarm. Someone'll be along pretty smart to help us out of this corner.'

Docherty nodded, but both thought the words sounded distinctly hollow. 'Best get to it, then.'

'Yes, staff corporal, best get to it. And tell them to take their helmets off. They offer no protection and they provide too big a target.'

The Boers were in no hurry to come rushing down. They moved now and then to draw fire, hoping to exhaust the British supply of rounds. Oates used his firepower as sparingly as he could. A half-hour into the skirmish he lost another man, shot cleanly through the forehead. He urged the others to stay calm, explaining that the Boers were expecting wild retaliation.

The sun climbed and, with no shade but their terrified horses, the water supply became critical as they slaked their thirst. Oates ordered them to take no more than a capful an hour. He regretted not instructing the wounded men to leave their canteens as well as bullets.

Docherty popped his head up, but instead of firing he slid back down. 'Flag of truce approaching, lieutenant.'

It was a young Boer, dressed in civilian clothes, a rifle slung over his back, a white sheet on a stick waving before him.

Behind the boy, Oates could see figures moving into position under cover of the Inniskillings's hesitation. 'Tell your comrades if they move again the flag won't count for a fig,' he yelled. He made a show of cocking the carbine to make the point.

The farmer looked over his shoulder and barked something incomprehensible. The scurrying stopped.

'And you. That's far enough.'

'Colonel Fouche presents his compliments,' the young man said in an accent so thick it was as if he was chewing the words. 'Colonel', Oates knew, was a self-appointed rank. There was no army and no consistent ranking system with the Boers. They didn't even possess proper uniforms. 'He says if you surrender you will be released and all your private property bar weapons guaranteed.'

Oates looked at Docherty, who shook his head. They had all heard tales of Boer perfidy with prisoners, even summary executions. 'Tell him to fuck off and stick it up his arse. Sir.'

'I'll rephrase if you don't mind, staff corporal.' Oates took a sip of water and cleared his throat. Then he stood up, exposing himself to the fire of the gunmen who lay in the scrub no more than a hundred yards away. Foolhardy, but it gave him a chance to spot their positions. 'Please tell the colonel, thank you for the kind offer. But we came here to fight. Not surrender.'

'Respectfully,' the lad replied, 'you are outnumbered.'

'Respectfully, only by Boers.' That gained him a guffaw from some of the men and a scowl from the farmer's son. 'So, please, tell Colonel Fouche to continue.'

With that he flopped back into the gulley, just in time to glimpse the bent figure trying to outflank them. He was a good two hundred yards along the river but Oates squeezed off four shots, causing him to scamper back the way he had come. The parapet of the riverbank above his head, meanwhile, began to spit dirt as hefty .303 rounds hit home.

'Well done, sir,' said Docherty.

Oates raised his eyebrows. He wasn't so sure it was the wise thing to do. But surrender had no appeal.

The fusillade lasted less than ten minutes and the Boers went back to pot-shots. They managed to take down a horse that had struggled to its feet, despite the best efforts of its rider. It whined pitifully and its cavalryman put a mercy bullet through its skull. The others looked away as he cradled the head of the dead animal before returning to his position.

Oates told the men roughly where he had seen the gunmen and

the British fired at their positions on an irregular basis. By midday, though, the first of Oates's troopers had run out of ammunition.

'Leave your water,' he told Wilder, the bullet-less trooper. 'And your carbine. Horse?'

Wilder pointed across to the site of the ambush, where the scout and several animals lay baking in the sun. 'Shot from under me.'

'Well, keep your head well down, run back to town along the river bed as fast as you can. Report to the colonel and tell them our situation. Take this.' He handed the lad his revolver. If the Boers got close enough for Oates to have to use it, he was done for anyway, but it might help Wilder if he ran into any stray commandoes.

'And ask them where the fuck are they,' Docherty chipped in.

'Tell Colonel Herbert,' Oates corrected, 'if it isn't too much trouble, we'd quite like a relief party.'

Wilder sprinted off, covering the ground like a primate, on all fours. He made it without mishap to the far bend where the course of the river kinked and, with a fast backward glance, he was gone. Oates listened carefully for the sound of sniper fire but, apart from two shots from their own tormentors, there was nothing.

Another of the group fired his last round an hour later, and Oates repeated the exercise, sending him along the river to gee-up Herbert. Docherty took a bullet to the shoulder shortly afterwards. Oates inspected it and found it a clean puncture, although clearly it hurt like a demon, because Docherty trotted out a stream of profanities escalating in intensity and explicitness till he slumped back against the bank. Only then did he allow Oates to stuff a makeshift bandage inside his tunic.

'Sir. Down to the last two rounds.' It was Peyton, a corporal.

'Off you go.'

Peyton looked offended. 'What if they charge the position, sir?'

'Well, at least you won't be here to see it. Bugger off. None of us is much use without ammunition.'

Soon after Peyton's departure, there came an explosion of distant rifle fire, borne on the hot breeze blowing from the West. That could, thought Oates, be a rescue party fighting its way through. Or being routed.

They took one further casualty shortly after that, a nasty neck wound to a trooper called Carlisle. Oates watched as a field dressing was put on it, but the white gauze and linen bandage was soon soaked crimson as it wicked up the blood. Now Oates, at last, began to feel fear, the possibility that none of them would make it out alive. Much as he was afraid for himself, he couldn't countenance the loss of a whole patrol.

'Docherty, I want you to take everyone back to town. Leave me the weapons. I can pretend to be the whole unit—'

'No, sir.'

'No?'

'Corporal Ronson is y'man. He'll take them. I'll stay here. Don't fancy four miles of crouching with this shoulder.' Oates knew that a pathetic excuse but let it pass. 'I'd best stay with you and Carlisle, 'cause he's too bollocksed-up to make it as well. If the others can get through, maybe they'll get the arses moving.'

Some of the troopers were equally reluctant to leave, but Docherty called them and their mothers unspeakable things and soon the three of them were left alone with the restless horses. Oates let the most troublesome gallop off after the retreating troopers. The remainder he gave a few splashes of precious water each.

Another hour crawled by, punctuated by probing shots from the Boers. Docherty and Oates took turns to check the enemy's progress, popping up at varying intervals along the bank – with and without helmets – to try to swell their apparent numbers. Apart from a splash of dirt in his eye, Oates remained unscathed. Carlisle, though, was beginning to moan. He gave the trooper some water, but his eyes were rolling and there was an unpleasant sheen on his forehead and upper lip.

'We might be in a fix, here, sir,' said Docherty.

'True. But we've got most of them away.'

Docherty took another peek over the bank and let out an exclamation of surprise.

'Sir. Take a look.'

Oates scrambled to the edge and popped his head up for a

61

second. Then he brought it up again, more slowly. Up on the ridges he could see the Boers gathering, and a string of horses was being led to them. He watched them mount and ride off with a feeling of disbelief.

'Lord above,' he said. 'What's got into them?'

'Maybe the fuckers' cows need milking,' offered Docherty.

Oates laughed. 'Maybe they do, staff corporal.'

He waited ten minutes before he risked standing. Then he brought the horses to their feet and walked over to Carlisle to see if the man was capable of getting himself in the saddle.

Oates saw the puff of smoke from the ridge moments before the sniper's bullet smacked into his thigh, spun through the muscle and crazed the bone, sending him to the ground into the brilliant light of absolute agony.

Seven

Beyond the Antarctic Circle

There was blood on the ice. Puddles of it glowed a garish red against the white background. Curlicues of vapour issued from the fresh pools as the warm liquid cooled and congealed. The greasy slick made for uncertain footing as the men, now dressed for the most part in their light but windproof Burberry gabardines, moved over the floe.

The corpulent crabeater seals barked and rolled away, confused by what was happening, but didn't take the sensible course of sliding into the sea. Another shot, the sound deadened by the great slabs of frozen water, and another spray of crimson splattered across the floe. That made six dead seals. Then the butchering began, turning the ice pink as the hot fluid from the entrails hissed across the frozen surface and diluted the blood.

Scott, swathed in greatcoat, cap and scarf, stood at *Discovery's* rail, watching as Wilson supervised the chop, as the doctor called it, creating a stack of seal steaks from one of the carcasses. The others would be skinned and hung from the ratlines, where they would freeze.

Raucous, pushy skuas were gathering, anxious for a share in the massacre, swirling and squawking. Skelton took a pot-shot at them and they whirled away, before finding their courage again moments later. Sinister sooty petrels patrolled above the mêlée, also waiting their turn at the feeding table, along with the more attractive blue-grey fulmars. A whale breached nearby. Scott wondered if it was a killer, drawn by the blood sliding down the five-foot edge of the floe and staining the green water black. It might explain why the surviving seals were reluctant to slither free. They were stuck between the murdering devils and the deep-cold sea, which glistened with submerged frazil-ice, the slush of solidifying seawater.

Scott's eyes ached from the glare. He had been up all night, unable to pull himself away from the ever-changing scene. The endless dance of light on ice was more fascinating than he had ever thought possible. As the sun skimmed the horizon for a brief time and then rose again, the shades went from crimson to burnished copper to salmon pink to a soft, rose hue. Sometimes bands of different colours played over the floes, like earth-bound rainbows, at other times a sea fog reduced everything to a dull grey. The harsh light when an unclouded sun shone on the pack was fearsome and he often had to wear goggles. Sometimes the same sunlight struck a mist-shrouded berg and caused it to glow with an inner light of jewel-like intensity and rays of sapphire and jade to shoot across the waters.

'All done, skipper.' Shackleton and Skelton, who had performed the shootings, returned onboard, cradling the rifles, their breath coming hard after the exertion of execution.

'We'll do the sheep next,' said Shackleton brightly. 'They can be skinned and frozen too.'

'Very well.' Scott caught the smell of seal guts on the wind as Wilson eviscerated a crabeater. 'I hope those things taste better than they smell.'

'A few months in and they'll taste just fine,' said Skelton. 'Even the skuas.'

'Well, I should wind up the electrometers. And perhaps take a pipe to get that stench out of my nostrils. Gentlemen.'

'Skipper.'

'Is he all right?' Shackleton asked as Scott moved to the wooden hut that housed the two self-recording clockwork quadrant electrometers which measured the earth's potential gradient on a roll of paper. Scott spent a long time watching the dots on the continuous sheet, recording the fluctuations in the planet's magnetic field. Apparently, he couldn't wait to set up his device for measuring the ionisation of the air.

'Skipper doesn't like the slaughter,' the engineer replied, recalling how he had barely tolerated the killing of the penguins on Macquarrie Island, en route to New Zealand. 'Bit of an animal lover, is our Commander Scott.'

Shackleton understood sentimentality about dogs and perhaps horses, but seals and sheep? Shackleton looked over the apparently endless floes and the bergs, which ranged from table sized to enormous mansions of ice, and at the dark channels between them. This ice-littered seascape appeared brooding and terrifying, but this was only the beginning. They had nudged through groaning, granular sea ice for two days and now they were on the edge of the far less accommodating pack ice, a confusing maze of black water and white tabulars. 'Nervous?' asked Skelton.

Shackleton looked at him. 'About the sheep or the ice?'

'The sheep won't bite,' laughed Skelton.

But the ice might give you a nasty nip. Those who had ventured to the far north had a refrain they were fond of repeating: *You can't trust the ice*. Shackleton knew all about the forty-six gruelling days it had taken for Ross to break through the barrier of floating ice to reach the solid mass of the ice shelf. He had heard Armitage's tales of ships crushed like hen's eggs in the floes. To Shackleton, the sea ahead was a white, blue and green kaleidoscope, where the currents and the icebergs seemed to flow in contradictory directions. It was confusing in the extreme, but Armitage had the eye. From his perch aloft, he could see clear water and safe passage where others saw only a treacherous icy trap. Or so he had assured them.

Shackleton peered up at the sky, a palette of pastel blues streaked with delicate strands of thin, white clouds. 'It's beautiful, though, isn't it?' he said.

Skelton grunted. Like many of the crew, the engineer struggled to see the wonder, complaining there was nothing to please the eye out on the ice.

'Whenever I think of the end of the world,' said Shackleton, 'I think of it burning, being consumed by fire. But it might be it will end in ice, frozen in permanent stasis.'

'Are you going to go all poetical on me again, Shackle?'

Shackleton pulled back the bolt on the rifle. 'I wouldn't waste my breath, Reg. The only poetry you like is the rhythm of crankshafts. Come on, let's get this over with before the skipper changes his mind and adopts them all as pets.'

They stepped around one of the bulkier items on deck and Skelton nodded at the shape under the tarp. 'Is he really going to use Eva?'

'I damn well hope so,' said Shackleton. 'Do you know how much it weighs? And all those cylinders to go with it? Took me half a day to stow that lot. He'd better use it.'

'A balloon, though. In Antarctica. He must be bloody mad.'

Shackleton threw back his head and roared, peering up at the icicle-encrusted spar masts till his condensing breath clouded his view. He slapped Skelton on the back. 'Not like the rest of us then, eh, Reg?'

After the seal and sheep slaughter and a series of hearty meals, came a late Christmas on 5 January, with skiing races and football and rum. Scott also finally revealed his plans which, whether they approved of them or not, at least lifted the uncertainty of the crew. *Discovery* would not be returning to New Zealand when night fell. It would overwinter as far south in McMurdo Sound as they could safely manage and then, come summer, sledging parties would be sent out to explore the volcanoes, the magnetic pole and perhaps probe south towards the pole. They would attempt to discover the relationship between the Great Ice Barrier and Victoria Land. The sledging parties would also aim to sustain a second winter, depending on their progress and the disposition of the rescue ship that Markham had promised.

On 'Boxing Day', *Discovery* broke free of the temporary grip of the ice and sailed on through the canal-like bands between the floes. Two days later, on an eye-wateringly bright day, the air filled with delicate snow petrels, Scott saw what he thought initially must be a mirage. It wasn't. It was Antarctica proper, the continent itself, rather than its protecting aureole of ice. The filmy curtain that had blurred the horizon for days lifted and revealed its mountains, sparkling and flaring in the low midnight sun as if created from frosting sugar. It drew every pair of eyes on deck, and men moved to the rail just to gawp. It was as foreign a world as most had ever seen.

'The Admiralty Range,' said Shackleton.

'Must be a hundred miles away or more,' replied Scott. 'And the Pole beyond it.'

'Well, Dr Wilson's God isn't going to make it easy for us to stand at that pole.'

'If we decide to go for it.'

'Of course.' The shore team had not discussed an assault on ninety degrees south, at least not formally. On the face of it, the physicists were more concerned about the magnetic pole and the variations in the earth's magnetic pull, the biologists about the new species of penguin or plankton, the geologists by the volcanoes and the age of the rocks; but, in their hearts, they all knew that the bottom of the world was the hard, glittering prize. 'But when we get back *Discovery* will be judged not by the science, or the new lands we have named, but by *how far* and *how long*. You know that.'

'We mustn't let such concerns distract us,' said Scott.

'Don't tell me you don't feel it?'

'Feel what?'

But Shackleton just continued to stare at the distant range of jagged peaks, letting some unseen magnetism tug at his soul, till the curtain of mist descended and obscured the land once more.

Eight

Aberdeen, South Africa

Dear Mother,

You may have heard the news, but I hope this reaches you before any other message. And certainly before you read the South African press, which if given a stick, contrives to get the wrong end of it. I am billeted in a house in Aberdeen, laid up for the moment. There was a bit of a scrap. I have broken my leg.

Actually, shattered was a more accurate word.

Not too bad, considering. Didn't hurt too much.

As he twisted in his bed and felt the fire streak up his thigh, Oates managed a rueful laugh. When they had finally reached him, several hours after he took the bullet, they re-set the splintered bone without so much as a tot of brandy. Then there was the ride back to town, every jolt bringing grinding pain.

Am being well looked after.

Colonel Herbert had pulled out and left him with the local doctor.
With too many Boers around for comfort, his hosts had decided
to transport him to the hospital at Naauwpoort. Three days, they
estimated. That was twenty-five miles on roads like baked corduroy,
then a train. And the bullet was still in there. Oates was not
relishing the prospect.

So mustn't complain. Apart from the fact I am losing fitness.

And three stone.

I am as weak as a kitten. Still, I am mentioned in despatches.

He stopped writing. When he had visited, Culshaw had told
him there was talk of a Victoria Cross. If only, he said, Oates
stopped complaining to all and sundry. Not that Oates was moaning
about his own pitiful condition. His anger was directed towards
the army. They had lost dozens of men that day on the patrols.
Oates had written to Kitchener, no less, arguing the army was
under-resourced and badly used. He doubted he would get a VC,
not after criticising his superior officer's so-called rescue attempt.
As if he cared about a gong. It had hardly been Rourke's Drift. He
would feel a fraud accepting it.

The men of my draft are calling me 'No Surrender Oates', but
please, just stick to Laurie when I get home. I don't like a fuss,
as you know.

Would his mother catch the superciliousness? The nickname
was certainly being used, but he would squash it as soon as he
could.

So, wish me happy birthday, although I shall spend it on my back.
Not quite what I had in mind. Don't worry, I'll be fine by the
time I see you in six or seven weeks.

He stopped and changed it to eight or nine. It was a long time. He'd be thoroughly bored with such inactivity. Or Boer'd. He laughed at that and incorporated it into the letter and then let an uncharacteristic cloud of gloom wash over him. He was bed-ridden, in continuous pain, facing an agonising journey and, so the senior medical officer had told him, the chances of a lifelong limp were pretty high. One leg, apparently, was shorter than the other. What a way, he thought, for a chap to spend his twenty-first birthday.

Nine

Hut Point, Antarctica

As Scott trudged up the snow-covered slope behind the three huts and the kennels they had constructed, he took stock. *Eva*, the balloon, had been a fiasco. Although he had gone aloft, he had seen little and the valve leaked hydrogen, depositing him back on the ice with a painful and embarrassing thump. Thirteen hundred pounds wasted and his pride bruised. Still, they had found a useful inlet, now named Balloon Bight. And, after all, he wasn't the only one who had made a fool of himself. Shackle's first attempts at travelling over the ice had not gone well. Shambles was the word.

'Skipper?' It was Shackleton, a few yards behind. 'You all right?'

Scott halted, catching his breath, and repositioned the skis and the long single pole on to his other shoulder. He was dressed in his sledging gear, with woollen underwear, flannel shirt, thick sweater, jacket and britches and a Burberry gabardine outer suit. On his hands, he had wolfskin mitts. It was hot work, climbing the slope, but by now Scott realised it was important to get used to the bulky clothing. 'Yes. Was I mumbling?'

'Yelling, more like.'

'I was thinking of your reconnaissance. You and Wilson and Ferrar in that tent.' The sailor, doctor and geologist had undertaken the initial sledging trial after the expedition had constructed their huts. 'Like a French farce.'

'It wasn't funny at the time.'

The effort of man-hauling, the clumsy dressing and undressing in the cramped tent, the three-in-a-bag sleeping arrangements and the ice-stiff socks and clothes they had to contend with had sapped their energy. The party had averaged one mile an hour and given the men their first taste of frostbite and Wilson of the terrible cramp the cold could bring on. Such pain was unbearable under normal circumstances; dealing with it while trying not to wake your colleagues in the reindeer-hide bag was sheer torture. There was one positive outcome: the trio had climbed White Island and were sure that the ice barrier which they had landed on stretched all the way south, down towards the Pole. There was no inland sea to bar their way. Just the distant, forbidding mountains. But were they capable of tackling those?

'We didn't do enough preparation,' Scott said. 'Enough practice at the basics.'

Shackleton knew Scott was flagellating himself, taking every setback to heart. As if it was his fault the three of them made such a mess of pitching the tent and operating the stove. 'You didn't have enough time.'

Scott hesitated before nodding his agreement, thinking of the deadlines and the furious preparation against rival teams that had, so far, failed to materialise.

'I'll race you down,' said Shackleton and began to stride confidently off towards the summit, his boots making the now familiar squeaking-crunching sound. The snow was reasonably deep and crisp, not like some of the sticky porridge-like mush that had hampered their earlier ski tests.

'Nansen told me when I met him in Norway that he thought no man walking could match another on skis. What do you think?'

Scott did not seek advice very often, but the question of skis and dogs had been occupying his thoughts ever since they had chosen this spot – Hut Point as it was christened – to overwinter *Discovery*. 'I think he's a man who knows what he's talking about. And to watch Skelton, you'd think it might be true.'

'Aye, he's good, is Reg. But Armitage says skiing is all nonsense, that it's one thing here, another out on the ice sheet. It'll be a race worth having. Foot versus ski.'

'And the dogs?'

'We'll see about them when we head for Cape Crozier.' Scott intended to leave details of where they were quartered, so a relief party might locate them. Markham had sent word to New Zealand that he had raised enough funds to ensure a ship would come the next summer to check their progress, bring fresh supplies and take off any sick or injured. 'We'll try the dogs then.'

They attained the summit, and Scott pulled down his wide-brimmed hat to shade his eyes from the low sun, which had stained the cumulus clouds a distinctive saffron and fringed the mountains with a dark purple. It had started to vanish below the horizon at midnight, a taste of twilight, presaging the long night to come, the half-light revealing the brightest of the stars that daylight had masked. Time was short if they were to try more sledging. But then, it seemed to Scott, time was always short.

He looked down towards the ship, still surrounded by limpid open water, and the rather depressing suburban prefabricated dwelling the men called Gregory's Villa. Next to it were the two asbestos huts for the physicists and the dog kennels, which, being contrary, the animals had spurned in favour of snow-burrows. Scott bent down and fixed the ski bindings to his boots, exposing his hands in order to close the fiddly buckles and straps.

He imagined performing this task when the temperature had dropped to minus thirty and the wind was howling and making it seem even colder. Dr Koettlitz had given them all a lecture on frost-bite, but Scott felt he had rather underplayed the dangers. The men were more interested in his toilet advice. The doctor, with pantomime help from Armitage, had explained carefully the necessity of cupping your privates when urinating and the advantages, when *in extremis*, of soiling your britches and letting it freeze, chipping it out later. 'But only', Armitage advised, 'if you're passing solids.' There followed an argument about whether such a thing would be possible with the lardy pemmican – a mixture of dried meat and fat that would be their staple on the ice – they had brought and the discussion had become a little too corporeal and bawdy for Scott's tastes.

'To the rocky outcrop and its little friend?' Shackleton suggested, indicating a cairn-shaped lump of ice with his pole, and the waddling shape next to it. 'The one with the penguin that doesn't realise just how close to becoming lunch it is?'

Scott shuddered. Much as he found seal unpalatable, especially the liver and kidneys, he still preferred it to oily penguin. He rolled the balaclava he was wearing under his hat down over his face. 'Indeed. Call it?'

Shackleton adjusted his balaclava and crouched into an aggressive position.

'Ready. Winner gets this slope named after him, eh? Scott Slope or Shackleton Slope?'

'Very well.'

Scott looked at the ship, where most of the men would remain quartered during the long night, at the growing pile of stores next to it, much of it being ferried to Gregory's Villa. He didn't want to take the chance of losing everything if the crushing winter ice took *Discovery*. Having already been trapped firm in the pack for a few days and subsequently lost in fast-freezing seas with a panicking crew, he had fresh respect for the power and capriciousness of frozen water. The polar dictum was correct: you couldn't trust the ice.

'Steady.'

Scott glanced north, the albedo from the sheets of smooth ice that caught the sun hurting his eyes, causing him to squint. Despite the glare from some of the surfaces, the smokeless, unsullied air was so preternaturally clear, the light so piercingly sharp, he could make out distant waves of sastrugi and even the seracs on the distant mountains, the fractured columns of ice-like pillars. It's a scene from *Childe Harold*, Shackleton had said, when he first gazed on this spot. The brooding conical shape of Mt Erebus with its sulphurous plume, and its aptly named companion, Mt Terror, much of it clear of snow, giving it a dark, sinister aspect, certainly lent the landscape menace.

Following the example of the pioneers before him, Scott blunted the impact of the unknown by christening the unfamiliar with hieratic zeal. The tip of the peninsula was now Cape Armitage, to the north of that, anchors held *Discovery* in Winter Quarter Bay, The Gap gave easy access to the ice barrier and the peak now charted as Observation Hill would enable the base group to watch over the ice barrier for any sledger's return. Castle Rock was an outcrop that straddled the ridge of the peninsula. It was like naming the Stations of the Southern Cross.

And yet sometimes, he looked at this place and felt the terror of early pagans contemplating the night sky. Perhaps they were pathetic to attempt to subdue it with their charts and bearings and friendly names. Antarctica was vast, brooding and hostile and it just was. Whatever tiny marks men could leave on it could and would be swept away with ease in no time.

'Go.'

Shackleton had barely begun the consonant when he launched himself off the crest and began poling frantically, pushing on either side of his body, like a crazed gondolier.

Scott yelled in protest at the gamesmanship and flung himself forward.

The pair plummeted down the slope, the huge wooden skis riding easily over the smooth surface, gathering speed as they went. Scott adopted a similar knee-bent position to Shackleton, who had clearly been watching Skelton, and he felt the wind keening in his face.

Around halfway down the incline he began to catch Shackleton, who had turned to his left slightly, losing vertical progress, before swinging to the right. Scott, gaining on him rapidly, suddenly appreciated what the Irishman was doing: slowing down to keep control. A vision of his colliding with the cairn – or worse, the penguin – suddenly came to him, a repeat of the ignominy of the balloon ascent.

He also threw his weight to the right and felt the ski edge dig into the snow and steadied himself with his single pole. There was a satisfying shushing sound, and a spray of ice arced up behind him.

He shifted his body again, pleased at the way he had carved a smooth turn. He was within yards of Shackleton now, and able to check his progress.

As he tried the next swoop, his right heel slipped, turning inwards and he felt the tendons strain. He moved his shoulders to correct the roll and pushed with his stick, but in that second his whole gait collapsed and the skis crossed with a loud clack, catapulting him forward.

His face hit the snow and its icy substratum, only the woollen balaclava saving him from damage. He rolled twice, and came to rest, his lungs burning. Shackleton hadn't noticed and continued on his way. Scott was facing down the slope, with a mess of skies and limbs behind him. The thick layers of clothing had absorbed much of the impact. It was only when he tried to shuffle round that the pain, like a bradawl stabbed behind his kneecap, caused him to gasp.

With excessive care, he pulled his legs round so he could reach the bindings. A yell of victory told him Shackleton had made the cairn. Scott touched his knee. Even through the Burberry and britches he could feel the pudding-like swelling and when he pressed, the flash of fire brought tears to his eyes. Not only tears of pain, but of frustration. He was no doctor, but even Scott knew he wouldn't be leading a dogsledding expedition to Cape Crozier any time soon. Robert Falcon Scott's first polar season was finished before it had begun.

Ten

Essex, England

When Lawrence Oates alighted from the train at Sudbury, a hearty cheer issued from the crowded platform. For a moment he looked around, puzzled, till a hand clapped his back. 'Well done, sir, well done.'

Now he could see familiar faces in the group, neighbours and employees of the house. He had assumed the gathering meant it was simply a busy day for the railway, but it seemed all of Essex and half of Suffolk had turned out to welcome him.

'Proud of you, Mr Laurie.'

'Thank you.' He smiled at the well-wisher and positioned his crutches in under his arms. 'Can I get through?' He looked for a porter, but the crowd was pressing closer. 'I have some bags—'

'Don't you worry there, Mr Laurie. Make way, make way.' It was the reassuring barrel shape of Davies, the family coachman, and behind him one of the grooms. Hal, that was it. The lad had gained a foot in height.

'Hal, I have a trunk—'

The groom leapt up on to the train and relieved the conductor of the case, while Davies gently took an arm and led him through the crush of people. 'Have the rig here, sir. Can you manage?'

Oates nodded, but in truth using the crutches without being able to get a good swing was tricky and the sheer number of people made that difficult. As he shuffled forward he was forced to put some weight on his damaged thigh and the twinge told him the healing wasn't complete yet.

'Do you mind?' Davies said, shouldering aside one of the more persistent admirers.

'Hold on,' said Oates, spotting a young lad hovering at the rear. He hadn't recognised him without a cap and his father's gun, broken, tucked at his elbow. 'Sam. Sam Aylett, come here.'

Sam, who was barely sixteen and thin as a whippet, squeezed through. 'Sir. Welcome home, Mr Laurie.'

'Is your father here?' He scanned the crowd for the man's friendly, weather-tanned face. 'No? Tell him to come and see me at the house, will you?'

The boy's head dropped and he mumbled.

'What?'

'Dad's dead, sir.'

Oates felt his mind scrabble. Dead? Death was something he was used to out on the veldt, but he hadn't imagined it coming to Gestingthorpe in his absence. 'When? How?'

'Month or more. His heart, sir.'

'My God.' He doubted the man was much past fifty. 'I wanted to . . .' He lifted the boy's chin. 'How's your mother?'

'Bearing up. You know. Bit of a shock, Mr Laurie.'

'I'll say so. Listen to me, Sam. Your father saved my life. Whatever shooting I was able to do, I did it because of him and the poor pheasants and rabbits of the estate. He was a good teacher and a fine man. Do you understand?'

The boy sniffled. 'Yes, sir. Thank you, sir.'

Gamekeeper Henry Aylett, Sam's father, had taught the younger Oates the rudiments of country life. He wasn't much taken with trapping stoats or weasels or indeed trudging the perimeters at dusk or dawn looking for evidence of poachers, but the fishing and the shooting he had taken to with ease. 'I'd like you and your mother to come and see me up at the house. You'll do that?' Sam nodded. 'Good.' He made the boy shake his hand. 'Tell your mother. Make sure it's soon.'

It took another five minutes to clear the crowd and get into the game cart. Hal loaded the trunk, strapped it down, and stood tiger at the rear.

Davies took the reins and started out for Gestingthorpe Hall at a brisk trot, the sleek Hackney in the limbers pulling the load with speed and grace. Soon they crossed from Suffolk into Essex and Oates took a breath of his home county's air.

'Good to have you back, Mr Laurie. Been in the wars. If you'll pardon the expression.'

'Yes, I suppose I have rather. What on earth were all those people doing there at the station? How did they know?'

'Been in all the newspapers about you. Been an outcry that you didn't get a medal.' He turned around. 'Your mother will be pleased to see you. Shocked, but pleased.'

'I won't have the crutches for too much longer, Davies. Be back in the saddle before too long.'

The look the coachman gave him was all too familiar. Lawrence Oates wouldn't be the judge of that. It would be up to the Mistress.

It was a lustrous day, the deep green of the hedgerows startling after the paler, sun-bleached colours of the South African interior. They passed duck ponds and thatched cottages, twisted ancient oaks and willows bent over lazy streams, fields of unripe corn and, on the sunnier slopes, saffron crocuses were being planted by lines of crook-backed women and children. The drivers of various gigs and dogcarts raised their hats as they recognised one of Gestingthorpe's carriages. Oates was glad his mother hadn't sent the rather grand Victoria she kept for funerals and other special occasions.

Oates found his eyes closing as the sun warmed his face. The sounds were gentle, unthreatening; the smells, from orchard and farmyard, familiar yet vivid; the palette the comforting one from his childhood, not that of a wild, unpredictable foreign country. Oates sighed to himself. He really was home.

As they neared Gestingthorpe, bunting and flags began to appear on the high hedgerows of the twisting lanes. Oates paid it no attention, till he saw a handwritten sign, welcoming him home by name.

Another mile further on, as they turned into the hamlet, a cluster of locals applauded, and a bunch of flowers was thrown into the cart. The bells of the church began to ring as Davies turned the horse into the driveway, past the severely clipped yew hedges and the lake where he had launched his leaky wooden ships only a few years before. There, beyond the lawns and the holly hedges, was the great house itself.

Oates was pleased to see it, still draped in virginia creeper and with its backdrop of proud elms and the avenue of two-hundred-year-old beeches to one side. The front lawn was as verdant as ever, but much of it was obscured by rows of tables that had been placed on it. The trestles were covered in gingham cloth and jugs of lemonade. There were more flags outside the entrance porch of the house, and at least thirty people who were stamping and whistling. Bryan, his excitable younger brother, was first to greet him, sprinting out of the doorway in a tangle of gangly limbs. 'Laurie, welcome home. Maybe you can talk some sense into Mother now, about what she wants me to do with myself. Her—'

'Now, now, Mr Bryan, don't rush out all your problems,' said Davies reprovingly. 'It's as nothing to what your brother has been through.'

Standing demurely in the shadows were his sisters, Violet and Lillian, both looking radiant and healthy. Stanley, the butler, was behind them, with Billings, his footman, and Mrs Melton, the cook, to his left. Oates raised a hand to his sisters and they waved back, but he could tell from their expressions something wasn't right. With Bryan hindering rather than helping, Davies guided him down and Oates positioned the crutches, telling Bryan not to make too much of a fuss about them, that they were mainly for show.

His mother finally appeared, as graceful and regal as ever, but looking far brighter than he recalled. The sombre clothes she had adopted since her husband's death were gone, replaced by sunny yellows and creams and she was sporting the first full grin he had seen for quite some time. As she stepped forward, however, her smile faded. A hand went to her mouth. Oates realised at once what he must look like to his sisters and mother.

Thin, bedraggled, crippled; a shadow of the fit young man she had sent off to Ireland.

'Hello, Mother,' he said.

'Davies, get these people out of here.'

Davies hesitated, not sure he had heard the Mistress correctly.

'There will be no party, Stanley,' she hissed over her shoulder. 'Make sure the children go off with some lemonade and biscuits.' She cocked her head, as if just noticing a strange sound. 'And tell the vicar to stop the bells.' A hard, bitter edge appeared in her voice and she gripped his shoulder, wincing at the feel of bone. Her eyes glistened with moisture. 'This is how Great Britain sends its heroes home, is it?'

'Carrie, I'm fine—'

She stepped towards him, and he caught the citrusy smell of her favourite perfume, so delicate compared to other women's. Caroline Oates reached up and touched his face and said: 'Don't worry, Laurie, you're home now. And safe.'

Much as he had looked forward to seeing his mother, Oates felt the familiar crushing sensation in his chest as she ushered him inside, snapping off orders to the staff. If Oates was to do the full convalescence as advised by the army doctors, it was going to be a long six months.

There was eventually a party, of course, several weeks after Lawrence Oates returned, once Caroline was certain her son could take the strain of frivolity and adulation. As Oates told his brother: 'It's more likely the strain of chicken broth and bad poetry will carry me off.' His sisters' regime had been unrelenting, with three a.m. feeds and copious quantities of Tennyson. Oates found he particularly hated *The Charge of The Light Brigade* – hardly the British army's proudest moment – although he quite liked the restlessness and grit of *Ulysses*. At least by the fourth time of reading.

The postponed celebration was finally held on a Saturday, and all the outlying villages emptied as people came to pay their respects. Oates was amused and embarrassed by the sheer number. Bryan estimated there were 120 children, or perhaps more, 'but they won't sit still to be counted' – which was hardly surprising, given the swings, donkeys and coconut shys they had been provided with – and Oates handed out nearly that many pouches of fine tobacco to the many male well-wishers. Lillian and Violet had spent the previous evening and morning supervising the maids tying small but elegant posies for the ladies.

The children had jam and cake at the village school at three p.m., while 275 adults sat down for dinner an hour later, with Oates at the centre. His appetite still feeble, he picked at the beef and mutton, although he enjoyed two glasses of rich brown ale.

Afterwards, they decamped to the lawn, where a small, bunting-draped dais had been erected. The desultory showers that threatened to blight the day had passed, and the sun shone on the honeyed stone of Gestingthorpe and the lightest breeze flapped the flags and banners.

The Reverend Bromwich made the first address to the satisfied throng. He stared out over a sea of flushed and grinning faces. 'I must thank Mrs Caroline Oates and her family for their remark-able generosity.' There were cheers and heartfelt applause. 'And it is an honour and a privilege to be allowed to officially welcome Lieutenant Oates home. A genuine example of an Englishman and a patriot, loyal and true to king and country. We were all very moved to read the accounts of his bravery.' He turned and looked at Oates directly. 'Indeed every other Englishman's heart must have soared when he read of your valour. My emotion left me choked, with pride and pleasure that this was one of ours. Yet look at him.'

Those nearest craned to see Oates, standing next to his mother, cheeks burning, a fixed smile on his face. If they had looked closely, they might have noticed he was taking discreet support from Caroline Oates and his brother Bryan, who had sandwiched him. Although he had devised a way of padding the shoe to make his legs equal length, putting his weight on the damaged left leg for any length of time still caused a nagging ache.

'This is a man who did his work without swagger, without fuss, without thinking of himself. It was as if he were doing some everyday task, not fighting for the life of his men. So we give thanks to God

82

for his safe return. And we give thanks to Mrs Oates once more. As part of the jubilations, she is—' Caroline Oates shot the vicar a glance, but he ploughed on. 'No, I have to say this. She is to fund the recasting of our church's poor cracked fifth and sixth bells.'

The roar of approval banished any doubts Mrs Oates had about the public announcement and she nodded to acknowledge the cheers.

Oates was feeling the effect of the sun on his neck, and longed to undo his collar. His knee was throbbing and he could feel the familiar spikes of pain in his thigh. 'I have to go in soon,' he whispered to Bryan.

'They want to hear you, brother.'

The vicar, though, was reluctant to vacate the stage, and ultimately it was left to Lillian and Violet to find a pretext to lead him away, to lubricate his hoarse voice. Oates hobbled to the platform and took the three stairs slowly, leaning on the rail. The crowd fell silent. He found he could think of nothing to say other than thank you.

'Speech!' someone yelled.

'No speeches. The good vicar has made a fine talk for all of us. And I would like you to remember that, although I made it back in almost one piece,' he tapped his leg, 'many of my friends and colleagues did not. I know what much of the continental press has said about our soldiers out in South Africa. Let me tell you, if there were a Boer here' – there were boos at the very thought – 'if there was a Boer here, he would agree with me that our soldiers did us proud.' Another cheer. 'So, if I could ask for a minute's silence for fallen comrades.'

Hats were whipped off and gazes lowered. Bryan winked at him. It was a neat ploy to diffuse the call for any more speechifying. When the sixty seconds was up, Oates said: 'I thank my mother, sisters and brother for nursing me back to health. I thank you for coming, because there are no folk like the folk of Essex. And I think you should enjoy the rest of the day!' He pointed towards the stream that ran through the property. 'The swings and roundabouts and amusements await you.'

Bryan was there to help him down as the clapping rang in his ears. 'Well done.'

Oates felt his head swim from the sun and the ale. 'Take me inside.'

Bryan tried to steer him to the drawing room, then the morning room, but Oates insisted on going into those parts of the house where carpet gave way to linoleum. He settled in the kitchen, where the staff was trying to make headway against the devastation left by the party. Amid the clatter of pots and pans and the barked orders from Mrs Melton, the cook, Oates accepted a glass of water from Alice, the scullery maid, and eased himself into a wooden chair, pushing his damaged leg straight out and massaging his aching thigh.

Bryan crouched down. 'Will you be all right? I should go back out.'

'Spotted a young lady, have you?'

'No. Yes.' Bryan blushed. 'And I dare say our war hero could have the pick of many a maiden out there.'

Oates sipped his water. 'You know the army's opinion on that. If I want to advance, I should delay marrying.'

'Marrying?' Bryan looked shocked. 'I was just thinking of an Essex Rose to mop your poor brow and keep you company.'

Such talk from his younger brother made him uncomfortable. 'Preferably one who doesn't know Tennyson.'

'I heard that.' It was Lillian, feigning horror. 'You are a monster. I for one, didn't believe a word of Reverend Bromwich's speech. You are mean spirited and ungrateful.'

He nodded solemnly. '"We cannot be kind to each other here for even an hour. We whisper, and hint, and chuckle, and grin at a brother's shame; however we brave it out, we men are a little breed." Forgive me.'

Lillian laughed at the quotation. 'So you were listening. Mother wants to know if you are well enough to rejoin the celebrations. Or if you would like to rest.'

'Please tell her not to fuss.'

Lillian laughed. 'If dinner for three hundred people isn't a fuss, I don't know what is.'

'And inviting the Dunwoodys.'

'Now, now,' she chided. The Dunwoodys were the area's most prominent Catholic family and Carrie had a history of antagonism with anything papal. Especially where her children were concerned. One of the Dunwoody boys had once taken an interest in Lillian. He was sent off with a flea in his ear, in double-quick time. 'That's all behind us.'

Outside, he heard Violet shouting their names up the narrow back stairs, thinking they had bolted to the servant's hall or even, reverting to childhood, the warren of storage rooms in the attic. 'Laurie. Lillian. Bryan. Are you up there? Uncle Charles is here. Wants to meet the hero!'

'I think', Oates stared at Bryan to make sure his brother appreciated he was serious, 'I would like to retire from being a war hero after this day. I'd prefer we didn't mention it again.'

'Then what shall you do?' asked Lillian with affectionate sarcasm. 'If you can't bask in your military glory? Or turn a pretty girl's head with a wound for king and country.'

'That's what I suggested,' said Bryan.

'Look what happened last time I turned a pretty girl's head.'

'Oh, Laurie, shush,' scolded Lillian. 'Don't get all maudlin. What are your plans?'

Lieutenant Oates thought for a moment. 'I shall buy some horses. They are a sad lot you have left in the stables. And as soon as I am able, I shall ride to the hounds.'

Bryan stood and clapped Oates on his shoulder. 'Welcome back, Laurie.'

Eleven

Hut Point, Antarctica

At the beginning of April, the last of the skuas disappeared north. Now the culled seals could be hung outside or placed in the snow-trench larder without fear of scavengers. As May loomed, the sun finally disappeared from the Antarctic sky for five long months. For weeks it had circled lower and lower, like a marble spun round a bowl, vanishing for longer and longer periods. Finally, as if in fond farewell, it had bathed Hut Point and its frosted hills in a soft, peach glow, making the ice look like tinted marzipan. Its departing flourish was a stunning blood-red horizon.

The film of elastic young ice that had surrounded *Discovery* eventually froze thick and firm, so that a skiff was no longer needed to ferry men and goods to shore. Ice anchors held the ship firmly in place.

Before the darkness fell there was a final seal cull, taking the toll to more than a hundred frozen carcasses, most of them stored in the trench larder. An entire seal lasted the crew about a day and a half or perhaps two. There was enough, Drs Wilson and Koettlitz reckoned, for the crew to have fresh meat four times a week. They might die of boredom, but they wouldn't starve. As daylight gave way to twilight, they fitted in the last football tournament before all games would have to be played by moonlight. Shackleton's McMurdo Rangers had won, thanks to putting Taff Evans in goal.

He might not be the fleetest of keepers, but the big Welshman was hard to get a ball past. Scott, his knee still giving him the odd twinge, acted as a linesman.

On the third day of total darkness, Shackleton followed the ropeway from ship to hut. There he fed the ever-truculent dogs – they had attacked and killed two of their own number for reasons nobody could ascertain – and checked the stores in Gregory's Villa to be sure he had a decent supply of paper and inks. Satisfied, he walked out on to the ice, away from the hut lights, letting the night envelop him. He found himself on the lower slopes of the ice-quarry, where each day an early-morning party dug out the frozen blocks that would be used for drinking, cooking and washing. He stood and watched the heavens, marvelling that it could hold so many celestial bodies. Then, the show began, as if he had taken his seat in the theatre and it was curtain up. It started with a flash of unfamiliar colours, hues he would be hard pressed to name, flickering like cold flames across the sky.

Next came the great sheets, sheer blue and green scrims of a sparkling organza-like material, blown by a cosmic wind, twisting, looping and drifting across the sky. 'My God,' Shackleton muttered to himself.

If God was up there, he was being very playful, rolling out fresh bolts of the sparkling cloth, spitting flashes of violet and magenta across them, creating dazzling multi-hued ribbons that tumbled over each other, snapped by an invisible hand.

He heard soft footsteps behind but ignored them. Ice dancers, the men called it, the ghostly echo of footfall, which seemed so real, you had to turn and look. Inevitably, there was nobody there. Just a trick of the ice, an auditory illusion.

Shackleton muttered to himself once more. 'Jesus, Mary and Joseph.'

'I'm sure they had a part to play in this.'

Shackleton spun around and peered at the figure standing behind him. It was no ice dancer after all. This man had on a camel-hair helmet, which covered all but the eyes and nose. 'Bunny?' It was the nickname for Bernacchi, the physicist, who shared Shackleton's appreciation of poetry. When the skies put on a show, he always came out to tend his electrometers, often with Scott in tow.

'It's me. Wilson,' the man said. 'Hard to tell under all these layers.'

Shackleton then noticed the small prayer book peeping from a tunic pocket. That was Wilson's giveaway. 'Bill. I was just admiring the sky.' Shackleton pointed to the tumbling bands of radiance. 'What do you think causes that?'

Wilson crunched forward till he was beside Shackleton. 'I don't know. You should ask Bunny for the science. One thing is certain, no brush could capture any of it.' He touched his prayer book. 'So I just like to enjoy God's presence.'

Shackleton remained quiet.

'You don't share that thought?' Wilson was aware that Shackleton, like Scott and Royds, had become Freemasons prior to the voyage South. He was also aware that sailors often sought Masonic brotherhoods not for theology, but because it was seen as desirable for fellowship and promotion.

'My faith isn't as certain as it once was,' said Shackleton. 'There was a time when I read my prayer book more than you do. I don't know if it's God or not, Billy Boy . . . but there is something beyond our ken happening up there. And, yes, sometimes out here I do feel . . .'

'Go on.'

'A spirituality. If Blake could find heaven in a wild flower, what would he make of all this? Although whether that spirit is your God or not I wouldn't like to say. But perhaps, as Keats said, God is the perfect poet. There's poetry up there, all right.'

'Up there. But on the Barrier? All that shadowless expanse of whiteness. Melville said white was the colour of atheism.'

'Melville was an old wind bag,' replied Shackleton.

Wilson's stiffened clothing crackled as he stepped forward. The huts were well behind them, but he knew the sound carried over remarkable distance. Words had wings in Antarctica. 'I hear you are to edit the paper.'

'Aye. *The South Polar Times*. You'll contribute, of course?'

Wilson's stock of drawings and watercolours grew by the day and the best were exquisite.

'I'll be pleased to.'

'The paper'll keep me busy. Along with barometer, anemometer and temperature readings, the theatre, the games, the lectures, the football and my turn as the pantomime dame. I don't think the skipper has left us a moment of idleness.'

Wilson wasn't sure if this was a criticism or not. 'I think that's the idea. It's why all have to take turns at the readings. It will be a long time before we see that sun again.'

Shackleton looked up at the glistening sky and spoke softly: '"For winter's rains and ruins are over, And all the season of snows and sins; The days dividing lover and lover, The light that loses, the night that wins."'

'It's his job to make sure the night doesn't win.' They stood quietly for a few moments. 'How do you think he is doing?'

Shackleton turned to examine Wilson's frost-ringed eyes, the lashes like tiny icicles. He knew Scott was having episodes of self-doubt. The expedition to Cape Crozier, the one he should have led, had been a disaster. Royds, the leader, had sent Barne and a team back when food ran low. Then Royds himself failed to make the letter drop. All had suffered frostbite, Barne had nearly lost his fingers and one man, the popular Vince, had lost his life. Trying to walk an ice ridge in his felt boots, he had slipped and plunged over a cliff into the icy sea. 'Did he ask you to come and ask me that?'

'No. Of course not.'

'No. He wouldn't.' Shackleton pondered for a while. It was only out here, in the solitude of the ice, that they could have these conversations. There were precious few moments of privacy on ship. He could afford to speak honestly. 'He's done well. I think the death of Vince hit him harder than anyone. The calamities could have tipped the expedition into despair. Not just the skipper's knee, but the whole sequence, from our efforts out there—'

'Please don't remind me. I blush.' There were times during their short and abortive foray on to the ice when Wilson had been incapable of undressing himself and getting into the wolfskins, used in place of sleeping bags, without Shackleton and Ferrar's help. 'We disappointed him, I think.'

'As he was sorely disappointed in Royds and Barne.' All the more so, he failed to add, because they were Navy men. 'And none of us has mastered the dogs, not really. And yet, he has somehow moved us along, away from dwelling on all that and looking to the future. Still, it's early days yet. Let's see how we are when the sun comes back. We'll all get tetchy. I'm not sure any of us is suited to confinement, least of all the skipper. Or me. I'm ashamed to say I lost my temper just two hours ago and threatened to strike a man.'

Wilson tried to keep the shock off his face. It was hard to imagine Shackleton turning belligerent, except inside a boxing ring. 'Who did you threaten?'

'That good-for-nothing Brett.' The cook was a foul-mouthed drunk who presented food either raw or burned. Scott had already clapped the man in irons, the harshest punishment the skipper had yet dished out. Mostly Scott used his tongue, as he had to numbing effect on Royds, for his failure of nerve at Cape Crozier.

'Understandable. Brett would try the patience of St Francis. And a lost temper happens to us all.'

On a stationary, trapped ship or in a cramped hut, it didn't take much to stoke a grievance. The way a man chewed his seal steak might start you off, a piece of tuneless whistling, a badly stowed piece of gear or a pair of damp, icy socks in the morning. 'Well, I have certainly mislaid mine from time to time, but not you, doctor.'

'Oh, yes. Even me.' He put a hand on the prayer book once more, as if in penance. The men knew him to be a good Christian, rather than the Sunday-only type they suspected the skipper was, and many of them came to Wilson for spiritual advice. Shackleton knew he didn't find this easy. He was a naturalist, not a natural father-confessor. 'But then, I am not too taken with Navy life, Mr Shackleton.'

'The skipper knows no other way. The Royal Navy made him what he is. Can an Ethiopian change his skin? I think the skipper is doing as good a job as anyone has the right to expect under the circumstances.' He didn't add that the circumstances were that their shocking ignorance of the rigours of ice travel had been cruelly exposed. 'But he makes it hard on himself sometimes.'

'Commander Scott isn't always an easy man,' said Wilson softly. 'But he's a good man.'

Shackleton nodded. He had no reason to dispute this. 'And remember, Bill, the Society almost appointed Royds as expedition leader. Look where we might be then.'

'Indeed.' Wilson felt disloyal agreeing, because the fastidious and usually cheerful Royds was a positive asset on the ship and he liked him. But they both knew what Shackleton was referring to. Since his failure to reach the letter drop at Crozier, and the experience of savage temperatures, crevasses, snowfields that could swallow a man up his waist, weather that could turn from benign to belligerent within a hundred yards and the terrible, crippling cramps of strained sledge-hauling muscles, Royds seemed cowed by Antarctica. A fear had seeped into him and Skelton was still murmuring about his 'girlish' behaviour on the ice. The stern tongue-lashing from Scott had also dented his confidence.

The fiasco had made Scott certain that improvisation was the enemy of polar travel. One man had died in the most hideous circumstances and, as Scott had told the company, only providence had kept the toll so low. Wilson had saved Barne's hands by soaking them in warm water for hours. It caused agony, as his screaming testified, but it was better than losing fingers.

Never again could Scott allow his men to go stumbling about without clear, defined orders. An improvisation – Barne being told by Royds to choose whichever route back he thought best – was what had almost killed them.

'Jesus.' A shooting star dashed across the sky, slashing a bright slit through the heavens, like a knife through a black safety curtain. 'Sorry. Did you see that? Now if you told me that was an angel's chariot, I might just believe you.'

Wilson felt his limbs stiffening and the familiar prickling feeling as the blood fled from the exposed skin around his eyes and the end of his nose. A promise of frost-nip. He rubbed his face and shuffled about to generate some warmth.

The doctor looked north again, along the peninsula, where a soft glow of red sometimes marked the summit of restless Erebus, stoking its volcanic fires through the long winter night. The only evidence of its plume was a wedge of darkness where the crystalline brilliance of the sky should have been.

A series of gusts scooped up the loose snow and ice around his feet, creating a low fog. A dog yowled mournfully and he heard a whisper of conversation, disembodied words passing by him into the night, blown from goodness knew where. Men were on the ship and in the huts, taking measurements, writing, reading, mending, gossiping, smoking, playing cards, arguing, cooking and dreaming. To be this far south, not only safe, but also comfortable, was remarkable. Despite the loss of poor Vince – a service and a memorial cross to the perished seaman had helped the crew reach some kind of accommodation with the first death on the continent – for the most part they remained optimistic about the season to come. It was quite an achievement, the true wonder of Antarctica, for that year at least.

'He's a decent man,' Wilson repeated to himself, as he trudged back over the ice, head down against the strengthening breeze, bound for the soft glow bleeding from its skylights that marked *Discovery*'s position. 'We are in good hands.'

'And God's hands,' offered Shackleton from behind.

Wilson, not sure whether he was being mocked, stopped for a second and looked back at the dark shape. 'Yes. Him too.'

Despite the stiffening wind, Shackleton stayed out a little longer, till staring at the ever-deepening heavens and the growing number of visible constellations gave him vertigo. Then he, too, returned to the ship. As he stepped over the compacted surface in Wilson's footsteps, careful not to turn an ankle in the deep scoring from the ice-quarry's sledge loads, he wondered if being a decent man in Antarctica was enough.

Twelve

High Top Stables, Yorkshire

The man selling the horses was called James Alexander. He was a squat Yorkshireman, dressed in a loud three-piece tweed suit. He struck Oates as a rather brash fellow, but his stables and stud at Harrogate were hard to fault. He had welcomed the Oates brothers to the Queen Anne house that fronted the property with a glass of Madeira and seed cake, saying they would have lunch once the proceedings had been concluded. Oates, walking with a stick, said quietly, 'If they are concluded.'

Alexander smiled. 'Lunch comes regardless. And if you see nothing you like here, my brother has a well-regarded stud near York.'

'Let's see what you have to offer first.'

There were twenty-five stalls in the main stable, each one with a brass plaque announcing the horse's name in a curlicue hand, as well as a subscript with details of sire and dam. At the far end was a large equine water-bath and exercise pool, of a size Laurie Oates had never seen before. Alexander was only too keen to explain the benefit to horses with joint problems.

Once Oates had managed to convince the garrulous man that he had heard enough, Alexander had one of the lads bring out Arion, a fourteen-and-a-half-hands colt, into the yard and they followed.

Bryan whispered, 'That's a handsome beast.'

Although he had to admit the three-year-old chestnut was attractive, Oates knew enough not to be smitten early. 'Looks aren't everything.'

Alexander explained the horse's immaculate pedigree, while Laurie Oates walked around, not touching the animal, letting his eye run from head, past withers to haunches and tail. The coat was certainly richly coloured, the haunches strong, but there were a few mis-proportions. The architecture, it seemed to him, was not without problems. The back, to Oates's gaze, was a mite too long, the neck beneath the carefully arranged mane somewhat skinny. Although there was no evidence for it, Oates always felt a thin neck on an animal gave it problems with delivering wind to the lungs. Culshaw used to point out that Derby winner Sir Visto was famously slender of neck, but Oates had always stood his ground.

He moved to the animal and fetched an apple from his pocket. It was gratefully crunched down in a few seconds.

'How much?'

'A hundred and fifty guineas.'

It was almost a hundred guineas more than he had paid for a better colt in Ireland. 'Rather steep.'

'You've heard the pedigree.'

'I'm buying the horse, not the parents.' It was easy to be dazzled by pedigree but, as he had found with cavalry officers from good families, the child isn't always the equal of illustrious forebears. Oates gazed into the mouth, then, with easy, consistent movements, stroked the flanks and ran a hand down the rear legs. He lingered over a couple of the joints. He'd wager Arion was spavined; only a little, but there it was, a marker of trouble to come.

'Take him out on the gallops,' suggested Alexander.

Oates considered, making one final circuit of the animal and looking into the large, unblinking and, it seemed to him, vacant eyes. 'I think I'll pass on him, if you don't mind.'

'As you wish.' If Alexander was irritated he didn't show it, nor did he attempt to bring the price down. Someone would pay one-fifty for Arion. Just not Lawrence Oates.

He rejected the next animal after looking into his eyes. As he later explained to Bryan, some horses have personality in there; others just exude dumb friendship or unknowable soul. The Trickster's gaze suggested a mean streak, confirmed when he tried to nip Oates as he examined the teeth and kick him when he touched the fetlock.

In the end, he chose the Angel Gabriel, who had been orphaned when his dam became colicky after his birth. He had been hand-reared by the stable lads with buckets of milk. Although suffering from the equine equivalent of a pugilist's face, he was sleek and strong in the body. The ears were attentive and mobile, and Oates could sense a keen intelligence. Still wary of his thigh, he let Bryan ride him. His brother was a steady, but unexceptionable horseman, but that made it all the more interesting to see how the animal behaved.

After criticising a few minor flaws, chiefly a turned-out left knee, they shook on a hundred and ten guineas. He spent another forty on a mare called Sorry Kate – so named on account of a trouble-some thoroughpin – at the same terms. So when Mr Alexander turned up with the two animals at Gestingthorpe, he'd have thirty days to hand over a hundred and fifty guineas.

It was at times like this he felt his mother's purse strings draw tight about his neck, as choking as any lariat.

To Lieutenant Oates, Gestingthorpe's drawing room was Caroline Oates's version of General Headquarters, her button-backed chair the CO's desk. It was here that staff were praised or scolded, family plans approved, the girls' suitors entertained, or more frequently dismissed, and finances and prospects – chiefly Bryan's – discussed. There were times when Lawrence Oates hated it, preferring the morning room, with its less precious furniture, the stable block or the kitchen, or even his bedroom. When, after the two horses had been paid for on delivery without a word of protest, his mother summoned him there, he knew there was another price to pay for the pair.

The room smelled of freshly polished rosewood and ormolu

overlaid with woodsmoke. A fire smouldered in the great hearth, as it always did, winter or summer. Caroline Oates believed chimneys only needed sweeping if fires were allowed to go out; a continual blaze, on the other hand, purged the passages of soot. That was why she employed Gilbert, whose job it was to keep the three largest fireplaces in the house burning continuously.

She was sitting by the window, novel in hand, the room's heavy crimson drapes pulled back to admit the maximum grey afternoon light. Oates had become aware that her eyes were failing, at least for reading small print, but she would not, as yet, admit to it. Caroline Oates had also reverted to her former mode of dress; almost everything she had on was black or charcoal. The only splash of colour was a ruby brooch, a present from her husband.

'You wanted to see me, Mother?'

She set aside her book and indicated he should sit. 'Yes. "Mother" is it now?'

'Carrie.'

'Better. Are you happy with the animals?'

'You had no need to pay for them. I arranged to have a pair of pistols sold at auction—'

'They are not yours to sell.'

'They were a present.'

'From your father.'

'To do with as I wish.'

'I would rather you kept them as a memento of him. I have cancelled the sale.'

He spluttered but no words came. Brough & Son, the auctioneers, would have carried out her instructions without question.

'Now, how are the horses?'

Oates closed his eyes for a moment till the red mist passed. 'I had Brooks look them over.' This was the local vet. 'He agrees. Angel Gabriel is a fine horse and Sorry Kate just needs more care than she's been getting. Brooks has prescribed a hock bandage and feeding up. They'll do me well. Thank you.'

Caroline Oates smiled in a way that showed she wasn't at all interested in the horses. 'Very good. If it helps your recovery, I am only too happy to oblige.' She frowned. 'But Laurie, I have heard something that concerns me from the War Office.'

Oates shifted in his seat at her little-girl-lost tones. Caroline Oates had never been lost, as girl or adult. He could guess what she was referring to. He had written to ask for a reconsideration of his convalescence period. 'You have heard from the War Office?'

'Informally. It suggests you are thinking of returning to your regiment.'

He felt himself redden slightly. 'Informally' meant some family friend had tipped her the wink about his request. She would not be pleased he had gone behind her back. 'As soon as I am well.'

'Lawrence.' His full name was a sign of real irritation. 'Six months is what the doctors said.'

'Yes, Mother, but that was a guess. An estimate. And you know how slow the army is—'

'How is the leg?'

'Fine.'

'Then the cane is for decoration, is it?'

He spread his arms to show he had no supporting cane with him. 'I only use it now and then. The built-up boot helps. I get the odd twinge.'

'The odd twinge is perfectly acceptable on the battlefield, then?'

He groaned impatiently. 'I should not necessarily be on the battlefield.'

'There is still a war on.'

'I would more likely be sent back to Ireland. There'll be precious little fighting there.'

'Then why go back so soon? Here would be more comfortable. If you fear inaction there is the hunt or sailing at Burnham.'

He could do both in Ireland, as well as race at Punchestown or The Curragh. 'I need to be with the men.'

'I am sure they can manage without you for two more months. Are you bored with our company so soon?'

'No, of course not.'

'Good. I know you hate confinement. But we will take better care of you than the army. And now you have your new horses.'

'Yes. Which I would have paid for myself.'

'Oh let's not go into that again.' She leaned forward. 'Laurie, you're not looking for her, are you?'

He didn't have to ask to whom she was referring. Little Edie. 'No, of course not.'

'Because that would make me very angry. Is that why you want to go to Ireland?'

'Mother, Carrie, I am in the army now. I go where my regiment goes.'

'I always wondered why you chose an Irish regiment.'

'Because they were the only ones who would have me. I haven't been scouring the country looking for her.' He desperately wanted to get off this topic. She could always tell when he was lying.

'You know, that whole affair broke your father's heart.'

The Big Gun had finally come trundling out. Guilt over his father's death, taken by fever in Madeira.

He adopted a conciliatory tone. 'I wouldn't have done anything definite without a conflab with you, you know. I was just testing the waters.'

'I understand. However, I think this chat will stand for the conflab, don't you? I think you should see out the full term of your leave. Just in case.' She flashed him a smile. 'Just for me.'

Oates sighed. Better a Boer bullet than Caroline Oates in full fury. 'Of course. It was just a passing thought. I'll let them know I shall be rejoining as originally scheduled.'

'Thank you. And could you tell Mrs Phelps we could do with some fresh flowers in here? There's a good boy.'

'Yes, Mother.'

As her son left the room, she picked up her book with a sigh of contentment.

Thirteen

Hut Point, Antarctica

It was a climb of more than a thousand feet over smooth ice, with a truculent wind tugging at them. Scott and Shackleton scrambled up Crater Hill, towards the glow that had been strengthening in the sky for several days. The long twilight that heralded the end of the even longer night was almost over. Neither man spoke on the ascent, their breath coming hard after months of relative inactivity.

The duo crested the broad-shouldered rise scrambling on all fours and rose to their full height. The sun, free of the horizon at last, was a deep, almost blood-red disc and it stained the ice in front of it. The highest peaks before them had begun to glow, like freshly lit gas mantles.

Scott breathed deeply, pleasure flooding through him. 'And I was beginning to think there was no finer sight on earth than silver moonlight on ice.'

The wind faltered and dropped and Scott pulled off his cap. He closed his eyes, letting the rays warm his pale, sun-starved face. Shackleton stared at the orb till his eyes hurt, then looked away. The vast emptiness of folded ice before them made him feel giddy after the closed horizons of life on *Discovery*.

'Cold frost and sunshine,' quoted Shackleton. 'Day of wonder!'

'Swinburne?' ventured Scott.

'Pushkin.'

'Ah.'

A seal barked, somewhere very far away, and others joined in. What little life Antarctica could support was returning.

'You did it,' said Shackleton. 'The furthest overwintering south.'

'All thanks to a bowl of hay.'

Shackleton laughed. The skipper's cabin, being situated over the engine room, was notoriously cold when the boilers were idle. Scott's habit of snuggling his chilled feet in a bowl of hay while writing had become a standing joke on the ship. It had even found a place in one of the wardroom revues. 'I was wrong to call it a fraud, wasn't I?'

Scott nodded. Shackleton had parodied 'Death, where is thy sting?' in a *South Polar Times* article, suggesting the reputation of Antarctic darkness was fraudulent. That had been early on. However, in time the constant lack of light had certainly dragged spirits down, despite moonlit football and golf.

There had been disasters, too: Scott's precious windmill had been plucked away by a gale. Bernacchi and Skelton had become disoriented mere yards from the ship in a blizzard and had been lost for two hours. Huge snowdrifts had almost swamped the ship and had buried the boats they had left on the ice. More than a few severe cases of melancholy had struck, one man teetering on the brink of suicide. Preventing that catastrophe had needed the best combined efforts of Scott's authority, Shackleton's bonhomie and Wilson's faith.

The last month of confinement had been particularly testing, so Scott had begun to make serious plans for the next season's expeditions, simply to keep the crew focused forward. He had designed a new dog harness and set Skelton the task of creating sledge-meters, modified bicycle wheels that would give a true reckoning of distance travelled. He set others the task of finding efficient ways of packing sledges and deploying tents.

'It's no fraud,' Scott said. 'But we have no casualties.'

'And no scurvy.'

Scott shuddered. He felt about the naming of the subject much as an actor felt about *Macbeth*. There had been continued dispute over the best methods of prevention, and whether this was consuming fresh meat and limes, as Koettlitz thought, and whether the real cause was a taint of supplies, as the Royal Navy medical authorities insisted. To be on the safe side, they had all consumed fresh, if often overcooked, meat four times a week – skua, seal, seal liver, penguin, all roasted, stewed, devilled and boiled – and Dr Wilson had assiduously checked all tinned supplies for spoilage.

'No, none of that evil, thank the Lord.' Scott pointed to the sun. 'And it's time to come out of our hibernation. We should start the reconnoitring.'

'You've done the figures?' Shackleton asked. Scott had been in his cabin for the last few weeks, hunched over his desk, estimating rations and loads. Every man knew he was working on the sledging programme for the spring and summer. But what had occupied him most was the amount of energy a man would need out on the ice, and just how much food they would have to haul or deposit along the way for the return trip.

'I have. A shade over thirty-three ounces per man per day.'

'Broken down how?'

Scott went through the proportions of pemmican, biscuit, cocoa and chocolate he had calculated. With a few extra days' in hand, it sounded reasonable, especially if the dogs pulled well. 'Wilson agrees?'

'Wilson and Koettlitz have been over the figures. Koettlitz thinks I may have been too parsimonious.'

'I'd wager he thinks the sledges too heavy as well.'

'Well, you know the doctor likes high rations and low loads.' The long night had revealed many true characters to Scott. That Armitage was by nature gloomy and livery; indeed, he could turn monstrous if anyone suggested another should try for the magnetic pole. That Brett the cook was a villain and that Koettlitz was by inclination an idler. Scott thought he, too, suffered from indolence, but he recognised and fought the condition. Koettlitz simply succumbed to the lure of pipe, port and berth.

Shackleton risked pushing Scott further, knowing he was not a man given to sharing his intentions until he was ready. 'And the sledging parties? You have decided?'

Scott walked forward a few paces, as if he could grab even more warmth from the low sun. He had written detailed orders for a dozen different forays on to the ice, noting every aim and permissible deviation, but hesitated to share the degree of his preparation. It was best that people had no time to dwell on or dissect orders, and that they just get on with obeying them. 'More or less, although I would prefer it remained private. I want health and constitutional checks once again before I make final assignments.'

Shackleton sometimes had to look beyond the words to establish Scott's agenda. Scurvy was what he was talking about. Although they hoped they had kept it at bay, he wanted to ensure it hadn't crept up on them by stealth during the slack months. It was an insidious and intractable enemy, all the more feared because of its baffling origins.

'There will be depoting runs, of course.' Food dumps were an essential part of the plan to travel long distances over the ice, which meant Scott was thinking the Magnetic Pole – theoretically northwest of them – or the Pole, due south, but Shackleton said nothing. 'And there is much still to be mapped. There is plenty for the sledging teams to do.' This was all so vague, the next revelation came as a shock, even delivered as it was, a quiet, almost offhand remark. 'I am decided, though, that a small party is best for the Pole.'

There, he'd said it. They were striking for the Pole. Which meant travelling over the ice barrier – the frozen sea – and trying to find a way through the mountains on to the continent itself. 'How small? Will you go yourself?'

'Yes. I thought two.'

Shackleton felt his chest constrict as he watched Scott's back. He resisted the urge to spin him around and ask him to come straight out with it. The idea of the Pole had grown in Shackleton's mind throughout their long winter as it clearly had in Scott's. The last truly unknown part of the world was at their feet. He hadn't come this far to be left behind at Hut Point, like a whaler's wife, awaiting news of her husband's voyages into the lands of mystery. But he had to accept it was Scott's decision. 'Just two?'

'That is my thinking. And I have asked Bill Wilson to accompany me.'

Shackleton didn't answer for a moment. He considered Wilson a friend and did not want to disparage him. Nor did he want his voice to convey his disappointment. But there was a truth that had to be faced. 'The doctor didn't find it easy last time out.'

Scott turned and faced Shackleton. 'He admitted as much. But I told him he would learn from those mistakes.'

'And I am sure he will.' It was difficult not to sound bitter, but Shackleton wondered, if it came to it, how much man-hauling Wilson had in him. 'But physically, is he the right choice?'

'He did say that, given his uncertain health some time ago,' – Shackleton assumed Scott was referring to the TB that nearly cost Wilson his place on *Discovery* – 'he would be happier if there was a third. With just two, any one man's breakdown would be a disaster.'

Shackleton allowed a flutter of hope to return. 'Did he? He's no fool, then. Three is indeed better than two, skipper. Did he have any suggestions?'

'He did.'

Shackleton knelt as best he could in his thick britches, and scratched at the ice with his glove. He etched the date: 22 August, 1902. As he stared down at it, he could still see the after-image of the sun, ghostly flames dancing over the whiteness.

'And I had some ideas of my own.'

The firm tone made Shackleton look up at his captain.

'I think we shall have a Feast of the Sun. Turtle soup, perhaps, some of the mutton. The Heidsieck '95. Armitage can do one of his punches, for those who have forgotten the effects from last time. And an entertainment. Young Gilbert can do his cabin-girl turn, if you feel our hearts can stand it. What do you think?'

'I think you are a most aggravating man, skipper.'

Scott smiled. 'Fortunately, Wilson's ideas and mine were one and the same. We both think highly of you, Shackle. Your name was on both our lips. But this is a big undertaking, the biggest there is. Will you—'

Shackleton leapt up and threw his arms around Scott. The other man gasped in surprise, not least because of the power he could feel even through all the layers of clothing. His arms were pinned to his sides. Scott made a guttural sound as the air puffed from his body. Shackleton stepped back, embarrassed.

'Sorry, skipper. Don't know what came over me. Cabin fever. I interrupted you.'

Scott cleared his throat as he recovered his composure. Wilson had greeted the news rather more equably. 'Mr Shackleton, will you be my third man in the party to journey south?'

'Well, skipper,' Shackleton furrowed his brow and stroked his beard. 'I'll have to think about it.'

The sun seemed to rise a notch up in the sky as the sound of the two men's laughter resounded over the icy hillside.

A huge shudder, half shiver, half spasm, pulled Scott from his troubled dreams. He opened his ice-glued eyes to a swirl of snowflakes, circling his head like moths around a flame. The wind battered his ears and when he tried to move, his frozen sleeping bag cracked, like a twig snapping.

Where was he? In the open. In a blizzard. His numbed senses struggled to think how he could have been deposited there.

A dog whimpered from somewhere out in the storm and he raised himself on one elbow. All he could see was the flickering white curtain of the storm that surrounded him. The tent was gone. So were Shackleton and Barne, his companions on this depoting trip. The aim was to cache food needed for the attempt on the South. Now he had lost them, lost his shelter. The cold seemed to envelop him, driving breath from his body. He had lost his life.

He yelled, but the wind took the words and ran with them. He had no gloves, no sledging clothes to protect himself, and snow was already filling the bag. The deep, sustained shivers of a body desperate to protect its core temperature began to afflict him. The tingle of early frostbite played over his exposed skin.

Then, something solid and real emerged from the maelstrom, a tantalising glimpse and it was gone. Scott stared at his feet and saw it again, a flash of material, followed by a crack like a gunshot. The tent. Then he realised it was still lying on part of the ground-sheet, even if it was buried beneath the snow. The tent hadn't disappeared completely, but the wall above his head had detached itself from its anchoring and blown over him, leaving him exposed. There was shelter just a few yards away.

Scott shuffled around with his elbows, trying to protect his hands, which were covered only by light, fingerless woollen gloves, from the ice. Replacing his arms inside the bag, he rolled himself like a sausage to the billowing apparition, and once he had reached it, he risked grabbing the canvas. The feeling went from his fingers within a second. He lifted the skirt and pulled himself inside, hoping to find warmth.

He discovered the storm within, howling like a trapped, demented animal, flinging itself against the walls of its prison. Shackleton and Barne were both in their bags, partly covered by drifts, struggling to get free, and the flap that sealed the 'tube' entrance had been torn back. 'Shackle—' he began, just as the wind lifted the whole bell of the tent and began to drag it away. Scott managed to grab part of the skirt as it lifted over his head. The other two, finally free of their snow cover, moved quickly to aid him. Then the wind, as if furious at being denied the trophy, changed into something altogether more ferocious. Scott felt himself pulled up and out of his bag, as if he were a peg to be taken alongside the rest of the shelter.

With gritted teeth, he forced the fringe down to the ground and managed to scrape some snow on to it as ballast. With an extra moan, the wind flicked it off with desultory ease.

'Try and get a decent amount of snow on it,' Scott yelled. 'But watch your fingers.'

Shackleton had wrestled his section to the ground, pulling part of it under his body, but still it threatened to lift his entire bulk and toss him aside.

'Mr Barne, your hands. Be careful of your hands.'

Barne nodded. His fingers were still damaged from the last dose of frostbite, which made them doubly vulnerable. But he couldn't let go of the tent. The three of them were barely enough to prevent it becoming airborne.

'One hand at a time, Mr Barne. Warm one at a time.'

Barne tried to slide one set of fingers under his armpit, but the wind sensed the weakness and flapped that part of the tent into his face. He yelled as the canvas sliced through the bridge of his nose.

'Get your mittens, Mr Barnes. We'll hold it.'

Shackleton laughed at that, but managed to swing a leg on to a loose flap of material, pinning it down. Barne quickly sorted through his scattered belongings and found his mittens. He showed them to Scott. They were filled with snow.

'Better than nothing,' he said, not entirely sure that was the case.

'Mine will be drier,' yelled Shackleton. 'Use them.'

Barne didn't argue. He found Shackleton's gloves wrapped in his night bag and slid them on. Then he threw himself back to the tent's hemline and began to shovel snow.

The gale was finding every crevice, and Scott could feel the sleeping bag freezing solid around him. His teeth began to chatter uncontrollably. He forced himself to bite down hard, locking his teeth, controlling the jaw muscles, till he could speak again.

Barne's cheeks were taking on a deathly pallor as the blood drained from them.

'Try and keep your face from the wind! Mr Barne!'

His words barely made it even across the confined space. He hoped the dogs were safe in their burrows.

'Skipper, watch your own hands.' It was Shackleton. He had worked himself up into a sitting position and placed his bottom on the tent edge. He was gripping it too, but keeping his fingers close to his body. With his head on his chest, he was doing his best to minimise the amount of flesh exposed. Scott forced himself to adopt the same position and encouraged Mr Barne to stop ruining the mittens by getting them wet and to sit out the storm.

It was four hours before the wind gave one last defiant wail, and then began to drop progressively, diminishing moment by moment, till all that was left was a residual roaring in their ears. Nobody moved, nobody could move, for many minutes. Eventually, Shackleton lurched forward and fell on to his face. He brought up his stiffened fingers and examined them. They had frozen into claws. 'Damn.'

'Let's pin the tent down and get something to eat,' said Scott, wrenching his own hand free and painfully straightening the fingers. Stabs of pain, like barbed wire dragged over the skin, shot up his arm and he bit his lower lip. Blood quickly filled his mouth.

With all the agility of a trio of Methuselahs, they weighted down the canvas fringe with heaps of wet snow, then moved around inside the tent, trying to find the rations and clothes that weren't ice encrusted. The stove had gone, whipped away out into the void, as had the biscuits. Scott's clumsy fingers managed to unwrap some chocolate, while Shackleton broke out slabs of pemmican.

Scott crawled over to Barne. Parts of his face had the death-white of frostbite, his lips were cracked, and his hands were causing him considerable pain. He remembered how Barne's ruined fingers had been after Crozier, like blackened sausages, with curls of skin flaking off them. It was as if someone had taken a wood plane to them.

Shackleton, too, had damaged his hands and his nose was frost-nipped. He pointed to Scott's cheeks and grimaced, to show there was marring. 'You know, Con, sometimes I think we are just like wisps of smoke out here; not men, but something diffuse and weightless, just waiting to be blown away.'

'Pushkin?'

'Shackle.'

Scott slumped back, exhausted. The overwintering had taken more from them than he had thought. After a day's sledging, they had simply been too exhausted to secure the tent properly. It had been a fine, clear night, so they had thought they could get away with it. Now they were truly spent.

You can't trust the ice.

There was a whimpering at the entrance and Brownie, one of the friendlier dogs, slithered in. She was shivering piteously and Scott gave her his last slab of chocolate. She slid next to him and pressed her body against his legs. Scott ruffled the fur between her ears. They had finally got to grips with using these beasts in the last few weeks, discovering to their cost just how vile and aggressive they could be if split into smaller, rival groups. If teamed correctly, though, they could make astonishing time. And on this short run they had worked well, despite the chaotic, pressure-ridged snowfields they had encountered.

Shackleton tossed a piece of pemmican, which Brownie snapped from the air. 'I think that's a deputation. From the dogs.'

'What do you think they want?'

'I think they want to go home,' said Shackleton morosely.

Scott looked at the scarred faces and at Barne's crippled fingers trying to snap the chocolate. He found it incredibly difficult to say the next sentence, especially as they had travelled so little south, without a single pound of the supplies on the sledge cached for the long march to come. Still, he knew that they were dangerously cold and afflicted by frostbite. Barne would lose his hands if they pressed on. And Shackleton, normally so resilient, looked beaten. Scott had no choice, even though every sinew of his own body cried for him to push on.

'I think the dogs are right. We go home.'

Scott was pleased to see *Discovery*, even so soon after leaving her, but their reception was muted. He hadn't expected bunting or cheering after such a circumscribed trip, but the way the crew avoided the gaze of the returning party seemed a harsh judgement on their aborted attempt south.

They quartered the dogs, made sure they were fed, and trudged back to the ship, where Wilson was waiting to examine them.

Scott sat in his cabin until Shackleton and Barne had been treated and tried, painfully, to write up his journal. His grip, though, was unsteady. It would take more than a bowl of hay to warm him through. He summoned Hare to draw him a hot bath.

He held his fingers to the oil lamp and then wrote a spidery account of the night they spent clinging on to the tent like beleaguered washerwomen trying to save their laundry:

> ... But the worst was poor Barne, whose fingers never recovered from last year's frostbite. To hang on like that for so many hours must have been agony.

He considered writing something about Shackleton's keenness to return, too. It surprised him. He was aware they had to drop food for the journey south, yet he had been the first to suggest abandoning the trip. Was it for Barne's sake? Or his own? In the end he decided not to commit to paper. Hasty judgements recorded in a diary were often wrong. Already, he had changed his mind about the crew, the dogs and possibly about the use of skis, even though in his early entries his opinions had been trenchant.

There was a tap on his door and a grave-faced Wilson entered. His expression alarmed Scott.

'How are they, Bill? How are Barne's fingers?'

'He's been lucky. Again. But I don't think you can risk him on the ice, not this season. Once you have been bitten in a place, it becomes far more susceptible to a return bout.'

'And Shackleton?'

'Blistered fingertips. And severely hurt pride.'

'Ah, I think that is contagious. I have caught it too.'

'Did you accomplish anything?'

'The getting of wisdom. I shall never be too tired to secure a tent property again. Waking up outside on the ice is not an experience I wish to repeat.'

Wilson stepped closer. 'May I?'

Scott turned his face upwards and Wilson massaged the pale spots that disfigured it. There was no blackness, no signs of necrosis. Scott winced at the pain as Wilson pressed harder. 'I plan to go back out again. The food depots must be laid.'

Wilson picked up Scott's swollen hands and grunted. 'There'll be no lasting damage.'

'I said I plan to go out again. Is there any physical reason why I shouldn't?'

Wilson pushed back Scott's upper lip and examined the gums. 'When did you last eat a proper meal?'

'Thirty-six hours ago.'

'You have suffered nothing that will prevent you doing so after some food and rest.'

Wilson said this with the bearing and gravity of a mortician, not a doctor. Scott thought of the glum crew and the downcast eyes. 'What is it?'

Wilson sighed.

'Bill, please. What are you keeping from me?'

'Armitage and his party returned shortly after you left.' His second-in-command had set off with a five-man skiing party to find a path to the magnetic pole.

'And?'

'We were hoping to save the news—'

Scott stood, fearing the tidings would be of another man's death, yet angry that anyone on his ship should try to protect him from serious developments. 'And so, Dr Wilson? So?' He grabbed the man's biceps, ignoring the pain in his fingers. 'What is it? Where is Armitage? Why didn't he report to me at once upon my return?'

'He is resting on my orders. All of them are. They, too, ran into blizzards. They were pinned down for days on end.'

'Frostbite?'

'Yes. But worse—'

Scott was fit to burst. 'Who have we lost?'

'None yet. All five returned.'

Scott loosened his grip. 'Then . . .?'

'There are sprains. Bruising. Bleeding.' Even before the confirmation came, Scott knew what Wilson had diagnosed. 'All of them have scurvy, Con.'

Fourteen

The Curragh, Ireland, 1902

Lieutenant Lawrence Oates thought his colonel was about to explode. His face had turned a deep red, almost mauve, and a vein had started to pulse alarmingly in his temple. Before he spoke he took in a huge lungful of air and catapulted the words into Oates's face. He caught the whiff of stale cigar. 'I beg your pardon, lieutenant?'

'I simply said it isn't terribly convenient at the moment.'

'Convenient!' The face darkened further. 'We don't run the army for your convenience, Oates.'

'Sir, with all due respect—'

Colonel Sterling leaned back in his chair. 'That would be a novelty.'

'Sir, when I returned after my convalescence, I was shipped to South Africa, where I did little more than get enteric while the war petered out, then I was shipped back here, on the under-standing I would be at the Curragh for some considerable time. I had my horses brought over and I have purchased more. I have just made arrangements to race Sorry Kate at Dundalk, and I am looking for a hunt. I thought a position at First Whip might help for when I get my own pack—'

Colonel Sterling propelled himself forward once more. 'Stop. Stop now.'

'Then there is my boat. I have bought a yawl, *The Saunterer*, Sixteen tons, built by—'

'Stop!'

Sterling stood and moved to the window. Rain was lashing against it, but through the blurred panes he could see the rolling countryside that reminded him of parts of Surrey. He often wished he were there. It was tiresome dealing with officers who thought the cavalry was a part-time job for idle sons of the wealthy. He had already hit opposition when he tried to change inspection of barracks, stables and tack from Sundays to Saturdays. Officers rebelled on the grounds that it would interfere with other activities. Such as Saturday polo. The word 'moderniser' was a term of denigration, and he often heard it whispered in the mess behind his back.

Sterling ran a hand over his thinning hair, a habit he had acquired when there was rather more on top. 'The army is changing, Oates.'

'I have noticed, sir.'

'Poor men with brains, that's what we need. Not rich men with hobbies such as hunting.'

'You will be hard put to get men with brains, rich or poor, to join a peacetime army. And it isn't a hobby. Hunting, I mean. The pursuit of the fox has many similarities to a military campaign. Riding to hounds teaches patience, endurance, strategy and fortitude. Major-General Parsons said so.' It was a well-rehearsed argument that he had used to solicit funds from Carrie, who sometimes suggested his was a dilettante – and expensive – approach to soldiering. Oates usually responded with a spirited defence taken from Parsons and the suggestion that he could always volunteer for the Front again. That usually calmed things down.

'Major-General Parsons is entitled to his opinion. For my part I think it pure sophistry. And I would suggest the Cavalry School at Netherton would do you just as well as any hunt.'

'But for six months, sir. I'll have missed the Military Cup, the Punchestown meet and the bulk of the hunting. And the King will be at Dundalk.' Oates risked a barefaced lie. 'He has an eye for Sorry Kate.'

Colonel Sterling muttered something about the King having an eye for most fillies. It was at the Curragh that the then Prince of Wales – Bertie – had discovered his taste for actresses, in a dalliance with Nellie Clifden. Edward often came across for the Irish races with the Queen or, occasionally, one of his mistresses, and the Duke of Gloucester.

'And BP is happy enough for me to represent the cavalry at the races.' This was a low blow, because Baden-Powell, the hero of Mafeking, was now Inspector-General of the cavalry. Everyone knew he often cited 'No Surrender' Oates as an example of British fortitude under fire. Both men appreciated that Oates could appeal to Baden-Powell directly and that the IG would overrule the colonel.

Sterling, sensing a rout, returned to his seat. 'And who will be riding this Sorry Kate?'

'I will be.'

Although a fine horseman, Oates had gathered quite a stable and didn't always ride his own mounts. 'I thought you had a trainer and jockeys?'

'Sacked them. BFs, the lot of them. They don't encourage. If a horse wants to run, they'll let it. And take the glory. But they don't motivate a ride that is holding back. I know more about how to get the best from a horse than they do.'

The colonel sighed. He didn't doubt it. While his fellow officers went to the dances and dinners that were always on offer from the local gentry, Oates preferred his hunting, polo and racing. Quite a number of his contemporaries had bagged – or been snared by – local beauties, with several engagements announced in the past month alone, something that was unlikely to happen to Titus. Still, Oates was but a lieutenant, too young and too junior to marry; perhaps he was better off with four-legged fillies, after all. And his equine activities were certainly preferable to dalliances with the Bushside Betties, the dubious women who camped around the barracks, or loafing about on the town.

'Very well, Oates, I shall postpone the Cavalry School. And the Musketry School too?'

'Where is that to be held?'

'Six weeks at Hythe.'

'In Kent?'

'Yes.'

'Oh Lord. If you don't mind.'

'I do mind.' The colonel scribbled on a piece of paper. Oates could hear his teeth grinding as he did so. 'Dismissed.'

'Thank you, sir.'

Oates, resisting the urge to grin, stood, replaced his cap, saluted, and turned on his heel.

'Oh, and Oates?'

'Yes.'

'Do let me know when it is convenient to send you, won't you?'

Oates nodded solemnly. 'Of course I will, sir.'

Once out of the office, Oates sighed with relief. He couldn't tell the colonel the real reason why he wanted to stay in Ireland. He would no more understand than Caroline Oates would. The thought of Carrie's wrath at his actions made his stomach contract and he was still mumbling to himself when McConnell fell in beside him.

'Sorry, Boots, didn't get a chance to ask about going on the rolls.' This would make his Boots an official member of the regiment, rather than a supernumerary whose future depended on his employer. 'Wasn't quite the right moment.'

'I understand, sir.'

'I will get you on.'

'I have no doubt of that. But it was something else, sir.'

'What is it?'

'There's a message, sir.'

'Can I see it?'

'By telephone. But don't worry, I took it. Well, I got it from McCleary, who is a good lad.'

'What message?'

'Well, here's the thing. The Mother Superior of The Immaculate Heart of the Virgin Mary says she can see you next week. As requested. Is everything . . . you know?'

Oates sighed. The steward clearly knew what St Mary's was. 'Oh, don't worry, McConnell. I'm just thinking of converting, that's all.'

'Converting—' McConnell stopped in his tracks and watched the young lieutenant stride on. 'Yes, sir. Whatever you say, sir,' he said quietly to himself. 'I just hope you know what you are doing.'

Fifteen

Hut Point

It was a marvellous sight, enough to bring a lump to every observer's throat. A dozen men and their five fully loaded eleven-foot ash sledges on the ice. Each of the wooden contraptions bristled with pennants, standing proud in the icy breeze. Some of the flags were personal crests, like Barne's, and others decidedly homemade, with mottoes such as 'Who Needs Dogs?' and 'Back In a Jiffy' painted on them. Largest of all was the Union Jack, presented to the expedition by Sir Clements himself. It was a clear day, and, away from the wind, reasonably warm. Most of the crew who had come out to see off the support party wore only their sweaters and woollen waistcoats, jackets and sledging britches being unnecessary.

Led by Barne, the support party's job was to carry extra food for the main group – Shackleton, Wilson and Scott – who would follow a day or so later. Scott intended to use dogs; Barne was relying on human muscle. Once the polar party had caught up, Barne was to offer support till Scott felt able to continue on with just his two companions. Barne would then return to the ship, rest, then set off to explore and test the fringes of the ice barrier that ran to the island – if it was an island – of Victoria Land to the West.

Meanwhile, Scott, Wilson and Shackleton would make the run to the Pole.

'October the thirtieth,' said Wilson, as if Scott wasn't only too aware of the date. 'Nearly November. The illness cost us dear.'

'It always does,' said Scott. 'But we beat it. Thanks to you and Armitage.'

'Oh, give Armitage the full due, please. He worked like a demon.'

Scurvy had sent the ships into paroxysms of activity. Although many complained about the four a.m. starts, the cleaning and painting and washing, few disputed the intentions behind the fully re-instigated RN regime. Scurvy had devastated many polar parties, and none on board wanted to be tainted with failure because of bleeding gums, swollen ankles and the terrible fatigue it brought. The ship was scrubbed from bowsprit to stern.

Bert Armitage, driven by guilt that his sledging party had succumbed first, used his resulting anger to good effect. He upbraided the cook and insisted on lightly cooked fresh meat every day. He set about slaughtering seals as if they were personally responsible for the outbreak and roped in skua and penguin as accomplices. Tinned food was used only as a supplement to the newly slaughtered creatures. The scurvy retreated before the onslaught.

'Could we still do it? The Pole?'

Scott squinted up at the high-circling sun and the cirrus clouds that speared it. 'Perhaps.' The Pole lay 740 nautical miles over an unknown landscape. The progress would have to be exceptional. However, they would be travelling in the best possible conditions with, if all went well, thirteen weeks' worth of food, pulled by what he hoped would become eager dogs. 'But if not, we can give it a good fright.'

He watched Shackleton talking to Barne and Lashly, the ever-reliable stoker, and their raucous laughter boomed over the ice. Shackleton seemed back to his old, easy, popular self. 'How is Shackle?'

If Scott noticed the hesitation, he didn't let on. 'He'll be fine. It's me I'm worried about.'

They joined in the three cheers for Barne and his party and it was a few moments before Scott could say, 'You? Are you not well?'

'Fit as Mr Hodgson's blasted fiddle. No, it's the thought of the

117

ice out there.' He nodded to the South. 'Nothing to sketch; no beasts, no trees, no rocks, perhaps. Blizzards, crevasses, perhaps even open water. I . . .'

'Go on,' Scott prompted.

'There are occasions . . .' The doctor sounded ashamed and his eyes went to the churned slush at his feet. He cleared his throat. 'I wake up in the night sometimes, suffocating at the thought of it.'

Scott slapped the forlorn doctor on the back. 'So do I, so do I.'

'You?'

'Yes, me. All of us, truth be told. Look at Royds.' The lieutenant had conquered his fear of the blizzards and returned to Cape Crozier, this time succeeding in leaving a message with their position for Markham's relief ship. The party had also located an Emperor penguin rookery, which had set Wilson all a-twitter. The fact that the doughty animals chose to overwinter, like *Discovery*, had created a bond between man and bird. 'He won't mind me telling you this, Bill. The night before he left for Crozier, he was sick as a dog. He came to see me, pale and drawn. To worry about soiling your britches and still to go. I think that's what we call courage, doctor, and I know you have plenty of that.'

'We'll see, won't we?'

'I know already. You have written your letters?'

'To poor Ory, yes.' This was Wilson's young wife. They had enjoyed but three weeks of married life together and Scott wasn't surprised by the trace of yearning he detected. Bill hadn't been able to stomach seeing Gilbert dressed as a pretty young girl. 'And Shackle has written to his fiancée Emily. He showed me. Rather maudlin, I thought. About meeting in another world should he not come back. And he mentions God a lot. Strange how He reappears at such moments such as these. You've written?'

'To my mother, and I have almost completed my instructions to Mr Armitage in case of . . .' Scott shook his head and smiled, bemused by his superstitions. He could face up to the possibility of failure and even death on paper; he simply didn't like to vocalise it.

'And you've made your peace with God?' Wilson asked.

Scott laughed. He knew Wilson didn't mean to sound pompous, but he sometimes couldn't help it, as if there was an elderly pastor trapped inside his young body. And Scott had no idea how you reached a settlement with God. His relationship with the deity was one of constant turmoil. Now and then he envied Wilson his uncompromising, and uncompromised, faith. 'God and I have reached an understanding. He says he won't mind if I go and take a look at his wondrous works down there. And I promised him you would take your prayer book and give due thanks. Come, let us wish Mr Barne luck.'

He crunched over the ice and shook hands with Barne, telling him he would see him at Depot A, if not before. The lieutenant declared himself ready to depart. Willing hands assisted with jerking the sledges forward, overcoming the initial inertia. The helpers set off with the party, running over the ice, till Scott thought half *Discovery*'s crew might go along too. These camp followers halted a mile away from the ship and stood, waving. Barne and the others pulled south, heads down, not looking back.

There was champagne in the wardroom that night, toasting the imminent departure of the trio who would strike for the Pole. Shackleton, for once, was very subdued and excused himself. He donned his outdoor gear and went out into the dark, where the sun had dipped low in the sky. He made sure he was well away from the ship's long shadows before he let the cough wrack his body, straining his lungs as he turned red in the face. It was nothing, he told himself. Nothing at all.

As he trudged back, feeling spent, the wind picked up and moaned through the riggings. The dogs joined in, a discordant and dreadful noise. Shackleton hacked once more and spat. Flecks of red glistened on the ice. He kicked over the marks, leaving a few faint pink streaks. A gust hit him in the face, making him grimace. A mist had veiled the sun, blurring it, and angry clouds had obscured Mt Erebus. In the far distance, yellow snow devils danced as local winds plucked at the ground. He could imagine the gales building, picking up their tiny pellets of ice, ready to dash at any man foolish enough to be in their tempestuous path.

A storm was coming.

Sixteen

Punchestown Racecourse

Oates loved a racetrack, especially an Irish one. For, unlike some of the genteel English races that liked to dress things up in social ritual, here racing was but war in another guise. A battle not only between horses and their riders, but also between owners and trainers, bookmakers and punters, rumour and truth. It was at once noble and squalid. And there was talk, reams of it, enough to paper over the Irish Sea, expressed in accents that ranged from the high-falutin' of the grandee landowners in the club to the almost unintelligible brogue of the crowd in the park.

He had arrived by jaunting car, pulled by Sorry Kate. She had won at Dundalk, given him a third at the Curragh's own track, another win at Dundalk, then a credible second at Leopardstown. At Fairyhouse, though, she had pulled up, and he detected a slight problem with the troublesome thoroughpin. It swelled a little the next day. He had rested her; he might even retire her from the track, but, in the meantime, he gave her an outing with the car.

His horse entered to race in the two-thirty at Punchestown that day had been prepared by Ernest Jefferies, his new trainer, who had the good sense to consult Oates before he took any major decisions. Unlike some of his contemporaries, he never forgot who was the owner and who paid for all the livery he was charging. The horse was Mr Daniels, a four year old he had bought at a selling race in Roscommon, cash down before the off; three weeks later Oates had ridden him to a third at Leopardstown. He had an odd, disconcerting habit of shaking on the line, as if he was cold, but once the flag had dropped he pulled well, with a long, loose stride.

The jockey was a local lad called Eamonn Dunnet, who despite two missing fingers – from a farmyard accident – was an up and coming name. The race was the Quinns of Dublin Steeplechase for the St Patrick's Plate. As always, Oates wished for the saddle himself, but with nine horses, he couldn't ride them all to every meet. Nor, given his above-average height, could he compete with the diminutive jockeys the Irish seemed able to produce for such races. He had decided to keep himself for events such as the various military and regimental cups, where he would be competing against fellow officers, not leprechauns.

He took the car backside, made sure Sorry Kate was looked after, and arrived at the saddling station to the usual chorus of whispered entreaties ('For the next time out, you need my boy, sir, Simon O'Connell'; 'I know this fine blood horse, dam out of Ramsey, untried, sir, untried') and unlooked-for advice ('Tell yer man to watch out for The Cubby, she leans hard on the rail, no matter who is in her way').

The course vet, Hugh Flynn, had given Mr Daniels his approval to compete, Dunnet had been put on the scales, the race secretary, one Harold Parrish, had decided the weight penalties. Oates found Jefferies and the jockey in the pre-race stall, saddling the horse. The lad rode in Mr Jefferies's colours, with an added Gestingthorpe sash of checked mauve.

'How does he seem, Mr Jefferies?'

'Good day, lieutenant. He seems happy enough. Just the odd shiver.'

'It'll pass. The only horse I've ever known with pre-race nerves. And how is our boy?'

Dunnet looked up and grinned. There was a slight cast to his eye, which made it hard to fix where his gaze was aimed. 'No shivers here, Mr Oates.'

Oates didn't correct the omission of rank. Unlike some of his friends, he didn't insist on being reminded every minute of the day that he was property of His Majesty's army. 'Glad to hear it.'

'You know they have posted that it will be the championship course?' Jefferies asked. 'Not the club? Ten fences, two miles two furlongs.'

It had been two miles dead, eight fences when he had entered, but Oates was used to the elastic rules they had in Ireland. No doubt someone fancied their horse a stayer, and likely to make good over a longer distance, so had called in a favour or two from the race secretary or chief steward. The change would have been published in some obscure newspaper or nailed to a distant fence post at the rear of the track, just to keep it legal. 'And still eighteen on the card?'

'Aye, but All Quiet is scratched, a non-runner. And there's Pegasus Rising come in.'

'What do we know about Pegasus?'

'Very handy.' It was the jockey. 'And Jimmy Smythe pulled the ride. He's a fine one.'

'As good as you?'

The lad shook his head vigorously. 'Oh, no, sir.'

'Then we'll be all right, won't we?' Oates stepped in and felt Mr Daniels's forelegs. They were cool and tight. But then he sensed that odd quiver pass through his hands. He stood and stroked Danny's nose, running a finger between those expressive eyes and the spasm passed.

'Right, Mr Jefferies, I shall go and see the first two races and be back down.'

'Very good, sir.'

Oates walked from the stables, through the paddock and into the owners' enclosure. There was the customary mix of uniforms, morning suits and tweeds, and caps, toppers, boaters and bowlers. Several people wished him good luck with a slap on the back. It was a bright, slightly blustery day but the rain that had threatened soft going had held off for two days now and if Punchestown had one thing going for it, it was good drainage. The ground, and the crowd's mood, had firmed up.

'Lieutenant.'

He spun at the bark of his rank. It was Colonel Sterling and his wife. For a second Oates felt guilty, like a truanting schoolboy, till he recalled he had no reason to be. He was an officer, legitimately racing his horse. It was just that he had a larger stable than most. Oates yanked off his bowler.

'Hello, sir. Ma'am. Didn't know you enjoyed the races, sir.'

'Only place I can get to see half my bloody officers these days.'

There was a pause before all three burst out laughing. The colonel's cheeks were flushed and Oates wondered if he had been at the whiskey or stout.

'It's my doing, Lieutenant Oates. My family are from Cheltenham.' Mrs Sterling was not a tall woman, a shade over five foot, but she was in perfect proportion, with a delicate doll-like figure and a sculptured face that, when she smiled, suggested a talent for mischief. He estimated her a good decade younger than her husband. This was no doubt a proper army marriage, with the colonel only seeking a partner when he had promotion and position within his reach.

'Really?' Oates regretted sounding so surprised. 'I mean, you know horses, Mrs Sterling?'

She shook her head. 'Not know. Who can claim that? But enjoy.'

'But you ride?' It wasn't a facetious question; most wives preferred the carriage and the jaunting car to the saddle.

'Not often enough. There is a lack of company. Charles rides his desk these days.'

Sterling tutted. 'Now, Felicity.'

'There are the hunts, Mrs Sterling. And many of the families around the Curragh ride.'

She glanced at her husband. 'Not always the right families, I fear.'

Sensing an old disagreement about to bubble to the surface, Oates replaced his bowler and touched the rim. A few niceties were the best he could manage with most women before he became tongue-tied, and domestic disputes floored him completely. 'If you'll excuse me, Colonel Sterling, Mrs Sterling. I'd –' he waved vaguely towards the front of the crowd, as if he had someone to meet – 'best be taking my leave.'

'Of course,' said the colonel. 'But before you do, how about a small wager on your Mr Daniels?'

'There're plenty of bookies who will take your money, colonel.'

'Not this kind of wager, Oates. In kind.' The colonel was smirking, far too pleased with himself for comfort.

'Such as?'

'If Mr Daniels wins, we'll forget all about Cavalry and Musketry Schools.' He said it as if the thought had only just occurred to him, but Oates sensed this might be a premeditated snaring.

'And if he doesn't?'

'Well, I hear Hythe has one or two nice pubs and a dog track for amusement.'

Despite himself Oates had to laugh. 'So if I lose I do my sentence?' The colonel nodded. 'If it gets you off my back, you have a wager.' The colonel held out his hand. Oates hesitated, unwilling to seal the bet just yet. 'Although, it rather distresses me that I will only gain a negative. There is no positive outcome for me. Should I lose, I go to two training schools. If I win, the status quo remains.'

Sterling considered for a moment. 'I do see. What do you propose?'

'If I win, you take McConnell on to the roll.' This would give his Boots the right to billet on-barracks and a decent monthly wage.

'McConnell? Your Boots?'

'Sir.'

'The civilian roll is full.'

'This civilian served in South Africa, sir. And he's met a woman. Wants to marry. He needs the security. It's overdue.'

'Oh, for goodness' sake, Charles,' said his wife impatiently. 'Just do it. What if this man costs you an extra half-crown a week?'

'Very well.'

The two men shook hands on the deal. McConnell, thought a confident Oates, and his fiancée would be very pleased.

124

Seventeen

Hut Point

The bad-tempered squall that engulfed *Discovery* kept them pinned down for the best part of two days, so it was 2 November before the three-man polar party assembled on the ice to set off after Barne. The sky was still grey and troubled, but there were hints of blue in the south and the fiercesome wind had abated.

It was ten in the morning when they were ready and the group looked, thought Scott, like a Caravanserai from another age. Again, the pennants that Markham had made for each officer, the Union Jack and the flags of the Royal Society and the Royal Geographical Society, fluttered in the spluttering breeze and once more the full ship's company turned out to see them off.

Fully mittened and helmeted the trio also wore the wide-brimmed hats that helped reduce the eyes' exposure to glare. Their blouses pulled tight and finnesko fur boots tightly sealed with lengths of lamp wick, Scott, Wilson and Shackleton posed for photographs in front of the train of sledges. 'Smile, we three polar knights,' exhorted Shackleton. 'Off to find another Holy Grail.'

The animals were yapping and restless, as if they knew all about the delays and postponements and were eager to get going. Their original names were lost mysteries, but now Scott could identify each of them by their new ones, bestowed by their handlers. For this trip, the sledges were pulled by Nigger, Jim, Spud, Snatcher,

FitzClarence, Stripes, Birdie, Nell, Blanco, Grannie, Lewis, Gus, Joe, Wolf, Vic, Bismark, Kit, Boss and Brownie. Scott even had favourites: the hard-working leader, Nigger, the charming Brownie, indefatigable Kit and the lovable, lolloping Lewis. Wolf, true to his name, was wild and unpredictable, Bismark lazy and Jim sly.

To think he had once called them vile, evil beasts and had discussed with Wilson the dog-eat-dog method of ice travel espoused by Nansen. Now, he could identify all nineteen. He was fully prepared to be proved wrong about the dogs and sledges; Markham, that seasoned advocate of man-hauling, would just have to live with the consequences.

The three of them checked the loads, each making sure their personal possessions were secure. Shackleton fussed over his camera and the double-burner stove. Wilson was most concerned about his sketchpad and pencils, whereas Scott rechecked the theodolyte and the thermometers for the third time in as many minutes. The sledges looked neat and efficient, thought Scott, a contrast to the badly loaded efforts they had put up with the previous season.

There were five linked units, the first two carrying 400 lb of dog food each, the middle one had the tent, kit bag, shovels and ice picks, the last two provisions, seal meat, skis, cooker and oil. The total weight was 1,852 lb, quite a load even for nineteen dogs. The plan was that at Depot A, where Barne was headed, they would replenish food stocks and strike hard for the South. If the weight was too much for the dogs, the men would pull too. And every night would see a reduction of more than 30 lb as both dogs and humans were fed. As they made their farewells, Scott went over the figures in his head again, for the thousandth time.

'Skipper.'

He turned. It was Tom Crean, the Irishman. Crean was softly spoken, often silent for long periods, but Scott knew him to be the hardest-working man on *Discovery*. Whether it was shooting seals, man-hauling or whitewashing, he always applied himself fully, with good humour. He also had the best singing voice on the ship. 'Crean. What is it?'

'I been watchin' the loading, skipper. Mr Shackleton did a good job for the most part. But I reckon there is one thing you ain't got enough of.'

If Crean proffered an opinion, it was normally worth listening to. 'What's that, Tom?'

The Irishman pressed an oilcloth pouch into Scott's hands. 'Baccy. An extra pipe a day'll make all the difference.'

Although Scott mainly smoked in the wardroom or his cabin, during the long darkness of winter he and Crean had once or twice shared a section of the pin rail up top, watching the Aurora Australis, or the gathering of yet another violent storm. Their time had been limited, because frostbite was an ever-present and insidious threat, but Crean had reminisced about life in Kerry and talked about how he would one day like to open a pub. This had been news to Scott: Crean was a singularly abstemious sailor. 'I'm sure it will, Tom. Thank you.'

'You show them Americans and them Norskies how you set records, sir.'

'I will, Tom. I will.'

'I wish I could be there to see it.'

The sentiment took Scott by surprise. Crean had never pushed himself forward. Yet any sledging leader would gladly have him along. 'Next run, maybe, eh, Tom? Our time here isn't over yet.'

'That's for certain, skipper.'

Scott raised his voice. 'Gentlemen? I think it is time we took our leave and let these good people get back to work.'

They left with the dogs harnessed in line, the heartfelt cheers of the crew ringing in their ears. With Nigger straining in the traces, the animals were the keenest Scott had ever seen them, all pulling hard and fast, the sledges running straight and true over the ice. Jogging alongside, the three men could hardly keep up. In the end, Shackleton threw himself on to one of the sleds, hoping his weight would check them. It barely did and as his feet pounded over the ice, Scott let out a whoop of joy at the pack's commitment. Once clear of the long line of well-wishers, the sledge-train swung south towards the nanatuk of extruded black rock and ice they called White Island. The floating barrier had formed pressure ridges and created hidden crevasses around it. Going too close was not advisable, so a dog-leg would take them round that barrier and track them beyond along the headland known as Mina Bluff and then they would be into the great unknown, the last truly uncharted place on earth.

Within the hour, the dogs settled into a more sustainable pace, but still they threatened to outstrip the humans. The animals took small, fast paces, their ears were up and their tails wagging. They didn't even break stride when they worked their bowels or bladders. Oft-times the spray of snow churned at the men came tainted with a scatter of undesirable particles as the other dogs ran through their colleagues' excrement.

The bicycle-wheel sledgemeter that brought up the rear, measuring distance travelled, was fairly humming. Scott tried the skis, but failed to find a rhythm that would enable him to stay alongside and he kept falling back. He had to admit to himself he was still wary after his knee injury. Hot and breathless, shortly after noon, they had an early lunch and set off again. Here, the fresh drift snow covering the ice gripped at the sledge runners and the speed over the ground diminished.

Late that afternoon the slash of brightness in the south had widened and they could see a severe blue sky. Still the dogs pulled well, so that it was impossible for Scott to find enough breath to speak other than to ascertain that the other two were comfortable.

'Ahead,' gasped Shackleton.

Scott raised the wooden slit-apertured goggles he preferred over the smoked glass ones that the others wore. He could see a series of dots in the distance, just before the jagged hump of White Island.

'What's that, Bill?' he asked, thinking it was a group of animals.

'Sledgers,' said Wilson.

It was the support party, well short of Depot A. The dogs had trounced them.

By the time they reached their colleagues, the surface of the ice had transmuted once more. Now they were travelling over wave after wave of sastrugi, sculptured ice waves. The sleds began to slither on them and the dogs found the going harder. But still they pressed on.

The twelve men ahead grew in size till Scott could distinguish them as individuals, and that some were on skis, the long single poles clearly visible, others on foot. Hands were raised in greeting. The advanced party dropped their traces and sat on the sledges or the ice while Scott covered the last few miles.

Scott caught his breath before speaking. 'Mr Barne.'

'Skipper.'

'I didn't expect to see you quite so soon.' Scott tried not to make it sound like an admonishment.

'That storm kept us in the tent.' It was Stoker Lashly, uncharacteristically glum. 'And this ice . . .' He kicked at the shiny, uneven surface with the toe of his fur boot. 'Can't get a good grip with these furs. But the ski boots, them's dreadful cold.'

Wilson quietly moved among the advance party, checking faces and hands for frost-nip or worse, but all seemed well. Only spirits had suffered.

Shackleton looked at the dozen already-weary faces. They had been gone three days. He surreptitiously glanced at the sledgemeter. It was horribly accurate, always undercutting their guesswork at how far they might have travelled on the ice. Sometimes a march of what felt like twenty miles turned out to be fewer than ten. By its reckoning Barne and his company had made terrible progress, less than a mile an hour. 'We should take some weight, perhaps,' he suggested. 'The dogs are performing well. They can handle more. It might even make it easier for us to keep up.'

'That might help,' agreed Barne. He pointed ruefully at one of the limp pennants. 'No Dogs Needed' it said. 'And maybe we'll take that down.'

'Don't be despondent, Mr Barne,' said Scott brightly. 'Let's have some cocoa while we redistribute the loads.'

Wilson and Shackleton set about the primus stove. Scott walked along the sledge train, whistling badly, identifying equipment and rations for the transfer, mentally calculating the weight savings.

'I reckon we can lighten you by a hundred and fifty pounds, Mr Barne. How's that?'

'Thanks, skipper.'

'Excellent.'

Lashly sat down on the edge of a sledge and began to roll a cigarette. Barne turned to him and whispered: 'You know, I'm not sure I don't prefer the Owner when he's depressed and liverish.'

After supper, Barne decided on a night march to make up for lost time. While Scott, Wilson and Shackleton pitched camp, piling plenty of snow on the tent's skirting, they watched the group harness up. The strapping consisted of a webbing belt, supported by leather braces, with an iron ring at the rear, on to which the sledge traces were attached. It was designed to put less strain on the neck and shoulders than the conventional rig.

Lashly struck up a song, the 'Southern Crosses'. There wasn't a man who didn't feel a chill in his bones as the usually powerful baritone was swallowed by the lifeless land surrounding them, save for a small echo that hovered around White Island. Like the men, his voice seemed tiny and insignificant in the vast, impersonal landscape. Barne took up the refrain, followed by Hodgson and the others came in one by one, their voices strengthening till the wilderness had to admit defeat. Still singing the mournful tale of lost ships and giant cetaceans, they tramped off, heading for Mina Bluff, beyond which Depot A lay.

Not wanting to waste time while the other party tried to put some distance between them both, Scott insisted on theodolyte practice. It was clumsier to use than a sextant, but needed no visible horizon. It also had a light-needled compass, far better than the heavier prismatic ones, which were reluctant to move where the earth's magnetic influence was weak. Shackleton initially protested at having to go over the basics, but quickly demonstrated that, should anything happen to Scott, he would be able to establish their position.

Wilson fed the dogs on the stinking dried stockfish that Nansen had insisted was the best diet for the animals out on the ice. He saw to Nigger first, aware of the snapping and growling that would follow if he didn't. Nigger sniffed the meal cautiously, clearly disappointed not to have the cod-liver-oil-laced dog biscuits they were used to back at camp. Reluctantly, it seemed, he eventually took it and the others followed suit.

After carefully making sure the tent's interior was free of loose snow, they prepared supper. The men dined on a reasonably thick hoosh of Bovril pemmican with a slice of thawed seal meat on the side. Scott ensured they put into practice some of the lessons of previous trips. Boots were carefully moulded into the shape of the feet, the apertures left open so that, if they froze, a foot could still be pushed in. Socks were changed and the day pair put close to the body to dry out as best they could. The reindeer-skin sleeping bags – separate, as opposed to the three-man model – had not been through the cycle of freezing and thawing that would become the daily norm, so for the moment they could be manhandled inside with ease and laid out. As they all knew, this situation wouldn't last. The bags would get heavier with the accumulation of frozen sweat, and would need to be thawed out by body heat each night.

The temperature began to drop with the sun and a few ice crystals from the cooking steam glistened on the inside of the tent. It was still relatively warm, however. Usually, they would dive for the sleeping bags before the last of the stove's heat dissipated. This evening, Scott stepped out for a final pipe, using Crean's tobacco. Wilson snuggled down into his bag. Shackleton did likewise, and then produced a volume of verse. Wilson opened his prayer book. When Scott returned, he had a copy of Darwin's *Origin of Species* with him.

The three men read to each other for a while, then Scott wrote the day's events in his small sledging notebook and bade the others goodnight. He couldn't nod off, however, and couldn't quite understand why till he examined his feelings. It was a sensation he had almost forgotten. Robert Falcon Scott was too excited to sleep.

That night, for the first time, he noticed Shackleton's cough.

*   *   *

131

November the thirteenth was a raw, cold day. Even the blank emptiness ahead of them was mostly hidden by a mist that had enveloped the land like a sea fog. For once, the two groups, Barne's and Scott's, were together, having leapfrogged each other all the way to Depot A, where the sledges were repacked. Still the dogs pulled, with hardly a slack trace among them, not even sly Jim. The dogs had managed eleven and a half miles in a day, despite the mist. At every stop the man-hauling party had appeared much later, their faces creased with the pain of their efforts.

Nobody took much notice when Scott, seeing the sun struggle through a break in the gloom, set about taking readings with compass and theodolite and then did them again as a horizon emerged from the departing fog. He invited Mr Barne over to double-check his calculations, and then he called the other thirteen men into a tight huddle. A cloud of condensation hovered over their collected heads.

'Gentlemen,' he said, 'Mr Barne and I are agreed. We might not be able to see much, but we stand within a whisker of the seventy-ninth parallel. The furthest south any human being has ever trod.'

A cheer went up and the seepage of cold caused by inaction was forgotten.

'And I am pleased you are all here to witness it.'

'Photograph!' yelled Shackleton.

'Splendid idea,' replied Scott.

Shackleton had experimented with using a thin rope to operate the camera lever and he quickly set up the tripod. He worried at the men like a sheep dog, until the sledges, pennants and the explorers were all perfectly framed. Then he walked back, positioned himself next to Scott, and operated the shutter.

There followed much shaking of hands. 'Congratulations,' said Wilson. 'Every step a new measure for man. Each footfall virgin snow.' He pointed south, where a wind was agitating the loose surface snow, causing it to flow in wispy sheets, like sand in the desert. The thought of the eternally white waste ahead of them was both invigorating and terrifying. 'Well done.'

Scott beamed. 'Indeed. Well done, all. Well done, dogs. I think we can let the support party go back tomorrow.'

'All of them?'

'You think that unwise?'

Wilson shrugged. He was aware of how lonely it would feel without knowing the others were either somewhere ahead or bringing up the rear. Three for the Pole suddenly seemed like a very small number and the barrier very large indeed. 'You could stagger it, Con.'

This seemed over-cautious to Scott, but he knew he mustn't let his own enthusiasm betray him. 'Very well. Half tomorrow. Half in a few days' time once we are sure all is well with the dogs and our skiing. How's that?'

'I think that best.'

Wilson heard Shackleton's bark of a cough. He reached up and pinched the bridge of his nose and squeezed his aching eyes shut, wondering why they should be so painful after such a short time on the ice.

Eighteen

Punchestown Racecourse

There was a false start that left the horses on the line jittery. Mr Daniels, though, resumed his position in the pack without too much fuss, and Oates was pleased to see young Eamonn Dunnet leaning over and whispering in the horse's ear, patting his neck as he did so. The off, when it came, was impressive; a surge more reminiscent of a cavalry charge than a race as they thundered towards the first.

As they went over, it was clear who were going to be Mr Daniels's rivals. Pegasus Rising had a strong, fluid stride and was an easy jumper. Cornish Beauty was less graceful, but tough, refusing to be crowded as they came up to the fence. And Mr Daniels? While accepting he was biased, Oates thought he displayed both attributes: courage and elegance. All the runners, though, had a degree of grit and there were still sixteen in contention by the third, with the bulk still bunched together as they took the right hander to the highest point of the course. Given the flatness of the countryside, this was little more than a small incline and gave none of them trouble.

Mr Daniels was fifth, instantly promoted when the leader clipped the top of the next and went down in a splay of limbs. The jockey rolled free and covered his head with his arms as hoofs thumped down around him. The Damsel twisted in mid-air to avoid him and lost pace. Eamonn pulled Mr Daniels right to avoid the confusion. Third now, with Candlemaker in the lead, Pegasus Rising second and the field spreading out. Mr Daniels, though, still had more to give.

Now the main body fell away, leaving four at the front, jumping cleanly: Howth Boy, Mr Daniels, Pegasus Rising and a strong Candlemaker. The whips came into play and the gap closed once more.

Another horse went down behind, causing more confusion in the chasing pack, leaving the quartet as the only contenders.

'Come on, Danny Boy,' Oates muttered.

Seventh and eighth fences seemed clean enough, but Candlemaker was still there, with no sign of distress. Pegasus Rising, too, had plenty of wind.

Then, in a sickening collision, Pegasus and Candlemaker were gone. They had jumped for the same space, and the front legs of the animals had crossed. Neither could pull free and they hit the ground together. The jockeys flew through the air as the chimera tumbled to earth. Pegasus was first to his feet, shaking his head. Candlemaker rolled, staggered, and dragged a hind leg as he limped to the rail.

Mr Daniels was clear. There was a roar of expectation from the crowd.

'Attaboy,' muttered Oates.

Fence nine was dispatched, which just meant the tricky tenth, and he was home. He took it well, but stumbled on the landing. Howth Boy was behind as they began the last sprint, Eamonn in the stirrups, the whip in his hand but, as instructed, he simply showed it to the horse. Daylight appeared between the two leaders.

And Mr Daniels hesitated, the stride breaking. Then he slowed. It was as if a net had been cast over him. Within three lengths, Howth Boy was past him, while Mr Daniels appeared to be running through molasses.

'Come on, come on,' was all Oates could say. The head went down, the front legs splayed, and Eamonn was forced to leap from the saddle. Mr Daniels folded into the ground while the rest of the horses galloped past him towards the finish.

The horse was breathing hard, his mouth flecked with foam. Oates knelt and cradled Mr Daniels's head, the enormous weight pinning his thighs. Hugh Flynn, the senior course vet, circled, stroking his double chin, his preliminary examination of the fallen animal complete. Eamonn Dunnet stood behind Oates, tears staining his cheeks.

'Never seen anything like it,' said Flynn eventually.

'He'll be all right,' replied Oates.

Flynn shook his head but said nothing.

'Lieutenant Oates, we need to clear the track for the next race.' It was Parrish, the beak-nosed race secretary.

'I know. Give us a minute.'

'I'm sorry, sir. He just went from under me. Nuthin' I could do.'

Oates looked over his shoulder at the distraught boy. 'I know that, Eamonn. It was a good ride. You did well. No blame attached, is that clear?'

The boy sniffed and nodded.

'Lieutenant Oates.' Parrish sounded impatient now. There was intermittent booing coming from the stands.

'I just need a moment.' Oates almost growled the words and Parrish backed off. 'Come on, fella. We've got to get you out of here.' He laid the horse's head down on the ground and the breathing became fast and shallow. He took the reins in his hand. 'Come on, Danny. Hup you come.'

Mr Daniels lifted his head six inches off the ground, teeth bared with effort, and then thumped back once more. A fresh batch of foam flecked the lips, some of the bubbles pinkish, and his flanks were shiny with sweat.

'What is it, sir?' Eamonn asked.

'I don't know.'

'There's damage to the ligaments, too,' said Flynn. 'His racing days would be over anyways.'

Mr Daniels gave a large shudder and his legs thrashed, as if trying to get purchase. The whinny that came from him was equally pitiful. 'Lieutenant Oates, we have to clear the track.'

Oates looked at Flynn who shrugged. 'We'll have to do it.'

Oates pointed over his shoulder. 'I'll not let your knackers have him.'

'As you wish,' said Flynn. 'My main concern is for the animal—'

'Then give him more time.'

'He's finished, lieutenant,' said Parrish softly. 'He can't get up.'

'He's right,' added Flynn. 'It'll be a mercy.'

Oates clenched his fists in frustration. 'But you don't know what it is.'

'No. But we can see what it's doing to him. The animal is in pain, Oates.'

'You don't need to be a vet to see that.'

'Then do something, man. Do something.'

Oates felt a hand on his shoulder. It belonged to Jefferies, the trainer. 'He's right, lieutenant. Maybe Danny was trying to tell us something. With the shivers an' all. And we just wouldn't listen. Didn't want to listen.'

Oates looked down at his fallen horse. The eyes had dulled, but the coat was wetter than ever. 'I'll do it. Fetch me the bolt.'

'There's no need—' the vet began.

Oates spun on Flynn, stepping so close that he could smell the trace of alcohol on the man's breath. 'I'll do it and I'll take him home, thank you.'

'That's not the arrangement here,' Parrish said. 'Mr Flynn has the rights to any animal put down on the track—'

'That's all right, Mr Parrish,' Flynn said, worried by the expression on Oates's face at the suggestion that the glue pot had first dibs on Mr Daniels. 'The lieutenant can take his horse with him. And I'm happy for him to put him down. I'll fetch the bag.'

Nineteen

The Great Ice Barrier, Antarctica

'What on earth do you think is wrong?' yelled Wilson.

The day was murky, with no horizon in sight, just a spongy greyness. To make it worse there was a southerly wind battering their faces, snatching words away, so that each man had to shout, a strain on already-dry throats. At first the thought that every single step was a new conquest, fresh lands never before explored, had been exhilarating. Now, it felt each pace took them further away from safety, into a world of naked hostility.

'What?' asked Scott.

Wilson lifted up his goggles and rubbed his gritty eyes. 'What do you think is wrong with them?'

Scott shook his head. They had paused to let the dogs take a rest, but several of them had slumped to the ground, panting, letting the snow drift over their haunches. They were barely two weeks out, the support party had been gone not much more than a day, and the dogs had suddenly developed a malaise.

'It's the snow,' said Shackleton, breaking out their lunch of seal meat, biscuit and sugar cubes.

Scott bent down, removed a mitten, and ran the surface between his fingers, feeling them tingle at once. 'No, they've coped with worse. And even the new sastrugi.' They had been traversing a novel form of ice-waves, steep sided and pointed, and it made the hauling hard for the dogs compared to the usual gentler undulations. Even so, they had knuckled down and got through the field.

After the men had eaten their hoosh, they tried again but the dogs, even Nigger, seemed to have lost heart. Several of them looked at the humans with imploring expressions, as if they were asking a simple question. Do you really expect us to do this?

'I'll have to use the whip,' said Scott.

On previous occasions just brandishing it had done the trick. These dogs were not stupid. But this time, even Jim refused to budge, and Scott steeled himself. He lashed out, caught FitzClarence on the rear, and the pack lurched forward. Scott, Shackleton and Wilson broke into a trot.

It lasted less than half a mile and they felt the progress slow. They went from a jog to a walk to a crawl and then Nigger flopped down. Scott cajoled and threatened, but the dog remained implacable.

Shackleton looked at the sledgemeter. They had barely made two miles since breakfast. 'It's the weight,' said Shackleton. 'We'll have to haul too.'

Scott nodded. He broke out the extra harnesses needed. Shackleton took the lead, with Wilson behind him. Scott, with the whip, took up a position at one side, just ahead of the lead sledge.

'On three. One.' They gave a preliminary jerk to free the runners. Two.' Another yank. 'Three. Heave.'

Shackleton leaned into the wind, hauling with every muscle and sinew. He looked over his shoulder and shouted, 'Hi-looo.' The whip snaked over them and snapped the air. Reluctantly, the dogs got the message and the sorry convoy gathered momentum, heading into a grey, featureless shroud.

'What if one of us skis ahead?' asked Wilson. 'Give them something to aim at?'

'That leaves only two hauling or one hauling and one steering the sledges. And we can't get too far ahead without disappearing into that muck.'

They fell into silent strain, working cold, reluctant muscles up to smooth pistons, not speaking again until a late-afternoon halt, and then they only exchanged a few words, before carrying on for the rest of the day.

The wind that had sought to beat them back faltered then dropped altogether and the temperature rose, up towards freezing. They all began to sweat in their clothes, soaking their undergarments, which would cause problems later when it froze. The dogs panted harder and some began to whine pitifully, the warmer conditions suiting them even worse than the cold. As usual, dog excrement seemed to coat everything, sledge, traces, animals and men.

Shackleton's foot sank through the crust with a sharp report that fled across the ice and he stumbled. The dogs stopped and a few began to growl. There came a dull, hollow sound, followed by a thrumming bass note that appeared to come from the earth beneath them. The rumble of a collapsing top surface grew and ice was flicked into the air, creating a low ground mist. The solid footing beneath their feet dissolved and Scott braced himself as they began to sink.

'Con—' Wilson started, before he, too, felt the earth drop away from under his boots.

The terrified howl of the pack blotted out all else as the entire train plunged through the crust.

Six inches.

The unexpected jolt jarred Scott's back. His heart was beating wildly under his jacket and he felt hot sweat trickle down his neck. Instead of a crevasse opening up beneath them, they had fallen all of half a foot. But that initial drop had shaken them all.

'Jesus,' said Shackleton. 'That gave me a start.'

Scott knelt down and examined the sub-surface. They had broken through a crust of brittle, compacted snow, passed into an air pocket and fine powder and on to another hard, icy layer. He could hear the basso profundo of more subsidence off in the distance.

'You know, this forms because there is not a single creature to disturb it. Like the skin hardening on a rice pudding. There must be dozens, maybe hundreds, of square miles of it.'

'Make the going even tougher if it keeps happening,' said Wilson.

'Grand,' said Shackleton. 'Just grand.'

Scott noticed the huskies had taken the opportunity to sit, heads on their front paws, as if they were settling down for the night. 'Let's move on.'

It was, as predicted, a hard day, with the friable crust collapsing every few miles, and, later, a persistent fall of wet, sticky snow which clung like porridge, binding the sledge runners and slowing the pace further.

Scott's croaky voice called a halt when they had reached the point at which they might not have enough energy to unpack the gear, let alone pin the tent down with ballast. The dogs collapsed into the snow and stayed where they lay, barely rousing themselves to protest that they were hungry. They knew from bitter experience that the tent came first.

The poles and canvas were duly erected and secured and the dogs fed. Wilson was unhappy that several of them merely picked at their food and Jim refused to eat at all, preferring to whimper plaintively and snap at any animal that came near.

The ice was melted on the stove, the pemmican, salt and pepper added, and they slowly thawed their fingers and picked the ice – frozen sweat – from their beards and necks. The mixture was almost at boiling when Shackleton gave a yell. His leg shot out, and the stove and its contents flew across the tent. The groundsheet began to sizzle and dance with flames, but Scott was on it in a second, smothering the spot and extinguishing the fire. Without a word he began to scoop up the hoosh.

'Sorry. Cramp.' They all suffered from it after hauling. It was one of the reasons why Wilson preferred individual bags, sacrificing warmth for freedom of movement if the terrible contractions struck. Scott remained a protagonist of the triple version because of the shared body warmth.

Wilson massaged the rogue leg, while Shackleton writhed in pain. Scott managed to recover most of the lost food, relit the primus and carried on cooking. At least he hadn't put the cocoa in the outer ring yet. That would have been far trickier to scrape up. But he was alarmed by the surge of anger that had almost engulfed him, although equally pleased he'd managed to chase it away. 'This is no good,' he said quietly.

Shackleton did his best to keep his own temper in check. 'I said I was sorry, skipper.'

'Not the hoosh or you. This, this hauling. You've seen the dogs. They're done in. We'll have to split the load. We'll have to relay.'

Shackleton groaned, but Scott wasn't sure whether it was the pain or the prospect of relaying.

Wilson moved away from Shackleton. 'How much?'

'We leave half the load. We go forward and deposit. Then come back for the other half.'

'Two steps forward, one step back,' said Shackleton. He gave a chesty cough. Even without a stethoscope, Wilson could hear fluids rattling in the tubes.

Wilson rubbed his stinging eyes as he calculated what relaying meant. Leaving half the gear behind then returning to pick it up, covering the same stretch of the ice three times in all. Constant packing and repacking, which often meant removing mittens, exposing the fingers to tie and buckle and tighten the loads. Frost-nip within minutes, its nastier cousin not far behind.

'It will be more than that. We will cover three miles for every mile we gain.'

'You have a better solution?' It was snapped out and Scott took a breath to calm himself. He had already thought this through. 'My apologies. But I can see no other way. We have provisions for weeks yet. The dogs are failing. But the load will get lighter as we consume the food and fuel. What do you think? Bill? Shackle? We three are in this together.'

The others knew what the alternative was. The ignominy of another early, defeated return. Shackleton sat up to accept the pannikin of hoosh that Scott offered. He took a spoonful and felt the familiar gag reflex as his body revolted against the fat. He forced himself to swallow. 'We relay.'

'Correct me if I am wrong, Bill,' said Scott as he applied the hazel-dine cream to his cracked lips, peering at his reflection in the single pocket looking-glass they carried. The stove was hissing, and he kept an eye on the time, ready to turn it off after it had boiled for two minutes, to conserve their fuel. The paraffin creep that caused the fuel to evaporate through the cork bungs at low temperatures was costing them dear. 'But weren't the dogs meant to haul us?'

Wilson laughed as best he could without smiling. The skin around his mouth was fissured and chafed. They had had poor sick Snatcher on the sled all day. The relaying was as dreary and dispiriting as they had feared and southerly progress was slow and slowing. They had been doing it for days, and seven miles was a good tally; in poor weather, it had dropped to two. Except for the fiercest of blizzards, Scott insisted they worked if they could, otherwise they would sit in the tent burning energy with no gain at all. 'I don't think anybody told the dogs that,' Wilson said.

'What do you think ails them?' asked Shackleton, running a comb through his tangled hair. Scott held up the mirror so Shackleton could see the snow and windburn on his face and the blackened, cracked lips.

'You have to stop licking your lips,' said Scott, passing the hazeldine. 'It doesn't help.'

'I see you doing it,' the Irishman replied tetchily.

'The food,' said Wilson emphatically, before a squabble broke out. One side effect from relaying was short tempers, which remained till a hot supper was inside them. 'I think it's the food that ails them.'

'The stockfish,' agreed Scott. 'They never liked it. Brownie vomited it back up today. It's tainted.'

'Good Lord, I believe you're right,' said Shackleton, as if the scales had fallen from his eyes. 'We are feeding them rotten food. That explains it.'

Wilson said: 'Then how do you account for the fact nobody noticed it had spoiled? The stockfish, I mean.'

Shackleton hooted at this. 'It smells bloody rotten when it's fresh. It must have spoiled in the hold in the tropics.'

'What shall we do?' Wilson asked nobody in particular. 'We can't spare any of our supplies. Not for nineteen dogs.'

Scott stirred the hoosh. It was watery. Preserving food and fuel had been on his mind as their rate of progress had plummeted. 'The land we have seen to the West – we must head there. There will be landmarks where we can make another depot we are sure to find again. We get rid of the dog food and leave supplies for our return.'

They accepted their pannikins and all ate in silence for a while, the only noise the scrape of spoon on metal and the crack of canvas as the wind probed the tent for weaknesses. Muscles were slowly coming back to life, ripples of cramp running through them. Relaying was all about repetition, going over the same ground time and time again. It numbed the body and the soul; it was when you stopped that the pain started. Occasionally, one of them groaned and massaged a thigh or rotated an aching shoulder. Feet either ached or burned with an intense fire that was followed by the most agonising itching that was impossible to scratch. If you started, you were likely to tear the flesh off before relief came.

Wilson finally asked the question that had been on all their minds. 'What about feeding the dogs? If the stockfish really is rotten?'

The look on Scott's face told them the answer, a mixture of distaste and horror at the only solution that presented itself.

'Really?' asked Wilson. 'We feed them to each other?' They had discussed it, theoretically, on *Discovery* because Nansen had insisted it was a viable method of travel. They had both agreed it was an abomination.

'I am being pragmatic,' he said.

'Or dogmatic,' suggested Shackleton.

For once, Scott didn't give even a polite laugh at the attempt to bring humour to a grim situation. 'Although I'm not sure I have the heart for it.'

Scott had no lack of heart; without him, they would already have turned back. His energy in relaying was remarkable. It was killing that turned his stomach. Wilson couldn't blame him for his squeamishness. He put him out of his misery. 'Don't worry, Con. If it comes to it, I'll kill the dogs.'

The next morning they awoke to find that Spud had chewed through his traces and gorged on a week's supply of seal meat he had filched from the sledges.

Twenty

Punchestown Racecourse

A dishevelled Oates found Colonel and Mrs Sterling just as they were leaving the enclosure, arm in arm.

'Sir,' he yelled. 'A moment.'

His commanding officer stopped and turned, propelling his wife around as he did so.

'Oh, you poor man,' said Felicity Sterling. 'I am so sorry.'

'Quite. A terrible business,' agreed the colonel. He took in the wild-eyed figure before him. 'Are you all right?'

'In the circumstances, sir. About our bet—'

'In the circumstances, Oates, I won't hold you to any wager.'

'What on earth was it?' asked Mrs Sterling. 'That could take him like that? One minute running so well, the next . . . what could it be?'

Oates had mulled over nothing but that question since Mr Daniels's collapse. He could only conclude it was a prior condition of his heart or liver or kidney. He would arrange for a post-mortem, just to be certain. He ran a hand through his already straggly hair. She saw blood on his fingers, but realised it wasn't human but equine. 'I have some ideas but I don't know. Neither did that horse-butcher of a vet.' He addressed the colonel again. 'And I want you to hold me to it, sir. The wager.'

'Well, if you insist.'

'Cavalry school. Musketry.'

'Yes, yes. We can talk about it at barracks. Come and see me tomorrow morning.'

'No!' Oates stepped closer and Mrs Sterling gripped her husband's arm in surprise.

'Steady on, lieutenant,' he warned.

'Sorry. Bit excitable. I'll go to any school you deem fit to send me to, sir. But first I want a veterinarian's certificate.'

Sterling had no idea what he was blabbing on about and wondered if the death of his horse had unhinged him. 'A what?'

'There is a cavalry officers' vet's course. I've heard about them.'

Sterling had seen Oates's logs, accounts and diaries. They were a mess, illogical and often illegible. He couldn't spell for toffee and his arithmetic was wayward. He tried to be as gentle as possible. 'You are a good horseman, Oates. One of the best, I'd venture. But the horse vet's examination? That's not an easy option, Oates. Not for anyone.'

'Nor is shooting your own horse,' he replied. 'We both know I'm not much for writing. Or reading. But then, neither are the horses. There must be a practical course, one without too much bookwork.'

Colonel Sterling considered for a moment. There were half a dozen centres that could issue the cavalry veterinarian's certificate, and no uniform method of examination. It was bound to vary in the division of practice and theory. 'Perhaps. I'll make enquiries, Oates.'

'Thank you, sir. Then I will attend your cavalry and musketry schools. A wager is a wager. Good day.' He tipped his hat to Mrs Sterling once more.

'Perhaps I can have a word about your man as well,' she said, ignoring her husband's filthy look. 'McConnell, was it? It seems a shame for him to suffer.'

He thanked her politely and hurried away, plunging into the crowd, elbowing his way through. He wasn't thinking about McConnell's extra cash. He was thinking of his powerlessness, of cradling Mr Daniels's head as he killed him. All Lieutenant Lawrence Oates wanted to do was make sure he would never again be in a position of such ignorance or at the mercy of lesser men.

Twenty-one

The Great Ice Barrier, Antarctica

The dogs fell silent as the three gaunt, hungry men approached, six aching legs shuffling over the ice. Behind them lay thirty-one days of relentless relaying; a living nightmare, as Wilson had described it. None took issue with him. Their bodies were sad, ragged things now. Every sinew, tendon, muscle and joint was overworked or overstretched. At night the pain played over them like shooting stars across the sky, stabbing brightly from one quadrant to the next, finding new ways of making them groan or exclaim in their fitful sleep.

Even Scott had admitted one more day of fetching and carrying the same load would have been beyond him. 'It makes Sisyphus's job seem preferable,' Shackleton had said.

Not many miles to the West now stood the great peaks of the real *terra incognita*, which Wilson had sketched and Shackleton photographed assiduously. At their rear, cached at Depot B, was the rotten stockfish and three weeks' supply of food and fuel for the humans, buried opposite a distinctive bluff. This was part of the seemingly impenetrable mountain chain they were now tracking alongside each day, wary of encountering the blue-lined chasms and giant ice-blocks that were a defining feature of such terrain, where the floating barrier butted up against the rocks of the continent proper.

As the trio reached the pack, Nigger gave a whimper, followed by a defiant growl and Jim barked, but the remaining animals just stared balefully, as if they knew what was coming and, somehow, accepted it.

'Jim?' asked Scott.

Shackleton coughed. He had kept them all awake the previous two nights with his rasping and hacking. All knew their nerves were frayed, so Shackleton didn't discuss it, apart from a sheepish apology over the breakfast fry-up. Wilson's cheer kept relations cordial, muting Scott's tendency to irritation and Shackleton's tired lashing out in response.

'Brownie?' he finally said. 'She's been vomiting.'

'No, pulling well, pulling well,' said Scott.

Snatcher had died of natural causes. Butchered by Wilson, he had lasted his companions three days and reversed some of the decline; three miles a day had become seven or eight. The last of Snatcher was gone now; this was to be the first cull.

'Grannie is weak,' Wilson said.

'Wolf,' said Scott and they all nodded. It had to be Wolf. Lazy yet aggressive, he had done little to redeem himself over the days of relaying. They had covered 109 miles south; to do that, they had walked well over 300. If it had been linear progress, thought Wilson, they might have made the Pole. But he could see no alternative to the back-and-forth; their own resources were seriously depleted, and hunger a constant companion. They could spare nothing for the dogs. But one thing was for certain, he didn't want the animals to die in vain. They owed them that. It was why Wilson always voted to continue on, despite the nagging cramps in his stomach.

'Come on, boy,' he said gently as he undid the traces. Wolf's eyes seemed more saucer-like than usual, and instead of the habitual nip, he gave Wilson's mitten a lick.

The doctor walked him over, past the tent, out to the last sledge, which he had detached from the others, dragging it well away from the animals. Gripping a handful of mane, he steered Wolf around the far side of the tent, out of sight to all, and sat himself down.

He took off his gloves and laid them behind him. Wolf placed his front paws on Wilson's thighs as the zoologist ruffled the top of his head. The ears went up and the tail swished through the air. It was the gentlest the doctor had ever seen him.

'Good dog. Shame it should come to this, eh? Maybe it's best to go, first, eh?'

The dog leaned forward to nuzzle him and Wilson put an arm around him and jabbed the scalpel under the ribs. The animal gave a squeal, a jerk and began to twist, but he pushed home into the heart with all his strength. He felt two strong pulses of warm blood, heard them splatter on to his boots and across the ice and then Wolf was still.

He swallowed hard, slightly sickened by the smell rising with the steam from the ground. He could taste the iron in his mouth. Wilson pushed Wolf away and let him drop down on to the snow, watching the patch under the belly darken and melt as the hot liquid flowed out of the dead dog.

He stood, put on his gloves, wiped his boots in a snowdrift, and went back to tell the others it was done.

They awoke the next morning to find they had all had food dreams, with Shackleton's being the most vivid. As Wilson cooked breakfast, he explained that there had been pies of every description flying through the air, steak-and-kidney puddings, three-cornered meat pasties, hundreds of them, whirling past him like leaves on an autumn day. Try as he might, he couldn't catch one. Even if he got a grip, the pasty somehow wriggled from his fingers.

'I was in a steak and porter shop,' said Wilson, pulling reindeer hair from his beard. 'But I had ordered venison. A great haunch of it and a bottle of best claret. As the meat was delivered, the waiter stumbled and the whole plate went skidding over the floor. At that moment, poor Wolf dashed from the kitchen and ate the lot.'

'Wolfed it down?' asked Shackleton, his laugh turning to a cough. 'I think I'd better help you with the next dog.'

Wilson nodded his appreciation. He didn't want the sole responsibility again. 'And then when I seek solace in the wine, the glass neck is solid, with no cork. It cannot be poured. There is no hole at all.'

'Did you see if the women were the same?' asked Shackleton, but Wilson ignored his bawdiness.

'I have worse than that,' said Scott, as he took his tea and the mixture of pemmican and biscuit.

'Worse?' the others asked.

'Yes, I sit down at a feast, a banquet and there is beef, lamb, swans, geese, all manner of delicacies. I gorge myself for hours.'

'You lucky man,' said Shackleton.

'But when I awake, I am as hungry as when I sat down. Every night I eat at this table of plenty, but still I am hungry.'

Shackleton's face took on a wistful look. He would clearly trade his own flying pies for Scott's imaginary repast. 'When we get back I want duck, crisp fried bread with salt and pepper, thick bread soaked in golden syrup, Porter House steak and onions with plenty of gravy. Huge salad of fruit. And also green stuff. Sirloin of beef with brown, crisp fat. Soaked bread in the gravy. Three-cornered tarts, fresh, hot, crisp. Jam hot inside. A pile of them with a bowl of cream. Jam sandwich, crisp but heavy pastry and jam between. The end of a porridge pot, providing there is plenty of milk.'

'You'll explode,' warned Wilson, 'if you try that in one sitting.'

Scott handed them a square each of seal meat. 'Put that in your breast pocket, let it thaw. It'll have to be your duck for today.'

After getting out of their night-gear, they changed into sledding clothes. Clean socks were put on and extra sennegras, the fine Norwegian hay, stuffed inside the fur boots as insulation. Once they had fitted helmets, inner gloves, mittens and goggles, they fed the remaining dogs some cuts of Wolf and set off with Shackleton steering. Scott and Wilson were in the harnesses, their stomachs barely satisfied and the food cravings made worse by the conversation.

'I don't think we should talk about food again, Bill,' said Scott to Wilson between clenched teeth. 'It doesn't help.'

To the right and ahead of them stretched the barrier of snow-covered mountains, marching off to the distant blue. It was still unseasonably warm, with strange variations in the snow surface that either aided or hindered them. Sometimes the wooden skis would work perfectly, other times they couldn't keep up with a man walking.

'No, perhaps not. It'll be Christmas soon, though. How do we keep our thoughts from that?'

They heard the whip snap behind them, felt the extra help from the dogs as they responded. 'Perhaps Shackle has smuggled a goose with us.'

Wilson laughed. 'The primus takes thirty minutes to make a hoosh and cocoa. How long for a goose?' He adjusted his goggles and pointed south-west. 'Look at that, the mountain. The twin peaks. So symmetrical. I will sketch that at lunch.'

The very word 'lunch' provoked a contraction in Scott's stomach. 'I made a new discovery last night.'

'Oh yes?'

'You can't smoke tea leaves.'

Wilson looked at him. 'Tobacco gone?'

'Mine and Tom Crean's. I look at my spare mittens and wish I'd brought tobacco instead.'

'The hunger will get worse.' Neither Shackleton nor Wilson smoked, but all of them knew that a good pipe or cigarette could ameliorate the pangs of an empty stomach.

'I think I am moving on to ravenous already. It's all I can do to leave my lunch alone.'

The pair trudged on, occasionally turning to shout at the dogs.

'I, too,' said Wilson, 'have found something new.'

There was a note of worry in the voice, so Scott said, 'What is it, Bill?'

'Your ankles.'

'A fine pair indeed. Have we been out on the ice so long you've forgotten Ory's?'

'You know what I mean, Con. I saw you massaging them to get them into your boots this morning.'

151

'That's nothing. Bit of swelling.'

'And when I was examining Shackleton about that cough, I looked at his gums.'

'You only do that Sundays.' It was part of their weekly ritual. Sunday prayers and health check.

Wilson didn't reply at once; he conserved his energy for a few minutes, concentrating on the hauling. 'Your ankles worried me. I think they might be the start of it. But Shackle's gums . . .' He shook his head in dismay. 'Inflamed and swollen.'

Scott spat out the next word as if he had a gobbet of rancid fat in his mouth. 'Scurvy. Just say it, man.'

'It's a long time since we had a decent amount of fresh food.'

'And you think it's that?'

Wilson shrugged. 'I can't imagine what else.'

'Damn.' There was a prolonged period of silence before he spoke again. 'Do you think we should turn back, Bill?'

'Shackle doesn't know about his condition yet, but he will soon enough. And that cough is a concern.' There was another lengthy pause while Wilson gathered more wind to speak. 'Should we turn back? It pains me, but I think perhaps we should.'

Scott looked ahead. He knew the eighty-second parallel was there for the taking, just in front of them, and to the West were the forbiddingly beautiful cliffs and elaborate, twisted ice cascade formations that deserved a look. Some of the steeper faces were bare of ice or snow, and it might be possible to take geological samples, to see how these peaks were related to the ones further north. He might also be able to make sense of the mix of mountains, glaciers, snowcaps and plateaux they could see at various times. It would mean going back with more than a valueless southing record. He pushed harder into the harness, willing the dogs to join in. 'Just a little further, Billy. Just a little further. Would you mind?'

'Very well, Con. Just a little further.'

They took the lunch of seal meat and biscuit out in the open in their sleeping bags, shivering as the sweat of their efforts cooled and froze into sheets. Wilson sat apart, sketching the mountain ranges. Despite the burning in his blistered fingers, he drew fast and firmly.

'You know, those drawings of Bill's really are quite special,' said Scott to Shackleton. 'I knew he was a fine one for capturing animals, but his landscapes astonish me. He has a remarkable eye for depth and they are geographically very accurate. I've tested his proportions by angular measurement. As accurate as any photograph.'

'He should watch his eyes. Two hours a day staring at the glare of mountains is not good for them.'

'I have warned him.'

Shackleton struggled up and crossed to stand behind Wilson. He watched his pen strokes for a while before he spoke. 'Billy, the captain says you're better than my camera. Shall we see?'

'By all means, Shackle.'

Shackleton set up the half-plate camera and took several photographs of the most prominent features and, satisfied, sat down to finish the last few crumbs of biscuit.

'Shackle.'

'Yes, skipper?'

'Don't tempt me like that again, eh?'

'How?'

'Get up and leave your biscuit. I'm only human.'

Shackleton roared with laughter.

'What?'

'Your face is black with snowburn, your nose is peeling, your eyes are as raw as steak, your hair is filthy and, if I might say, very ungroomed. You look more monkey than human.' He scratched his own beard. 'We all do. So, point taken.' He licked his own blackened fingers. 'I will tempt you no more.'

'Good. I shall take some sightings before we move on. Four point five miles this morning. Well done.'

'Billy will steer this afternoon. I've done with whipping for now.' None of them liked driving the doomed dogs.

'He said that?'

'No, but he will.'

This meant putting Shackleton in harness, which, if Wilson were right about his scurvy, would rapidly deplete his energy levels.

'I think we should carry on as we were.'

'Why?'

Scott was momentarily lost for a decent reason. Eventually he said: 'We made good progress as it was.'

'There are three of us in the group, you know. You can't keep Billy to yourself. That's what you are doing, isn't it? I hear you talking, laughing. We all need another to converse with.'

Scott was taken aback by the venom behind the words. 'You are being a fool, Shackle.'

'And you are the biggest bloody fool of all. You give me words, I'll give them back to you tenfold.'

Scott felt his anger drain away and trepidation replace it. Shackleton had never been the most mature of men as far as he was concerned, often quick to take offence, but this was something new. Something irrational. He spoke slowly and clearly. 'No slight was intended. Nor did I mean to deprive you of company.'

'Then Billy Boy steers.'

'Bill steers.'

That afternoon they were visited by an exotic beauty. It was a vision so extraordinary it tested their credulity, making them wonder if hunger was fostering hallucinations on them. But they all saw the same thing. It began with a sudden drop in temperature that forced them to close all fastenings and pulls on their clothing and yank down their caps. Then the air took on a strange, hazy quality. The sun dimmed so rapidly, it was almost possible to look at it without the goggles.

'Ice crystals,' said Shackleton, attempting to grab a handful from the air in front of him.

Now Scott could feel them on his face, a million tiny needle points. Colours began to dance in the cloud that enveloped them, light broken apart by the prismatic effect of the crystals and water droplets. Then, lines and circles and arcs dissected the heavens, as if God was playing with a geometry set. A glowing double halo embraced the sun and, above it, hovering to the left and right, were two other discs.

'Mock suns,' Scott said. 'I've heard of them, but never—'

He had to stop as more strange lines appeared, glowing links joining real sun to false sun. Wilson appeared running at their side, breathless. 'Do you see it? I must sketch it. It's magnificent.'

So they halted while Wilson carefully set down a record of the phenomenon, and marvelled at the shifting hues both in the sky and all around them. Now and then, despite themselves, they reached out to try to touch some dancing fire or dark shadow, but it dissolved away, to be replaced by an apparition even more beautiful and ethereal. They felt privileged to be seeing the phenomenon, as if nature was putting on a three-man show, just for them.

That night Dr Edward Wilson went snow-blind.

Twenty-two

The Curragh, Ireland

Lawrence Oates stripped off his jacket, rolled up his shirtsleeves and began with Sorry Kate's hoofs, noting that she would have to be re-shod soon. He cleaned her cornets and began brushing her down, enjoying the feel of the animal's muscles rippling with pleasure as he did so.

Oates had cancelled his racing entries for two months following the demise of Mr Daniels. Animals died, he was quite sanguine about that, but the manner of their dying concerned him. So, during the week he attended the veterinarians' course in Galway, where practical ability accounted for three quarters of the final mark, and he spent the weekends back at the Curragh riding Sorry Kate and then grooming her. They had enjoyed a decent canter that morning, before a slanting drizzle had blown in from the West.

While he brushed, he sang softly:

> *I'm Burlington Bertie, I rise at ten-thirty*
> *And reach Kempton Park around three.*
> *I stand by the rail, when a horse is for sale*
> *And you ought to see Wooton watch me.*
> *I lean on some awning, while Lord Derby's yawning,*
> *Then he bids two thousand and I bid Good Morning.*
> *I'm Bert, Bert, I'd buy one, a Cert,*

But where would I keep it, you know?
I can't let my man see me in bed with a gee-gee
I'm Burlington Bertie from Bow.

'Oates.'

He looked up to see his old friend Culshaw, now a captain.

'Sir.'

'Oh, knock that off, Titus. How are you?'

'Not too bad.'

'I hear you passed your horse veterinarian's examination.'

Oates shrugged. 'I've had nothing official yet.'

Culshaw gave a broad grin. 'I did a stint as the colonel's adjutant, remember? I hear you have passed your horse veterinarian's exam.'

He had been reading Sterling's papers. 'Oh. Good.'

'I also heard you reduced the examiner to tears.'

Oates had to smile at the memory. His written exam had, of course, been borderline, so for his viva he had been required to criticise some poor nag they had brought out. He had been very thorough in his appraisal and critical of the conditions that could have been cured. 'Keeping an animal in discomfort just so someone can diagnose summer itch is not right in my opinion. I told him that. Quite strongly, I fear. I thought they must fail me.'

'Apparently not.'

There was something about the way the captain had his arms wrapped around his body that concerned Oates. He was shivering, too.

'Are you all right, Culshaw? Are you ill?'

A heavier downpour began, beating on the stables' iron roof with an insistent pulse.

'Bit of trouble in town.'

'The pox?'

'Oh, I wish. That would be easy. I'd go and see one of those witches in Temple Bar for a few powders. Look, I hope you don't mind me talking like this. Don't know who else to speak to. You've always been a good sort. Hold up.'

157

They watched the Saunterer, the horse named after his boat, being led in by Trooper O'Neill who had taken him out to the gallops. Both were drenched, but O'Neill had a smile on his face.

'How was he?' Oates asked.

'Very good, sir. Very keen.' O'Neill wiped the moisture from his eyes. 'He'll make a fine hunter.'

'Good. Just take the saddle off and throw a blanket over him, I'll be there in a while.' Oates turned back to Culshaw, his voice low. 'It's a girl, then.'

'That obvious, eh?'

'Usually is. Pox or a girl. How far gone?'

'Two months, perhaps.'

'Marry her?'

Culshaw snorted louder than Sorry Kate. 'I have a fiancée.'

'Fiancées can be unhad.'

Culshaw shook his head. 'Not this one.'

'Babies can be unhad.'

'Catholic.'

'Oh Lord, Culshaw.'

The captain hissed at him. 'It's all right for you, Oates, you've always kept your pecker in your pants. The rest of us don't have that luxury—'

'Or don't choose to.'

The captain snarled now. 'Whatever. What can I do? She's from a good family.'

'Do you love your fiancée?'

'I suppose. She's one of the Caldwells.'

Oates didn't know who the Caldwells were, but no doubt they were another prominent family on a par with the Sheffield Steel Culshaws. 'And this Irish girl?'

The wistful look on his face and the glint in his eyes gave the answer. 'There you are, then. You choose love.'

'You don't fully appreciate what that would mean at home, it would ruin me to be with this girl. Her family is nothing away from the bogs.'

'You are ruined either way, Culshaw. Go with the one where your duty lies.'

The captain frowned. It wasn't what he wanted to hear. 'I shouldn't have said anything.'

'I won't breathe a word. And there are places where she can be confined, you know.'

'I am aware of that, Titus. But it's hardly your area of expertise, is it? Women, I mean. Forget I mentioned it, would you? There's a good chap. You don't understand.'

Oates waited till Culshaw had gone before he muttered: 'Don't I?'

He returned his attentions to Sorry Kate, brushing with even more vigour. Culshaw's dilemma took him back to his own. The meeting with the mother superior had been another dead end. Edie Roslin, the girl he sought, had left no trace of her passing in the convent or any other such establishment.

'You heard about the orders, sir?' Trooper O'Neill asked as he walked past.

'No. Not another khaki jacket?' Oates replied and the private laughed. There had been five changes of jacket style in the last year, with the fifth one being remarkably similar to the first. The British Army, Oates had decided, was totally cracked.

'There's to be a detachment of the sixteenth deployed in Belfast. But they—'

O'Neill stopped and looked around for any stray ears of rank. It was amazing how the men often knew more than the officers and spreading gossip – no matter how accurate – was frowned upon.

'Go on, you can tell me. I won't spill the beans.'

'No, I know that, sir. They say it's only a stop-off. Belfast, I mean. Not much call for cavalry there. It appears that the unit in question is to join a squadron to go to Egypt.'

'Egypt? Really? What's happening there?'

'Turks have taken some of it, so I hear. And a few uppity tribes need a taste of the lance.'

'Egypt,' Oates said, mainly to himself. 'That might be something to see. The pyramids and the Nile.'

O'Neill winked salaciously. 'An' a lot more, so I hear from thems that been there.'

Oates remembered he had been due to go before the committee of the Kildare Hunt, with a view to a post as chief whip. 'Do they hunt there, do you think?'

'I dunno. Desert, innit? Do you get foxes in deserts? But there's a racetrack in Cairo. I know that. And polo grounds.'

'Is there, indeed? Yes, that rings a bell. Where did you get all this from? About the orders?'

O'Neill looked slightly abashed. 'The *Cork Examiner*, mostly.'

'Ah. Well, it must be true, mustn't it?'

Detecting a note of scepticism, O'Neill said: 'Well, those papers often seem to know what we doin' before we do. They get tip-offs from the War Office, so Corporal Houghton says.'

'I'm sure the Corporal of the Horse is right.'

He slipped O'Neill a sixpence for giving the Saunterer a workout, retrieved his jacket and headed out for a word with Higgins, the squadron corporal quartermaster. As always, he'd know what was really afoot and how best to get his name on the list for attachment. At that moment, with chill rain squalls hammering on the roof and the trail of Edie colder than ever, Egypt didn't seem like too bad an option. At least it would be warm.

Twenty-three

The Great Ice Barrier, Antarctica

Scott found himself yelling impatiently. 'Keep still, man. Keep your hands from your eyes.'

Wilson was lying in his sleeping bag, his feet thrashing, his face screwed up in agony. He had been grinding his knuckles into his eye sockets, and Scott had smacked them away. Now he was leaning over Wilson, examining his corneas, which looked like a river delta drawn in capillaries. 'I'm going to put some of the cocaine in there.'

'Don't touch the eye,' pleaded Wilson.

'Shackle, hold his arms.'

Scott fetched the small vial of cocaine solution from Wilson's medical kit. They had all had some symptoms of snow-blindness, mainly the scratchy, sand-in-the-eye sensation, which caused agony when blinking. Wilson's, though, was by far the worse case; it was likely the glare had burned the retina. He said it was as if someone had scored the conjunctiva with a razor blade and then thrown salt into the wounds.

'I'm going to try and lift up the lid so I can get the liquid under it.'

'Be careful.'

Scott had only touched the puffy membrane when Wilson let out a yelp. One of the dogs replied from outside with a heartfelt howl.

161

'How come the blasted huskies don't get it?' Wilson moaned. 'They don't have goggles.' But he knew they had nictitating membranes, a third eyelid, to help protect their corneas.

'Look, Billy, Christmas tomorrow,' said Shackle, his voice low and raspy from serving his continuous tickly cough. 'You'll need your eyes for that.'

'Oh yes,' said Wilson, with uncharacteristic cynicism, 'I wouldn't want to miss the tree and decorations. Aargh. Scott, you bloody oaf.'

Scott had never witnessed Wilson swearing before. It was as unlikely as hearing his mother curse. 'All right. Doctor, heal thy self. Do you want to do it?'

Wilson stopped squirming. 'Sorry, Con. Go ahead.'

Scott managed to prise the lid up enough to squirt a good dose of the cocaine into the eye. 'There. I'll do the zinc sulphate later.'

Wilson continued to roll about and complain for a few minutes, but soon the drug had the desired effect, numbing the pain. Shackleton indicated they should go outside. The dogs stirred, expecting food, but the pair walked on, automatically striding further south, if only for a few paces. 'We'll have to take another dog soon,' Scott said.

'We?' Shackleton said, bemused.

'It's a sordid business. But I'll give it a go.'

'You'd mess it up, skip. You have to be bold, so Billy said.' He mimed stabbing with a ferociousness that made Scott flinch.

'We are going to be pretty short to the Pole, aren't we?'

They both examined the great exuberance of mountains and ice fields that lay to the West. Appropriately enough, much of the dusting over the soaring peaks seemed like marzipan on a Christmas cake.

'We have to find a way to get past those first. It's like God is guarding his crown jewel, keeping the Pole from human eyes.'

On the few occasions they had deviated and headed for land, their route had always been blocked by fearsome fields of ice-blocks and dizzying crevasses crossed only by unstable snow bridges. Even when they were roped together and climbing with ice axes, the obstacles defeated them.

'Should we turn?' Shackleton asked. 'Given Billy's eyes?'

'The noon latitude was eighty-one point thirty-three South,' Scott reminded him.

'And you want eighty-two.' It wasn't really a question.

A muffled moan came from inside the tent. Surely the cocaine would last longer than that?

'I do. You don't?'

'What does Billy think?'

'A little further.'

'Did he say that before or after his eyes were replaced by hot coals?'

'He'll walk blindfold if he has to.'

'I know he will,' replied Shackleton. 'But should he have to?' He tapped his cotton jacket. Through all his layers he could still feel his ribs. Stabs of deep pain, too wretched to be mere hunger, were plaguing his abdomen. He felt as if he were consuming himself from within. 'We're starving, skipper. You know that.'

Scott nodded. His urine was a strange colour now, and he could tell his muscles were wasting. 'Yes. But we have plenty at Depot B for when we turn. It needs to be a little blacker before we give in.'

Shackleton resisted the urge to laugh in his face. His own lungs and throat were burning. Wilson was blind and Scott, with his hollow cheeks and burned, wrinkled skin, looked like an old man. They'd all either chipped or cracked teeth on semi-thawed seal meat and could only sleep with heavily tightened belts. How much blacker did it need to be? But having been the one who curtailed the expedition last time, he kept his silence.

Scott interpreted the lack of reply as agreement. 'So we go on. We should feed the dogs and make supper while Bill's quiet.'

'Yes.'

'And put your goggles on if you are going to stare at the ice.'

'I will.' But Shackleton stayed where he was, watching the clouds scurry over the corkscrewed mountains, feeling a sharp blast on his face, stinging like shotgun pellets. He pulled the improvised windguard on his helmet forward. A wire ring held the cloth a few inches away from the face, so that he now saw life down a canvas tube. But it cut the exposure and the chance of frost-nip. Shackleton spoke to himself softly, reciting the poem he had written during the long night that now seemed so distant: 'We leave our pleasant homelands, for the roaring south-east winds, all words of love and friendship, for yearning hearts and minds, for clasps of loving fingers, dreams must alone.'

He saw fingers of spindrift reaching out from the distinctive peak they had christened Mt Longstaff; a pair of them, like the devil's horns. All around him the surface ice blew like sand, a fine mist tracking over the wastes. As the same wind found the cracks in his clothes, he prayed his mentor and sponsor would never be unlucky enough to see his namesake.

Shackleton took four paces, opened the front of his britches and, careful to cup exposed flesh in the fur of his mittens, made the snow yellow. He'd already had a bad bout of diarrhoea, and a frost-dappled arse to show for it. He didn't want anything else on his body turning black and blistering. That would be rather difficult to explain to Emily on their wedding night.

He realised rather guiltily that it was some days since he had thought of her. Over winter, especially when he read mildly erotic verses on the *Discovery*, she had been a constant presence. As for most of the men, Gilbert's turn as a cabin girl during the winter shows had aroused in him old urges. But Emily's spectral presence hadn't followed him out on to the barrier. Starvation had the effect of diminishing sexual hunger.

'There's not sufficient here for the dogs,' he heard Scott yell. 'Wolf's pretty much gone.'

'Brownie?' Shackleton shouted back as he fastened himself up.

'Brownie,' Scott confirmed.

'I'll do it.'

'You sure?'

Shackleton mumbled his reply. 'One of us has to be man enough to do it. And they call Royds girlish.' Then he raised his voice again. 'No problem, skipper.'

Shackleton sighed, coughed, and went to fetch the blood-marked scalpel from the sledge. He hoped he got Brownie's heart first dig.

*   *   *

Shackleton didn't write up his account of Christmas Day till the twenty-sixth, after he had milked his companions' surprise at his resourcefulness for all it was worth. Against all odds, the spirit of the day really did descend on the tent. Wilson recovered in one eye and managed with a bandage on the other, so he looked like a sun-ravaged pirate.

Shackleton smiled at the memory of his friends' faces and, while the Boxing Day breakfast cooked, he jotted into his notebook:

Christmas Day
Beautiful day, the warmest we have yet had – clear blue sky. We have made our best march, doing today ten geographical miles; we are entirely doing the pulling, the dogs being practically useless.

Started breakfast at 8.30, Billy cook.

Christmas breakfast: a pannikin of seal's liver, with bacon mixed with biscuits, topped with a spoonful of blackberry jam; then I set the camera, and we took our photographs with the Union Jack flying and our sledge flags – I again arranged this by connecting a piece of rope line to the lever. Then four hours' march. Had a hot lunch. I was cook:- Bovril, chocolate and Plasmon biscuit; two spoonfuls of jam each – Grand! Then another three hours' march and we camped for the night. I was cook and took thirty-five minutes to cook two pannikins of N.A.O. ration and biscuit for the hoosh, boiled the plum pudding, and made cocoa. I must, of course, own up that I boiled the plum pudding in the water I boiled the cocoa in, for economy's sake, but I think it was fairly quick time. The other two chaps did not know about the plum pudding. It only weighed six oz. And I had stowed it away in my socks (clean ones) in my sleeping bag, with a little piece of holly. It was a glorious surprise to them – that plum pudding, when I produced it. They immediately got our emergency allowance of brandy so as to set it on fire in proper style. We turned in really full.

The hunger came back, though, and Wilson's eyes plagued him again over Boxing Day breakfast. Shackleton, too, had been feeling the grit of snowblindness. While they were packing up, he surreptitiously touched his aching gums and came away with blood on his fingerstips. He quickly wiped it off.

They moved on, Shackleton leading, a blindfolded Wilson also pulling with Scott steering and whipping the increasingly reluctant dogs. A silver fog surrounded them that night and persisted till they made camp on the last day of the year, when it finally lifted.

All around them they heard the booms and groans of the ice flexing and the strange miniature earthquakes that froze the heart. Sometimes they were convinced they were like fleas or lice, walking over the back of a giant creature, one that occasionally shifted and scratched at them.

The cliffs of the coastline, where ice barrier met land, were magnificent, often streaked in red or a dark brown. Scott estimated they were ten or twelve miles away, and they looked as formidably impenetrable as ever.

Scott took his sightings, checked the sledgemeter and announced his findings. 'We are at eighty-two point sixteen South.'

Lips cracked once more as a smiling – and relieved – Shackleton and Wilson shook hands and then crossed to Scott. They were well past the eighty-second parallel. A new Farthest South by a great margin.

'Well done, Con,' said Wilson.

Scott gave a ridiculous little dance, spinning with an imaginary partner, drilling a hole in the snow, then fell down laughing, panting with the exertion. 'But I think we have shot our bolt,' Scott gasped. 'We have two weeks' worth of food to get us back to the depot. We must turn.'

There was no argument. Shackleton seemed to stagger at the news. When he took off the hat that had been shading his face, Scott was shocked at how liverish he looked. He struggled to his feet.

'But shall we ski on a few miles?' Scott asked. 'To be certain? Shackle?'

'Very well.'

'I think not,' said Wilson softly, putting a hand on Shackleton's shoulder. 'Rest might be better. Given your condition.'

'Is that the physician speaking?'

'Physician and friend.'

Shackleton was about to object, but then he slumped down on to the lead sled. 'I'll look after the dogs. You two go.'

'Sure?' asked Scott.

'Yes.' Shackleton put his head between his knees. He let himself cough freely for a whole minute. 'I'll be cook. You go.'

Wilson and Scott strapped themselves on to the wooden skis and set off, goggles carefully positioned. Wilson's right eye was still covered by cloth, the other red and swollen.

They shushed through the snow, making good progress, till, after an hour, a fog bank loomed ahead. Under their skis, cracks had appeared in the ice, radiating from the mountains ahead, or so it seemed. Another ten minutes produced furrows, as if an ice-farmer had ploughed his fields, and the skis began to lose their grip as the land rose slightly to an incline.

They stood silently for a few minutes, watching the atmosphere play its tricks, distorting distance and size, taunting them to come on. Just a little further. The mountains are really close. You can reach out and touch them. One more push, boys. There really were sirens in this world, luring men to certain death, Scott thought, but not always at sea.

As soon as he thought that, a fog came down, obscuring the cliffs and shrouding the mountains, reducing them to distant silhouettes, a long, long way off. The mists seem to move, alternating in density, revealing some peaks, while obscuring others. It was just the high winds, he knew, but it was like watching a dance of the seven veils.

'I think this is as far as we can go, Bill. It's reached the tipping point. Every day I have weighed it up. On one pan, the danger of going on. The other side of the scales, the drive to go further, to achieve Farthest South or find a route through those mountains. You understand? I have always looked at the equations, Bill. It's not blind ambition.'

Wilson realised Scott was apologising for bringing them on so far, for the pain it had given them. 'I appreciate that. If I thought you were risking our lives unnecessarily, I would have said so.'

'I hope so, Bill. I hope so. And now the scales have moved.'

'He's all done, you know. Shackle. Like a balloon slowly deflating.'

'I know.'

'You must not be too hard on him.'

'Am I being?'

'No more than on yourself, perhaps, but he feels your disappointment in him. Or imagines he does.'

'We all have our crosses.' Scott gently tapped Wilson's shin with the big ski pole. 'How's the leg?'

Wilson had been gamely trying to hide a limp since Christmas Day. 'You noticed? Comes and goes. The ankles?'

Scott grimaced at the thought of the constant throbbing throughout the night he had endured. 'Sore as hell. I'm ready, too. It's almost 1903, Bill. We've been gone two months. It's time to go home.'

Wilson touched the prayer book in his jacket and hoped they hadn't left it too late for all three to return safely to *Discovery*. Despite what he had said, he feared the margin was too thin. So, although Wilson hadn't guessed it, did Robert Falcon Scott.

Twenty-four

Egypt

The sky, previously so clear and blue, was quickly darkened by the arrival of the swarming pigeons. The treacly air pulsed with their massed wing beats. Lieutenant Porter stepped from the shade of the makeshift hide the Sheikh had arranged, shouldered his rifle, and began firing into the flock. Three birds instantly detached and spun down to earth.

He heard his fellow officers following suit, and soon a steady rain of dead birds was littering the desert floor. His gun empty, he handed it to his native loader and hesitated. 'Can you smell burning? No, not the rifle.'

The loader indicated a plume of smoke hanging over the nearby village. Something was ablaze. They were on the edge of the small hamlet of Denishwai, not far from Tanta. The troop of mounted infantrymen was en route to Alexandria and had come here as a flag-waving exercise and to allow the officers a little innocent pigeon hunting.

Porter waved at Smithwick and Bostwick, who were some fifty paces either side of him. Further on his left side were Major Pine-Coffin, a man who had heard every variation on every joke about his name, and Captain Benjamin 'Bonza' Bull. Porter snatched the fresh rifle and began firing again. The pigeons were thinning, but he could see from the distant smudge in the sky they were turning.

The feathered idiots would make a big loop and come over once more to be exposed to the guns.

It was when he lowered his weapon that he felt the first hard clump of mud hit him in the face. 'Bloody hell.'

The loader pointed and exclaimed something Porter didn't catch. He didn't have to. A moving wall of local villagers seemed to be heading towards the British soldiers, sticks and farming tools held aloft. A stone arced over towards him and he stepped aside. He heard his loader cry out as it struck him. The man yelled something else unintelligible and took to his heels, dropping the spare rifle as he went.

The fellahin continued to stream forward, splitting into smaller groups, each moving to target one of the hunters.

Porter dropped his empty weapon and picked up the fully charged piece the loader had abandoned. He levelled it at the mob, but they carried on coming. He could see there were angry young men at the front, but behind them were women, children and the heavily creased faces of the village's elderly.

He considered firing over their heads, but he thought it might be interpreted badly. Two stones and more mud hit him.

'Steady on! Just calm down, will you?' he yelled.

But the villagers continued to hurl abuse and rocks.

His fellow officers were already hidden from view but Porter could see the cab drivers that had delivered them over the heads of the crowd. He raised an arm and signalled one of the native drivers. Perhaps they could force their way through. Sure enough the carriage began to move. It was a second before he realised that the drivers were heading away from the crowd, not towards him.

'Hey there!' he shouted, but the grumblings of the fellahin drowned him out and the drivers disappeared from view.

He could smell the gathering now, the sharp tang of anger and hot blood. A woman hawked and spat at him, finding her target on his cheek. He felt sick as he wiped the slime away with his sleeve. One of the men pointed with his stick towards the thickening smoke coming from the village and let out a stream of invective.

'Hold on, you can't think we did that ... Does anyone here speak English? English, anyone?'

The bodies pressed closer, forcing him back. He swung the rifle to face the stomach of the most insistent native, but the man arrogantly pressed his belly against it, as if daring him to pull the trigger. The damned Egyptians held their lives pretty cheaply, so he took another step of retreat. He felt the canvas of the hide against his back. Someone else spat, but missed. Porter knew he had to diffuse the situation.

'All right. Look, I'll tell you what.'

He took the rifle in both hands and presented it, almost ceremoniously, with a bow. 'To show I mean no harm.'

It was wrenched from him and roughly passed back into the mêlée and seemed only to incense the villagers more.

'Does anyone here speak—'

The sound of the discharge caused his heart to jump. A woman screamed. He was aware of people leaping back as at least one body fell. A hush fell over the gathering. Now they formed a circle. There was a woman and, in her arms, a small baby. Both were covered in blood.

'Oh my, God. I put the safety on—' he began. The roaring resumed as his tormentors all cried out at once, a great whoosh of anguish and fury.

That was when the first heavy stick smashed into his jaw and he went down to the mob.

There was no turf on any of the three fields at the Ghezira polo grounds, just hard-baked earth. That meant there was no requirement for the ritual of the spectators being allowed to press the divots back into the soil. However, the genuine polo aficionados, not wanting to break with tradition, still walked the field between the third and fourth chukkas, even though there was little to stamp down but dust.

It was during this invasion that Major Collins finally located Oates. The quarter final of the Lord Sutton Cup was a close-fought match. Oates's team was three–two down; the Hussars were playing well, but he was confident the Inniskillings would even things up in the fourth.

Oates and the others moved into the shade of the stand and drank a pitcher of water each. It was scaldingly hot out there. Oates made sure each of the horses received plenty of liquid from the grooms.

'Lieutenant Oates.'

Oates turned at his name. He tipped the remains of the water over his head, where it seemed to evaporate in a flash. 'Major Collins, sir. Nice of you to come along. We need the support.'

The man's toothbrush moustache twitched. 'I'm not here for the polo.'

'Oh.' Oates knew this perfectly well. Collins was one of the new army 'professionals' who thought polo frivolous. 'Pity. What can I do for you?' He looked over his shoulder; the crowd were rapidly vacating the field. 'Don't have too long, I'm afraid.'

'You'll have as long as I need.'

'Sir.'

One of the umpires rode over, indicating they were ready to resume, but Oates shouted. 'A minute here, please.'

'No longer,' came the reply. 'This is most irregular as it is.'

'You were saying, sir?'

'I need you to take fifty troopers to Denishwai. It's on the Alexandria Road.'

'When?'

'I'd like you to start as soon as possible.'

'I shall go straight back to barracks after the seventh, sir. Will you excuse me—'

Collins grabbed his arm. 'British soldiers have been beaten by natives. Severely. Captain Bull has died of his injuries.'

'Bonza Bull?'

'You knew him?'

'Of course. An eight-goal handicap. Fine polo player. What happened?'

'Well, it seems the locals got upset by our lads shooting pigeons.

172

Then someone blamed them for a local fire. One of the men handed over his rifle—'

'He did what?'

'I know, scandalous behaviour. It went off, killing a woman and her baby. All hell broke loose. The rest were lucky not to be murdered as well. Seventy-five have been arrested. There'll be a tribunal. Things are pretty hot up there. You'll be assigned to help the police maintain order.'

'Sir.' His eyes flicked out to the polo ground. His three fellow riders were already in play and the umpires had signalled for the throw-in. Whyman was frantically waving his mallet at him.

'Go on, then, man, finish your damned game.'

Oates unfastened his helmet and took it off. He realised he'd been playing the fool for so long, enjoying getting up the noses of the stuffed shirts, that it had almost consumed him. The actor performing the clown and the clown itself had become indistinguishable. He signalled to young Lieutenant Moores to take his place. 'No. I'll pick the squadron this afternoon. We'll be on our way first thing, sir.'

The executions took place an hour after sunrise, before the mid-summer heat had time to hit its full, debilitating intensity. Oates supervised the cordon around the execution site. It was a patch of scrubland, not far from where Bull had been beaten to death and pretty much on the spot where Porter had been severely maimed by the mob after making the mistake of handing over his rifle.

The Royal Engineers had erected a gallows in the centre. The mosque aside, it was the sturdiest structure for miles around. Near it was an equally stout wooded triangle. There were four tents. One, open sided facing the gibbet, housed the press, both local, international and the Reuters agency. Also within were the sentencing tribunal, which had consisted of a judge advocate, who was a British officer; Sir Malcolm McIlwaraith, judicial adviser to the Khedive, the nominal ruler of Egypt; an English judge of the Native Appeal Court and the President of the Native Court of the First Instance, who happened to be Armenian. The second bell-tent held the prisoners and the third housed the commandant of the police, the supervising British officers and the Mudir of Menifiya, a local dignitary.

The fourth canvas structure was busily being erected by a brace of bony-looking men who had brought a cart piled with shrouds and water butts. These would handle the bodies of the executed.

Oates had arranged his men into a circle with a triple-layered circumference. He ordered the first row to kneel and fix bayonets, the second and third to be ready to fire. Since before sun-up, fellahin had been drifting to the area. Now they were mostly sitting or squatting, staring at the cordon. In the last half-hour, with prayers over, their number had swelled considerably.

'How many of those buggers do you think there are, sir?' his staff corporal asked. 'Must be thousands.'

Oates checked his timepiece. They were running late. 'There might be a thousand by the time the execution happens. Pass the word: I don't want anyone handing his rifle over to a mob. If there is trouble they get one, I repeat, one, warning shot over their heads. The next volley is right at them. Understood?'

'Sir.'

'Four executions then the floggings. Shouldn't take too long.'

Justice had been remarkably swift for Egypt. Of the seventy-five arrested, four had been sentenced to death, thirteen to be flogged and subsequently imprisoned, another nine flogged only.

Oates patrolled from behind his men, whispering to them. He had spaced out his troopers and corporals so that there was one man every few yards, with infantry and police between them. He expected the Inniskillings to lead by example.

After an hour, Oates's thigh began to ache. The old wound was never a problem on a horse, but if he had to stand for long periods it began to throb. That was when the limp returned.

'Here we go,' said his staff corporal at last.

The prisoners' tent opened and two Egyptian policemen, with rifles and fixed bayonets, led out the first of the condemned. Even Oates was shocked at how old he was. It was difficult to judge the age of the natives, given the drudgery and misery of their lives, but this man must have been seventy if he was a day.

His escort led him first to the wooden triangle, where his wrists were bound to the wood.

A burly army sergeant major stepped forward to administer the flogging. He carefully cut through the man's jellabah and exposed a square of brown, sagging skin.

Oates had seen floggings before. He didn't want to watch another. Instead, he kept his eyes on the crowd.

He heard the swish of the lash going back and then the snap as it cut into flesh. There was the smallest gasp from the observers. Another whip-crack, this time louder and a cry of anguish from the victim. The sergeant major had his eye in now, judging the distance perfectly with each stroke. The crowd shifted, but Oates was puzzled. He had expected something more demonstrative.

A fifth and a sixth strike of the whip followed. Oates risked a glance over his shoulder. Wet stripes glistened across the hide of the old man. He had slumped against his bindings already. Oates willed the whiphandler to stop; this was surely enough. But still the blows came, and the jellabah became soaked, as the entire top layer of skin disappeared. Now he was whipping muscle and fat and gristle, driving the tip deep, exposing the bone in places.

The signal was given to stop at twenty, and the man was cut down and taken to the gallows. He could hardly stand; he was dragged up the steps on jelly legs and needed support while the charge and sentence was read.

Asked if he had any final words before the black hood was drawn over him, he stood straighter and yelled a short sentence. The crowd responded, the volume deafening, and Oates saw some of the guards shift their rifles. 'Easy,' he said.

With the sack in place over his head, the noose around his neck, it was the Mudir who gave the signal to the British executioner. The trapdoor gave a creak, sprang open and the rope twanged taut.

Now, Oates thought, they'll react now.

There was nothing but silence, during which he could clearly hear the flies buzzing around him. Not one of the natives moved. They stayed unnaturally still and equally quiet while the second, younger, prisoner was brought out and flogged with the old man's body still swinging from the gibbet in full view. He suffered twenty-five strokes, before being hauled up to take his place at the end of the rope.

And all the time Oates watched the fellahin, realising there were subtle changes taking place. Their eyes were hardening, their faces growing more sullen and angry. By the time the final man was hanged, there was so much hatred directed at him and his men and the officials on the site, he felt the intensity of it outdid the sun beating down on them.

For the first time in his life he knew what it was like to be truly despised.

That night he wrote to his mother, describing what he had witnessed. He had no doubt that a punitive action had been required following Bull's murder. Otherwise more British officers might die at the hands of fellahin mobs. But he had been unnerved by the passive yet aggressive spectators, who had not seemed at all cowed by the harsh retribution. In fact, they appeared to draw strength from it and grew more arrogant. When the mob had dispersed, several of his men had been 'accidentally' shouldered aside.

He glossed over his feelings of unease about the whole process, though, and reported the facts. Then he remembered he had other business to address.

Thank you for shipping Sorry Kate from Ireland to Mr Hallick. Tell Bryan that Hallick has entered the Angel Gabriel for Sandown. Might be worth a flutter, he's a ripper horse.

I am enclosing a letter from a boy called Frank Chester. He was a young lad who had an accident on the way over to the Cape and still cannot work. The army discharged him without a gratuity of any sort. Could you have him brought up to the village and boarded and see if perhaps we can find a position for him? He was a teetotaller and bore a very good character. The regiment won't help him. But we have to do something or he will starve.

The army, Oates had already noted, did not always look after its own. Not in the case of the men, anyway.

Did I tell you our drum horse died? Been carrying the drum since '96. Wouldn't be surprised if it was the heat that took him. The Mounted Infantry are disbanding and I have been chosen to pick the best of their horses. There are Arabs, Barbs and Syrians. I might even find one or two for myself. Plus it is a chance to go out into the desert. It has an extraordinary effect on me. I think I like barren places. Colonel Brooks has appointed me Acting Adjutant as well. Who knows, I may be Captain Oates soon. I shall have to take the examination, but some awful fools are passing now, so why not I?

His mother would like him to have a worthwhile promotion, but he felt he had to prepare the ground for her subsequent disappointment. For the first time in his life – or at least since Edie had come and gone – he felt the bonds with Caroline Oates loosening.

And there are rumours that an India posting will follow Egypt. It sounds all very exciting from afar, no doubt, but it isn't. India is worse than here by all accounts. I feel the army is moving on without me. I know I have polo and my motorcycle, but it isn't enough. You know me, the more work I do the better I feel, but the kind of work we have here is not to my liking.

He wondered if that was just his distaste for the floggings talking. But he pressed on.

If I could think of something else to do, I would, but for the moment I am only qualified for horses and cavalry. It is just that

I went straight to war when I joined the Inniskillings and in peace-time the routine is so deadly dull. How those who don't like polo or shooting manage, I will never know. So there, I have said it. I won't do anything without consulting you, of course. Just to prepare you, though, one day a real adventure opportunity will come along and I intend to take it.

He read the last line and signed off. He had no idea what kind of adventure would appeal, but Lieutenant, soon-to-be Captain, Oates was certain he would know it when it found him.

Twenty-five

Great Ice Barrier, Antarctica

'Shackle, get up. Come on. It's not penguins. It's men.'

Shackleton, sitting at the rear of the sledges, his role reduced to braking by digging his ski pole into the snow, groaned.

'I'll stay here, I think.'

'Can't do that, old chap,' said Scott. 'How would it look for you to be half asleep on the job?'

'Come on,' said Wilson. 'Or the gilt will be off the gingerbread.'

Scott and Wilson reached down with their ravaged hands and lifted him on to his unsteady feet. Then they dismantled the makeshift sail that had helped propel them for the past weeks. Without a man acting as a tiller, the gusts from the south sometimes sent the sledges careering out of control, so Shackle had been some use. But his pride was rubbed as raw as his face.

'It's people,' repeated Wilson. 'Someone must have seen us from Observation Hill. It's a welcoming party.'

'As I say, best not be lying down for this one. You don't have to pull.'

Shackleton nodded, understanding that the skipper wanted a more dignified homecoming than two men at the end of their tethers dragging a sick companion reduced to a brakeman. He shuffled over to get into the harness.

There were no dogs now; Jim and Nigger had been the last to go. There had been tears of remorse and anger. The three men had made a vow then. Never again. They would never put themselves, or the animals, through such a degrading ritual. Nansen had claimed dogs were good companions out on the ice. That was true. The problem was you had to murder your new friends, then worse, help the surviving ones indulge in canine cannibalism. On several occasions they had been reduced to hauling a sick and vomiting dog, keeping it alive as fodder for the remaining animals. *Never again.*

'Ready?' asked Scott. 'Let's heave.' Out of habit he stretched the last word, as if encouraging a pack of phantom dogs.

It was a diamond-clear morning, the land pin-sharp in the light and their snow-blighted eyes could clearly make out the two skiers hurrying towards them. It was nine days since they had seen the familiar plume of Mt Erebus, the eternal beacon, standing straight in the sky like a giant exclamation mark. It told them they were safe, if they could just hold on. Their spirits were buoyed by the extra food and the letters Armitage and Royds had left at Depot A for them.

The ship thrived, it seemed, and much exploration and scientific work had been done. Shackleton had rallied then, but had suffered a relapse overnight, his scratchy cough once again a continuous background noise that had disturbed the others. At one point Wilson was convinced he wouldn't last the night. But Shackleton had confounded them all, coming back from the brink time and time again. Some days he had been more enegetic than his companions, but that day the malaise had struck at his lungs again.

'Nearly there, Con,' Wilson said.

Scott realised he had slowed, like a horse tiring with the finish line in sight, and doubled his efforts against the sledging straps, his breath coming hard. Shackleton said nothing, his jaw set in solid determination as he walked alongside, willing his legs to work. They had coped with temperatures of minus 50 and blizzards so malevolent, it felt like a personal assault. At one point they had been down to one good eye between the three of them. It was hardly surprising they were somewhat careworn.

Scott and Wilson hauled for another ten minutes before anyone spoke. It was Shackleton, and the one word he uttered was full of anguish. 'Skipper.' He stumbled and Wilson caught him. They lowered him into the snow. 'Sorry.'

'It's not a problem. Let's pitch the tent,' said Scott. 'We'll let them come to us. And we'll brew up some cocoa.'

It was Skelton, the engineer, and Bunny Bernacchi, the physicist, who had made the effort to greet them. They skied into the hastily erected camp and, quickly undoing their toe straps, embraced each man in turn. If they were shocked by their appearance, they gave no indication, which Scott interpreted as them looking even more dishevelled and starved than he feared. Had they merely been battered, Skelton would have made jokes about them. Their condition was clearly beyond jest.

'Did you . . . ?' Bernacchi began.

'No,' Scott admitted, enunciating carefully to preserve his raw lips. 'We didn't make the Pole.'

'Eighty-second, though,' croaked Shackleton, before Bernacchi could express disappointment.

'Beyond the eighty-second,' corrected Wilson. 'And seventeen minutes.'

'A new Farthest South. Well done, skipper,' said Skelton, hiding his disappointment. 'Well done all of you.'

'The ship is here,' Bernacchi said.

'Which ship?' Scott asked.

'Markham's relief ship. *Morning*. *Discovery* is still packed in tight. So *Morning* is standing off in open water some miles away. There are fresh supplies, though, that they've hauled over the ice. Meat. Vegetables.'

'And news,' said Skelton.

'What news?' Wilson asked.

They drank the cocoa brewed boiling hot for once, with no regard to the amount of paraffin consumed. Skelton and Bernacchi tripped over themselves as they told them stories from the outside world; that there was a new prime minister, Arthur Balfour, that Cecil Rhodes, the great Empire builder, was dead, of the treaty to end the Boer war, the coronation of Edward VII. They also learned of the events on the ship, including sledging, tobogganing and shooting contests between men and officers and the first-ever Antarctic Athletics Contest. It hadn't been all fun and games. Royds had returned to Cape Crozier to investigate the Emperor penguins. Skelton had been part of the western party led by Armitage that had ascended to over nine thousand feet, on to the ice cap proper of Victoria Land; they had found a way past the mountains. During the exploration, Petty Officer Macfarlane had suffered what appeared to be a heart attack, although he had recovered well. Plus *Morning* had brought mail from home, both heartbreaking and uplifting. Babies had been born, sons and daughters married, parents died, wives deserted. The three exhausted men wondered what their own postbags held.

After thirty minutes, the stream of conversation slowed to a trickle. The initial euphoria dissipated and Shackleton, who had seemed more animated than of late, fell silent once more. He hunched broodily over the remains of his cocoa.

'Well, gentlemen,' Scott said. 'There is clearly much to tell and discuss. Let's proceed to *Discovery*.'

Scott and Wilson were taken aback when Shackleton leapt with gazelle-like grace to his feet and began to dismantle the tent. 'Come on, chaps,' he announced. 'Last one back is a soggy biscuit.'

Skelton and Bernacchi were at a loss to understand why Scott and Wilson found their companion's admirable vigour so amusing that they couldn't stop laughing through their scabbed lips for the next five minutes.

As they rounded the hump that had obscured it from their view, the party stopped in its tracks when it saw *Discovery*. The men viewed it through a fog of condensed breath. Her rigging was a mass of fluttering pennants, snapping in the wind. It was a cheering sight and Shackleton exclaimed with joy.

'Every flag is out,' said Bernacchi. 'And every man.'

As the group surged forward, they heard a low rumble, almost like the strange tremors they had experienced out on the barrier. It was a while before Scott identified it as the distant roars coming from the crew hanging in the rigging. The ship looked magnificent, a bold testament to the spirit of exploration, and the welcome for the three was almost overwhelming in its intensity. *Discovery* was crammed, its usual company swelled by *Morning*'s crew, including her captain, who had journeyed over the nine miles of still-frozen sea that separated the two vessels to join in the welcome, speculation and gossip.

Although eager to bathe and sleep, the polar trio accepted hot drinks and hearty congratulations. Scott borrowed some tobacco from Tom Crean, prepared a fresh pipe, and pronounced it superior to tea leaves at least.

Within the confines of the galley, mess deck and the scientists' work station where the two crews gathered, the noise of the company was deafening. The chatter of excited voices boomed along the low wooden ceiling and most had to shout to make themselves heard, adding to the cacophony. As Scott answered the inevitable questions – 960 miles covered, 300 further south than anyone else, but still 480 miles from the Pole – he caught sight of a crumpled Shackleton wedged into the corner near the galley, leaning against a stack of wooden packing cases stamped 'Tomatoes: tinned'. He was talking to Macfarlane, the lad who had suffered a possible heart attack. The pinched face under his bleached hair showed he was flagging and from the way he gasped between words, it was obvious his breathing was painful once more. Scott moved across and politely but firmly sent the petty officer away.

'Are you all right, Shackle?'

'It's a little overwhelming, isn't it?' He nodded to the galley area. 'Have you noticed the smells? How much more intense they are after being on the ice.'

Scott nodded. 'I would imagine we smell pretty strong to the lads as well. It's ninety-three days since our last hot wash.'

'I suppose we must be pretty rank.'

Scott sucked on the pipe, still relishing the sensation of hot tobacco smoke in his mouth. 'You don't have to do the dinner, you know.' Both knew there would be a celebratory feast in the ward-room, with calls for speeches, anecdotes, jokes and plenty of drinking.

Shackleton looked grateful. 'I'm not up to the mark, really.'

'Off you go. Come back if you do feel up to it.'

'Thanks, skipper.'

Once Shackleton had left the mess room, Scott found Wilson, busy describing their expedition and their subsequent condition to Koettlitz, his fellow medical man.

'And you, captain?' Koettlitz asked. 'How are you after your ordeal?'

Scott simply smiled to show he was well, but he could see Koettlitz trying to peer in his mouth at his rough gums as he did so. 'Ordeal is too strong a word.'

'Not for Shackle, I hear.'

'Perhaps not.' He turned to Wilson. 'Bill, can you look in on him in a while? Once you have bathed. He's not going to make dinner.'

'You think scurvy taint?' asked Koettlitz. 'You think it caused the collapse?'

Wilson stroked his beard, fondly anticipating its removal. 'It's most likely. But the cough is something else. The blood he brings up is worrying. I'll pop in, of course.'

'Thank you,' said Scott and then put a hand on Wilson's shoulder. One thing had been bothering him during the last thirty minutes, a nagging sense of emptiness and loss. 'I wish we had managed to get some of the dogs back.'

'I know, Con. It mutes the achievement somewhat. Just be grateful we got here ourselves.'

As Wilson moved off, Scott could see his leg dragging. Wilson was so stoical, Scott sometimes forgot how he must have suffered, with his eyes and his leg. The doctor was a different man from the one who had been unable to change his clothes without assistance on his first sledging trip with Shackleton. And Shackle?

184

He was a different man as well, but not in the way Scott had anticipated.

Scott had a delicious bath, shaved and had Hare cut his straggly locks before attending the evening's main event, the dinner hosted by Colbeck, the *Morning*'s skipper. There was mutton and fresh vegetables in both mess and wardroom. The two meals turned into raucous celebrations of the group's safe return, with many toasts, not all of them coherent. Scott felt the unfamiliar alcohol fuddle his brain and sipped rather than gulped. Despite a nagging concern about stomach cramp, he found that both he and Wilson far outstripped the others in the consumption of food.

'Does this always happen with sledging parties?' Captain Colbeck asked as yet another plate of mutton and potatoes passed Scott's lips.

'Only if you are sledging with the skipper,' said Armitage.

Scott joined in the laughter, even though he wondered if there was a hidden jibe in there. Did Bert Armitage think they had won Farthest South by too narrow a margin for comfort? That he had risked lives with meagre rations? There was another toast and he dismissed the thought.

After plum puddings and jelly and glasses raised to the King, the evening passed over into musical entertainment and increasingly ribald parlour games. When they began to play The Bishop in His Belfry and Roll the Topsail Gallant Down, which always ended with britches being removed, Scott excused himself. His head spinning with tiredness, he left the room to much painful backslapping. His ankles had grown tender and each step caused a jolt of agony. He walked as if he had gout. As he passed Shackleton's door, he tapped on it. There was no reply, but he slid it open. Shackleton lay in his berth, a thin pillow over his head. The little cabin smelled strongly of soap. Shackleton opened a red-rimmed eye, saw Scott and swung his feet down. 'Don't move. You should eat something. Sardines on toast?' he asked.

'I think I might manage that,' said Shackleton with a lazy grin. Sardines were a luxury usually reserved for the night watchman.

'How do you feel?'

'All done. You?'

Scott shrugged. 'My eyes hurt and my feet ache and my gums are sore.' He patted his stomach. 'And now my belly gripes. Tiptop, I'd say.' Although he knew the answer to the next question, he asked it anyway. 'Did Bill come along?'

'Yes.' Shackleton raised himself on one elbow. 'You won't send me back, will you?'

There was a roar of laughter from behind Scott, so forceful he felt as though he were buffeted by a gale. Someone on the mess deck had come up with a new set of filthy lyrics for 'The Boy Stood on the Burning Deck' and there came insistent demands for a repeat performance from the wardroom. Armitage seemed to have dismantled some of the traditional distance kept between the two messes while he was away. Scott wasn't sure he approved. 'I'll get Hare to call you when the sardines are done.'

'Skipper.' Scott stopped halfway out of the doorway, keen to be gone. He didn't want this discussion. 'We know you're sending a few of the black sheep back on *Morning*. But Macfarlane thinks he won't be allowed to stay on either. Because of his heart.' This was true. Armitage's initial verbal report of his journey was pretty conclusive. They could not risk a recurrence on another expedition. Macfarlane had become a liability. 'Don't send me back as well.'

'Nobody is talking about that now. All they are talking about is what we achieved. Farthest South. We covered almost a thousand miles. Not always well, but we covered it. Enjoy this moment; our record will not stand for ever. Now, sardines on toast coming up.'

Scott slid the door shut, seriously contemplating for the first time the consequences of sending Shackleton back. He would hate him for it. But that didn't mean it wasn't the correct course of action. He worried for another few seconds, then put the dilemma out of his mind. The decision would wait till they were fully recovered, as would *Morning*.

Shackleton banged the table, almost upsetting the oil lamp on Scott's desk. 'It's not fair.'

'Keep your voice down.'

'Dammit, I will not.'

They were in Scott's cabin, the door slid shut, but both knew sound spilled into the wardroom through the slats. 'I don't take this decision lightly—'

'Don't be such a prig. It's me, Shackle. You can't send me back. The men wouldn't stand for it for one thing.'

Despite his weariness, Scott felt the old hot flash of temper. 'It isn't up to the men. It's up to me.' Once Scott remembered just how low Shackleton was, he recovered his equilibrium. It had been a stupid thing for him to say. The man didn't normally try to capitalise on his popularity. 'Both Bill and Koettlitz—'

'You brow-beat them into it.'

'I can show you their written comments. Bill was reluctant, yes, but then he's your friend.'

'As I thought you were.'

Scott winced at that. 'Mr Shackleton. It took me three whole weeks to find my usual energy levels. Bill slept for ten days solid and is more or less his old self. But more than a month of good food and rest has left you still well below par. Look at your hands, man.'

Shackleton instinctively slipped the shaking fingers behind his back. 'I might have failed out there, but if it wasn't for me and Bill . . .'

'What?'

'You and those dogs. Was that not a failure by you?'

'I offered to do my part.'

Shackleton laughed and leaned in towards Scott. 'You couldn't do it. You haven't the heart for it. You said so yourself. You were weighed in the balance pans and found wanting. Yet it's me who is going back.'

'I have made my decision, as your commanding officer and friend.'

'You'd best add rival to the list.'

Scott frowned. 'How's that?'

'You send me home, skipper, and I'll have to come back to this godforsaken place. Just to prove you wrong.'

'Well, I wish you good luck.'

Shackleton banged the table again.

Scott picked up a piece of paper and handed it to the lieutenant. 'This is part of a letter to the Royal Geographical Society.'

The Irishman read it carefully.

Mr E. H. Shackleton, who returns much to my regret, should be of greatest use in explaining the details of our position and of our requirements for the future. This gentleman has performed his work in a highly satisfactory manner but unfortunately his constitution has proved unequal to the rigours of the polar climate. He was and remains a valued member of the party. I trust it will be made evident that I am sending him back solely on account of his health and that his future prospects may not suffer.

'It still makes me sound weak.'

'It isn't meant to. Nobody who knows you will think you weak, Shackle.'

'You know why I made it back in one piece?' he asked. 'I heard you and Wilson talking. Bill said he doubted I would last the night. Remember?'

'Yes.'

'I swore I would prove him wrong. And you.'

'And you did,' said Scott. 'And I'm glad of it.'

Shackleton stood to his full height, looking partly mollified. He slid back the door. 'You'd better reach the Pole next season, skipper, or I'll be snapping at your heels like the devil himself.'

The cabin shuddered as he rammed the partition back home.

The day of *Morning*'s departure dawned grey and overcast. Every rope and spar of the old whaler was clearly outlined against a darkening sky. Thick snow was blowing and a thin layer of fresh ice had formed around the ship's hull. The *Discovery* crew, all thirty-six of them, gathered on the floe to bid her farewell. They cheered when, with a creak and a shudder, she reversed, smashing the tentative hold the ice had already made.

'Just in time,' said Mr Barne. 'Another day and she might have been frozen in with us.' The imprisoned *Discovery* had still not broken free into clear water, despite the use of ice saws and explosives. It wasn't a concern this year, as Markham had sent permission for them to overwinter for another season, but it might be a problem when they wanted to go home. At the back of Scott's mind was a concern: what if this ice-free anchorage had been a one-off freak occurrence? That the ice rarely retreated so far south? It might be that *Discovery* would have to be abandoned, a possibility he really didn't want to face just yet.

Scott raised a hand as his men cheered the departure. 'How was Shackle on the journey here?'

'Shaky,' said Mr Barne, who had accompanied him over the ice. 'And gloomy.'

'It's understandable.'

Scott had said his final goodbyes to Shackleton on board *Discovery*, rather than on the ice, fearing a public outburst. The man had still railed against his removal, but had accepted he had no choice. The captain's decision was final.

Now, Scott could see Shackleton standing on *Morning*'s deck, and next to him an equally despondent Macfarlane, the latter waving half-heartedly. Not Shackleton. Both his hands were over his face; he was weeping. Scott took this as a further sign of a man still not fully recovered. The old Shackleton would have plucked his eyes out before making such a display.

'I am sorry to see him go. And Hare. He's a good boy. Too good to be a steward and drawing baths for the rest of his life. The rest are crocks.'

Brett, the despised cook, was pulling out, as were Duncan, Page and Hubert, three misfits who never rubbed along with the others, and Buckridge, an Australian troublemaker, too clever by half to ever be caught in his mischief. All had elected to return on *Morning* and would be replaced by members of her crew. Armitage, whose formidable wife was involved in some scandal at home, should have been among them, but he had flatly refused to go. He had accused Scott of trying to weed out all the Merchant men and of wanting to keep the best sledging expeditions for himself. Scott had assumed this was his upset at his wife's errant behaviour talking.

Scott was quietly pleased with the remainder of his crew. Royds was a changed man since his success at Cape Crozier, and gratified when it was his message that *Morning* had found, telling them the location of *Discovery*. And Barne's fingers had once again recovered and he was back to his cheery self. Even the most bumptious of the scientists had settled down. All he had to do was remember not to play bridge with Koettlitz, a sure source of friction.

The *Discovery* crew cheered themselves hoarse as the ship turned north and quickly receded, steaming the first few miles of the long voyage home. There wasn't a man on the ice who didn't both envy and pity those leaving.

'Look at it. Have you ever seen such a heartbreaking sight?' asked Wilson.

'Yes. Eighty-two degrees south.'

'We were still four hundred miles short, Con. There was no way we could have made it. Not over the mountains and the bergschrund.' This was where the barrier reared up against the land and created the treacherous fields of fractured ice and crevasses.

'I know. But at the time, it seemed so much nearer than that.' He made a fist. 'Within our grasp.'

'You don't blame Shackleton?'

He thought for a moment. 'No. Not at all. Or you, before you start thinking it, Bill. I might sometimes judge in haste. But in the end, you know, I only ever blame myself.'

'It's a shame! A shame!' It was Frank Wild, still drunk from Shackleton's farewell party. He and Shackle had always got along well. 'He shouldn't be going, skipper.'

Scott ignored him, knowing it was the alcohol in charge. Others calmed Wild down and his head drooped. Scott was glad he had declared a holiday. Quite a number of them had rumheads to sleep off.

Scott waited till the final hurrah had faded, turned south and flinched as the wind from the Pole cut into his face and moulded his clothes to his body. He pulled out the windbreak from his helmet. The company gave one last look at the rapidly diminishing *Morning*, bowed their heads into the icy blast, and marched off over the floe, singing balefully as they went, back to the ship that was to be their home for another year, steeling themselves for a second long Antarctic night.

Part Two

'The object of this expedition is to reach the South Pole and secure for the British Empire the honour of that achievement'

Robert Falcon Scott, 13 September 1909

Twenty-six

The Western Front, 1917

Kathleen Scott came very close to getting Teddy Grant killed. It was two days after their initial meeting, and he was part of a four-plane patrol charged with protecting two camera-laden reconnaissance planes. They were antiquated FE2bs. The pair lumbered along at barely seventy miles an hour. The Germans called them pigeons. They were somewhat easier to shoot down than that.

There was a tin-coloured ceiling capping the whole of the front, which forced them down lower than was desirable. It also gave the Germans somewhere to hide. The FE2bs, however, could not seek the protective cover of the cloud. The pilots had a clear mandate: to capture images of the new German artillery installations and head for home as fast as they could. Perhaps the overcast sky could help shield the British then.

A flaming onion was discharged as they crossed the first trenches of enemy lines, whooshing through the sky and bursting ineffectually behind one of the Sopwiths, leaving a wispy stain in the sky. A stutter of machine guns followed, but they didn't have the range, the tracers drooping well before their target.

Grant armed his Vickers and began to weave, back and forth, at the rear and slightly below the older planes. One of the observers raised a hand, but Grant didn't respond. The fool shouldn't be

195

waving at friendly planes, but looking over his Lewis and checking for hostiles.

He had finished reading Lady Scott's manuscript and also gone over his own diaries, but had done nothing yet by way of corrections or additions. He wasn't sure why he was so reticent. Something didn't seem quite right about the whole business. Her explanation of why she had come to him seemed spurious. After Amundsen, the British were less likely to trust a Norwegian, no matter where his allegiance lay, than an Englishman. Grant's involvement could actively damage the book.

There was another thing. Her asking him about the state of the bodies, to describe her husband's condition when they found the tent, now seemed oddly calculated. She had seemed genuinely upset when he had done so. Yet he was certain that Atch – Atkinson, the surgeon – had written to her with a full description and that Cherry had also discussed the matter. In fact, he recalled Cherry telling him just how difficult it had been, but how he felt he owed it to her to be honest and straight. And Tom Crean, too, had sent a letter.

Lady Scott was lying to him.

The bullets from the Spandau light machine guns entered the canvas of Grant's Sopwith with a hiss, followed by sparks and the ping of released tension as another burst severed part of his cat's-cradle of bracing wires.

He recalled Soldier saying that women filled your brain with flummery and distracted you. Captain Oates had been right. Lady Scott had taken him out of the moment.

Grant pulled the stick back and took the Sopwith up towards the cloud cover, aware that more rounds were puncturing his plane. He waited till the propeller was spinning through the first tendrils of mist and then pushed forward, taking it down into a dive to the right.

Now he could see the dogfight laid out below him, with the bleak, treeless countryside as backdrop. One of the reconnaissance planes was in trouble, trailing a thin stream of oil. The other was frantically circling, trying to allow the rear gunner a clear shot at the two little planes harrying it. Fokker Triplanes. About as easy to hit as gnats.

A third hostile was heading straight for Grant, its Spandaus winking. He yanked the scout to the right with all the force he could muster, feeling his face distort as gravity and wind tugged at it.

The wounded FE2b lost a top wing. Grant watched it tear free of the struts, flap wildly when a couple of stubborn wires refused to give and then spin away, tumbling end over end, as the eyelets ripped out. The plane flew on for a few seconds, wobbled, turned upside down, and began a slow, terrifying arc down to the ground.

He knew the Fokker would have turned after him, but he concentrated on trying to save the vulnerable second photographic plane, firing a burst as one of the acrobatic little Huns sped by in a blur of red-and-blue livery.

Pull left, gain height, he thought.

Another Sopwith flashed in front, guns blazing. It was Cyril Meadows, he registered, good flyer, but Grant's Fokker – or another one – was close behind him. Grant felt the airframe twist as he pulled around and latched on to the pursuing Triplane. He let the guns chatter for a second, just to let the German know he was there.

Another burst from behind him pinged through his airframe. It was like a train now, four planes shackled together by invisible links: friendly, hostile, friendly, hostile, with him at number three. It was time to break the chain.

He cut the ignition and pushed the nose down, waiting for the airspeed to drop. The scarlet Fokker skimmed over his head, the undercarriage missing his rising propeller by inches, but exposing its compact belly. He refired the engine, raised his snout and fired. He watched as a puff of canvas and wood burst from it.

For a few moments, Grant thought his Vickers had had no effect, but the hostile faltered and yawed to the left. The engine continued to turn and there was no sign of smoke, but it fell almost elegantly away from the formation, before entering a spin that looked to be fatal. He'd hit the pilot.

There was no time to think about that or the victory he would be due. A flaming onion exploded to his left, buffeting him, the orange fingers of fire clawing at his wings. He had to make height again.

Below him the second of the photographic planes had ploughed into the earth, and the Fokkers were regrouping. There was no sign of another Sopwith. Any second now the Triplanes would be coming for him. As he raced for the safety of the clouds, hot oil from a puncture peppering his face, he fought to stay focused. It was only when the gloomy half-light had engulfed him and Grant turned the faltering Sopwith towards what he hoped was home, that he allowed the question that had been nagging him to surface.

Why was Lady Scott lying to him?

Twenty-seven

London, 1907

The novelist with the strange accent, part strangled American, part clipped English, leaned forward as he asked his question. Everyone around the lunch table had been allowed one of the explorer, so as not to hog him. Scott was well used to this. In a roomful of artists and authors, it was the adventurer who drew the interest. 'Well, Captain Scott, let me see,' Henry James drawled, stroking his beard. 'What was the worst moment of the expedition?'

All swivelled to hear his answer. He was at one of Mabel Beardsley's luncheon parties. She was on his right. His great supporter and advocate J. M. Barrie was at the far end, between an unknown woman and the rather smug and dandyish Max Beerbohm. Two foppish poets, Carling and Thripple, a trio of minor illustrators who called themselves the Hoffman Set and James, the American writer, completed the group.

Scott had toured and lectured about *Discovery* for almost three years and he was certain there wasn't a question he hadn't been asked on the subject. His answers were now well rehearsed and sometimes well worn.

'It must have been the crevasse,' said Barrie. 'That's my favourite.' The *Daily Mail* had run a lengthy piece on Taff Evans and Scott plunging into a massive ice ravine during the second season. The image of them dangling over the blue abyss, held only by leather traces had been a powerful one. But Scott had never thought he was going to die, not with ever-reliable Lashly hanging on to them.

'That had its moments. But it wasn't till the final scene that the worst time came. After *Morning* and *Terra Nova* had arrived.'

'The rescue ships?' interrupted James.

'The relief party, yes,' Scott replied, trying not to sound too prickly. The RGS and the Admiralty had sent two ships the following winter, ordering him to abandon *Discovery* if it couldn't be freed from the ice that had imprisoned the ship for the best part of two years. A combination of explosives and a providential sea swell had eventually broken her from the prison and saved Scott from the ignominy of returning shipless. 'After the ice dispersed, a freak storm drove us on to rocks, beneath the cliffs. Our engines were not fully up to steam when we were swamped by a wave that blocked the inlets. It was a race between getting the boilers working again and being smashed on the ice by the gale. *Discovery* grounded and looked to be dashed to pieces. Fortunately, we managed to slide off just in the nick of time. But that, of all my moments, was the lowest.'

Beerbohm said, 'Which is saying something, captain.'

'And Captain Scott, if I may. Will you be going back? To try for the Pole again?' asked Carling.

Scott shook his head. 'I have said categorically no.'

'But we read about sledge trials in France, do we not?' It was Henry James again, smiling at having caught the explorer out.

Scott shook his head. 'The Navy are, of course, interested in motor sledges as a way of crossing ice. And as I have some experience of cold conditions—'

'Oh, come on, Con.' It was Barrie. 'I hear tell that every man who returns from the ice swears for six months he will never, ever go back. After that, he feels the pull. Do you not feel it? The pull of the South?'

'There are things one misses. The silence, the beauty of the mountains, the changing play of light on the ice, the companionship.' He stopped himself before he began to sound too wistful. Despite his new stellar acquaintances, he sometimes found himself longing for the robust humour and good common sense of men like Bill Lashly, PO Taff Evans and Tom Crean. He had got to know them well during the last, very successful sledging season, especially Lashly and Evans. There was nothing like hanging over oblivion to form bonds between men. And Barne and Royds had both come good, contributing excellent work in the final summer of exploration. He hadn't, though, tried for the Pole again; he wouldn't be bullied by Shackleton's threats to beat him. 'But I have a command now and a naval career to resume.'

'And besides, your Mr Shackleton is en route down there as we speak,' said James. Ernie Shackleton had put together his own polar exploration party – the British Imperial Antarctic Expedition – and had departed for the ice in August of that year, aboard a tiny converted whaler called *Nimrod*, to try to make good on his promise.

'So he is and I wish him well.'

'Do you not feel he is treading in your footsteps?'

'Mr James, really. One question each was agreed,' protested Mabel, but she was ignored.

'He has promised me he will not use the landing site at McMurdo Sound or huts from my expedition—'

'And why not, if you have no need of them?' asked Barrie, enjoying himself. He wanted to trap his friend into confessing he had unfinished business down there. Barrie's imaginary Antarctica was like an ice-bound version of Neverland, and he inhabited it vicariously through Scott. The explorer sometimes thought they should swap places and have done with it. The thought of living by writing had its attractions. 'Why not just give them up?'

'Because it is a convention in exploration', said Scott, 'that one does not trespass on another's chosen territory. Even the foreign expeditions accept that the Ross Sea is English and that McMurdo Sound is reserved, for the time being, for any sequel to the *Discovery* voyage. The same applies to our winter quarters. Shackleton has given me a written undertaking he will stay well clear of our bases.' Only after an intervention by Bill Wilson.

Shackleton had subsequently begged Wilson to come with him. The man had a bottomless supply of hard cheek.

'And if he makes the Pole?' James asked. 'Shackleton? How would you feel then?'

'He won't.'

The new voice shocked everyone into silence. It came from the woman sitting next to Barrie and Beerbohm. For the first time Scott noticed how deeply tanned she was; at first he had assumed it was a dark powder, but now he examined her properly, he could see she had been in a hot climate.

'Shackleton won't make the Pole.' She said it with absolute conviction. 'Don't you agree, captain?'

The table waited for his reply. He thought for a moment. 'I couldn't possibly say. He is a resourceful man. Not a great one for the detail, but he has imagination. And he inspires, let us not underestimate that. As I said, I wish him every success, and always have. We are friends and colleagues.'

This was no longer quite true. Relations had started off cordial enough once *Discovery* had returned, but Shackleton felt Scott's account of their Farthest South maligned him. Scott considered that this imagined slight – he never intended to suggest permanent weakness – as much as polar or scientific ambition had fuelled Shackleton's *Nimrod* expedition. Such was his drive, Scott wasn't convinced that the Irishman would keep his undertaking not to use Hut Point, especially if no easy alternative presented itself.

'But why, Captain Scott?' James asked. 'Why do you people do it? Put yourself through that hell? I couldn't countenance it, even if I wasn't bedevilled by my back. If I were twenty-five and fit you couldn't tempt me. What drives you down there?'

'It is important that the British Empire—'

'No, no,' interrupted James, knowing very well the imperialistic urge that drove the British to claim any uncharted part of the world. 'I don't mean the grander motives. I am wondering what you personally find down there that is so irresistible.'

Scott fiddled with his glass of dessert wine. It was the one question that he always found tricky to answer. 'Apart from the beauty and the majesty? Yes, it can be hell, but it can heaven, too. You will see sights that no man has ever seen.'

'That must be true of other places.'

'Perhaps. Not like Antarctica, though. But there are other reasons.' He took a sip of the Sauternes. 'There is the science. Of finding out how the planet works, of its geology. Many secrets are held under the ice. Then there is the biology. We discovered hundreds of new species, on land, in the air and in the sea. And geography. I don't think there should be blank spaces on our maps. I don't think nature should scare us or hold us back. I think it is one of our greatest assets, as a species, that we are able to test ourselves, to find our limits. That's what happens down there. You have to confront your own limits and those of others. I think you feel more alive in those situations.'

'Here, here,' said Barrie.

James, clearly dissatisfied, made to speak again but Mabel Beardsley clapped her hands together like a schoolmistress bringing an unruly class to order. 'Now, I think that is enough questions of Captain Scott.'

As the table split into smaller hubs of conversation, Scott leaned over and thanked Mabel. Then he nodded towards the woman next to Barrie. 'Who is she again?'

'Kathleen Bruce.' She looked at his face and saw the shine in his eyes. 'Oh, no. She's not for you, captain. My goodness, the choice of women you have.' Since his return, he had certainly been to more dinner parties and soirées than he would have dreamed possible, including ones at Balmoral and within J. M. Barrie's illustrious circle. Antarctic exploration gave you as much an entrée, it seemed, as penning such successes as *Quality Street*, the *Admirable Crichton* and *Peter Pan*. And, there was no doubt, Scott's exploits seemed to fascinate many women, something that had helped breach his usual reserve around them. Shackleton had been right: the men of the ice did very well for themselves upon their return, in all spheres.

'Who is she?'

'She calls herself a sculptor. Actually that's unfair, she's really rather good. Friend of Max's. Greek descent, I hear, which accounts for her wild streak. Lives alone in a flat in Cheyne Walk, if you can believe it.'

'Then we are near-neighbours.' He had found a house for himself and his mother in Oakley Street, Chelsea, although paying for it, as well as helping his sisters, was a constant struggle.

'She studied under Rodin in Paris. And I do mean under.'

Scott knew that Mabel was a great one for spicing up her sexual gossip. 'Is that true, Mabel, or are you being wicked?' He glanced over at Miss Bruce and she smiled back, a fleeting, dazzling burst of white teeth. She knew they were talking about her and seemed not to mind.

Mabel gave a small shrug. 'He's famous for it.'

'But is she?'

'She is a friend and intimate confidante of Isadora Duncan. You know—'

'I know who she is.' The past few months had accelerated his knowledge of the arts, even stretching to include a working knowledge of infamous, scantily clad dancers of a bohemian bent. 'Quite captivating. So I am told.'

'There's more. I hear Kathleen allowed herself to be taken on a tour of the opium dens down by the docks by young men.'

'I know for a fact you have done that. So far you are damning her by association.'

Mabel puffed out her cheeks in frustration at his sanguine replies. 'And she has been to war. To the Balkans. As part of the relief fund. A nurse.'

His eyebrows shot up. 'Really? How interesting.'

Mabel laughed. 'I'm not doing a very good job of deterring you, am I? I tell you she has rebuffed a great many men. Aleister Crowley was bewitched by her. He claims she has supernatural powers. He told me she is a terrible tease.'

'It sounds as if Mr Crowley was simply frustrated.'

Mabel placed a hand on his. 'She is not right, Con. Chalk and cheese, chalk and cheese.' The actress gave a bright smile of her own, and he could see why a younger Mabel had so captivated

New York a decade earlier. 'What about the widow Marie-Carola d'Erlanger?'

Scott grimaced at the memory of his abortive courtship. 'Not to be. The family disapproved of me. Apparently my fortune was insufficient. In that I don't have a fortune.'

'Just as well. Her two children were an obstacle. A ready-made family is not easy. Remember, captain, you always have me to turn to.'

'As does your husband.'

Mabel roared with laughter at this. 'You see? You're far, far too conventional for the likes of Kathleen Bruce. Royal Navy captains do not marry into bohemia. You need someone to keep home while you are away. Not a woman who attracts men like bees to the honeypot. Now, tell me about this accident you mentioned.'

'You don't want to know about that. Regular Navy life is far too dull.'

'Oh, but I do, Con, I do. I have a thing for sailors.'

As he embellished the tale of the collision of the *Commonwealth* with his ship *Albermarle* during night manoeuvres in the Mediterranean – an accident for which, after a few nervous weeks, he had been absolved of all blame – the party began to break up. It was a few minutes before he realised Kathleen Bruce had gone. He made hasty goodbyes to Mabel, accepted his coat and hat from the housekeeper and hurried out. He saw her down the street, turning the corner into Claverton Street. He followed at a brisk pace, careful not to break into a run. When he finally made it to the junction, she was standing there, just out of sight. A wry smile played on her face and sharp, cornflower-blue eyes peered from under a wide, velvet hat adorned with roses.

'Miss Bruce—' he gasped.

'You should catch your breath, captain.'

He put a hand on his chest. 'Yes. Forgive me.'

'Not been doing too much man-hauling lately?'

'No. Speeches in Middlesbrough and Dundee for the most part. Long dinners with many toasts. It is not conducive to fitness. Are you walking home? I live in Chelsea, too.'

'I thought I would stroll, yes.'

'May I walk with you? I'm sorry we weren't introduced properly.'

'I think Mabel Beardsley would like to keep you all for herself.'

'I am afraid I am very public property now. She can't.'

'Well, then.' She held out her hand. 'Kathleen Bruce.'

'Robert Scott.' They gave a pantomime handshake.

'There, that's over. Of course I knew who you were straight away. I saw you in *Vanity Fair*.'

'Oh, Lord. That scandal sheet. They are always trying to marry me off.'

'No success?'

'Not yet. Tell me, where on earth did you get your sunburn?'

'Vagabonding in Greece.'

'Vagabonding?'

'Sleeping under the stars.'

'Alone?'

She stopped and gave him a quizzical look. 'That's really none of your business, Captain Scott. But since you ask, there would normally be a companion nearby, with a gun. If I was in any danger, I would bang on a petrol can with a stick and he would discharge the gun. Although we never actually had to use the device, captain.'

'My friends call me Con. I wanted to ask you something. How do you presume to know about Shackleton, Miss Bruce?'

She waved a hand to dismiss the question as if the answer were obvious. 'I have heard about his financial woes, of course. He seems like a man who doesn't bother with the finer points of finance. If that crosses over to his planning, well . . . And, of course, I've read your book.'

'Really?' *The Voyage of the* Discovery was selling well, but he had presumed to a mostly male audience.

'People have, you know. Or do you think they purchase it as a mantle ornament?'

'I am deeply flattered you have read it, of course. I was just surprised it would have any interest to a person like you.'

Her eyes widened provocatively.

'I mean, an artist.'

'I'll have you know I have had one or two adventures myself.'

'So I hear.'

Kathleen tutted. 'Please don't believe everything you hear.'

'What if I like what I hear?'

'Go by what you experience, Captain Scott. Not second-hand impressions from others.'

'Well said.'

She stopped and examined the window of a dress shop, her eyes not really taking in the goods on display. 'I don't think Shackleton will make it. He has something to prove, to you, I think. But I am not sure that is enough. He'll turn back, see if he doesn't.'

'I can't wish him ill.'

She continued walking. 'And then you will go back. You will return South, Captain Scott.'

He had to laugh at her certainty. 'I feel that I should cross your palm with silver. How do you presume to know my future plans?'

'It's in your book, captain. You have earned the country's respect. But not your own self-respect.'

'That's in there?'

'Yes. For all to read. But most won't. Not that part. You have something to face down there. You must go back, or you will regret it for the rest of your life.' She hesitated. The light was going, and the chill of an autumn evening descending on them. 'I am having a pot pie at seven-thirty tonight. And some Wagner. I have a new gramophone. If you care to join me.'

Mabel had been right. She did have a wild streak, inviting a man she had barely met to her quarters. Where, he recalled, she lived alone. 'Alas, I have promised to dine with my mother.' Hannah Scott would not countenance a cancellation, not for a dinner in his honour at the Savoy hosted by H. G. Wells. She might despise the man's politics, but she relished his celebrity.

'You are a dutiful son.' She could have been mocking him, he wasn't certain. 'Is there no way . . . ?'

'You haven't met my mother.'

'Well, then. I am sure I can find another to share my pot pie.'

He felt an unfamiliar spasm in his chest. 'I could . . .' He ran through alternative scenarios. All involved watching Hannah Scott's face crumple with disappointment. And what would the upright Victorian lady make of an exotic creature like Kathleen Bruce ruining her night? 'No, I'm afraid no easy solution presents itself. We'll have to do it another time. If you would still be interested.'

'I am back to Paris tomorrow. Then Brussels. I shall be away for three weeks.'

'I shall be at sea by then. On the *Albermarle*.'

'Well, there we are, sailing in opposite directions.'

'So I won't see you again?' The note of desperation surprised him.

'Oh look, there's Gilbert.' She waved at a tall, blond man in a checked suit across the street. He instantly swerved towards her, a huge, lopsided grin on his face. She signalled for him to stay where he was and prepared to launch herself between the drays, omnibuses and chuffing automobiles. 'I have to go. See if Gilbert likes Wagner. But, yes, we will meet again, Captain Scott. Be sure of it.'

As she darted across the street, deftly weaving between the traffic and side-stepping the horse droppings, he suddenly felt terribly bereft, as if something vital had just walked out of his life.

Twenty-eight

Holland Park, London, 1908

Charles Shannon put his brush down and waited for Kathleen Bruce, who was sitting at the window seat, to notice his sudden inactivity. The sun was streaming through the grubby panes, catching dust motes and illuminating her hair, which was cascading around her shoulders. She looked wonderful, the painter thought, but there was something missing. The vivacious woman he had sketched out on canvas over the last three sittings was not in residence.

Shannon began to wash out one of his brushes, clacking it noisily in the jar.

'You've stopped, Charles,' she said at last, glancing up at the studio clock. 'Are we done already?'

'You don't love me today,' Shannon said with mock-petulance.

'Nonsense, Charles. You know that you and Ricketts,' she replied, referring to the other half of the Rickysan painting duo, 'are my two favourite Charlies in the world.'

'You aren't loving me. The paint isn't loving you either. You are somewhere else.'

She took two great handfuls of hair and flicked them over her back. 'I'm sorry. I saw my captain again yesterday.' She had met Scott at tea at Mabel Beardsley's, ten months after the initial encounter. They had seen each other a half-dozen times since, going to the theatre, galleries and concerts as well as attending readings at fashionable literary salons. He seemed hungry to fill in the gaping holes in a naval education.

'Your gallant explorer?'

'I took Gilbert along this time. Tea at the Goring. Gilbert, I am afraid, is not going to go quietly. He was excessively charming and witty yesterday.'

Shannon raised his eyebrows and swished the brush vigorously. Like most people who had met the young playwright Gilbert Cannan, he was very taken with his beauty. 'Well, I always thought Gilbert was more suited to you than a naval type. Not quite as much as a successful artist, mind.'

'Charles, don't waste your ardour on me.'

He smiled to show he was half teasing. 'Then our love shall remain chaste. And purer for it.'

'That's more like it.'

Kathleen stood and walked over towards the easel. Shannon stepped into her way.

'No, you can't see. I'm not pleased. I am very unhappy with you bringing your personal life in here.' He stuck out his lower lip, a comical effect in a middle-aged man. 'Besides, I am having trouble with your hands.'

She held them up and examined her fingers. They were perfectly formed, but larger than her frame might suggest. 'I have a man's hands.'

'You have a man's soul, Kathleen, but a woman's wiles. It is a fatal combination. So, what was the outcome? Was there a duel between suitors? Or did they behave like twentieth-century gentlemen?'

She had furrowed her brow, and ignored his question. 'Trouble is, he'd be perfect.'

'Gilbert?'

'Captain South Pole Scott. What do you think of that scheme?'

Shannon tutted. 'I understand you might need someone more, um, stable than Cannan. He can be very erratic. He's been a promising playwright for just a little too long now, hasn't he? Time to

210

fulfil that promise, I'd say.' He cleared his throat, aware she might not like what was coming next. 'On the other hand, Kathleen, alas, I can't see you as the doting naval wife, knitting socks while . . .' His face lit up as a fresh thought came to him. 'A-ha. A husband who is away at sea and God knows where else for long months might be an ideal situation, might it not?'

'That's a beastly thing to say, Charles.' A sly smile dimpled her cheek, though.

'And you can carry on your dancing and your vagabonding.'

'When I am married I shall be very good,' she said forcefully. 'But he would have to accept me for who I am.'

'And would he?'

'I'm not sure. Some days I think yes, others no. And for a great explorer he is wracked with self-doubt. Thinks he's not worthy of me.'

'Who is, darling, who is?'

'And there is his mother.'

Charles tutted. 'A mother. Oh, dear. The curse of our age. Tell me she isn't an upright God-fearing widow who regards the arts as Satan's spawn and anyone with designs on her son a harlot?'

'I haven't met her. But I suspect you are right. He has to support her. And the sisters.'

'Oh. Will you be poor?'

'One can't be poor, can one?' she mused. 'No, I couldn't stand that. But I still think he might be the one I had in mind. There must be a great inner strength in him. I shall have to digest what he has said and done these past weeks. He is going to write to me from his ship. I'll see then.'

'And Gilbert?'

She sighed, imagining the younger man's crushing disappointment. 'Poor Gilbert.'

'Do you love him? Captain South Pole?'

There came a hammering on the studio door. 'Don't peek,' said Shannon, indicating the incomplete portrait, as he crossed to see who was making such a racket.

Gilbert Cannan burst in like a wild-eyed bedlamite, breathless and dishevelled. 'There you are! I've looked everywhere from Sloane Square to Richmond for you.'

Kathleen, unfazed said: 'Gilbert. You've met Charles, haven't you?'

Cannan's head swivelled as if he had only just noticed the owner of the studio. 'What? Yes. Hello. Sorry to interrupt.'

'Not at all, my dear chap. It's only a sitting after all. Can I get you something?'

'No. Would you excuse us?'

Shannon looked nonplussed at being dismissed from his own premises, but said, 'I'll see if there's any tea.'

As soon as Shannon had left, Cannan grabbed Kathleen by the shoulders. He towered over her, far taller than Scott. 'I have a solution.'

'To what?'

'Our predicament.'

'Which predicament is that?'

'You don't know which of us to choose. The steadfast rock or the interesting author. The dull penny or the shiny sixpence.'

'You'll be the sixpence, I take it?'

'Yes. He's the penny because he seems more substantial, heavier. But the weightiest coins aren't always the most valuable.'

Despite herself she had to laugh.

'Oh, he's a dear, clean thing, but he just doesn't see life the way you and I do. Does he know Socrates or Euripides? Muriel Paget? Beethoven? Where is the joy in him? I sense a melancholy, don't you? Dark thunderclouds.'

She didn't disagree.

'Whereas you and I, we burst with life. With freedom, truth, purity and light. And my life is for you. I dream of you. I will troubadour under your window every night—'

She sensed one of Cannan's more elaborate flights of fancy. 'Yes, yes, Gilbert. And your solution?'

'You can have both of us,' he announced. 'We three can live together.' He caught the flicker of dismay on her face. 'Or you can live with the captain while he is home from the sea and with me the rest of the time.'

'A ménage à trois? That's terribly modern.' For some reason, she wasn't shocked by the suggestion. Kathleen enjoyed having the attention of men and with a few exceptions – Mabel, Isadora – she preferred male company. The prospect of two husbands, therefore, didn't sound quite as grim as it might to others. But it wouldn't do. 'I don't think Captain Scott would agree to that.'

Cannan threw out his arms wide in frustration. 'Oh, hang him. Tell him to take it or leave you. I saw the look in his eyes. Besotted. As am I. You are enough woman for two men, Kathleen. Think about it. Don't leave me. Please.'

She moved to the window and looked out over the garden and the skeleton of timber beyond it. A new row of four-storey houses was being built, which would cut the late-afternoon light to the studio at certain times of the year. The two Charlies had railed against it, but it seemed property speculation took precedence over mere art.

'No. It's not right. He can't have two fathers. It would confuse him. Thank you for the offer. I think you should go.'

Cannan looked puzzled as she ushered him towards the door. 'Who can't have two fathers?'

'My son, of course.'

Early in the morning, the map room of the RGS at Number One Savile Row was always gratifyingly empty. Scott knew he would have it to himself for at least an hour. He selected the Des Barres map of the southern hemisphere and unrolled it on the table. He used the lead weights provided to hold down the corners. His eyes roamed over the chart, till his gaze located New Zealand and tracked south. His eyes came to rest on McMurdo and he stared down at the fringes of white continent.

The last news he had received was of Shackleton's ship, the *Nimrod*, being towed south from Lyttleton in New Zealand. Towed! The vessel was so small it couldn't carry enough coal to get it to the Antarctica ice pack. Scott had admired the speed and enthusiasm with which Shackle had put together his expedition, but rumours had reached him of unpaid bills and rash promises, of hasty provisioning and last-minute recruits. Still, he knew all about that. When you were preparing for the South, a kind of immorality gripped you. It was all about getting down there, by fair means or foul and hang the consequences. They could be dealt with later.

'Where are you, Shackle?' he whispered, his voice shaking with the anxiety that was present whenever he thought of the man. He ran a finger over the coast to the east of McMurdo, to Balloon Bight. 'Where are you?'

'It won't speak to you, you know. Won't tell you where he is.' Sir Clements Markham's voice boomed off the wood-panelled walls.

Scott looked up. 'It hasn't yet, true. Good to see you, Sir Clements.'

'And you, Con.' The old man shuffled in on his sticks. His mutton-chop whiskers and heavy topcoat marked him out as a man of the middle of the last century, as did his weary, painful gait. 'There will be word eventually. You'll have to be patient.'

'Alas, not one of my virtues.'

By the time he reached the map table, Markham was huffing like a steam engine. Both his physical and mental powers, once so formidable, were on the wane. 'He'll be on the ice b'now.'

'But where?' Scott asked, his hand hovering over the ice shelf. 'Where will he have landed?'

'Wherever he sees fit, I would imagine. Now, Con, you must prepare yourself for the fact he might make it to the Pole. It'll be a bad blow if he does it by using your foothold. I was as angry as any man that he didn't consult you about his plans. But he might do it anyway, regardless of where he makes his base.'

Scott felt his stomach sink to his boots. 'I know.'

Markham removed the lead weights and let the map curl up once more. 'How long have we known each other?'

Scott considered. They had first met when Scott was a midshipman in the Training Squadron and had won a cutter race some twenty years previously. That was when Scott had first come to Markham's attention, but that wasn't what the old man meant. 'It's ten, no nine years, since we bumped into each other in the street and I said I was interested in going South and you took up my cause.'

'Nine years. I remember you then. Whip smart, ambitious, a naval man through and through. Shy, somewhat, though you fought it well enough. Restrained.' A bushy eyebrow arched upwards. Scott wasn't sure what he was driving at. 'And now, look at you.'

'What?'

'Oh, the doyen of the drawing rooms. The best boxes at the theatre. Soirées and receptions. Opera and ballet, I hear. The ballet. Man about town. And I hear rumours. Of a woman.'

Scott flushed slightly. 'Yes.'

'A suitable woman?' he growled.

'An interesting one.'

'Oh dear,' laughed Markham. 'That's exactly the phrase I heard used. Do navy captains want interesting wives?'

'This one does.'

Markham's smile faded. 'You are not the same man you were, back in *Discovery*—'

'I haven't grown soft. I'm as fit as I was.'

Markham pointed to Scott's stomach. 'Down there.' He tapped his temple. 'But up here?'

'What's your point, Sir Clements?'

'I know you are hoping he fails. Not that he suffers. But fails. But even if he does, I am not sure you should go back. You got away with it once, Con. By the skin of your teeth, sometimes. But you were hungry then, had no other life, no high and mighty friends. And once you have a wife—'

'Shackleton has a wife.'

'You are not Shackleton. Don't look at me like that. I don't mean that as an insult. Just that you are different. You, Con, are my friend and my protégé. I see the thinking behind your claim of primacy. Know the temptation you must be under. But don't be pushed into something in haste by what Ernest Shackleton does or doesn't achieve.'

Scott rolled the map into a tighter shape and pushed it into its tube. 'I won't.'

'Do you love her? This Bruce woman?'

Scott nodded. 'Yes. Yes, I do.'

Markham's eyes sparkled. 'See, bloody disaster already. She loves you, I suppose. How could she not love Captain Scott of the *Discovery*?'

It was a question he had asked himself a dozen times. He had thought her lost to him, but now her letters were full of ideas of marriage. Did she love him? Or the idea of him? For his own part he thought a woman like Kathleen Bruce might find it terrifically easy not to love Scott of the *Discovery*. Especially as he had never achieved anything as concrete as the Pole. And then he felt the stab of fear once more. Where the hell was Shackleton at that moment?

He forced himself to smile at Markham as if the answer to his question was a foregone conclusion. 'Shall we take tea, Sir Clements?'

Lunch was at the Café Royal and Scott was there first, having tired of Sir Clements' cataloguing of his medical problems. He watched as Kathleen entered and made slow progress through the gilded room, stopping at every other table, it seemed, to share a greeting or an anecdote, her booming laugh infecting all around her. He wondered why he found her so captivating. He knew she wasn't conventionally beautiful or dressed in the height of fashion. There was something intangible about her, a force that electrified him, even across a crowded room. But then, love was always intangible he supposed, no matter what definition of it you used.

Was Sir Clements right? Was he going soft? No, he was not. Which is why Kathleen was perfect for him. This was not a woman who would allow him to sink into comfortable old age. This was a woman who would challenge and encourage him.

Kathleen dropped down in front of him ten minutes after he had first spotted her. 'Sorry,' she looked around and raised a hand at a friend across the room. 'Perhaps we should have chosen somewhere more intimate. Oh look, they've given me a menu with prices.'

'Really? I'll change it.'

'No, don't worry.' She leaned forward. 'Perhaps they think I am a suffragette.'

They both laughed at the thought.

'Dover sole, I think. You know, Con, I decided today that we shouldn't get married.'

The burble of conversation around them seemed to fade and the room spun slightly. 'Oh.'

'I mean we are horribly different, aren't we? In all ways. The artist and the man of duty. What a match. Then I thought about the look on your poor face. Look, there it is. Like a bloodhound. I meant, I thought we could do something altogether more romantic. Just live together. But then I imagined what your mother might say. So, I thought of a compromise.'

'What's that?'

'I think we should get married. Perhaps next year. Or sooner. We need to start making babies straight away.'

Scott opened his mouth but not much came out beyond a squeak.

'Come on, Con. Aren't you going to order? Although don't you have the Dover sole as well.' She laughed and widened her eyes. 'It's frightfully expensive and we've got a lot of saving up to do.'

Dear Mother,

Now, my dear, I must tell you that I want to marry Kathleen Bruce. She and I are agreed that if we do marry, under no circumstances must your comfort suffer. You are my first priority. Now I have two women to look after. I would like you to get to know her, of course. Yes, she is unconventional, but I feel that is good for me. But we must move beyond this condition of strain we have been living under, knowing I must marry one day but you worrying about how it will affect you. Money will not be a concern, be sure of that. I have looked at the cost of two persons living in a small house in London. It is £329. With the income from my book and even at half-pay when not at sea, that leaves enough to contribute to your upkeep, especially now you are in Henley rather than Oakley Street. So can you please write and ask her to call on you as my prospective wife? I am now near forty, she is but twenty-eight. She is a bright and joyous thing. But a lady by birth, with ties to the late Archbishop of York. I have appended her family history. Quite exotic in parts, but also a very good match for an ageing sea captain.

We will live in London and so be near you. Kathleen says she wants me to go back to the Pole. What is the use of all my energy if I can't knock off a little thing like that? she says. But, of course, it all depends on what Shackleton achieves and we won't know that for some months. Not till after the wedding. Please offer your congratulations. There will be no announcement till I hear back from you and you are quite settled in your mind, as I am in mine, that this is the right thing for me to do.

Your Son,

Con

Twenty-nine

From the *London Graphic*, 7 September 1908

FAMOUS EXPLORER MARRIED

Huge crowds gathered to celebrate the wedding of Polar hero Captain Robert Falcon Scott at Hampton Court last week [2 September]. One hundred and fifty guests were present in the Chapel Royal, including several of Captain Scott's colleagues from the *Discovery*, J. M. Barrie and, on the bride's side, the famous sculptor Auguste Rodin and his wife as well as well-known literary figures Max Beerbohm and Gilbert Cannan. The King sent a telegram of congratulations. The bride wore a dress of white satin trimmed with Limerick lace and a body of chiffon, a wreath of natural myrtle and a tulle veil. The groom surprised many by choosing morning coat over Naval uniform. The service was conducted by Rosslyn Bruce, brother of the bride, and she was given away by a second brother, Lt Wilfred Bruce RN of HMS *Arrogant*. Captain Scott's best man was an old friend from HMS *Majestic* Captain Henry Campbell. After the ceremony the couple left by motor car for a honeymoon in Paris & France to cheers by the large number of well-wishers. It is understood that the marriage will make no difference to Captain Scott's future plans with regard to Antarctic Exploration.

Thirty

Portsmouth, 1909

The London train was late. It was March, and the steel rails glistened in a very English drizzle. Captain Scott consulted his pocket watch, checked it against the large Smiths model suspended above the platform, and tried to contain his fury. Having left HMS *Bulwark* once and for all, he was desperate to get back to see Kathleen now there was good news.

Her letters had become vague and dissatisfied for the most part, shy on detail of what she had been up to or whom she had seen. Scott abhorred jealousy, but he could sometimes feel its first seeds taking root in his heart. *Danced till two-thirty*, she might say, without specifying whom she had partnered. *Saw Max Beerbohm and his friends for long lunch. Quite jolly*.

While he had been in France with Royds and Skelton, testing the new motor sledges (which prompted a new round of press speculation about his intentions), there came letters ripe with the disappointment of a pregnancy that had failed to materialise. *At least nobody could claim we HAD to get married in a hurry*, she had written, which he took as a chiding.

When he castigated himself in reply, called himself a clod and a clown, she replied with cheery letters telling him he was the most wonderful man and how the house was empty without him. *I even miss your pipe ash*.

This had been terribly confusing, especially when their letters crossed. It was no easier, he had decided, being a naval captain than a naval wife. Not when the wife was as determined and headstrong as Kathleen. And then there was the news from Lyttleton. Shackleton had used McMurdo after he had promised not to. It was treachery. In fact, he would have been flung into a terrible dark funk, had not news come that changed everything. *'My dear love, throw up your hat and shout and sing triumphantly for it seems we are in a fair way to achieve my aim.'*

The 'my' made him bristle, and he had said so, but he did rejoice, wrestling a flabbergasted Lieutenant Humphries to the floor. Kathleen was pregnant. A child was due in the autumn.

'Skipper.'

It was Petty Officer Tom Crean, his coxswain for the past two years, kitbag over his shoulder. 'Crean, my goodness. Are you up to London too?'

'No, skip. It was you I was looking for. See if you'd seen the news?'

'From *The Times*?' There had been recent criticisms of the worth of *Discovery*'s scientific measurements. Some of it was justified, as there had been a few basic meteorological errors that had proved embarrassing. But much of it came from the dual snakepits of the RGS and RS, and were designed to embarrass Sir Clements and, by default, Scott. 'We can't worry about that, Tom. We must move forward.'

A crackling announcement told them the London train was due in ten minutes.

Tom Crean put down his bag and took out a newspaper from the top of it. 'Not *The Times*. You'd best see this, skipper.'

He handed over that day's *Daily Mail*. 'I didn't have you as one for reading this sort of thing, Tom.'

It was the *Daily Mail* that had promulgated the lie that Scott had unfairly maligned Shackleton over his collapse on their Furthest South. He had boycotted it ever since.

'I couldn't miss it, sir. You didn't see the hoardings on the way up?'

'No.' He had been daydreaming about Kathleen and her

pregnancy. Now, as he looked at the front page, Scott felt a huge jolt at the main headline. *Shackleton Fails To Make Pole*. 'I'll be damned,' he muttered, his voice cracked and full of contrary emotions. 'But he's safe. Stopped short, it says.'

'Just. He used McMurdo,' said Crean. 'And our old hut, as a forward base.'

'I know. That takes the bun, doesn't it? So much for paper promises,' Scott said distractedly. He was still trying to absorb the gist of the story, cobbled together as it was from telegrams sent from New Zealand. 'He found a new route up on to the plateau. They have the Magnetic Pole as well. Old Armitage will be sick about that. And they climbed Erebus.' Despite himself, he felt a flush of admiration. 'My word, he was busy.'

Then he found the part he wanted. 'Ninety-seven miles short. Kathleen was right.'

'Skipper?'

'Nothing, Tom. Well, it's a remarkable achievement, if true. A new Furthest South.' He scanned the account once again. 'It doesn't say whether statute or nautical miles. This is all *Daily Mail* geography. Still, it must have been a difficult decision, to turn back.'

Scott felt his spirits lift. It was hard to enjoy another man's failure, but the confusion and ennui of the past few months fell away. He now realised what he had been doing all those weeks. Simply biding time, paralysed by the thought of what Shackle might achieve. Well, the Irishman had done magnificently, but he hadn't got the Pole. And he had only got as far as he had by using Scott's peninsula and his old hut.

Ninety Degrees South was still there for the taking. And Kathleen, she had her baby. She had achieved what she wanted most from their union and she would love him for it, he was certain. It was the most propitious timing. He was already rehearsing his announcement to the RGS: *My Lords, ladies and gentlemen. The object of this expedition is to reach the South Pole and secure for the British Empire the honour of that achievement.*

And he knew where he should make his proclamation. There was bound to be a gala dinner for the returning hero. He would announce his own plans there, before Shackle had time to catch his breath and consider returning to finish the job. And damn whatever Sir Clements thought about the wisdom of the undertaking or his suitability for the task.

The train appeared, wreathed in a collar of steam, chuffing its way into the station, fat sparks flying from the funnel, hissing into the rain. He handed the paper back to Crean.

'Well, skipper?'

'Well, Tom,' he said softly, his words almost drowned out by the impatient shushing of the locomotive. 'If you are agreed. The Pole still awaits the arrival of an Englishman. I think we'd better have a crack at it next.'

Thirty-one

Burnham-on-Crouch, 1909

Lawrence Oates was scrubbing down the wooden deck of *Saunterer*, prior to a sanding and a fresh application of varnish, when he felt the boat rock as someone came aboard. 'Billings? Is that you? You should be doing this, you lazy good for nothing—' He knelt up to deliver his final tirade to his hapless crew face-to-face then halted.

'Hello, Laurie. Need a hand?'

'Not from the likes of you.' Oates threw the bristled brush into the bucket, leapt to his feet and wiped his hands on his tatty jumper. He held out his hand to his brother. 'Hello, Bryan.'

'Sorry I couldn't make the trip. How was it?'

Oates had taken *Saunterer* to France and across to northern Spain. 'Quite hairy, some of it. But great fun and *Saunterer*'s come through it well. Ignore what I said about Billings, he's a good chap. Come below, we have coffee. Or tea?'

'Tea please, Laurie.'

Oates hesitated, thrown by his brother's unusually diffident manner. The bouncy enthusiasm seemed to have been drained from him. 'What is it, Bryan? Is it Mother?'

'After a fashion.'

'She's not unwell?'

'No. I have some news.'

'Very well,' said Oates. 'But I warn you. So have I.'

They settled in the galley below, each with a wide-bottomed porcelain mug of tea, with *Saunterer*'s name on the side. They had been a birthday present from Bryan, bought at a chandler's in Dover Street, London. The flared base made them more stable in rough seas.

Bryan picked up a thick volume from one of the berths. 'You've taken to reading?'

'A Life of Napoleon,' said Oates. 'My new hero.'

'Why would you have a Frenchman as a hero?'

Oates shrugged. 'He was a great commander.'

'As was Wellington.'

'Wellington is too obvious. And he didn't like the cavalry,' said Oates. 'Come on. You go first. Your news.'

Bryan sipped his tea. 'Very well. I am in love.'

Oates choked on his drink. 'With a girl?'

'No,' said Bryan sarcastically. 'A horse.'

'Now you are making sense,' laughed Oates. 'Does Mother know?'

'Yes.'

'Hence the long face.' Oates could guess that Caroline would only approve of a princess or above for Bryan. 'Tell me everything.'

'It's Alma Kirby.'

'The vicar's daughter?'

'Yes.'

Oates slapped his thigh. 'But that's grand. She's a good catch. Handsome. And her father in the clergy. Why, even Mother can't object to her.'

'No. It isn't her she objects to. It's me.'

'You?'

'She says I must have a career. A real one, before marriage. You recall how scathing she was about Ranalow?' Frederick Ranalow had married their sister Lillian despite objections from Carrie that, as a professional singer, he couldn't afford even to keep her daughter in hats. 'Well, she says it would be hypocritical of her not to consider my financial security. So I must find a position before we can announce an engagement.'

'I see. You've no thoughts?'

'The Thought Vault is empty, Laurie.'

Oates considered for a moment. 'My friend Hugh Kingsland left the Dragoons last year. I hear he is doing well at his father's bank . . .'

Bryan was ahead of him. 'Would you mind, Laurie? Having a word before you go back to India?'

'Don't remind me.' He had been home four months and the thought of a return to drudgery in India depressed him. 'But I shall be up in town in the next few days.' The boat moved again and he shouted up through the open hatch. 'Billings, can you finish preparing the deck?'

There was no reply but a few moments later came the enthusiastic scrape of bristle on wood.

'So consider it done. And congratulations. She's a fine girl.'

'What about you?' asked Bryan.

'I don't think I'll be announcing my engagment just yet.'

'No, you fool. You said you had news.'

'Ah, yes.' Oates drank the last of his tea. 'You know I haven't been too happy with the army.'

'I think you mentioned it once or a hundred times.'

'I have decided on something new. I haven't told Mother yet.'

'Don't worry, I'll be tight lipped. Told her what?'

'I have applied to join Scott.'

'Which Scott's?' Bryan asked, thinking it must be another merchant bank.

'The British Antarctic Expedition. Captain Scott.'

Bryan's eyes bulged with amazement. 'That Scott? You? Laurie, are you serious? It's all sailors and sledges and ice and goodness knows what else.'

Oates spread his arms out to indicate *Saunterer*. 'And this is what? A horse and carriage? I know boats. I'm a sailor.'

That explained the summer jaunt to France and Spain. Oates had wanted to get his sea legs back. 'Mother will be—'

'Yes, yes.' He was well aware of what Carrie's reaction would be. 'And I know dogs.'

'Do they fox hunt in Antarctica? I don't think they use beagles, do they? And you've just bought a new pack to ship out,' Bryan reminded him.

'And there are plenty of officers in India who will buy a good pack of hounds if I am accepted.'

'But Mother?'

'Bryan, it's time Mother took a step backwards. It has been for years. You know I looked for Edie? Or at least her whereabouts, what is it? Fourteen years ago? Fifteen, goodness.'

Bryan sounded as if he was frightened to ask the next question. 'You found her?'

He shook his head.

'Well, thank the Lord for that.' His brother glared at him with uncharacteristic spite and Bryan decided to change an awkward subject. 'I read thousands have applied to join. Scott, I mean.'

'Eight or ten thousand, so they say.'

'Then why should they choose you? A cavalry officer?'

'I told you, I know boats, dogs, horses. I have given them good references.'

'Who?'

'Algernon Rayner-Wood at Eton.'

'But he's our cousin.'

'They won't know that. And he won't lie. We've already agreed what he will say, and it's pretty much the truth. Energetic, reliable, that sort of thing.' Oates looked down at his mug.

'And? There's something else?'

Oates nodded and looked a little shamefaced. 'I have offered them a thousand pounds if they'll take me.'

Bryan's eyebrows disappeared into his hairline. 'How much? Do you have one thous— You'll ask Carrie? Oh, please remind me to be somewhere else that day.'

'I'll need about one thousand five hundred. I said I wouldn't draw a salary. They are very short of money. Scott is off fundraising and coming back with meagre purses.'

'Better and better. South with a pauper. And you think Carrie will . . . ?'

'I won't ask if I can help it. I'll sell my horses. And those damned pistols. I can raise it, if you'll help put some things up while I am away.'

'Of course. Will the army grant you leave?'

'If I am shrewd enough. My CO won't like it, but I can use our friends at the War Office.'

'Mother's friends, you mean. If she'll let you.' He thought for a second. 'But she will, in the end. She loves you, you see.'

Oates grunted. He had no doubt of that. It was the way it manifested itself that was gnawing at him.

'Of all of us, you remind her most of Father. You understand that, don't you? It's why she keeps you close. And the only way she knows how is by money.'

'Since when did you get so perceptive?' He considered Bryan's thought for a moment. 'It might be true, but I've volunteered now and I have to follow through.'

'What on earth possessed you?' asked Bryan. 'It's bloody chilly down there, isn't it?'

'I hear they get the odd cold snap. After India, it will be a blessed relief. It's a healthy climate.' Oates thumped his chest. 'Good for a man.'

Bryan shuddered at the thought. He didn't much care for Essex winters, let alone those of polar climes. 'I think you are completely crazed. You'll try for the Pole itself? Is that the idea?'

'Is there any other point to going? They gave Shackleton a knighthood and he was a hundred miles away. Sir Ernest. I hear Scott was pretty banged up about that. Still, imagine what they will do to those who actually stand on it.'

'Is that the idea? Is that why people do it? Glory?'

'Independence.'

'Be serious for a minute. What about your leg?'

Oates gave the old war wound a tap. 'Fine and dandy.'

'Not first thing in the morning. I've seen you limping.'

'Then I shall get out of bed later in the day.'

Bryan laughed and shook his head, knowing there would be no dissuading his brother. Already there was a fire in his eyes, and, no doubt, in his belly. 'There is only one saving grace.'

228

'What's that?'
'You'll never get in.'

Captain Lawrence Oates was back in Mhow, India, when the long-anticipated telegram finally arrived, indicating that the few remaining obstacles to him joining Scott – such as paying his passage home and that of his replacement out – had finally been overcome. His argument that the Navy were taking all the glory of the Pole when it was, strictly speaking, a land-based affair, had swung the day. As he suspected, the army would like one of its men to stand at ninety degrees South. The cable was sent from the War Office, which had been liaising with his CO, the C-in-C India and Teddy Evans, Scott's new number one on the *Terra Nova*. It was about as terse as it could be, but it was the best thirtieth birthday present he could have hoped for.

OATES ACCEPTED. PROCEED AT ONCE.

Part Three

'*I have learned that something called friendship really exists and I have come to know men willing to sacrifice themselves for their country and for their convictions*'

Fra Tjuagut til Sydpolarferer
(From *Boy to South Polar Explorer*, Tryggve Gran)

Thirty-two

Norway, 1910

The afternoon stopping service to Christiana wheezed to a standstill, one halt short of its final destination, to take on water and discharge passengers. It was January, and despite the plunging temperatures and the sleeting north wind blowing through the small station, there was a sizeable crowd on the platform, all pressing against the windows, trying to peer inside the carriages.

'He's here!' a yell went up. 'At the front. Next to the loco.' The mob surged towards one end of train.

The lanky lad who had made the announcement, Helmar Hansen, quickly sprinted towards the rear. 'Come on,' he hissed at his young friend. 'I bribed the porter to tell us where he was. Carriage F, compartment fifteen.'

'You sure?' the other asked.

'I'll want a refund if not.'

The pair of them entered the second carriage from the brake car and burst through into the compartment. Sir Ernest Shackleton looked up in surprise and his wife let out a small gasp of apprehension. Both of the newcomers found themselves momentarily tongue-tied, as if they hadn't really expected to come face to face with the celebrated adventurer.

'Yes? What can I do for you, gentlemen?' He gave a smile. 'Is it our tickets you'll be wanting?'

'Oh, no. We are from—' Helmar began.

'Your names?'

The elder of the two took off his hat. 'Tryggve Gran, at your service, Sir Ernest, Lady Shackleton. And this is Helmar Hansen.'

The train gave a whistle.

'We are from the *Verdens Gang* newspaper—' Gran started.

Shackleton silenced him with a raised hand. 'I'm sorry, I cannot talk to journalists.'

'We're not—' Helmar began, but Gran elbowed him in the ribs.

'We have been asked to do a polar map. Of your journey. And there are a few questions we need to ask. Such as where you lost the horses. And we want to put on Mawson's trip to the Magnetic Pole. And—'

Shackleton shook his head regretfully. 'Journalists, I have found, print all there is to know about the trip, leaving me precious little to say at my talks. Why would the audience come if they could read all about it in the newspaper? In their own language, to boot.'

Another whistle, longer this time.

'I have a ship,' blurted Tryggve.

'I beg your pardon?'

'I have a ship. Ready for a trip South. Roald Amundsen is going to the North Pole, so it is not worth competing with such a great man. But South—'

'You have a ship?' Shackleton couldn't keep the surprise from his voice. 'How old are you?'

'He's twenty,' said Helmar.

'Twenty-one in a week,' Gran added huffily.

'But he has experience at sea. And all his family are sailors.'

And rich, thought Shackleton, if they can fund a boy having a vessel of his own. He suspected the Grans were more than mere Jack Tars. 'So are you reporters or explorers? Which is it?'

They hesitated. 'I am a trainee reporter. We really are doing a map. But Tryggve is an explorer,' said Helmar.

'Would-be explorer,' corrected Tryggve, colouring slightly. 'And skier. A good skier.'

'A great skier,' insisted Helmar.

Shackleton looked wistful and turned to his wife. 'What was I just saying, dear? If we'd had skis and used them like the Scandinavians, we might have made it all the way.' The train gave a jolt, preparing to move out. 'Are you coming with us?'

'No,' said Tryggve. 'But I'll be at Loge Hall tonight for the lecture. Will you see me?'

His wife whispered something in his ear, but he shook his head. 'Emily is worried that your king takes precedence. I say nobody should get in the way of a fellow explorer.'

Tryggve beamed at being included in such company.

'Wait till I have finished and shaken a million hands, then perhaps we can talk about this ship of yours.'

Shackleton proved to be a most entertaining speaker, with a clear, resonant voice. He was a born storyteller, breezy, self-deprecating and able to build tension where needed. He was received for the most part in rapt silence, but, because this was a country that knew the cold and ice, there were a few hostile questions at the end, mainly concerning the use of dogs, skis, ponies and the automobile he had taken.

Roald Amundsen, a seasoned iceman and the pioneer of the North-West Passage, was particularly scathing on one aspect. 'Your clothing of cotton and canvas was a strange choice, Sir Ernest. If furs are so useless, Sir Ernest, as you claim, why did you complain of the cold so much on the journey South?'

Shackleton thought for a moment, a finger on his forehead. 'Perhaps because it was fifty degrees of frost with a blizzard blowing and we had all but run out of fuel.'

The audience tittered and even Amundsen smiled. 'But nothing is warmer than fur.'

'True. If dogs are pulling you. When you man-haul, you sweat, no matter how cold it is. When fur has soaked up sweat and turned to ice, nothing is colder or heavier.'

'Then next time,' said Amundsen, gaining the laugh, 'I suggest you choose your underwear more carefully.'

The great Carsten Borchgrevink, the first man to overwinter in the Antarctic, queried the use of horses over dogs. Shackleton admitted that the Norwegians had the edge when it came to efficient use of the huskies, but said nobody knew horses like the English.

Otto Sverdrup, the captain of Nansen's legendary Arctic exploration ship, the *Fram*, was allowed the final question. 'Sir Ernest, how difficult was it to make the decision to turn back when you had the Pole in your grasp?'

'Not sure we had it quite in our grasp. To keep me going, I kept thinking of Browning: "To feel the fog in my throat, the mist in my face. When the snows begin, and the blasts denote I am nearing the place . . ."' He cleared his throat and, for a fleeting moment, his face showed the memory of what that painful decision to abandon the Pole had cost him. '"I was ever a fighter. So one fight more." Yes, we could have gone on, perhaps. But we were living, if you could call it that, on pony maize. Adams had dysentery.' He looked around the room. 'I don't have to tell some of you what it is like to share a march, and a tent, with a man who has dysentery.'

There was a burst of rueful laughter.

'And you know, a medical thermometer starts at ninety-four degrees. Below that, you are a corpse. For three of us, the mercury did not move. Technically, we had frozen to death. How difficult was it to turn back? It hurt worse than anything the ice did to us. But as I said to Emily upon my return, I am sure she would rather have a live donkey than a dead lion.'

There was applause and Sverdrup led the standing ovation.

Afterwards, once the King had shaken his hand and departed, the audience descended on Shackleton for more questions and autographs. Tryggve Gran hung back, kneading the rim of his hat, wondering how he could possibly get through the crush.

'I hear you have a ship now, young man,' said a voice in his ear.

Gran turned and found himself looking up at Fridtjof Nansen, a great Viking of a man, still fit and handsome at close to fifty, with fine blond moustaches and intense, piercing eyes. They had corresponded and Gran had met the older man at lectures, pumping him for information and advice till Nansen begged for mercy. 'Well, yes, Herr Professor. You gave the *Fram* to someone else.'

Nansen laughed at the boy's cheek. He had loaned his ship to fellow-countryman Roald Amundsen for his next Arctic venture. He would hardly have given such a prestigious vessel to an untried newcomer. 'You want to go South?'

'Yes, sir. Peary having made the Pole.'

Nansen looked doubtful.

'You don't think he did?' There had been rumours that neither Robert Peary nor Frederick Cook – both claimants to having planted the Stars and Stripes Furthest North – had not, in fact, stood at the Pole.

'Peary, perhaps. Cook, I think, is a fraud. A claim-jumper, like in the Wild West. But that is what Roald will discover, I believe. There is much left to do up there.' He pointed at the back of the crowd. 'Shall we go and see the great English explorer?'

'He's Irish,' Gran said, keen to show he had done his homework.

'Only when it suits him.' Nansen took Gran's arm in his huge hand, wrapping his fingers around his bicep. 'If he had made those last ninety-seven miles, would he have done it as an Englishman or an Irishman?'

Gran thought for a moment. 'Both.'

'Aye. Both.'

Nansen, with Gran firmly in his grip, ploughed through the people as though he was the *Fram* nosing through the pack ice and forced them to the front. Gran was introduced to Amundsen. He already knew his brother Leon Amundsen, who was helping him source timber for his ship. After an abortive conversation with the taciturn explorer, he moved back to Shackleton once more. When they had a moment alone, Gran asked him: 'I know I am young, Sir Ernest, but what would you do in my position? I fear I am not taken seriously, because of my youth.'

Shackleton accepted a glass of cloudberry liquor from one of his hosts. 'I will neither encourage nor discourage you, Mr Gran. But I would not set out without some experienced polar seamen. An ice pilot, for one. A first-rate dog handler. And sledgers, lots of them, men who have travelled over the ice either North or South. I can provide a list of some recommendations, although Norway has no shortage of good candidates. With old hands around you, your age need not be a handicap, my young friend. How far along is the ship?'

Gran looked down at his feet and mumbled.

'Beg pardon?'

'It is but drawings as yet.'

Shackleton laughed and knocked back the cloudberry. He gave a shudder. 'Not bad.' He looked around for a refill.

'I'm no dreamer.'

'I didn't say you were. Ah, thank you.' He accepted a new glass, which he also polished off. 'But if it's the Pole you're after you had better go ahead with your plan and go now. My hut at Cape Royds stands and is full of good things.'

Gran's jaw dropped. 'I could use it?'

'Of course. I think we owe it to each other to co-operate, not to deny our fellow adventurers any possible advantage. That is very small minded. Drink?'

'No, thank you. I wish everyone thought like you. I tried to engage Mr Amundsen about the South, to ask his advice, but he didn't seem interested. I asked for an appointment to see him and he said no.'

'His eyes and mind are on the North. You would be a distraction with your questions. But there are others looking to the South, my boy. You know that.'

'Scott.'

Shackleton nodded. 'Amundsen said Scott, too, is seeking an appointment with him. Which can only mean one thing. He wants to co-ordinate their efforts, to run simultaneous experiments North and South.'

'I suppose he'll see Scott,' Gran said sulkily.

'Oh, I doubt it. Not from the way he was speaking. Amundsen

does not like to be beholden to another. He knows Scott will come with a timetable of experiments and a catalogue of instructions. Such a straitjacket is not for Roald. So, when would your ship be ready?'

'I have employed Skaluren to build it. They constructed the *Fram*. But it will be more modern. Capable of ten knots at least. Sail and steam. If I give the go-ahead tomorrow, she would be ready in July of next year.'

'Best hurry, my lad. Best hurry.' He looked around and saw Nansen towering over Emily, his head bowed as he whispered something to her. 'Now, if you'll excuse me. I need a cigarette.'

Shackleton moved away and scooped up his wife. Gran went in search of a drink but before he could locate one, Nansen pulled him aside. Gran gave him a summary of the conversation he had had with Shackleton.

When Nansen spoke, he kept his voice down to a low rumble. 'He's a brave man, Sir Ernest. And that Farthest South was quite an achievement. There is no doubt about that. But he isn't always right.'

Gran was well aware that Nansen had thoroughly briefed Shackleton before he went South and that the younger man hadn't always take the advice. Had he done so, Nansen thought, he might have made the Pole. 'About dogs, professor?'

'That. And furs. And skis. But also about hurrying. It's an English disease. Both the *Discovery* and the *Nimrod* expeditions were put together in haste. It is not the way to prepare for the Pole, son.'

'What do you suggest?' Gran feared the old explorer was going to try to dissuade him.

Nansen looked the lad up and down. He was keen, all right, and bright, but not yet the calibre of man who could inspire the hardy Norwegians; he would need to make a decent fist of a polar assault. The boy needed roughening up and he needed experience. And he knew just who could give it to him. 'Can you come to Fefor in a few weeks?'

This was a village near Lillehammer, north of Christiana. Gran had skied there several times. 'Yes. Why, sir?'

'There is a trial of some new-fangled motor sledges. Idiots think they'll replace dogs over ice. Ha! But there is someone I'd like you to meet.'

'Who?'

The big man winked. 'Robert Falcon Scott.'

Thirty-three

Fefor, Norway, 1910

Fridtjof Nansen knocked on the door of the Scotts' suite at the Hotel Fefor. Instead of the captain answering, it was his wife, her fingers pressed to her lips.

'I have just put Peter down. Come in, come in.'

He hesitated. She was wearing a white shift with, as far as he could tell, nothing underneath. A wet patch indicated she had been breastfeeding. Her hair was down, cascading like an auburn river to her waist, and she was barefoot. Kathleen Scott was hardly in a position to receive a gentleman in her bedroom.

'Come on, come on.'

Nansen walked in and crossed to the crib, where a small bundle of blankets snored softly. 'Lovely.'

'He is a very good boy. I was just admiring the lake.'

She moved to the window. Out on the frozen ice were two black shapes, the tractors they had brought for testing.

'I thought Captain Scott was here.'

She turned and looked at him. 'You have the most amazing eyes.'

Nansen was taken aback. 'Thank you.'

'Con is with that young lad. Gran.'

'That's what I wanted to talk to him about. Or you.'

'Move over to the light. Here.' She grabbed the explorer by the

241

sleeve and manoeuvred him over so the ice-reflected light illuminated his face. 'Sit.'

He did so.

'Why did you send him? The boy?'

'He is a fine young man. He knows skis. He has ambitions to
go South, but ideas beyond his years.'

'Don't move.' Kathleen ran her hand across his forehead. The
blond hair was beginning to thin, but matched with the startling
eyes, one moment blue, the next steely grey, he was a fine Nordic
specimen, powerful and manly.

'I know you have influence—'

'Ssshh.'

She let her fingertips glide over his cheekbones, across to his
ears, and followed the line of his jaw. It was electrifying. Nansen
shifted uncomfortably.

'Keep still. So, about the boy?'

'I know that the Captain had trouble with the skis before. But he
had no skins, no waxes. Gran knows all about this. Did you see how
quickly he skied to the village yesterday to fetch the new stub axle?'

'Con did comment on it. My goodness, what neck muscles. Like
iron hawsers.'

'Mrs Scott—'

'Kathleen.'

'It should be Lady Scott, I think.'

Kathleen laughed. 'My husband would agree with you. But it
will have to be Mrs for now. Or Kathleen.' The warmth of
Shackleton's welcome, and the honours he received, compared to
those afforded Scott after the return of the *Discovery* sometimes
rankled. She could see it in Con's eyes. *He turned back*, they said,
yet his reward was a knighthood.

'Very well, Kathleen, I know you have influence, perhaps you
could have a word.'

She let go and stood back. 'About?'

'About Gran.'

She looked impatient. 'You want Con to take him? Yes, yes, that
can be arranged. Will he provide his own equipment?'

'Yes.'

'And money?'

'He will not have to draw any wages, if that is what you mean.'

'Well, consider it done. I shall have a word with Con. But there is a price.'

'Name it.'

Kathleen Scott walked back and forth in a semicircle, admiring the visage from various angles, pondering which was his best side. She bent over, till she was level with his ear and whispered: 'You are a magnificent specimen.'

The door opened before Nansen could reply. It was Scott, stripped of his outer layers.

'Darling,' she exclaimed. 'I was just saying I would like Mr Nansen to sit for me. A head. Would you mind terribly?'

'What?' Scott asked distractedly, pulling off his braces. 'No, fine, whatever. Bloody cams have gone again. They run wonderfully for half a mile then, putt, something else goes. Most frustrating.'

Nansen got to his feet. 'It's a shame. But I am beginning to think you might be right. When they are reliable, such sledges will have their place on the ice. But I wouldn't like to try and get one up a glacier. You'll still need dogs.'

Scott was tired of hearing the same argument. 'Was there something?' he asked the Norwegian.

'Nothing urgent.'

'Kathleen, you should put something on,' Scott said, noticing her lack of clothing for the first time. She reached for a shawl.

'Forgive me,' Nansen said, 'I barged in, thinking you were here.'

'So there was something?'

'There was, but Kathleen, Mrs Scott, answered it for me.'

'Oh?'

'You'll join me for dinner tonight?'

Scott sighed. 'Very well.'

'Thank you. Eight o'clock. Till then.'

After he had gone, Scott said: 'What was all that about?'

Kathleen had moved back to the cot and was staring admiringly at her snoozing baby. 'Just an old man who can't bear to see someone else living the life he once had, Con. Nansen was once the great ice explorer. Now he wishes he were you.'

Scott nodded. 'Yes. I suppose he does.'

Kathleen turned and smiled at Scott, knowing it could drive all other considerations from his head. 'What do you make of that lad Tryggve Gran?'

Thirty-four

India Docks, London, May 1910

Captain Lawrence Oates stood at the bottom of the gangplank to the *Terra Nova*, reporting as instructed. The little ship seemed tiny next to the grand ocean liners that shared the berth. She was filthy, too, a dirt-streaked little urchin in need of a bath. Even from the bottom of the gangplank he could smell the stench of ancient seal oil and blubber. She was riding low in the water, yet judging from the provisions still on the dock, they hadn't completed loading yet. Given the crates and boxes lashed on the decks, it was hard to see where anything else would fit.

He walked up the plank and felt curious eyes on him. He had on a bowler hat and an Aquascutum gabardine, neither of them of the first rank. Several of the sailors on the deck stopped and stared at him.

'Official tours begin tomorrow,' said Charles Williams, the nearest AB. 'You can buy a ticket at the harbour master's office.'

'I'm Oates,' he said.

'The soldier?'

'Aye.'

'We were expecting the Charge of the bleedin' Light Brigade,' laughed Williams. 'Where're your spurs? And boots?'

'Up your arse, if you don't mind your manners,' replied Oates with a wink.

245

The crew sniggered at this. 'I'm assuming you need a hand with getting some of the gear,' Oates pointed to the stacks of crates on the quayside and then to the *Terra Nova*, 'on there.'

'We do, we do.'

Oates heaved his kit on to the ship and rolled up his sleeves, ready to start toting.

'Not so much haste. We allow our people to settle in first, Captain Oates,' said the man coming down to meet him. 'I'm Bill Wilson.'

Oates held out his hand and they shook.

Tom Crean scooped up Oates's bag. 'Welcome to *Terra Nova*, soldier,' he said. 'Tom Crean, sir.'

As they stepped on board there was a flurry of introductions from Wilson. 'That there is Petty Officer Edgar Evans. We call him Taff because there is one too many Evanses on the ship.'

Evans gave a mock salute. 'I'm the best of them, though.'

'That's mutiny,' said Wilson. He pointed to a short-legged, stocky man with flaming red hair and a vast nose, not unlike a beak. He was heaving a case around as though it was empty but stamped on the side was the legend *Wolseley Motor Co: Wheels and Bearings*. 'That's Lieutenant Birdie Bowers, late of the Indian Marines, direct from Bombay, strongest man on the ship. If he annoys you, just show him a spider. Turns to jelly.'

Next Wilson indicated a young man with a bobble hat and a white, cable-knit sweater stained from his attempts to scrub the deck. Despite his grimy appearance, he exuded the healthy glow of the well fed and privileged. 'This is Tryggve Gran, our skiing instructor, all the way from Norway.'

Gran wiped a grubby hand on his sweater and held it out, but Oates ignored him. Wilson frowned but moved on.

'Up on the bridge is Mr Campbell, our First Mate. This way, Mr Oates. Or is it Captain? We've never had an army chap on board before.'

'Titus,' he replied. 'They call me Titus.'

'They call me Uncle Bill, but I don't like it,' Wilson said as they descended the gangway to the ship's interior. The smell of rancid seal guts and blubber grew overwhelming. 'Makes me feel about a hundred and ten. Titus? You sure?'

'It'll do till they think of something worse.'

'Oh, I'm sure they'll do that.'

Below decks he met the scientists and Teddy Evans, Scott's number one, who took him to his berth.

'Glad to see you are travelling light,' said Evans.

Oates looked around the cramped quarters. It was even smaller than he had expected. Room to lie down and take two paces in any direction. He opened his kitbag and extracted his bust of Napoleon, and placed it on the single shelf. 'Just as long as there is room for Boney. You'll be wanting a hand with loading the stores.'

'Yes. Get some cocoa first.'

Oates dropped his voice. 'I might be a soldier, but I know something about boats. She's pretty much up to the gunwales, isn't she?'

Evans nodded and gave a conspiratorial wink. 'Don't worry. We've painted out the Plimsoll Line so nobody will know. I'll see you up top.'

Oates laughed to himself. As if painting out the line that warned of overloading was any kind of solution. 'Madness,' he muttered.

'There's worse,' said a calm voice from the doorway. 'We are sailing as a yacht rather than a merchant vessel. That way we avoid maritime regulations. I'm Apsley Cherry-Garrard. Cherry.'

This one was even younger than the skier, a lad barely old enough to shave, with glasses that gave him an owlish cast.

'Oates.'

'I know. I'm in the Nursery next door. It's what we call it. I thought I'd come and apologise in advance. Four of us in there. Gets a little boisterous.'

Oates shrugged. Nearly ten years in the army would make anyone immune to boisterousness. 'And what do you do?'

'Oh, this and that. Assistant Zoologist to Dr Wilson, for the most part. I'm like you.'

'How's that?' asked Oates, as he took out his biography of Bonaparte and put it next to the bust.

'Another paying guest. Bed and board at a thousand pounds. But, without us, there would be no expedition, I fear.'

Oates rolled his eyes to the heavens, indicating the deck above his head. 'Why do we have a Norwegian? Did he pay?'

'No. Apparently impressed the britches off the Owner with his skiing. Brought him along to teach us all.'

'To ski?'

'I believe so.'

'Well, he can stay away from me. I have no desire to move around on planks of wood and even less to speak to Norwegians.'

'I rather like him.' He was too embarrassed to tell Oates that Gran had saved him from sleepwalking over the side of the ship. His nocturnal ramblings – both verbal and perambulatory – had already earned him plenty of teasing, not least from Teddy Evans. 'For a foreigner.'

'Is the Owner here?'

'Not yet. Singing for our suppers somewhere. Hope he gets some cash out of the buggers. He's in a frightful mood if he comes back with only fifty or a hundred pounds. So we all pray for a generous patron. Still, he's not a bad stick apart from that. You'll meet him soon enough.'

'Someone mentioned cocoa.'

'Follow me.'

'Then I suppose we'll see just how much we can fit on this ship of ours.'

'Don't worry, she's been down before.'

'Down where?' he asked in alarm.

'South. She was one of the two ships that relieved *Discovery* after its second winter trapped by the ice. His old ship.' Cherry pointed forward. 'Oddly enough, she's berthed just along the dock. Just to show us how much better they had it then. Bill Wilson says it's a palace compared to this.'

'*Discovery*'s here? Then why aren't we on that?'

'Hudson Bay own it. Wouldn't lease it back. So little *Terra Nova* it is. Let's get that drink.'

Teddy Evans blocked the doorway, a lopsided grin on his face.

248

'Come along, you two. We've found a spider the size of a small chicken, we're going to set it on Birdie and watch the feathers fly!'

Cherry was out the door as if the cabin was aflame and Oates heard the thump of excited feet as the men pushed up top. Clearly this wasn't going to be any ordinary ship. There might even be fun on her. If she didn't sink with all hands.

'The complaint about Petty Officer Edgar Evans and his drinking duly noted,' said Scott. 'I'll reduce him to half-pay. That will save us some cash into the bargain. If we can get the rest of the crew blind drunk and do the same, it'll help the purse no end.'

The others in the room laughed, with the exception of a stern-faced Teddy Evans. They were assessing each *Terra Nova* crew member in turn. There were sixty-four men on the ship. Of those, thirty-one officers, scientists and crew were to overwinter as the shore party while *Terra Nova* sailed back to Lyttleton. Scott had instituted the review because he did not want to repeat the mistake he had made with Brett, the foul cook on *Discovery*, or the scheming and indolent Buckridge.

Assembled in the Victoria Street offices of the British Antarctic Expedition 1910 were Teddy Evans, his First Mate Victor Campbell, navigator Harry Pennell and Bill Wilson. In the corner, bouncing a bonny boy on her knee, was a beaming Kathleen Scott.

As with the *Discovery* office on Savile Row, the place was crammed with supplies and samples, many of which still had to be found a place on the ship. Mr Heinz wanted his beans photographed on the ice, so a corner would have to be found for them, along with Mr Fry's chocolate, Huntley & Palmer's excellent biscuits and Alfred Bird's various custards.

'So, that's Taff Evans. Who's next?'

The Owner took the complaint against Taff with a pinch of salt. He liked and trusted the Welshman, despite his weakness for what he called a 'bevvy'. That didn't matter out on the ice. And Teddy Evans had already lost him Reg Skelton by refusing to serve as captain with a man who technically ranked higher than him. Scott had reluctantly conceded because he needed the monies Evans had raised for his own embryonic expedition to Antarctica. He was pleased that Skelton understood, even though he had made every effort to convince Evans that Reg would be a willing subordinate. Evans had stood firm.

'The Norwegian,' said Teddy Evans.

'I'll vouch for Gran,' Scott said, looking down the list. 'Because we won't see his full use till later. He's pulling his weight?' There were murmurs of assent. 'Now what do we make of our Soldier?'

'Titus? I'd say a good fella,' said Campbell. 'As far as I can tell.'

Teddy Evans nodded his agreement. 'You know, Birdie said he thought he was a farmer up from the country when he first saw him. Still calls him Farmer now and then. Lashly refuses to believe he is to the manor born. Says he must be an impostor. I think it was a shrewd move on Oates's part not to come on with his airs and graces.'

Scott laced his fingers together. 'Bill?'

Wilson thought for a moment. It was interrupted by a solid belch from young Peter Scott. 'Oates seems very sound.'

'The men like him,' added Harry Pennell. 'Does his work without complaint. Mucks in with the ratings. And he's up the rigging like billy-o. You wouldn't know he knew more about four legs than square sails.'

Scott noted the comments in his log. 'I was going to send him out with Meares to choose the horses. He can join us in New Zealand.'

'Shame,' said Campbell.

Evans shook his head. 'He's a bit of glue 'tween wardroom and mess deck. Pity to lose him. Meares knows horses, surely?'

'Dogs,' Scott said, thinking aloud. 'But he speaks Russian and Chinese, so he could negotiate for the beasts.'

'I'd hate to lose Titus,' said Campbell, extracting his pipe pouch from his jacket. 'All for him standing there in some godforsaken part of Siberia listening to a lot of jabber he don't understand.'

'Please don't smoke around Peter,' said Kathleen to Campbell. 'Makes him cough. He's a strong boy, but it's his one weakness. Even Con has to smoke outside now.'

250

'Oh. Sorry.' He put the pipe down on the desk, his craving heightened by the sudden denial.

'Thank you. You know, Con, Wilf would go to help bring the animals to New Zealand,' said Kathleen sweetly. 'He's good with horses.'

Wilfred Bruce was Kathleen's brother, a naval officer. Scott liked him, knew he was capable, but had resisted her blandishments to use him, as he was very conscious of any charges of nepotism. Eight thousand applicants and you choose your brother-in-law? It hardly looked impartial.

'What do you think, Bill?' Scott asked, aware that the company would creep up to sixty-five; an extra berth would have to be found for Wilf Bruce.

Wilson felt Kathleen's unnervingly even gaze on him. He tried to ignore it and give a balanced view. There was no way on earth he would have allowed Ory to sit in on such a meeting. But then Ory wasn't Kathleen. Something Wilson was very grateful for. 'It's not a bad idea to use Lieutenant Bruce. We'll need decent officers on the ship for her return to New Zealand during winter. This way we could leave Oates where he is. He'll be good company for us on the way down.'

Scott shook his head and dropped his bombshell. 'I'm not coming with you. Sorry to spring this upon you, Teddy. And you, Bill. Change of plan.'

The four men looked at each other and across at Kathleen, as if this revelation were somehow her fault. She smiled back at them as the boy Peter gurgled loudly.

'Not coming? Why is that?' asked Wilson.

'We still have money to raise and contracts for newspaper syndication and cinematography to sign. Ponting has driven a hard bargain.' The renowned Herbert Ponting would take photographs and moving pictures of the expedition. Scott hoped that a travelling show would later generate profits to help defray the expedition's rapidly accumulating debts. 'Between you and me, we can't match the wage bill at the moment. Thank the Lord there are men travelling for free. I had to borrow to find funds for the dogs and horses

Meares will purchase. We are reduced to appealing to school fund-raisers and that takes meetings and speeches.' The thought left him looking exhausted. 'The British public have not been generous. Apart from the Welsh, for some reason. Which is why *Terra Nova* will leave from Cardiff.'

Teddy Evans laughed, suspecting a joke. His smile faded when the Owner failed to participate.

'That's hardly on the way,' said the first mate.

'Cardiff is giving us coal, Mr Campbell. For free. And has raised a thousand pounds. I shall see you off there. You'll manage, Teddy?'

'Be sure of it,' Evans replied confidently.

'Harry?'

'Of course.'

'While you all whip the crew into shape, we'll catch a fast mail boat and join you in Cape Town,' Scott said.

'We?' asked Wilson, thinking Scott intended to keep him back.

'He means me,' said Kathleen Scott, holding her baby aloft, making him giggle as she tickled his ribs. 'I'm coming with you.'

Thirty-five

Polhøgda, Bundefjord, Norway

It was the cruellest day of Fridtjof Nansen's life. He was standing on a venerable, much-repaired watchtower that soared above a rocky promontory. The lookout point traditionally protected the entrance to the fjord by warning of approaching ships. But Nansen was here to watch a departure, not an arrival. It was midnight, and the sun was ready to dip below the horizon for the long summer twilight.

Below him, moving slowly out to sea, was the *Fram*, the ship on which he had proved polar drift was possible and achieved Furthest North. Nansen had been observing the shore below Amundsen's home through a spyglass for several hours. He had watched them load timber and supplies and what looked like a hut for living quarters – a strange thing to take to the North, where you would be erecting it on unstable floating ice – before *Fram* had finally cast off.

Her sails were furled, the slow clank of the overhauled diesel engine pushing her forward clearly audible. There were men on the spars and in the rigging, though, ready to deploy the canvas once *Fram* was clear of the headland. There, she would turn south, for testing and calibration, before Amundsen took her around the Horn and north to the Bering Strait and Arctic waters. It was typical of the man to put everything, from sledge to ship, through exhaustive trials before he pronounced himself satisfied. Amundsen had been singularly obsessed these past months, even refusing as 'a distraction' a meeting with Scott, despite the latter donating equipment so that they could run comparative measurements at opposite poles.

Fram looked strong and clean after her refit, proudly displaying the cross of St Olav, her national flag. Gone were the days when she had to skulk away under a Swedish ensign before the blue-and-white cross on a red background could be displayed. Despite his sadness, he felt a surge of pride in his small country. It was Independence Day, after all, a fortuitous choice for the sailing.

As the ship drew level with the Polhøgda tower, there came the sharp squeal of a steam whistle, which echoed around the mountains like a Viking blowing horn. From across the water, Nansen heard a ragged cheer, muffled by the wind and water, and he raised his arms above his head, his eyes moist. They were saluting him. A flare arced out over the water with a hiss, staining it red for a few seconds as it hung in the air. It was joined by a blue and then a white one. The three hotspots burned into his retina before they fell into the sea, leaving only fading smoke trails. Norwegian colours.

All across the world, it seemed, men were heading for the ice. Robert Scott and Teddy Evans from London – although they had now combined forces – had their eyes on the Pole. Mawson was planning a foray out of Australia. Flichner was raising money in Germany. From Japan, the formidable Nobu Shirase was making rumblings about another expedition. Nansen believed he should have been among them. He had allowed himself to believe that he was too old, that the polar regions were best reserved for young men. He had announced his retirement at a low spot, just after his wife died. He should never have said that, never given up the *Fram*. Although, he supposed, it was for the best that a Norwegian had picked up his baton.

What a strange assortment the men of the ice were. Amundsen was what the British called a 'Pole bagger', not interested in dressing up his expedition as anything other than a desire to stand on the Farthest North, to make a claim on the Pole that could not, like

Peary's or Cook's, be open to dispute. Science was secondary to him. He was focused and shrewd, endlessly improvising and improving. As with most of them, money was a problem, but there again Roald wouldn't let a shortage of cash deter him. He had borrowed heavily and had even taken a charge on his home to fund this trip.

Shackleton he liked. A blarney-spouting buccaneer, he was like a latter-day Drake, a privateer. He was a restless spirit, the sort of man who would never be able to resist the pull of the unknown. He'd be back on the ice, Nansen would wager. Actually, he wouldn't wager. He'd have nothing to do with Shackleton and money. The man just didn't understand it. With debts to pay and some of the *Nimrod* crew still not reimbursed, he had given most of the money from his Norwegian speaking tour to a children's charity in Christiana. The gesture had increased his status immensely, of course, but popularity never fed a hungry crew.

And Scott? He respected the man well enough, although Sir Ernest was better company, not being constrained by naval etiquette. Scott had a real curiosity, a striving for knowledge and progress. The motor sledges showed that, as did the number and scope of scientists he recruited. Scott, too, had been infected by the unseen bacterium that lived in the cold regions, a micro-organism that infiltrated the body and brain and would never let a man rest till he brought it home again. It was as dangerous as scurvy.

Captain Scott was certainly courageous and, although he wouldn't admit it, highly competitive. His stamina was impressive. Nansen had seen him out on the lake, pushing himself to his limits, working on the temperamental machines till he blistered his fingers on the freezing metal. And he had Kathleen. With her behind him, who knew what he might achieve? He still recalled her whispered words: *'You are a magnificent specimen.'* That night, at dinner, she had explained she had meant as a subject for a bronze bust. He was flattered, although he would have been equally happy with his first interpretation. She was like no other English woman he had ever met, unrestrained and forthright, solid yet sensuous.

'You are a magnificent specimen.'

The memory of that voice caused a strange sinking sensation in his stomach, as if he was falling from a high building. For a second, he felt a touch of vertigo as he looked down into the darkening waters of the fjord, riffled from his old ship's passage.

Nansen stayed on his cliff top till *Fram* dwindled away, swallowed by the deep blues of the summer twilight, his orphan, cast among others. As he wearily descended the lookout tower, he realised he had learned two things during his farewell vigil: he still wanted to explore, still possessed that relentless fire in his ageing belly, and he was in love with Kathleen Scott.

Thirty-six

Cardiff, Wales

Tryggve Gran found Oates in the smoke-drenched Carpenter's Arms, the fifth public house near the docks he had tried. Titus was sipping from a pint of mild and Gran was amazed how easily he fitted in with his down-at-heel surroundings. He had on a worn tweed suit, his battered bowler, hobnail boots, and an undershaved chin. Dark streaks remained on his face from the choking, despicable task of coaling they had all helped with. Nobody would take Oates for an officer or a gentleman and, looking around at the rough-house clientele, Gran supposed that was the idea.

Oates had chosen the pub well. All the others had photographs or banners wishing *Terra Nova* and her crew well. Any man associated with the ship would never have to put his hand in his pocket. But he also became public property, forced to acknowledge how the City of Cardiff had helped and no doubt answer questions about the rumoured leaks plaguing the vessel.

'Titus,' he said. 'Skipper sent me. We need to get back to the ship.'

Oates waved a hand at the barman. 'Have a drink.'

'Why?'

He nodded at his pint. 'It'll save me having to talk to you while I finish this.'

Ignoring the insult, Gran ordered a gin, having to repeat the order twice.

'Make it a large one,' Oates instructed the surly server.

'It's all over, Titus,' said Gran. Oates had shied off the mayor's banquet for the crew at the Royal Hotel. 'Safe to come back now.'

'Good. Bunch of bloody socialists, the lot of them.' It was the standard jibe from army types who didn't trust the social changes occurring around them. 'Let me buy,' he insisted as the gin arrived, slopped on to the bar. 'More money than I know what to do with.'

'Generous socialists they were,' Gran reminded him. He sipped his drink. 'Do you think they'll have ice here?'

Oates wrinkled his nose at the strange request. 'I doubt it. They probably put coal in their drinks. It gets everywhere else.' Coaling was a filthy business; nobody blamed the captain for finding some official lunch or other while it took place. 'Hold on a few weeks, though, there'll be plenty.' He took a gulp of his mild. 'The only gentleman I have met here so far has been the man who laid the telephone on the ship. Other than that we get mayors and counsellors and their bloody wives. Women, eh? Empty your mind and fill it with ribbons and feathers. Mark my words.'

'I hope you make an exception for Mrs Scott.' Gran had rather taken a shine to her in Norway, especially for the way she enthusiastically pursued his case in Fefor for coming South with the expedition. She had looked bored at the banquet and then succumbed to a fit of the giggles when Taff Evans had trouble with the giant dragon flag he had been given, spilling it across the table.

Oates narrowed his eyes. 'I do. She's a different kettle. She's even more frightening.'

'Why is that?'

Oates wagged a finger. 'A woman who thinks like a man? More powerful than those Dreadnoughts we sailed past.'

Terra Nova had cautiously steamed through the line of the fleet in the Solent, a staggering display of naval might that had awed them all. The new battleships were like the monsters of the deep, dredged up, armour plated and given sixteen-inch guns.

'Taff gave a good speech at the banquet. Said there were very few men he would follow South again. But Scott was one of them. Said he loved him. Had them cheering. Then he drank enough for the entire table and it needed six men to carry him out to the ship.'

'He should watch it. Teddy Evans has it in for him. He'll find any excuse to get rid of him.' Taff had found a mistake in Teddy's inventory of skiing equipment. Instead of quietly telling the other Evans about the error, Taff had taken a drink or two and announced it to the whole crew. Scott had then given Taff some of Teddy's responsibilities. Oates had no axe to grind with Teddy Evans, he thought him a splendid fellow in the wardroom, full of tall stories, but from his behaviour on deck, something told him he knew how to bear a grudge.

'It'll be hard to leave Taff behind after that speech. The Owner reckons it might have added three or four hundred to the pot. Anyway, we are wanted back at the ship. We leave tomorrow, remember.'

'I know. My mother is here for the occasion.'

'To wave you off?'

'Not publicly. We've said our goodbyes.' He tapped his pocket. 'She gave me . . .' Carrie had given him money, hundreds of pounds, but he told her there would be nowhere to spend it. She didn't believe him and had pressed it on him. Then she had cried, pleading with him to change his mind. It had taken all his resolve not to agree. She had promised to come and view from the dock-side at a discreet distance, to save him any further tearful displays of motherly concern. 'Why am I telling you this?'

Gran finally realised Oates was a little tipsy. Although he inevitably joined in the fun and games with the crew, and the port, Gran had never seen him the worse for wear. He could only imagine it had been something to do with his mother being there. It seemed to Gran that Englishmen had very complicated relationships with their mothers. Still, he reckoned it might be a good time to raise something that had been nagging at him. 'Titus, why don't you like me?'

'Who says I don't?'

Gran sipped some more warm gin. 'You refused to shake my hand the first time we met. You don't think I'm worth talking to.'

'Nothing personal.'

Gran laughed so hard that the darts and domino players paused to look at the strange pair at the bar. 'How am I meant to take it?'

'You can't help being foreign.'

'Just like you can't help being English.'

Oates smirked. 'How do you know I didn't choose it? Eeny-meeny-miney-mo?'

'I don't think God consults. It's the luck of the draw.'

Oates brooded for a while. 'I suppose it is. I just believed that the expedition should be all-British. You aren't a bad sort, Trigger.'

'Just foreign.'

'As you say. Just foreign. The thing is, if a war came, tomorrow. Who would you fight for?'

'Between Norway and England?' He finished off the gin and shuddered.

'No. England and, I don't know. France. No, Germany. War with Germany. Your neighbours.' He almost spat the final word.

'I think you are thinking of Denmark.'

Oates furrowed his brow, trying to picture a map of Europe. He had been away so long, it remained blurred. 'Am I?'

'Yes.'

'No matter. Who would you fight for?'

'England.'

'Really? But you are on the Continent. Don't you all hate us?'

Gran sighed. It was true that the self-centred jingoism of the British Empire was hard to warm to, but not the individuals who made up the country. At least, not his strange and endearing collection of shipmates, men like Crean, Taff, Archer, Clissold, Lashly and, yes, Oates, Cherry, Wilson and Scott. 'Like it or not, Titus, I am part of the British Antarctic Expedition. Always will be, now. I have a job to do and fine crewmates. As long as it does not involve betraying my home or family, then I would proudly stand alongside Englishmen and fight for their king and their country.'

'You would?'

'You have my word.'

Oates held out his hand, his words slightly slurred as he spoke. 'And you, Tryggve Gran, have a friend.'

Thirty-seven

Melbourne, Australia, October 1910

The *Terra Nova* bobbed and weaved at anchor, close enough to the dock that the voices of the men on board, if not their exact words, could be heard clearly on the quayside. Between land and ship, however, was a dark unsettled sea, foam flashing in the night as the wind sliced the tops of the waves. The little motorised cutter, intended to ferry the party gathered at the stone steps, was rolling and pitching; it was as inviting as mounting an unbroken horse.

The four passengers gathered for the ferry journey, already wet through with spray, hesitated.

'I think we should wait,' said Ory Wilson.

'It's all right for you,' said Kathleen, drawing her shawl around her. 'You have your husband here.'

'And yours will be ashore soon, I am certain,' said Bill Wilson.

'I have not seen him since Cape Town.'

'Well, who is to blame for that?' snapped Hilda, Teddy Evans's wife.

'Ladies, please,' said Wilson. Plans had changed in South Africa. Scott had taken back command of the *Terra Nova* from Teddy Evans, and charged Wilson with chaperoning the three wives down to New Zealand, with a port-of-call by both parties for fund-raising and supplies at Melbourne.

'Con meant no slight when he resumed command,' said Kathleen, knowing that it had caused some resentment. 'He told me he was pleased with the way the crew had butted together.'

'Without him,' Hilda said tartly.

'Yes, which is why he needed to establish himself once more. You see plots where there are none.'

Wilson looked between the two of them. Hilda was the more attractive, beautiful even, with a waspish tongue at times. Kathleen was more forceful and with an enticing charisma that she used to great effect. On balance, he was glad to have his Oriana, who he believed combined the virtues of both without the vices.

'Please God,' said Wilson, 'never let me run more than one wife at a time, ever again.'

Ory giggled. Only she had heard the muttered prayer.

'Either way, I am going out,' said Kathleen. She leaned into the wind and bellowed down to the young sailors in the cutter. 'Quite safe, is it?'

'Safe. Aye. Choppy, though. Have you had your dinner?'

'No.'

'Just as well, ma'am. Or you'd be saying hello to it again.'

'I have been seasick enough to last me a lifetime,' said Mrs Evans.

'I think I agree with that,' said Ory.

Kathleen turned on them, fists clenched. 'Oh, you, you . . .' she struggled for a suitable insult. 'Women!'

'Women who know their places and capabilities. Not some suffragette.'

'Pah. Don't insult me.' Kathleen hated the lumpen, graceless champions of women's rights. She cocked her head to one side. 'Listen.'

'What?' asked Wilson. He could hear nothing but wind and water.

'That's my man.'

'Which one?' muttered Mrs Evans.

Ory laughed again. They had joked about a Mr Hull who had paid Kathleen much attention during the voyage from Cape Town.

They thought she had done scandalously little to discourage the lovesick puppy.

Her face became a ball of fury. 'I have left my baby on the other side of the world to be with Captain Scott. I am not going to let a patch of rough water separate us. Do you understand?'

Ory found herself nodding meekly.

'I'm coming down,' Kathleen shouted. Her leather soles slipped on the top step and she nearly tumbled in.

Wilson caught her elbow. 'Steady, there.'

'I suppose Teddy will frown upon me if I don't come too.'

'And I can't let you two women go out alone. The skipper would toss me overboard.'

Ory sighed. 'And I am not standing here by myself.'

Wilson pulled the strap of the mailbag he was carrying over his head, to make it more secure. 'Then we all go.'

It took ten minutes to get the party safely into the motor launch, and when it did cast off, it had trouble making any progress. The lights on *Terra Nova* refused to get any closer. As far as they could tell the cutter's bow was plummeting up and down, but making no headway. 'It's like deadwater,' said Wilson, remembering the phenomenon from the Antarctic.

Mrs Evans put her head over the side and dry-retched. Kathleen sat tight lipped, not giving them the satisfaction of showing how queasy she felt.

Eventually, after an exaggerated zigzag by the cutter, the *Terra Nova* loomed larger and, with a few deft tugs on the rudder and judicious use of reverse, the boat was brought alongside.

'Con!' shouted Kathleen.

'You need a hand there?' It was Birdie Bowers, looming over the rail, nose first.

'Yes, please,' said Ory Wilson.

With the aid of ropes – and Oates, whose watch it was – the four were transferred from cutter to deck in no time. Their faces were dotted with globules of spray, their hair damp and clothes soaking. Oates laughed when he saw them. 'We should have piped you aboard.'

'Where is my husband?' Kathleen demanded.

'Below, ma'am.'

Wilson took off the mailbag. 'Tell him there is correspondence and cables.'

Kathleen hurried below and met a half-dressed Scott coming up. He had on his shirt, but unfastened, with no tie. His face split into a grin of pure joy when he saw her. 'Kathleen! We were just getting ready to come ashore.'

'I couldn't wait that long.'

They kissed and he put his arms round her. For a second, the ship fell away and they were half a world distant, entwined, never wanting to separate. Her heart beat so fast, he could feel it against his chest. Tears stung his eyes and she felt a small catch in her throat. Scott took a huge, shuddering breath, which broke the spell. 'You're wet.'

'Don't fuss. It was worth it.'

'How was the crossing from Cape Town?'

'Dull without you. Yours?'

He shook his head in dismay. 'She's a handful.'

'And still smells.'

'Not for want of trying. Come down to the wardroom while I finish dressing.'

She followed Con down below decks, careful with her footing as the ship rolled. His hair was failing ever more; she could see the sovereign-sized disc of scalp at his crown grown noticeably bigger. She felt a rush of affection for him. He was under such strain. None of the men – with the exception perhaps of Bill Wilson – appreciated just what it took to organise such an undertaking and to make it, as he insisted, scientifically worthwhile rather than just what Barrie would no doubt call an 'Awfully Big Adventure'.

'I have a letter from your mother. The boy thrives.' The mutual frostiness between Hannah and her daughter-in-law had thawed with the arrival of Peter. Being asked to guard the precious son while she was away had helped turn the corner. 'She sends all her love. As do your sisters.'

'Excellent. Did Bill bring the rest of the mail?'

'He did. And – oh—'

The most extraordinary sight greeted her in the wardroom. Teddy Evans was standing up to his full five foot seven, his legs spread wide, his sleeves rolled up, his eyes looking fit to pop from his head. In his mouth was a belt. Still attached to the belt was a furiously blushing Cherry, his feet kicking in thin air. Looking on, either bemused or roaring with laughter, were Herbert Ponting, Bernard Day, the mechanic, Tryggve Gran, Atch, the surgeon, and half-a-dozen officers she didn't know by name.

When he saw Kathleen, Teddy released his grip and Cherry crashed to the floor, losing his glasses and causing more hoots of laughter. 'Sorry, Mrs Scott,' said Teddy.

'Just a wager,' explained Cherry, retrieving his spectacles, getting to his feet and brushing himself down.

'It's always just a wager,' said Scott, slipping into his cabin and sliding the door shut. 'Ignore them.'

'Oh, don't mind me,' said Kathleen to the men sitting around the table. 'Looks like great fun. Is that your party piece, Teddy?'

Now he coloured as he pointed to the upright jammed in the corner. 'I'd rather play the piano, but that's what nature gave me. Strong teeth.'

'I'm sure strong teeth are more use on the ice than a quick rendition of "Boiled Beef and Carrots". Mrs Evans is up top, Teddy.'

'Right.' He rolled his sleeves down. 'Excuse me, gentlemen. Mrs Scott. Duty calls.'

He squeezed past Wilson, who had come down with the mail sack for Scott to read. There were greetings exchanged between the doctor and the company, and he joined Scott in his tiny cabin.

The room fell into silence, as it always did when a woman was around. Kathleen resented this, but her attempts at camaraderie back in England – such as teaching them the slightly bawdy songs she had learned in the Balkans – had been treated with even more suspicion. She was the Owner's wife and they were more comfortable if she played that part.

To relieve the thickening atmosphere, she sat down at the pianola, which had been dragged out of the 'Nursery' for a sing-song, and executed a deliberately ham-fisted version of 'Kelly From the Isle of Man'. Cherry, bless him, sang a couple of verses, giving cover for the others to slip away and resume their duties.

One of them stopped by before he did so, a muscular handsome chap. 'Don't stop playing. I'm Frank Debenham. Geologist. Just joined. Pleased to meet you.'

'And you,' she said.

As the last note died away, she heard raised voices in Scott's cabin. He emerged a few seconds later, his face disfigured by a strange, baffled expression. Behind him, Wilson had the look of an undertaker. 'Where's Gran?' Scott demanded.

'He went on deck, I believe,' stuttered Cherry.

'What is it, darling?' Kathleen asked.

'I'm not entirely sure.'

He passed the cablegram to her and as she read she felt a terrible foreboding descend on her. It was so terse as to be cryptic; but in her heart she knew it couldn't be good news.

BEG LEAVE TO INFORM YOU FRAM *PROCEEDING ANTARCTICA.* AMUNDSEN.

Thirty-eight

Letter Written from Madeira by Roald Amundsen to Fridtjof Nansen, August 1910

Herr Professor Fridtjof Nansen,

I have dreaded sending this letter, but there is nothing for it now. I beg you to read it carefully and consider my position.

Cook and Peary, with their claims for the Pole, killed my enterprise in the North stone dead. I was dismayed at the news.

This meant with the North probably gone, or at least sullied by claim and counter-claim, there remained only one goal left for me. The South.

So, it pains me to admit, in September 1909, I decided that I would change my ambitions from the conquered North to the unconquered South. Since then, there has not been a day when I haven't been tempted to blurt out the truth. I even wished Scott would somehow discover my new plans, because it would mean an end to subterfuge. Of course, I intend to rendezvous with *Terra Nova* and explain myself.

It is not my intention to follow in the footsteps of the English. If I am to succeed for Norway, I must forge my own route. I will not use Scott or Shackleton's bases or landing points.

I hope you understand, no other option was open to me.
All this has been done in the utmost secrecy. I have written to the King to explain my change of plan, but even my crew have been kept in the dark. I shall announce the new mission shortly, and see how they vote. At the same time my brother Leon will inform the press and Captain Scott.

So again, I beg you not to judge me too severely. I am no thief nor, by nature, a deceiver. The change of events has forced this upon me. I beg forgiveness for any ire I may have caused. Perhaps my work in Antarctica will in some way compensate for the manner of my arrival there.

With my most respectful greetings,

Roald Amundsen

Thirty-nine

Melbourne, Australia

'What do you make of it?' Scott asked.

The wardroom had been cleared of all but Scott, Wilson and Kathleen while Tryggve Gran read the cablegram. He did so three times. Nothing changed. Being a Norwegian did not allow him insights beyond those few words on paper. He was as mystified as Scott and Wilson.

'It was sent from Christiana,' said Gran slowly.

'So he hasn't left yet?' Wilson asked. 'Does it mean he is coming down next season?'

'Why go to the expense of a cablegram if something isn't imminent?' asked Kathleen.

'Good point,' conceded Wilson.

'*Fram* sailed before we were in Cape Town. The Norwegian consulate there told me. Amundsen was heading for Cape Horn, with a stop for a refit at Madeira.'

'Madeira?' Scott asked. 'Are you sure?' Madeira was a more usual stop for those heading South to Australasia, not the Horn, where ships tended to work down the east coast of South America.

'Am I being stupid?' asked Wilson. 'Are you saying this was sent while *Fram* and *Terra Nova* were both at sea?'

'I am.'

'It's very sly,' offered Kathleen.

'I think . . .' Gran began. The others waited while he stroked the poor attempt at a beard he had been cultivating. 'I think this was sent in all likelihood by Leon Amundsen. His brother. From Christiana. While *Fram* was at sea.'

'Why?' asked Scott.

Gran didn't answer, at first, because he didn't like the thoughts crowding into his brain, squirming like rats. The cablegram announces Amundsen was for the South, but it didn't give Scott time to do much about it. His planning was finished, his crew and ship, all set. It explained why Amundsen wouldn't see him or Scott. Either he didn't want to lie to their faces or he was scared of slipping up and his true intentions emerging. 'I don't know for sure. I can go and see the Norwegian consul here, see if he knows more.'

'Yes, good idea,' said Scott.

'And you should cable Nansen,' Gran suggested.

'And ask what?'

'If it means *Fram* is to conduct scientific work in the area of Antarctica before going north or if Amundsen is heading for the Pole. The South Pole.'

Scott considered for a moment, even rereading the cablegram, to see if it revealed its inner meaning. 'I shall do so. But even if it means that, I am not being panicked into altering our plans. I am not anticipating a race. This changes nothing.'

Gran realised Scott hadn't fully appreciated what kind of man he was up against. As far as he was concerned, it changed everything.

Later that evening, Gran found Oates on deck, staring out to sea. The clouds were clearing, stars poking through the lacunae, and the swell had subsided. Scott, Wilson, the wives and many of the other officers had gone ashore to dine and subtly solicit funds from their hosts. The whole ship, though, had felt the new tension.

'So, are you going to tell me what all the fuss was about?' asked Oates.

Gran explained about the message.

'How did the skipper take it?'

'More evenly than I would have.'

'What's he like, this Amundsen?'

Gran couldn't keep the surprise from his voice. 'You've not heard of him?'

Oates smiled. 'His fame didn't extend to India, no. I didn't hear him mentioned till I joined *Terra Nova*.'

'He is a fierce competitor. Driven, I think you say. He has been south to the Antarctic before, you know. With the Belgica expedition. That might be why he thinks he has some priority.'

'I see. That does rather change it. Still, something not quite right about the way he has done it.'

'Agreed. But he is a giant of an explorer. If he has his eyes on the Pole . . .'

Oates watched a cutter motor past them, heading out to one of the other ships. He returned a wave from a passenger. 'You think he'll beat us to it?'

'He'll have dogs.'

'We'll have dogs.'

'Not enough. Dogs, horses and those.' Gran pointed at the shrouded shapes of the motor sledges. 'The motors are temperamental, or were in Fefor. Horses, I am not sure about either, not on the ice.'

'Shackleton took them.' Oates said it in a mimic of Scott. He sometimes tired of the way the man was used as justification for every decision. If Shackleton did it, it must be the correct way. It wasn't just Scott; half the company were mesmerised by those ninety-seven miles. And the knighthood.

'And they did not perform well. But, of course, they didn't have you with them to coax them along.' The Norwegian grinned.

'That would be their first mistake,' he replied. But Oates felt a little twinge of apprehension as he said it. Being the equine officer was a far larger responsibility than he had originally envisaged. How the horses – his horses, once they arrived – performed might determine whether they got to the Pole or not. To be blamed for a shortfall would be intolerable.

'And, as I say, I saw the motor sledges break down in Norway. Sometimes after a few kilometres, sometimes after a hundred metres. If I was planning this expedition, I would have two hundred dogs. What is Mr Meares buying? Thirty-some.'

'Well, Trigger, if this Amundsen gets there first it won't just be the dogs coming home with their tails between their legs. We can't let a bloody Norskie beat us. No offence meant.'

But Gran's shoulders had slumped and his face dropped. 'You see, this puts me in an awkward situation. If I had known he was coming down here, I would never have agreed to join Scott. Everyone will think like you.'

'I was joking, Trigger. Nobody will blame you.'

'You asked about fighting in a war. Who would I back? I said England. Well, this is a war, but now it is Norway versus England. What do I do?'

He looked so glum Oates had to laugh. 'It's not a war. It's a race.'

'The skipper does not want a race.'

'Well, if your man—'

'He's not my man,' snapped Tryggve.

'All right, all right. The Owner might not have a choice. He might have a race forced on him. You have to agree, it's pretty rum if he is trying to steal a march.'

Cherry joined them at the rail. 'I just heard about the bloody feint.' It was unusual for Cherry to swear.

'You know Amundsen has been to Antarctica before,' said Oates.

'So's the skipper.' Cherry bristled.

'Prior to Scott,' added Gran.

'Are you defending him?' Cherry demanded.

'No. He's not,' said Oates with some force.

'No, of course not. Sorry, Trigger. How's the skipper about this?'

'Dining with the mayor of Melbourne,' said Oates. 'Looks like business at usual.'

'Talking of which . . . Ovaltine, anyone?'

The mention of a hot drink made Oates realise how cold he had become. 'Yes, why not? Trigger?'

272

'I'll be down in a while.'

From behind the packing cases came another voice. 'We should cut and run I say, sir.'

The glow of the pipe and the soft, rounded accent told Gran it was Tom Crean.

'What's that?'

'Pack up now, go get the ponies and dogs. Not twirl around for town three weeks more, trying to raise a few coppers. Tell the folks here what we're up against. They'll put the hands in their pockets. I know Australians and New Zealanders and they'll dig deep if he tells them he's had the rug pulled from under him by this Amundsen fella. That's what the skipper should do.'

'Have you told him?'

A snort. 'Don't get me wrong, I yield to no man in my admiration of Captain Scott. I shared a tent with him out on the barrier after that second winter. You get to know a man out there. You ever go down a crevasse, young sir, you want Captain Scott or Birdie Bowers on the end of your trace. Neither will let you go or they'll come over with you.' He took a noisy suck on his pipe and a few sparks drifted heavenwards. 'But there are too many voices yapping in his ears on this voyage. Officers. Scientists. Bankers. Politicians. And not forgettin' the wives. He's not going to listen to the likes of me.'

'Perhaps he should.'

Crean gave a small laugh. 'Maybes. But I've spoken out of turn. Must be that nip of rum.' The pipe flared once more. 'I'll leave you to your thoughts, Mr Gran.'

'Thank you, Tom.'

Gran stood on deck for another half-hour, feeling wretched. He had grown to like these mad Englishmen with their strange rituals and wardroom high jinks. Apart from the wise heads like Crean and some of the scientists, they were overgrown schoolboys, really, so very different from the types Amundsen would have with him. The whole English ethos was alien to Scandinavians; the English wanted to win, but it was a bad show to be seen to put too much effort into the enterprise. The lucky amateur was what they all aspired to. The Norwegians, though, would be hardened, professional ice men and dog handlers. Some of them would have a decade or more of driving Greenland huskies. Most of the *Terra Nova*'s crew had never seen pack ice, bergs or polar conditions before. Amundsen would have a whole shore party of expert skiers; Scott was, ironically, relying on him, a Norwegian, to teach the others.

He decided it might be best if he left the ship. A lot depended on Nansen's reply to Scott's enquiry. Had he been party to this? Had everyone but the naïve Tryggve Gran known Amundsen's true intentions? Was his whole country duplicitous? If so, he would give up his dreams and go home.

He heard lusty singing from below and went down. He could hear Titus holding forth. Oates and Atch often ended up with the men in the mess, despite Scott's disapproval. The habit had started while the Owner was on the mailship and Teddy Evans in charge.

Then came Lashly's voice. 'Who doesn't like women? Why, Captain Oates. Why not? Because he prefers goats!'

The roar of approval shook the ship's timbers.

He hesitated, thinking of joining them, but went to his berth instead. It all depended on Nansen. If he had been involved in the sleight-of-hand, Gran was determined to resign from the Scott expedition.

In the event Tryggve Gran had already left the *Terra Nova*, still a troubled young man, by the time the reply came from Nansen. It was no matter; it hardly helped clarify the situation. Scott had asked a series of questions about Amundsen's intentions. Chief among them was: did Amundsen intend to try for the Pole? He received a reply even less illuminating than the original Amundsen cablegram. It was a single word.

Unknown.

Forty

Quail Island, off Lyttleton, New Zealand

The horses and dogs purchased in Manchuria were delivered, after a harrowing journey, to a small quarantine island just outside Lyttleton harbour. When Oates, Birdie Bowers and Scott arrived at Quail Island, they found Meares and Wilfred Bruce, Kathleen's brother, had pitched a tent and were brewing tea. Bruce had the most alarming black eyes and a swollen nose.

'What happened?' Oates asked.

'Take care with the one with the dark blaze,' replied Bruce, pointing up the slope to the tethered horses, where a diminutive man was grooming one of the ponies. 'Caught me a hefty kick.'

'And watch out for any of the dogs,' Meares said, pointing to the thirty-three snapping, snarling animals, already lunging against their chains.

'They never change,' said Scott with a sigh, taking a mug of strong black tea. 'Thank you. Is there such a thing as a sweet-tempered husky?'

A stranger emerged from the tent. 'Good morning,' he said in heavily accented English.

'This is Dimitri. One of the men I cabled you about.'

'Splendid,' said Scott. 'The dog driver.'

Dimitri nodded. 'I can drive dogs, yes.'

'Even these ones?'

He smiled. 'Even these. They have had a long journey.'

'Well, show me around the huskies then,' said Scott.

Oates took Bowers aside while Scott examined the new arrivals. 'When I tip you the wink, the answer is linseed, OK?'

'What?' the little man asked, confused.

'Linseed.'

They watched Scott walk among the huskies, sidestepping a lunge every now and then as if he were dancing a bizarre quadrille.

'Well, the dogs look to be the mustard. Shall we examine the horses?' asked Scott.

The three men moved up the slope to inspect the line of teth-ered ponies, which were clearly tired and irritable. The groom introduced himself as Anton. He, too, spoke thick English. 'All white,' he said.

'All right?' asked Oates.

'No,' the Russian said again. 'Horses all white. As asked.'

'Yes, all white,' said Scott. 'Shackleton's dark ponies died before the lighter ones. So I asked for white Siberian ponies.'

Oates tutted at this superstitious nonsense, earning him a glare from Scott.

'They are Manchurian,' said Anton. 'Mostly.'

They were also slightly bigger than ponies, but Oates said nothing. The enormity of getting them to the ice intact was only just dawning on him.

As the skipper walked among them, there was plenty of irrit-able snorting and angry nips. 'They look splendid,' Scott announced.

The animals had been en route from Vladivostok for seven weeks, most of it standing. They looked bedraggled and thin, thought Oates, far away from top condition. 'First class,' said Oates sardonically.

'Glad you think so,' said an apparently oblivious Scott.

'They need a damn good feed, skipper.'

'You did the calculations?'

Oates passed over a piece of paper, which Scott scrutinised. 'What's this?'

'The calculations.'

'It's illegible, man.'

Oates felt himself redden. His arithmetic was worse than his lettering. 'Figuring was never one of my talents.'

Scott screwed up the note. 'Just tell me how much you need in total.'

Oates walked over to the nearest animal. He could hear wind whistling in its tubes. 'How much did you pay?' he asked Anton.

'One hundred twenty-five roubles,' said Anton and nodded towards Meares. 'He say that five pounds a pony.'

Five pounds. 'Not enough, yet too much,' muttered Oates before he turned to Scott. 'We need forty-five tons of fodder.'

'Impossible,' said Scott. 'We don't have room. Not now we have built the icehouse for the mutton.' The construction of the freezer to hold beef and mutton had eroded the available deck space even further.

'Then it's a waste of time taking the ponies. These ones, anyway.'

Oates moved among the animals, logging up the faults as he went, careful not to get a kick or a bite for his trouble. Windsucker. Spavined. Narrow chested. Pigeon toed. Stiff hocks. Old. Lame. Aged. Ringboned. One of them sounded as if there was a bag of nails loose in his lungs. 'Forty-five tons.'

'You are just an old pessimist, Oates. Not an ounce over thirty. Or we'll pay for it in coal. Birdie, you'll organise getting it shipped over here, eh?'

'Sir,' said Bowers. Scott called him his little treasure, because of his unquestioning willingness to work. 'What sort?'

'I have been offered a good price on compressed.'

'It should be linseed,' objected Oates as he stroked the coat of the nearest animal. It felt stiff with dirt. 'The horses need the oil.'

'Linseed? That's a lot more. What do you think, Birdie?'

The little man flinched. Oates tipped him the wink. Bowers hated conspiring against the Owner, but he was sure Oates knew what he was doing. 'Oh, aye, sir, the Farmer's right. Should be linseed.'

'Linseed,' agreed Anton.

Scott sighed. 'Very well, thirty tons. Of linseed. Let me know how much that will cost. Titus, I think you should organise some training of the animals. For the sledge-pulling.'

As Scott walked back to the dogs, Oates whispered to Birdie. 'Get thirty-five.'

Bower's eyes widened. 'But—'

'Get thirty-five, but the bill made out to thirty. Skipper won't be able to tell the difference with his naked eyes. I'll pay for the five out of my own pocket.'

'You are a wicked man, Farmer Hayseed.' Bowers liked to tease Oates about his continuing affection for scruffy dress, but after years of well-pressed and polished uniforms, he was enjoying being slovenly.

'And we need bran, two tons, oilcake, six tons, and two tons of hay.'

Birdie wagged a finger. 'You'll be in trouble.'

Oates shook his head. 'We'll be in trouble if we don't get all that, at least.'

'Titus!' Scott shouted from down the hill. 'We need to name them and assign a school. Birdie has the list of patrons. Meares and I will do the dogs.'

'Right, skipper.' As with the huskies, each pony had been sponsored by a school or college. Eton had one, Bedales, Liverpool. St Paul's, as well as a few individuals and gentlemen's clubs.

'This is a beggars' expedition,' said Oates, taking the list from Bowers. 'You know I have to write to Trafalgar House, Winchester to thank them for funding my sleeping bag?'

'It's been a terrible worry for him,' said Birdie, indicating Scott. 'Come on, let's christen them and apportion them a sponsor. Look at that one. With the teeth and the flared nostrils. He looks like he went to Eton.'

Oates laughed, not wanting to tell him the nostrils were actually split. Five pounds a horse. He wouldn't give five pence for some of them. Crocks, at least till he could see what a good feed and decent grooming could do. But they were what he had to work with and, ultimately, it wasn't their fault that the wrong men had been sent to buy the horses.

Before they left Port Chalmers, Oates wrote up the events in his diary.

> It seems the Owner upset protocol when he didn't ask Mrs Evans for the first dance at one of those dreadful balls. This, she claimed, was a terrible snub for her and her husband. Teddy Evans backed her up, much to the Captain's dismay. Then, Mrs Scott and Evans have had a magnificent battle, a draw after fifteen rounds. Mrs Wilson flung herself into the fight after the tenth round and there was more blood and hair flying about than you see in a Chicago slaughter-house in a month. The husbands got a bit of a backwash and there is a certain coolness which I hope they won't bring to sea or into the hut with them.

It had been Cardiff all over again. Banquets, inspections of the ship by sightseers who marvelled at how small and crowded every-thing was, stupid questions.

He had heard someone ask who he was and Mrs Scott's tart reply. 'That's Captain Oates. Hard to tell, but he is an officer.'

He had distracted himself by helping build the horse stalls, squeezed in between sacks of coal, beneath the fo'c'sle. They were comfortable enough, which was more than could be said for the men below them. The deck planks were spaced so wide, waste from the horses ran down into the hammocks and the mess room. Bowers had called him plenty of names when he got his first mouthful of hot piss while asleep. They were going to have to caulk up the planks.

Oates wished he had played a part in the horse selection. But Captain Scott had his own way of doing things, he supposed. White-only ponies indeed.

'Farmer! Come up here,' Birdie shouted. 'Almost two-thirty. We're casting off.'

As if to underline his words, the engine began to clank away.

Oates closed the notebook and went up top. There were few to see them off; most of the crowds had gathered at Lyttleton for the blessing, which had taken hours. Here, there were no more than two dozen, although there were numerous craft out at sea.

'My goodness but you look smart. And shoelaces, too.'

It was Kathleen Scott. She would be taken off with the other wives at the heads. Oates looked down at his old uniform, which, as requested, he had brought along for high days, holidays and fund-raising banquets. 'Thank you.'

'You can look like a dashing cavalry officer when you want to, then.'

She had been rude about him and his hobnail boots at the races in Melbourne, even though he won his event. 'When required. Aren't you drawing this out till the bitter end? Staying on till the last moment?'

'I suppose I am. Wife's prerogative.'

Kathleen Scott's prerogative, Oates thought, but said nothing. He had, rather begrudgingly, come to admire the way she did things according to her own lights.

'So, if I don't get another chance, good luck, Captain Oates.'

'Thank you, ma'am.' Oates squeezed himself between men and machinery and stores. There was hardly room to place a foot between the provisions and equipment and it was easy to turn an ankle whenever the boat moved. The Plimsoll Line was a long-forgotten concept, submerged permanently below the waves. The icehouse was surrounded by the three motor sledges and scattered around them two-and-a-half tons of fuel for the experimental machines.

Overloaded, said some of the ratings. Even more so than *Discovery*, and she had been dangerously top-heavy. Oates didn't want to think about the crossing facing them. Whenever men talked about the legendary storms of the Southern Ocean, he changed the subject.

Eventually, he zigzagged his way across to witness the gangplank being pulled up and the ship finally turned towards her destination. What a relief that would be. It was the closing days of November now, six months since he had joined the expedition.

One of the dogs went for him and he slapped it aside. The huskies never missed an opportunity for a snap and there wasn't room to separate man and beast properly on board. They were chained wherever there was a free post. Dimitri, the Russian dog-driver, did his best to calm them, but he said they wouldn't be happy till they were on the ice. He wondered if the same would be true of Meares, who seemed to have become a full-time pessimist.

Oates reached the plank and glanced down at the dock. There was a familiar figure standing at the bottom, looking up nervously, as if deciding whether to take the first step to come up it.

Tryggve Gran.

'Ahoy there,' Oates said quietly. 'Isn't that what we sailors say?'

'I believe so.'

'Are you coming aboard?'

The Norwegian shrugged. 'Am I welcome?'

'I don't know.' He turned to Birdie and Crean and Taff. 'Lads! Is this no-good Norskie welcome on board?'

'That bollocks?' said Crean. They all laughed. 'I suppose we can squeeze him in with the horses.'

'Or in the icehouse,' said Bowers. 'Get him used to the cold.'

'I think that's a yes,' said Oates.

Gran strode up the gangway, and Oates shook his hand. From the bridge came the barked instructions that began the sequence that would finally get the *Terra Nova* underway. The tugs fore and aft – the *City of Christchurch* and the *Dunedin* – let loose with their whistles and the waters at their sterns began to churn.

The *Terra Nova*'s deck vibrated with increased urgency as Lashly stoked up its engines. A shriek of steam escaped from the whistle on the funnel. The dogs began to whimper and the gulls screeched back at the ship. The gangway was pulled up and secured. The ropes to the tugs sprang tight and *Terra Nova*, her own lines and chains now neatly coiled on the deck, edged away from the dock.

There was a cheer from the quay and a louder one from the crew. It somehow managed to convey hope, excitement and apprehension.

'Welcome back, Trigger,' said Oates as she moved towards the breakwater. 'Let's go to Antarctica.'

Kathleen stood on the stern of the brig and raised a hand in farewell to her husband. Scott waved back from the bridge of *Terra Nova*, which was rounding the heads, followed by a flotilla of small boats, trailing like gulls.

'There they go. It'll be two years or more before we see them again,' she said.

'I think I might be hysterical,' said Hilda Evans, sniffing into her handkerchief.

'What, even more than usual?' asked Kathleen.

'Please, Mrs Scott,' admonished Ory Wilson. 'Haven't we had enough unpleasantness?'

They had indeed, and not just because of the imagined snub at the ball. Taff Evans had fallen in the harbour during the blessing of the *Terra Nova* by the Bishop of Christchurch. Teddy Evans had demanded his dismissal, which Scott initially agreed with. Then came rumours that Teddy had pushed Taff in. Wilf Bruce swore he had seen the nudge that unbalanced the drunk.

Kathleen had repeated this and caused a flaming row between both the wives and between Scott and Teddy.

At the end of the day, Taff was back on the crew roster, although reduced to quarter-pay.

By way of revenge, Teddy Evans had brought up the incident of Mr Hull, the young man on the steamer from Cape Town who had made eyes at her. Hull had written her a very unfortunate and hot-headed letter, full of inappropriate poetry and declarations, which made even Con angry. Jealousy was not one of his faults; but she had, he said, goaded him beyond reason.

Still, she had calmed things down between them. She forced on him a two-hour walk. Talking calmly, slowly, she had told him of her love as they strolled arm-in-arm on the cliff, hundreds of feet above the estuaries of the Avon and Waimakariri. Far behind them were the Kaikoras, the peaks snow dipped, the light shifting the aspect every few minutes. Despite her best efforts, she had found New Zealand suffocating and suburban. But if its society was parochial, she had discovered its natural beauty could restore her spirits.

As they walked, pressed together for the last time for at least two years, possibly as long as three, she explained that, unlike the other wives, she liked the company of men. Hull had been interesting, an expert on Australia. She had been curious about the Aborigines. Scott shared her curiosity and so must appreciate that.

He had forgiven her, although she thought there was nothing to forgive. She never thought of marriage as a vow of silence. It was not, should not be, a nunnery.

'You know, I think perhaps the wives should be chosen as carefully as the men if they are to come along.'

'Or have none,' he said.

'Not even me?'

'No. You can come. Captain's privileges.'

'I have a confession to make, Con.'

He narrowed his eyes. He wasn't sure he wanted to hear her confessions. 'What is it?'

She spoke softly, so as not to alarm him. 'When I first met you, my main thought was, here is the man who could be the father of a son I could love.' She put a finger to his twitching lips. 'No, don't say anything. I think I convinced myself that I loved you. I certainly felt something, but I don't think, in retrospect, it was love.'

His voice was the merest whisper. 'Go on.'

'Well, the strangest thing happened. I find that I love the man who gave me the son every bit as much as I love the son himself. More, perhaps.'

He should have been angry, but couldn't bring himself to be. There had been an initial deception, perhaps, but nature had made amends. 'You sound surprised.'

'Grateful.' She had stopped them and stared into his eyes, which flashed green like the ocean below them. 'If anything happens, or seems likely to happen, don't worry about us. We'll be all right. Peter and I. You know that, don't you?'

'You won't miss me?'

'Like my own heart. That's not what I mean. The other wives don't understand, with their ceaseless wailing. You have enough to worry about out there, without a weak-willed wife distracting you. You will come back to me, I know. But if you don't, we'll honour you every day. We will survive it. So you must not fret for us.'

He'd laughed. 'I think I understand.'

'The others don't. They think I don't care. I will not kiss you goodbye on the ship, Con. There is a finality, a sadness in that. Don't expect it. I don't want anyone to see us parting in sorrow.'

'Just as long as you kiss Peter for me when you see him.'

'I shall smother him in kisses. And I'll kiss you now.'

And, on the bluff above the harbour that held *Terra Nova*, the tiny speck of a ship that would carry Robert Falcon Scott away south, she had done just that.

Part Four

'*Scott used to say the worst part of any expedition was over when the preparation was finished*'

The Worst Journey in the World, Apsley Cherry-Garrard

Forty-one

Paris, 1917

The City of Light was full of soldiers. Actually, it was full of officers, Tryggve Gran noted, not regular soldiers. There were French and Belgian, of course, but also English, Irish, Ulstermen, Scots, Canadian, South African, and plenty of dominions he did not recognise. The beds of the Empire had been emptied and there were many pillows that would never see a young man's head again. How many soldiers in the trenches had lasted as long as he had? A handful, so he heard. Most of those who survived the first Mons were taken at the Somme or Wipers. The war might miss you at a particular skirmish or battle, but the killing machine got you in the end.

He stopped at a café on the rue de Rivoli. There were Americans in it, ones who hadn't yet seen action. He could tell by their eyes, by the jokiness, the relaxed shoulders. It contrasted with a table of Englishmen, drawn and pensive, without the energy for the hysterical celebration that sometimes took hold of soldiers on furlough. There were other signs of the war. The waiters were old, or infirm, with eye patches, missing fingers or, like the one who served him, the strange clonk of a wooden foot.

Millions of men maimed and killed. And here he was still fretting over five that died a lonely, some might say useless, death at the bottom of the world. Why did those men still matter to those who never knew them?

287

He finished his coffee, paid his over-priced bill, and walked swiftly to the Crillon, Lady Scott's manuscript tucked under his arm.

Kathleen Scott was dressed in a shapeless blue shift, barefoot as usual, her hair down. She had a suite on the first floor, with a view over Place de la Concorde, which looked bleak in the thin winter sunshine. He refused an offer of more drink and shrugged his coat. The room was white and gold, with richly brocaded chairs, a tapestry on the wall, Louis XV cabinets and deep, swirling Beaveau carpets on the floor. He felt a touch of nausea and the world became muffled, as if his head had filled with fine sand.

'Are you all right, Trigger?' she asked.

'I need to sit. Do you have any water?'

She fetched him a glass from the other room and he drank gratefully. 'When we came back from the ice, there was this strange effect. You were overwhelmed. The smells first of all. Flowers, fruits, vegetables, women's perfume so strong it made you gag. You had been deprived of these things for so long your body had become super-sensitive. And the colours. After months, years, of white, the world glowed, like a deranged oil painting. After the frontline, this room is much the same.'

'I understand.' She waited while he recovered, her eyes glancing at the fat envelope he had placed on the coffee table. 'You've read it.'

He nodded.

'And?'

'Why did you argue with the other wives? I don't understand.'

Kathleen sighed. 'That? Oh, it was all silly. There were incidents, slights, snubs. And Hilda Evans was a woman who would hear no word against her husband. The loyal little wife. She wanted, because he wanted, a guarantee he would be one of those to go to the Pole. Con would give no such undertaking. I am sure that now she is pleased with the way it turned out.' Now she spoke in a rush, as if to get the sentence out before she changed her mind. 'And to be frank, I was jealous of Bill and took it out on poor Ory.'

'Jealous?'

She nodded. 'It wasn't till the voyage home I realised it. There was Bill, already having been out on the ice for two years with my man. Now he was going out again. And I wasn't allowed. No place for women.'

'It isn't.'

'Till the first woman goes out and proves you wrong. Perhaps even a Norwegian woman.'

He laughed. 'Perhaps.'

'Apart from that? How did you rate the book?'

'I think it is fair. Accurate. But I can't add to it.'

'No?'

'No. I drew a picture of how we found them. That is all.'

'I think there is more.'

'Why?'

'Atch says you behaved very strangely. Insisted on going out to look for Oates. With Cherry.'

That explained why she had been so keen to take him back to finding the tent on their previous meeting. She wanted to know why he had seemed peculiar to the others. 'We found his sleeping bag.'

'And that's all. Atch thought you were being foolish. No, not foolish. He says you had a haunted look.'

'Haunted?'

'That's what he said.'

'I was worried we might be caught by weather, that was all.'

'There's something you are not telling me.'

'I could say the same.'

Kathleen Scott stood up and moved to the window. She took a deep breath. 'I happen to know that Caroline Oates is about to stir up trouble. A book.'

'Another book?'

'By a vicar. Criticising my husband. A vicar! She has given him letters from her son that he is to use. She is a bitter woman.'

'A book can do little harm, surely.'

'She is also talking about initiating an official inquiry. A public tribunal to apportion blame.'

It was true there had never been an RGS inquest into the deaths of the five men. By the time the national outpouring of grief and pride had subsided and heads had cleared, a war had begun that was taking the lives of millions. 'Now that, Mr Gran, is a can of worms we could do without.'

He couldn't help but agree. What was done was done. Who would benefit from the Government or a learned society going back over such well-trodden ground? 'But surely, not in the midst of this . . . this carnage?'

'She has the ear of the Royal Coroner who, I am sure, can pressure some of his lesser colleagues. And some anti-Markham factions in the Royal Geographical Society would love to see the bones picked clean.'

'Sir Clements is dead.'

'Barely cold in his grave. But Mr Gran, he was a giant. His ghost walks those corridors still. I think there are those who demand an exorcism. Think who would be called, think of the expense, think of the damage that could be done.'

Now his perceived role was making sense. 'You think I know something that might stop her convening an inquest?'

She turned away from the window. 'If I am honest, yes. I am sure Lawrence Oates was no paragon of virtue.'

He tried not to sound too angry at the slur. 'Her son was an honourable man, Lady Scott. You cannot play one man's reputation against another as if this was a game of bezique. The five who died are one. That's how they would want it to be. Oates might have written letters against the skipper. But we all had to have some kind of . . . I don't know the word. Release?'

'Pressure valve.'

'Yes, something to let off steam. Your book is worthwhile, without debasing it with rumour and conjecture about a very brave man.'

Kathleen strode over to him and placed her hands on the arm of his chair. 'So I do nothing?'

'Against a woman deranged with sorrow? No. I know what you are thinking, Lady Scott. That your husband's reputation is Peter's legacy. Captain Scott's stature is intact. He made mistakes, who hasn't? Nobody, and I mean nobody, who has been south has not made mistakes. I include Amundsen and Shackleton. Both blundered. They got away with it. Shackleton by the skin of his teeth and by the hand of some God who looks out for fools and madmen. No, that's not fair. But, by rights, by any rights, Shackleton shouldn't have made it when he lost his ship and was stranded on the ice. If your husband had had a tenth of his luck, he would have survived. But, be assured, while Cherry and Crean and Lashly and Priestley and Ponting and the others who were with him, who knew him, are still alive, then you have nothing to worry about from vicars or inquests.'

He slumped back in the chair, the force of his words having drained him.

'You won't help?'

'The book should be yours, not ours. And I don't think you should start a feud with Caroline Oates. It would be unseemly. But if you want me to say what I thought of the skipper, I shall send you some of my diary. It's in there.'

'Thank you, Trigger. And the inquest? You would appear?'

He considered this. 'If I live through the war, yes. But Lady Scott, think of what trouble the Government might be making for itself if it did convene an inquest. Caroline Oates feels her son died unnecessarily. Due to poor leadership.' She was about to speak, but he raised a palm. 'Her feelings, not mine. There are probably a million others out there who feel the same after Passchendaele and the Somme. Two million, perhaps. Are we to bring all our leaders to account? Will General Haig or John French be called to account for themselves?'

'I take your point. It would be a precedent.'

'It most certainly would.'

'Very well.' She sighed, sensing there was little more to be gained from the audience. 'What will you do now?'

'I have some leave due. I will go to London. Then home, before I am posted to Russia.'

'Stay well.'

Realising he was dismissed, he stood and fetched his coat. 'I will. You too.'

As he left the over-opulent confines of the hotel, he was already thinking about boat trains to London and how best to get out to Gestingthorpe. Tryggve Gran was going to see Caroline Oates, and settle matters once and for all.

Forty-two

Terra Nova at Sea, December 1910

It was the coal, the precious coal that nearly did for them. Cherry came to see Oates, as he was feeding the horses. The look on the young man's face told him something was wrong. 'The barometer is making me feel queasy.'

'Falling?'

'Plummeting.'

Oates looked out at the sea. For the moment the swell was long and lazy, like the South Downs sculptured in water. Even so, *Terra Nova* was making hard work of the waves, rolling enough to terrify the dogs and make the horses skittish.

Within an hour, the soft mounds of water had become more jagged, the troughs deep as a river valley and a wind was hunting across the top of them, flicking spume and foam. Now the horses were complaining, in a series of snorts and whinnies. Anton, the groom, was also in difficulty, heaving his insides over the bulwarks. The ex-jockey would be of little use if he carried on like that, Oates thought.

The first sizeable wave hit two hours later, just as night came upon them, falling on the *Terra Nova* with the force of a brick wall tumbling down. It broke over the deck with a crack, sweeping away a section of pin rail and belaying pins. Oates found himself up to his knees in water that tugged and pushed at him as it swirled away. The light faded as the sky darkened and a fine drizzle began.

'Sheet,' said Dimitri, the dog-handler. 'Doesn't look good.'

Now, Oates had lost track of the number of vast waves that had broken over them. Even with the topgallant and mainsails furled – just the jib and staysail left – and oil released to try to calm the waters, the ship was twisting and turning, driven this way and that by a gale with no sense of direction. Another column of water loomed over the fo'c'sle and came down like a mallet, with Oates and Dimitri the pegs to be driven through the decks. Oates clung on to the sides of the horse stalls as icy water swirled up to his chest, before draining away.

'Dimit—'

Another roller, this one snatching one of the dogs. The animal choked as its chain tightened, and then howled as the lead broke. Oates looked into its terrified eyes before the sea took it.

Dimitri stood, looking out into the vicious ocean, his mouth working as if he wanted to say something.

A spout seemed to spin around then, like a tornado, followed by another deposit of water. There was a mighty thud and there, in front of them, was the dog that had gone overboard, looking dazed and confused, as well it might.

'My Lord!' exclaimed Dimitri and fell on the husky before the sea could change its mind. He dragged the animal off in search of something to secure him with.

As he considered this small miracle, a heavy object crashed into Oates, pitching him into the horses and sending him sprawling. A stray hoof hit his ribs. As he stood, he felt his footing go again, and clung on to Willie to steady himself. All around the animals' legs were black lumps, bobbing like excrement. Coal. The coal sacks were breaking free.

One of them flashed by his head, borne on a column of water that seemed alive, and smashed into one of the motorised sledge's crates. The sack's contents scattered, flying through the air like oversized buckshot.

The decks were full of men trying to re-lash the cargo, but the storm wouldn't let them be, yanking ropes from their grip, squirming the jute sacks as if they were possessed by demons within.

As the frequency and size of the waves increased, the ponies began to rear and buck in their stalls. Oates tried desperately to calm them, and to keep them on their feet. If they went down, they'd drown.

A fist seemed to strike his head, a savage punch and he saw a circle of stars for a second. Another bag of coal had broken free and caught him. Now it split and spewed its lumpy black vomit into the water.

The noise became unbearable, a combination of the shriek of the wind round the masts and spars, the crashing thump of tons of water on wood, the drumming of the ponies' hoofs on the stall sides, the yapping and howling of the dogs and the shouted instructions of men. It filled Oates's brain, leaving no room for rational thought.

He began to lose track of time, as he flitted from pony to pony, sometimes leaning against one to try to stop it being bowled over. His ribs ached, his eyes stung and his teeth were chattering with cold. He couldn't feel the tips of his fingers when he stroked the horses; the gloves he was wearing were soaked through.

Anton, his stomach emptied, but his face still a sickly colour, helped as best he could, pausing only to dry-heave.

Then he felt it, the sudden change in the ship. It began to wallow. There was no vibration through his feet, no faint chuff of the boiler. The engine had stopped. They were powerless. As if to drive home the point, the biggest wave yet, a moving green-black cliff, struck *Terra Nova* amidships, submerging the deck completely, casually tearing away a section of bulwark.

Even over the roar of water and splintering wood, he clearly heard the limb snap. He had to wait till the sea had released him from its grip before he could wade across to see which one had been injured. It was Bonce, donated by South Hampstead School for Girls. He could see a small hook of bone jutting through the skin and the horse began to mew, a sound more feline than equine.

'Trigger!' he shouted at a passing figure, who was scouring under the rails for something.

The Norwegian, drenched and bedraggled like him, stopped. 'I need buckets.'

'What's happening?'

'We have to bail.'

'Bail?'

They paused while a fresh mound of water enveloped them. Now the injured pony began to thrash and the panic level among the others increased as they heard his pain.

'The coal dust had blocked the bilge pump. Hand pumps, too. Water up to the boilers. Had to douse them. Must bail—' Gran lapsed into Norwegian and Oates lost him. He had the drift, though. They might well sink with all hands, all because of coal dust in a bilge pump.

'I need a gun!' Oates yelled. 'A pistol.'

He pointed to the tortured pony and Gran nodded. 'See what I can find.'

A half-dozen drenchings later, it was Scott who appeared with a revolver. His face was smeared with black, his clothes ruined, but his eyes were strangely calm. 'You want me to do it?' he asked.

Oates saw the relief on the Owner's face when he shook his head and took the revolver.

'You sure you don't need me? It's all very well saving the ponies, but if . . .'

Scott placed a hand on his shoulder. 'Not yet, Titus. Stay with your charges. I'd best get back.'

Oates waited for another influx of the sea, so that the other animals were distracted. He placed the gun against the horse's head and pulled the trigger. A spout of black blood briefly cleared the surface of the water, and the animal gave one spasm and lay still.

Oates moved to the rear of the ship, stepping over cans of petrol slithering about, and, over the fearful racket, he could hear a sea shanty. Buckets were indeed coming up from below and being cast over the side of the ship, only to be returned fifty-fold in the next wave. It was like trying to drain a ship with a straw. As he looked below, he could see a chain of men stripped to the waist, their bodies blackened by the coal dust in the swirling water, working fiercely to a strict rhythm.

'Welcome to *Dante's Inferno*,' shouted Priestley. 'Teddy Evans and Bowers and the others are going to break down the bulkhead to reach the pump.'

'Can I help?' Oates asked.

Charles 'Silas' Wright, the Canadian physicist, answered from further down the chain. 'We bookworms need the exercise. We'll be fine. Go.'

Oates struggled past dogs being alternately choked and drowned, and Meares and Dimitri trying to hold their heads above the water and getting mauled for their trouble. A huge gash had opened on Meares's cheek, but still he cradled each of the animals in turn.

When Oates made it back to the stalls, another horse was down. Anton was desperately trying to pull it up with a set of reins he had slipped on, but the animal wouldn't budge. He put his weight under the belly and heaved, using the moment of the surging water to pull him up, but he refused to go.

As the next wave hissed around them, he felt a second pair of hands under the horse and another encouraging voice. 'Up y'come, m'beauty.' Like a newborn foal, the pony struggled upright.

'There,' said Atkinson, the surgeon. 'Skipper sent me to help you.'

'Thank you,' he gasped. 'I need it.'

'I think what you need is a good canvas sling to get under the animals. We could use one of the dodgers.' He pointed to a flapping windbreak.

'Good idea.' The rescued animal gave a lip-smacking whinny. Oates leaned against him, stroking his face. 'Don't worry, Nobby,' he said. 'It'll soon be over.'

Atch ducked as he took another soaking. 'One way or another, Titus. One way or another.'

The storm, after gusting Force 10, broke in the early hours and, by dawn, the pumps had been cleared and were working. The bailing party was finally stood down, although most of the men could no longer move. They had gone beyond exhaustion to the point where they had become inflexible machines. It took many minutes for them to climb up on to deck or stumble to their hammocks or cabins, where only more wet clothes awaited.

Wilson, Taff Evans, navigator Harry Pennell and Bowers took an inventory as the feeble sun broke through the clouds. The party shuffled wearily around the deck, running on the last of their reserves. Scott was at the stalls, inspecting the ponies when Wilson reported. 'Uncle' Bill Wilson was shocked by Oates's appearance. Nobody on the ship was unscathed, but the ponies had battered Soldier black and blue and his eyes were raw from saltwater and lack of sleep. He was limping, too.

'How long have you been on deck?' Wilson asked him.

'I don't know.' His words were slurred with fatigue. 'Thirty hours. Perhaps more.'

'Get some sleep if you can.'

Oates nodded. There was one more unpleasant task before he could rest.

'What losses?' asked Scott.

'About nine tons of coal lost, I estimate,' said Wilson.

'Perhaps ten,' said Bowers.

Scott touched his head. His fingers came away black with coal grease. 'Much of it in our hair, I fear.'

Wilson could only grunt an agreement. 'And sixty-five gallons of petrol, and three cases of tinned provisions.'

'Including a case of ginger wine,' added Taff.

'And the two horses,' said Oates morosely. They had lost a second pony during the night when its lung expired, too congested to continue the fight. He wasn't looking forward to the task of dumping the corpses overboard through the fo'c'sle hatch. He felt that he had failed them.

'Only two?' asked Wilson, looking at the poor beasts, their eyes still wide with terror.

'Davy and Jones, m'be,' said Birdie.

Oates glared at him, despite recognising the graveyard humour behind the comment. Bowers had also had a rough time down in the bilges, along with Teddy Evans, but didn't show it. The little man was as tough as tenpenny nails.

'You did well, Soldier,' said Wilson.

'And only one dog gone,' said Scott. 'Although Osman is in a bad way.' This was the dominant hound, a feisty if unpredictable animal. 'Meares has buried him in hay to try to revive him.'

'We got off lightly,' said Wilson, with wonder in his voice.

Scott nodded. The crew had worked miracles, in saving animals, machinery, provisions and the ship itself. Winds had touched over sixty miles an hour and *Terra Nova* had rolled to forty-five degrees. Not a man had flagged and not a spirit had broken. 'We were very fortunate. And we've found out one thing.'

'What's that?' asked Wilson.

'We might have a handful of a ship.' Scott looked around at the tattered *Terra Nova*, her equally roughed-up crew and the unsettled, heaving monster of a sea around them, with undisguised pride. 'But we have a shipful of heroes.'

Forty-three

Letter from Robert Scott, December 1910

Dearest Heart,

Just a little note from the ocean to say that I love you. I have been almost too busy to draw breath but once on the barrier there will be long hours in which to think of you and the boy. I hope you don't forget me. Everything is going pretty well for the present, although we have had one or two frights.

We are just over a week out of New Zealand. The sea is calming at last, which shows the ice cannot be very far off. Air and water at thirty-four degrees, just above freezing. The Antarctic animals have appeared: McCormack skuas, sooty and black-brown albatrosses, hour-glass dolphins are following the ship. Bill Wilson has spotted an Antarctic petrel and a fulmar, and there are whales blowing in the distance, their spumes easily mistaken for icebergs in certain lights. We rode out a rather disastrous storm, but I am happy to report the crew remain cheerful, despite deep discomfort. One hears laughter and song all day long – it is delightful to be with such a merry crew. The singing is surprising: it is odd that such an unmusical group should enjoy it so much. Oates sounds like one of his horses. Ponting plays the banjo, an instrument of torture.

Teddy Evans has settled down now, although he seems incapable of being quiet for more than a minute. His efforts at the pumps when we were in trouble were remarkable. Bill is his usual wonderful calm self. The men come to him with problems as they did on *Discovery*. He now tells me he found it strange I could share a sleeping bag with Lashly and Crean on the last expedition. He says he thought the men would have found it awkward, but I have no evidence of that. Oates, on the other hand, gets on well with the ratings. He and Atkinson spend time in the mess room. I suppose because one is a civilian and the other a soldier they do not follow RN ways. Cherry-Garrard is still rather shy and keeps himself to himself. I am sure the ice will open him up a little. Bowers is a treasure, immensely strong, even more so than Taff, and he is a Trojan. Ponting turns out to be quite a splendid fellow, very reasonable about everything except his photography. On that front, he brooks no interference. The crew sometimes complain in a jocular fashion about 'Ponco' making them stop what they are doing and pose, no matter how cold or wet they are.

We intend to land at Cape Crozier, where the Emperor penguin colonies are and where Royds set up our 'post office', if possible and not use our old hut. This is a new expedition and I feel we should start afresh. Of course, we have the pack to get through but I am confident we can forge a way. If it traps us I shall put out the fires and wait. At this time of year it is breaking up.

It is hard to realise this letter will not reach you for many months, will not start its journey until *Terra Nova* returns to New Zealand. What pains me most, apart from not seeing you, is that I shall miss the boy growing. How tall he will be when I return. Try to interest him in nature rather than the Navy.

I had a dream last night about the early days just after we had met. When I used to walk along the Embankment and stare up at your lighted window, not daring to knock on the door. Do you remember that? It is strange how memories come back in fits and starts.

It is a little later. I was called up because Evans (T) spotted two icebergs on the port beam, only visible from the masthead. They were tabulars, perhaps sixty to eighty feet high, and even at a distance one could see the blues and greens playing off the sides, which were highly fissured. It was oddly cheering to see them, to know we are nearly at the real start of our journey at long last and the sooner it is over the sooner I will be back with you. There is a strong ice blink in the sky. The pack is ahead. We will hit the first floes within ten to twelve hours and try and batter our way through. I shall write again soon, my love.

Forty-four

The Antarctic Ice Pack, January 1911

Oates laughed at the barked instructions from the increasingly frustrated Norwegian. '*Ooop the fut, oop the fut.* Speak bloody English, man.'

'I am speaking English; you must up the foot,' said Gran.

'What have you put on these skis? They smell worse than the ponies.' Oates and Anton had shovelled out three-foot mounds of horse excrement from the stalls when the animals were let out of them for their first exercise in weeks.

Oates and Gran were half a mile from the stationary ship, which glistened in the sun as her icing of frost slowly melted. The *Terra Nova* was not only held fast by ice anchors, but she was also pinched by slabs of shiny congelation ice that refused to yield to her bow. The ship was a captive of the floe; skiing was one way of distracting their thoughts from the predicament.

'Special recipe. Linseed oil and tar. It stops them slipping. Now, again.'

'Hold on.'

Oates put down the poles and pulled off his sweater and under-shirt. His outer jacket lay on the ice next to Atkinson, who had come out to join the fun. Oates's body was white, his Indian tan having long faded, but the cavalryman's muscles were still there, honed by hard manual routine on the ship. He had rarely felt fitter and hardly noticed his old leg wound. As he had told Anton, shovelling shit was good for the lungs.

'Hot work, this,' he said to Gran as he dropped his unwanted layers.

'Not if you do it properly.'

Oates adjusted his goggles, leaned slightly forward as Gran had instructed, began to pole and move his legs. The skis went back and forth, but he stayed where he was. 'No wonder there aren't many Norwegians. They don't get to meet each other to procreate.'

'You'll wear a hole in the ice. Watch me.' He leapt forward, the skis gliding over the fine powder that lay on top of the ice. Within a few minutes, he was a distant figure, almost at the edge of their floe, scattering a group of Adelie penguins that had stopped to watch this strange creature. He swivelled round, raised his poles above his head in salute.

'Bloody show-off,' said Oates.

Suddenly Gran bent down and began to massage his thigh. Cramp again. The lad seemed very susceptible to cold and cramp. Captain Scott had made a few disparaging remarks about it, which had upset the young man. The Owner didn't like physical weakness, which is why he pushed himself so hard and why he admired powerhouses such as Bowers, Taff, Crean and Lashly.

'Hold steady now.'

It was Ponco Ponting and his camera, aiming to capture Oates on film.

'If I hold steady I'll freeze. Atch, Mr Ponting wants to take your picture.'

Atkinson was still playing with his bindings and had not yet shed any layers. Wilson had set up an easel next to him and was sketching *Terra Nova*, which did look magnificent against the background of floes and bergs and, in the far distance, a pair of sunning leopard seals. There were two things Wilson would probably leave out of the finished article: the ragamuffin flags of sailors' clothes draped in the rigging, finally drying after weeks of being damp, and Cherry on the ice, skinning the penguins Wilson had 'pithed', a technique that involved stirring a metal rod in the brain to kill them. The young man whistled while he did his gruesome work, occasionally stopping to eye the skuas, patiently waiting for their pickings to begin.

Feeling the cold prickle his exposed skin, Oates put some effort into the strange motion and, to his delight, began to slither over the floe. His progress wasn't as elegant as Gran's, but he certainly had the speed. He let out a whoop as his poles dug in and he found a certain rhythm that propelled him forward. He felt the slipstream against his face, and poled harder.

'Hey, Norskie. Look at this!' he shouted.

The crack and creak of breaking ice didn't reach him till it was too late. It sounded no louder than a thickish branch bending then snapping. The hole immediately opened up beneath his skis and he plunged in, almost head first.

The shock of the freezing cold made him gasp and he sucked in a lungful of sea. He managed to fling the poles away and thrash in the water, but he could feel the skis dragging him down. He began to pump his knees, hoping the thin planks would act like flippers, but they suddenly seemed inordinately heavy. He was going down into the thick, icy depths.

He could hear men shouting, although he couldn't make out words.

'Help!'

With some difficulty Oates got both his arms on to the ice and managed to anchor himself there.

Wilson was running towards him and Gran was speeding over on his skis, his cramp forgotten.

'Whales, Titus.'

Oates tried to pull himself out but he could get no purchase and slipped back. He managed to pull up a leg and yank off one of the bindings from the ski boot, even though he could hardly feel his fingers. The wooden ski bobbed to the surface.

'Whales!'

There he was drowning in an ice-cold sea and all Wilson could think of was some whales which must have surfaced somewhere on the edge of the floe.

As he got the other ski free, a penguin popped its head up near him and made a disparaging squawk.

'Bugger off,' he tried to say. 'This is my ice hole.' But it came out as a wordless roar from between blue lips and the penguin slipped back down into the green water.

'Killer whales!'

And then he remembered. Ponting had been taking a picture of a berg close to the edge of a floe and a fearsomely huge black and white shape had burst from the water, thinking him an Adelie-with-camera.

'Oh fuck,' he muttered, an obscenity he hadn't used since India.

Oates didn't remember getting out of the water. One second he was up to his neck, the next he lay steaming on the ice, his body turning blue to match his lips. Wilson had had the presence of mind to bring Oates's clothes and he rubbed him with the under-shirt. Ponting and Gran stood around him, with concern on their faces, but also smirking.

'What is so amusing?'

'I have never seen any animal get out of the water so fast,' said Ponting, finally allowing himself a guffaw. 'Now you know how I felt.'

'You were like a rocket,' said Gran, miming his escape with his hands. 'Whoosh.'

'I wish I'd caught a picture of that.'

'Well, Ponco,' said Oates, through chattering teeth. 'Once I get dry, I'll do it again more slowly. How's that?'

'If you don't mind.'

'My pleasure.' A terrible shudder went through him.

'We'd best get you back to the ship,' said Wilson.

He stood, finished drying himself with the undershirt and pulled on his sweater. Atch, who had managed to ski over, after a fashion, took his fingers and rubbed them till some feeling came back.

'Three weeks we've been trying to get through this,' said Oates, indicating the floes. 'And now I fall through it.' He looked at *Terra Nova*, still fixed firmly. 'How much longer?'

'It'll let us through when it feels ready,' said Wilson, well aware that *Discovery* had rammed her way through much more quickly. But that had been later in the season, when the pack was rapidly dissolving. 'You have to be patient. But look on the bright side.'

'What's that?'

'Perhaps your little dip shows it is breaking up at last. Come.'

Wilson led him back towards *Terra Nova*, while Ponting and Gran rescued the discarded skis and Atch carried on trying to master the planks of wood he had strapped to his feet.

'Ridiculous things,' said Oates to Wilson, his voice quivering slightly.

'Except when used properly. We found them useful on *Discovery*, although hauling with them is even trickier than using them normally. Trigger says it can be done, with practice, but we never mastered it completely.'

'Hmm. Doctor,' said Oates.

'Yes?'

'Trigger was born with a pair of skis on, you know. They are, the Norskies, so he says. Has it occurred to you that if all the Norwegians ski like Trigger . . .'

'Then, if he gets through the pack, Amundsen might beat us to the Pole.'

Oates nodded.

'It has.'

'And have you mentioned it to the skipper?' asked Oates.

'Not yet. You think he doesn't realise it?'

'I find it hard to know what he is thinking at times.' Scott had become withdrawn and pensive during the past few weeks, as if depressed and mystified by the behaviour of the ice.

Wilson knew what the problem was. Scott was not blessed with patience, and the failure of the ice to yield was causing him great anxiety. 'Some might say the same of you, Titus.'

'Aye. They have, as well.' Oates began to shiver uncontrollably. They had reached the spot where he had discarded his jacket and he quickly pulled it on. 'Lord, I'm cold.'

'You were lucky. Eighteen thousand fathoms and freezing cold. Men can die in minutes in that water.'

'Even without a killer whale chewing on their privates.'

'Indeed.' Wilson stopped them just short of the ramp to the ship. He lowered his voice. 'And Soldier.'

'Yes?'

'What you just said about the Norwegians? Keep it to yourself, eh?'

'Good God, that stinks,' Oates proclaimed over the amplified crash of the surf hurling itself on to the basalt shore.

'It's not as bad as I recalled,' said Scott.

'The Emperor rookery is just over that cliff,' Wilson explained. 'Thousands of them, all sitting in their own guano. You get used to it.'

'Not sure I want to, Bill,' said Atch.

'Enough to make a maggot gag,' muttered Oates. 'And it's hardly a hospitable spot.'

Wilson nodded. 'Indeed. The Good Lord alone knows why the penguins have chosen the most windswept place on the planet to make their home.'

'You'll have to pull harder than this.' It was Tom Crean putting his back into keeping the whaler from the exposed rocks. That's all there were, black evil-looking rocks, backed by the columns of basalt, all hemmed in by an inlet of high ice cliffs. A large piece of sea floe had beached and was sitting over the best landing spot. This was Cape Crozier, the place they'd tolerated twenty days stuck in the pack to reach. It didn't look worth the effort.

'I've got a crab.' Cherry and his trawling net. 'No, two.' Then a screech. 'Ow. They are rum little nippers.'

Oates laughed as Cherry sucked his thumb. His glasses were misted and salted from the spray and he looked like a schoolboy who had caught his finger in a desk.

'Look, look,' yelled Wilson, pointing to the land. 'It's a chick. Can't we get in closer?'

An adult Emperor and its offspring were on the edge of the stranded ice floe, peering at the men.

'We'll be smashed, sir.' Crean again.

'We've never seen a chick like that. I could try to rope it.'

A wave dashed over the side and the swell rocked the boat with new violence. The noise of the surf echoed off the ice faces, multiplying its crashing, making it sound even more ominous than usual.

'It's moulting,' insisted Wilson excitedly. 'Look at its head and chest.'

'Look at those rocks,' said Oates.

'There's far more ice here than in *Discovery*'s day. We can't get any closer, Bill,' said Scott, scanning the mess of rocks, floes, cliffs, ice shelves, ice tongues and bergs. 'We certainly won't be able to land from *Terra Nova* with all this—'

The roar of the calving cliff face drowned him out. A crenellated block of ice the size of a large mansion split from the main body and crashed into the water, creating a disturbance that battled the incoming waves, resulting in a small maelstrom. Crean insisted they row away as quickly as possible, and all the oarsmen put their full effort into it. The newly born berg bobbed in the sea and, driven by the tide, began a stately progress towards the rocks. The Emperor and its baby had fled.

'The whole area is unstable,' said Scott. 'You'll have to come overland for your chicks.'

'It's the eggs I'd really like to see. But does that mean –?'

Scott nodded. Like *Discovery* and *Nimrod* before them, fate was pushing them west. There was only one place to land. McMurdo Bay, site of Hut Point. *Terra Nova* was going back to where it had all began.

Forty-five

Cape Evans, Antarctica

Dearest Heart,

I thought I would drop you a note about how we are living. It might help visualise me as my face fades over the months. Nearly four hundred miles through the pack ice and stuck fast for Christmas. We had the most splendid dinner, with soup, stewed penguin, plum puddings and mince pies, asparagus, champagne, liqueurs. Then singing again until one a.m. I may have partaken of a little too much of the liqueurs, because I found the banjo playing quite pleasant.

It is two weeks since we began to land stores at the cinder rocks at what was the Skuary, now renamed Cape Evans (Teddy wasn't as thrilled as I'd expected). It is around fifteen miles north of our old hut, separated by Glacier Tongue and two shallow bays of sea ice. We could not go much further south because of the risk of *Terra Nova* being iced in. If she is caught for the winter, my love, this letter will be sorely delayed.

I went across to Discovery Hut with Meares and the dogs. A good run, but how melancholy the place seemed. Someone – Shackleton, I think – left a window open and the place has filled with snow. How infuriating that anyone could be so careless. We will clear it out and use it as a forward base, no doubt.

I have sketched a plan of the new hut, similar to the one in my log. It is almost complete. Fifty foot long, twenty-five wide and nine foot to the eves. It is well insulated. I doubt a finer hut has ever been built in polar regions.

There is a line of packing cases separating the men of the shore party from the officers and scientists. Some of the latter were surprised at this, because out on the ice all is equal. But it was Crean and Wilson who first mooted it. The men like their privacy as much as the rest of us and to be allowed to carp and gripe if need be. As I said to Crean, we'll ignore anything we hear short of mutiny. He said he couldn't promise that, not after a couple months of seal dinners.

Oates, Bowers, Meares, Atkinson and Cherry sleep in the same area. They are already firm friends. They call the bunks The Tenements, because of the overcrowding. Gran was disappointed not to be included, but he is with Taylor, Debenham, Nelson and Day. The Norwegian thinks we wash too often and I find his posing when teaching skiing irritating. However, he has slotted in with the others well. They call their den the Ubduggery and call themselves the Ubdugs. When we ask them why they just burst out laughing.

Ponting has built a darkroom and sleeps over it. Some of the men object to posing when taking readings, but are generally astonished when they see the results. He has tried colour film, but the scenery is too bright. After complaining that the *Terra Nova* was no ocean liner, he now says the hut is not the hotel he is used to. At first everyone thought him far too prim. Now they simply rag him and he takes it in good spirit.

Plan of Hut

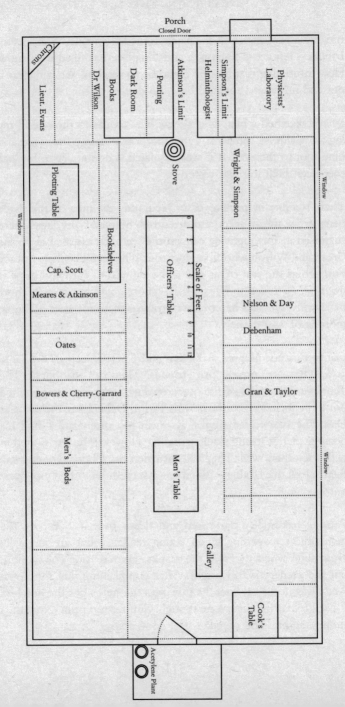

Porch
Closed Door

Chrons

Lieut. Evans

Dr. Wilson

Books

Dark Room

Ponting

Atkinson's Limit

Helminthologist

Simpson's Limit

Physicists' Laboratory

Stove

Wright & Simpson

Window

Ploting Table

Bookshelves

Officers' Table

Scale of Feet

0 1 2 3 4 5 6 7 8 9 10 11 12

Window

Cap. Scott

Meares & Atkinson

Nelson & Day

Debenham

Oates

Bowers & Cherry-Garrard

Gran & Taylor

Men's Beds

Men's Table

Window

Galley

Cook's Table

Acetylene Plant

I share a space with Bill Wilson and Teddy Evans and a linoleum-covered table at which I am writing. I can hear hammering outside. That is Oates and Atkinson building the last of the horse stalls on the north side of the hut – the winds mostly coming from the south at this spot – for the seventeen surviving ponies, which they have fitted out with a blubber stove designed by Atkinson. It really is most efficient, its main drawback being the smell of blubber, of course. But you learn to tolerate that. The stalls are roofed with canvas and rafters but the walls are made of bails of fodder and coal bricks, to be replaced by wood as they are used. I am worried about the state of the ponies, the poor brutes, but there could be no better man to look after them than Oates. He might be a person of few words, and those he does speak tend to be gloomy, but I don't know what we would have done without him.

We have one more motor-sledge to unload and then we shall plan the march south for the depoting, which must be completed by March. Then we will discover just how worthwhile horses, dogs and motor-sledges are.

Nobody speaks of him but we all wonder where Amundsen is. I think he must have landed at the Weddell Sea. I cannot see how he could do otherwise, with the pack the way it is. Still, I am determined the best way to treat him is to pretend he does not exist. We must not be panicked by what might be an imaginary rival. Nor must we compromise our science.

What madness this all seems sometimes. But what an adventure. I must finish now. Give my love to the boy.

Forty-six

Cape Evans, Antarctica, January 1911

Herbert Ponting was fussing with the bellows of his telephoto apparatus. He had discovered that the oil froze in the mechanism and so had drained it. Now it squeaked as he moved the mechanism.

Ahead of him was the ship, sitting hard up against the edge of the floe, held firm by the ice anchors, with men unloading the final batches of the stores and the last of the motor-sledges under the direction of Harry Pennell, the hard-working navigator who would take the ship back to New Zealand to overwinter. Scott had no desire to risk *Terra Nova* being iced in like *Discovery*.

Behind Ponting was a scene of improbable desolation and grandeur, the magnificent Mt Erebus and the sculptured vista of ice and rock that ran from it, down to their new home, the incongruous hut. To the south were the islands of the sound, encircled by ice, and beyond them peak after glorious snow-capped peak as far as the crystal-clear air allowed him to see. The sky was a rich royal blue, with just two banks of low cloud. Ponting had positioned himself close to the edge of the ice, but not too close. He had seen the black fins of killers breaking the water, racing up and down in their hunt for seal and penguin. He had no wish to be mistaken for a bipedal lunch again.

Scott was standing next him, talking away, but Ponting, concentrating on his focusing device, only caught one word in ten.

'And then I think yours will be a ten- or twelve-day photography expedition.'

'What?' asked Ponting, the mention of his own discipline finally getting through to him. His tongue was still thick from when he caught it on a metal flange of the camera in the ice pack. It had stuck fast and pulling away had ripped off the tip. He had filled three handkerchiefs with blood.

'To Cape Royds.'

'What about it?'

Scott looked annoyed for a second. He wasn't, Ponting knew, the most patient of men. Repetition galled him. 'My dear fellow, I was saying that there will be four parties. I will head south for the depoting, hoping to leave food and fuel as far south as eighty degrees. So I will be some time gone. Meanwhile, an Eastern party will be led by Campbell and five men. They will explore King Edward VII Land. A Western party with Taylor, Debenham, Taff Evans, Silas Wright and others, will explore the far side of this sound. Both expeditions will be taken by *Terra Nova* to a suitable landing site. And I have you, Lashly, Day and Nelson down for the photographic party to Cape Royds. There are some wonderful ice extrusions to be captured and more ice caverns.' Scott knew Ponting was very taken with the icicle-fringed ice cave he had found and used to frame *Terra Nova*. 'I have logged all this.'

Ponting adjusted his trademark tweed hat. 'And how are you referring to me in your log?'

Scott shrugged. 'Herbert Ponting, the well-known photographer.'

Ponting licked his lips and Scott flinched at the site of the damaged tongue. The tip was a lurid pink; it reminded him for a second of Peter's newborn complexion. 'You've seen my pictures so far?'

'Of course. The one in the ice cave in particular—'

Ponting didn't let him finish. 'Do they look like ordinary photographs to you, captain?'

'They are *extra*ordinary.' Scott glanced back at the ship. The motor-sledge was down on the ice and Day was fussing with its treads. Ropes were being attached to haul it over to join the others on solid land. The machines were temperamental still and it would take Day a number of hours to check the condition of the engine and fuel and cooling system on each before starting them. So it would be some time before they could join in the hauling.

The horses had proved the hardest workers when it came to shifting stores from ship to storage, thanks to Oates, with the dogs a poor second. They were out of condition, exhausted by the lightest load and driven mad by penguins, which came up to taunt them. It was as if the waddling birds could calculate to an inch the length of chain holding an animal, so that when it leapt to bite, it was pulled up a fraction short. It was torture for the huskies; it was tempting to think it was a form of cabaret for the penguins.

'So please, Camera Artist.'

'I beg your pardon?'

Ponting's moustache twitched. 'We have been over this. Not photographer. I don't work on a pier, a shilling a portrait. Camera Artist.'

For a second, Scott wished the killer whales had actually got the insufferable man. But he was right. They were no ordinary pictures. He still smiled when he thought of Atkinson's comments after the incident on the floe. 'What irony of fate to be eaten by a whale thinking one was a seal, only to be spat out because one was a mere photographer.' It might well have been that little dig which brought on his pique. 'Very well. Camera Artist it is.'

'Thank you. You know Cherry found one of my Jungfrau pictures in an old newspaper? Asked if he could keep it.'

Scott almost smiled. Cherry had shown him the clipping, remarking what a coincidence it was that Ponting's shot should be on the reverse of a beautiful one of actress Marie Lohr. It was Marie who was displayed next to his bunk, not the mountain, although Ponting clearly hadn't noticed yet. 'Yes. Got a good eye for composition, has Cherry.'

Over the few hundred yards that separated them from the ship came the chant of the eight men hauling. Overcoming the inertia of an empty motorised sledge was even more difficult than shifting a fully laden wooden one, and even that often required spine-snapping jerks. But the tracks were moving now and the voices rang out strongly over the white plain.

'Damn, this wasn't a very good spot to choose.'

Scott followed Ponting's gaze down to the ice. Water was bubbling up through tiny fissures, hissing as it came.

'It's rotten,' said Scott absent-mindedly. Then he remembered Tom Crean saying he had put a foot through the crumbling ice that morning and Lashly going up to his knees. 'Oh, no.'

'What is it?' asked Ponting.

But Scott was already running, his feet skidding as he tried to get purchase from the felt boots. 'Day! Watch out! Day!'

Bernard Day was on the machine, still examining the engine. Neither he nor the men hauling could hear him over their singing.

'Day, stop!'

The gunshot cracked and fled over the ice in all directions, causing even men within the hut to look up in shock.

Scott was still fifty yards away when the second sound reached him. A groan.

Day leapt off the machine just as one end jerked and tipped, like a horse going lame, and there came the slurp of liquefying ice. The tractor was floating on granular slush.

The song died in the men's throats. The eight of them turned and pulled the ropes taut, as if they could hold back tons of metal. There came the squeaking of ice sheets sliding over each other as the hole enlarged. The sound rose to a scream.

Day plunged in up to his waist and began scrabbling frantically at the crumbling fringes of his ice hole. Keohane also dropped into the sea, the shock driving all air from him.

'Let go!' said Scott, as heels were dug in to take the strain. 'It'll take you down with it.'

The front of the motor-sledge reared up and the tail hit the water. For a few seconds it lodged there, jammed. All held their

317

ROBERT RYAN

breath, as if a loud exhalation could cause it to shift. Scott had stopped running. He took a step forward on tiptoes. All might not be lost.

Then, almost silently, the great machine simply slid away into the opening, leaving only two large bubbles that burst from the green water. Scott imagined it sinking into the darkening depths, spinning as it went, lost in hundreds of black fathoms.

The men stood around, open mouthed, astonished that the ice had swallowed such a mighty machine the way the Orcas took their prey. Lashly and Keohane lay on the treacherous ice, steam rising from them as they shivered.

'Get those men to the hut,' Scott instructed.

'Aye, sir,' replied Petty Officer Evans.

'What a bloody disaster,' Scott said with feeling. Because Scott knew what it meant: from now on he would be relying on the ponies, the hardest workers. And that meant Captain Scott would need Captain Oates more than ever. And Titus wasn't convinced about the ponies' capabilities. Not one bit of it.

'A bloody disaster,' he repeated.

Forty-seven

London, 1911

Peter was naked that afternoon, as he often was. He loved to run around free and unencumbered and, to Kathleen, it seemed the most natural thing. Not everyone agreed. When he came to tea, Sir Clements Markham thought it inappropriate and Hannah, Con's mother, had scolded her on several occasions for under-dressing him when they went to feed the ducks in St James's Park. She blamed the influence of Isadora Duncan. Even Peter's nanny, she was sure, had doubts about the decorum of his wardrobe. Kathleen didn't care. Her main concern was that the little boy was happy. He had been so overjoyed to see her returned from the south, he had kissed her, before running off to get Con's picture and making her kiss that, too.

It was Bellamy, her houseman, who informed her that she had a visitor. She was taken aback when he told her the stranger's identity, and instructed him to make tea once the guest had been shown in.

'Professor Nansen,' she said as he swept in. 'How nice to see you.' Peter streaked from behind the curtains and gripped her leg. Nansen crouched down to Peter's level. 'Hello, young man. My goodness, but you look like your father.'

'Daddy not here.'

'No, I know, he is doing great things. Great things.'

'I shall call Nanny to dress him.'

'Why? He'll be wearing clothes for the rest of his life soon enough.'

She laughed at this. 'That's very true.'

'You know, my five were always running around like that. In the snow, even. He has nothing I haven't seen before.'

They sat and Kathleen felt unnerved by the direct gaze from the pale eyes.

'So, I have come for my sitting.'

'Your sitting?'

'You wanted to do my head.'

'Oh. Yes, I did.' The nerve of the man. As if she could drop everything. 'I will, one day, I am sure. Just now . . . I have a large commission. Charles Rolls. Of the motor car? He died in an airplane crash—'

'I am teasing you, Kathleen.'

'You are?' she said with relief.

'Yes. I am not here to be sculpted. Not today.'

'You had me worried. Between all the lunches with other wives and this commission and Peter and dealing with correspondence about the expedition, everything seems such a rush.' She put her hand to her throat, the thought of all the letters to be written to sponsors and well-wishers making her breathless.

'Forgive me,' said Nansen slowly, wondering what had happened to the woman he had met in Norway. Something had changed in her. The fire had dimmed somewhat. 'It was a poor joke. You won't have heard much from your husband.'

'Not yet.' She had heard a lot from debtors, his family and other Antarctic wives, who needed to cling together during the long months of silence from the south.

'I hope Tryggve is managing all right. You know he taught Queen Maud to ski?'

'He said.'

'I bet he did. He's young. He does like to boast now and then.' Ah, now he had the reason for her coolness. His nationality. A little improvisation was called for, perhaps. 'I have come to say I am embarrassed.'

'Really?'

'About Amundsen.'

'That was hardly your doing.'

'It was my ship. Had I known, I might not have loaned it. Or, at least, I would have said he must come out in the open.'

Kathleen wasn't sure what to say. She had been furious about it for so long, but now her anger had burned itself out.

'You know there are those in Norway who disapprove? Many people. There was a request for money to the government. It was refused. We all wish it had been done differently. But Roald, he is his own person. I just wanted to reassure you, we aren't all like that.'

'I have no doubt of it. Why are you in London? You're not returning as ambassador?' Nansen had spent two years at the Norwegian Embassy shortly after the country's independence.

'No. A lecture. At the Royal Geographical Society. About crossing Greenland. But it will be overshadowed by Amundsen, I am sure.'

The tea arrived and she sent Bellamy away. She enjoyed pouring; it also offered her a distraction from that unnerving gaze.

'And the voyage back?' he asked. 'How was it?'

'Oh, it had its diversions. There was a tiresome young man in Ceylon who fell in love with me.'

'I am not surprised.'

She reddened. 'Does it always happen in Ceylon, then?'

'No, I meant . . . You are teasing me now?' He roared with laughter and slapped his thigh.

She busied herself with the tea. 'Milk, sugar?'

'Black. No sugar. So, no other adventures?'

'I stopped off to see Isadora, Isadora Duncan, in Paris but she had just left for America. I went around my old haunts. But then I had this terrible urge to get back to Peter. As if something might happen if I didn't. Did you ever get that with your children?'

Now he understood. The fire hadn't dimmed, it was just redirected, towards a son and, perhaps, a man on the other side of the world. He was familiar with this feeling. 'Every day while I was on the ice. But I was in no position to do anything about it.' He hesitated, as if building up his nerve. 'Will you come? To my lecture?'

'This is Daddy.' Peter toddled over with a photograph of Con in uniform.

'I know. We are friends,' said Nansen, examining it.

'And Mummy?'

'I'd like to think so, yes.'

'Daddy away.'

'He is. I envy him.'

Kathleen, not sure what he envied, asked Peter to go and find Nanny. She took the framed photograph and set it on the table. 'When is it, the lecture?'

'Friday night. Then I thought we could have dinner.'

She shook her head. 'I promised Con and his mother I wouldn't get noticed. Having dinner with one of his rivals—'

'I am no rival!' he exploded.

'No, sorry.' She handed the tea across. 'But given the feeling here about Norway. You must appreciate, it could be difficult. As if I endorse what Amundsen has done.'

He gripped the saucer, making sure their fingers touched. 'I understand. But I am also talking in Paris. In Berlin. This waiting and brooding. It is no good for you. No good for anyone. It eats into your soul till you end up hating the ice for taking your lover away. And you should never hate it, whatever happens, it isn't its fault. So, there are other cities. Might you come to one of those? I promise you it will do you good.'

She hesitated. 'I wouldn't want to leave Peter again so soon. Not this time. Perhaps we could take tea again while you are in London.'

'I would like that. Now, I need some recommendations for the theatre while I am here.'

'You like the theatre?' She was surprised. It had taken several attempts to get Con to appreciate it. Her husband was a man fascinated by the minutiae of ocean currents and cloud formation but

322

bored by Ibsen. Obviously not all polar men were cut from the same cloth.

'I adore it. Is there a new Barrie or Shaw?'

'Shaw says he is working on something for next year. I can ask James for a recommendation. He is Peter's godfather, you know.'

'I didn't. How marvellous to have Peter Pan as your godfather. And if he recommends something, would you accompany me?'

She sighed, but there was no anger in it. 'You are very persistent, professor.'

'It is a trait of polar explorers. One your husband has in large measure.'

'I will see if Mr Barrie will come too.'

He mimed a long face for a second. 'I would be delighted to meet him.'

The talk of Con had caused her butterflies, the familiar fear, to return. She thought of him trudging through blizzards or huddled in a tiny tent, a dot in the vast whiteness. The passages in his account of *Discovery* sometimes came back to her, the casual mentions of the hunger, the cold and the frostbite, and she wondered how a man could go through it twice. Yet she'd encouraged him. Because, she told herself, it was what he needed, the only way to make him whole again. 'So where will Con be now?'

Nansen considered the date. It was not yet spring in London, which meant autumn in the South. 'He will be laying down food dumps on the ice barrier for his return trip. He will be training the animals. And the men. He will watch them all closely, see which one has it.'

'It?'

'The stamina, the mind strength to make it to the Pole. Not everyone can do it. He will be discovering that motor cars do not belong on the ice. And if he has any sense, he'll be thinking of you.'

Kathleen was simply not in the mood to be courted. There was something very pleasing about this man's directness, so very different from the preening and fawning of the boy in Ceylon.

But it always came back to Con. 'I should be giving Peter an afternoon nap.'

'Won't Nanny do that?'

'I like to put my son down myself. I even like to bathe him. I know, it is considered strange.'

'Not in Norway.' He placed the tea down and stood. 'I should not keep you from the lad. So, the lecture. On Friday. Can I at least have a "perhaps" to be going on with?'

She felt a pang of guilt as she said it but, nevertheless, the word slipped from her lips. 'Perhaps.'

'And the theatre.'

'Not this time. Please don't take offence.'

He leaned forward and took her hand. 'No, no, of course not. Tell me, can I write to you? Just while Captain Scott is away.'

'Yes. It would be nice to have a friend who knows what he is going through.'

He bent down and kissed the back of her hand. 'You certainly have that, Kathleen. And more.'

'A friend will do for now.'

Professor Fridtjof Nansen took his leave and, like all men in love, clung on to the slenderest thread of hope that his affection would be returned. '*For now*,' she had said. '*A friend will do for now.*'

And it would. For now.

Forty-eight

The Great Ice Barrier, February 1911

The sight of Atkinson's heel made Scott feel queasy. The young surgeon winced as Wilson slipped off his inner sock. It was crusted with blood. In the green-tinged half-light of the tent, the foot seemed rotten, like mouldering cheese. The top layers of skin had all come away and what was left was a pus-filled bag the size of a tennis ball.

'Oh dear,' said Wilson.

'When did this happen?' demanded Scott. They were barely days into the depoting trip. He had been forced to face up to the breakdown of the remaining motor-sledges, the poor condition of some of the ponies, and now this. 'Why didn't you say anything?'

'I thought I could walk through it.'

'How are the eyes?' asked Wilson.

'Better, thank you.' Atch had also suffered snow-blindness, thanks to badly positioned goggles, within forty-eight hours of leaving Cape Evans.

Scott's old temper bubbled to the surface. 'If you were a horse I'd have you shot.'

'If I were a horse I'd deserve it,' the young man replied, his voice tremulous and full of shame.

'You are a blithering idiot.' Scott gave a rueful laugh. 'Let this be a lesson. Bill, a word.'

They left the tent and stepped into the camp. Around them were the canvas triangles of the other tents and the humps of resting dogs. Oates and Gran were building a snow wall to keep the ponies out of a wind that hadn't yet arrived. It would, though. For the moment, the sun burned in a clear sky, glinting off the undulating surface of the ice, and the temperature see-sawed either side of freezing. It was a balmy day on the barrier, but that could be turned on its head within minutes. They had all discovered that the winds in Antarctica either blew fierce or gentle; there was no in-between, no moderation between off and on.

'Why do they do it? Why do they keep such things to themselves? Concealing their ailments?' Scott asked Wilson.

Wilson smiled. 'It's your fault, Con.'

'Me?'

'You set a high standard for yourself. They try to match it. Someone like Atch doesn't want to seem weak in front of you.'

'Well, he does now. There's one young man who has damaged his chances of the Pole next season.'

'He knows that, Con. That will be hurting more than his wound. They see how you value Birdie and Taff, strong lads who don't complain. They all want to be the same. Oates and Gran, look at them. Both feel the cold, you know, feel it hard. Never a complaint. As I say, you set a hard example to live up to.'

Scott grunted. 'I wish it were so.'

'It is. Look, each man here has one thing to worry about. His horse. His dogs. His stove. You, you have to worry about it all. I don't know how you keep it all in your head.'

'It leaks sometimes,' Scott said.

'You could have fooled me. What shall we do about Atch?'

Scott considered for a moment. The ponies were liability enough; he didn't need sick, crippled men. 'Crean! Tom Crean?'

Crean emerged from one of the tents. 'Sir.'

'Young Atkinson is not too well. Bad foot.'

'And a fever,' said Wilson.

'I need you to take him back to Hut Point and wait for *Terra*

Nova.' The ice between Hut Point and Cape Evans had gone, a fact disastrously revealed when Wilson had tried to return to the new hut to collect the snowshoes to fit on the horses. Despite Oates's doubts the plodder of a pony they called Weary Willie had performed well on them, but by then the disappearing ice meant it was too late to fetch some more. Scott had berated Oates for only bringing the single pair.

Crean looked disappointed. 'Sir.'

'Don't worry, no reflection on you, Tom. I just need a good ice man to make sure he gets back.'

'Sir. Thank you. When?'

'In a while,' said Wilson. 'I'm worried about the suppuration on Atch's foot. We don't want blood poisoning. I'd best go and lance it. We'll see how it is then. After it's drained of pus.'

Scott grimaced. 'You won't mind if I take a back seat for that.'

He watched Oates lead one of the ponies towards the snow wall, and saw how its hoofs cracked through the soft ice crust. Each high step was three times the effort of walking on the flat. The equine snowshoes would have been ideal. Now he had no shoes and a sulking Oates.

The dogs, on the other hand, despite their usual viciousness, had been performing well. Cherry, in particular, said he thought sledging with dogs – at least as a passenger – great fun. Gran guided Weary Willie over to the shelter, and he certainly lived up to his name, shuffling, then stumbling through the snow. It was agony watching a horse up to its belly in the snow trying to pull itself free, as had happened on the slopes to the barrier. It would happen again, too, when they hit the deeper drifts between the pressure waves out on the barrier proper.

Guts was led over the ice crust with the snowshoes on. He slithered a little, but remained on the surface without plunging through. 'The miracle of the snowshoe,' Scott shouted across. Oates ignored him. Well, nobody liked to be proved wrong.

Scott crouched and examined the icy surface. It was slippery from the sun beaming on it. He pressed and his hand sank several inches with ease. 'Tom.'

'Sir.'

'Pass the word, will you? This is too soft for the horses by day. We'll switch to night marching. We leave at midnight.'

'The noise will drive me insane,' said Oates, as the canvas of the tent cracked and whipped. 'I should go and look at the ponies.'

'There is nothing you can do,' said Gran.

'It's poor out there,' said Bowers. 'I'd best go.'

All three men were in their sleeping bags, their faces illuminated by a storm lamp. The tent's material lent them all a greenish sheen, which Oates found oddly comforting, as if they were hiding in the hedges of Gestingthorpe's maze. They had been taunted and prodded by the tail-end of storms, but the first proper Antarctic blizzard caught them at Corner Camp, the point at which they had avoided the disturbances caused by the ice pressing against White Island and could move south. Except they couldn't move anywhere in the current white-out conditions. All they could do was hibernate in their green cocoons.

'I'll go,' said Oates.

Bowers put a hand on him. 'Last time your nose nearly dropped off. Now me, I'd be pretty glad if this one fell off.'

They all knew, though, that Birdie Bowers had an incredibly high tolerance for the cold. Where other men's skin would blacken and blister, his remained ruddy and fresh. Bowers levered himself out of his bag and pulled on his outer clothing. Oates helped him tie the puttees that closed the bottom of the trousers.

'Have you seen the dogs?' Oates shouted over the roar of the wind.

'No.' Gran had tried to go outside in the blizzard and discovered what everyone had warned him about. The noise, the stinging ice, the buffeting winds of forty or more miles per hour, temperatures dancing around minus thirty or forty, meant you were lost in a whirlwind of pain and disorientation within six paces.

'The bloody animals are snug in burrows. They are treating this as a rest. As should we, I suppose.'

'Is it right we should just sit here?' asked Gran.

'There's no way even those skis of yours'll work out there, Mr Gran,' said Bowers.

'It is very confusing,' said Gran. 'I thought I was here to show skiing, but the captain doesn't seem interested now. He can't seem to decide, horses, dogs, men, skis.'

'I think the Owner should consult the senior men more than he has so far,' mused Oates. 'If he keeps us in the dark about his plans, he'll run into trouble on the way to the Pole.'

Bowers made a disapproving grunt. He was too embarrassed to look at them directly, so he spoke to his mittens and his helmet as he put them on. 'I think the Owner is a fine man. He knows what he is doing. There can only be one leader. Nine is eight too many. Loyalty is what we need now. There is nothing I wouldn't do for him. I think he is just splendid.'

He undid the ties that secured the short entry tunnel and the storm entered, carrying giant flakes that fluttered around like deranged moths. Bowers was out in a second, before the temperature could drop too much, and they retied the flap. They heard his faint voice. 'I'll try and get them to eat. And there's—' But the rest of it was drowned in the howling.

'I think we upset him,' said Gran.

'That's the Navy for you,' replied Oates. But they were unsettled by the uncharacteristic outburst by a junior officer. They fell silent. Oates struggled with his biography of Napoleon and Gran composed verses that he hoped Cherry would accept for the expedition's re-launched *South Polar Times*.

Oates's stomach began to grumble and cramp. He would soon have to decide whether he could risk going outside to defecate or risk his dignity by trying to perform his duties in the tent. It was not an attractive choice.

'Titus?'

'Yes?'

'Atch was lucky, wasn't he? If that happened further out on the ice and he couldn't walk . . .'

'Hmm,' muttered Oates.

'What do you think should be done if a man is a danger to his party?'

Oates looked up. 'Done?'

'Yes. One man is sick, and threatens the lives of the others.'

Oates didn't hesitate. 'A pistol should be carried. The wounded soul should be given the opportunity to help his comrades. That's what we did in the cavalry.'

'I don't doubt it,' replied Gran glumly.

'I have to go outside,' said Oates, clutching his stomach.

'I'll turn my back if you'd rather.'

'No.'

Oates had just struggled to his knees when Bowers returned, looking grim. He had bad news to deliver through his frozen lips. One of the horses was dead.

After they had negotiated ridges of snow fifteen or twenty feet high, they had laid another depot at Bluff Camp, which meant Gran had made it further south than any other Norwegian. He thought it best not to make too much of the fact. They struck camp at midnight, their departure signalled by two sharp blasts from Scott's whistle, and battled through a heavy snow fall, the ponies once more struggling up to their bellies. As usual, the horse caravan departed first, with the dogs, which made better progress, setting off later, so that they all reached the next camp at the same time.

Scott was leading Nobby, Bowers had Uncle Bill, named after Wilson because of his placid temperament, Oates Punch, Cherry led Guts, and Gran slogged on with Weary Willie. Three other ponies had been sent back, thin scarecrows that could scarcely manage to drag two hundred pounds apiece. Oates had argued that Blossom, Jimmy Pigg and Blücher were so weak that they might not even make it home, but Scott had sent Teddy Evans, PO Keohane and Forde with them.

Gran quickly found himself falling behind. Weary Willie was plodding on gamely, but he had the heaviest load on the eight-foot sledge and it seemed to stick with alarming frequency, so he was forced to drive the horse on to free it.

Willie was snorting and coughing as they went and, despite the weakness of the low sun, he began to sweat. The sweat would freeze on his coat as soon as he stopped, making the poor animal even more miserable.

Gran, skiing ahead of the animal, began to sing to him, in English, the verses he had written:

> Night has come – the distant mountains
> Have lost their golden fairy glance.
> The Barrier lies cold and endless,
> The wind is sighing in the South.

Gran could see the others ahead, small black marks bobbing up and down like spray of moving ink globules against the whiteness.

> Camp is broken – muffled figures
> Bending, faces homewards turned.
> Skis are moving, creaking, sliding,
> The wind is singing in the South.

He turned to see how Willie was enjoying the song, but he was fifty metres back, had stopped dead still, and was half buried in the white, his sledge stuck fast.

'Oh, was it that bad?'

He shushed over and, reluctantly, smacked the rear of the animal with a ski pole. The horse stumbled forward and he did it twice more and the sledge squeaked free, moving ahead again. It was like swimming through talcum powder. He tried to sing once more but Willie made wheezing noises loud enough to disturb his rhythm. 'Wonderful. My horse is a music critic.'

He gripped Willie's lead and skied alongside the animal. The depth of the snow lessened and they began to make good time, with Gran slipping into an easy, repetitive motion. His mind went into a kind of reverie then. He knew it was possible to dream as you poled along, as he did when cross-country skiing through the

331

forests at home. He often imagined himself in Norway, in spring, in a garden full of flowers and heady scents. There were cherry trees, the petals falling like the Antarctic snow, carpeting the lawn. It was a shock to fall out of the vision and find the petals had become a sea of ice.

He checked on Willie, still plunging into the small drifts with admirable grit. His eyes, though, seemed duller than usual. Gran tapped his flanks with his pole, but he didn't react, just thumped on in steam clouds of heavy breathing, gaze fixed on nothing, like the pictures you saw of soldiers after battle. Gran wondered what horses dreamed of when they were in such a state. Green pastures and firm going, perhaps.

His stomach was rumbling by the time he saw the distant signs of a bivouac. Scott and the others had halted for food. He redoubled his efforts, but the distance refused to shrink. It was another trick of the light, the telescoping of distance that plagued men on the ice barrier. Then a haze of ice crystals blew over and obscured the vision altogether. One mile or five to go? He couldn't tell.

Willie began to make strange blowing sounds and there was foam flecked around his mouth. Gran swore he felt the whole ice barrier shake as the sorry animal keeled over and thumped into the snow.

'Come on, boy, no time to lie down.'

But as far as Willie was concerned, that was exactly what it was. Gran peered south, but the infuriating haze was still there. It could be that Scott's encampment, where Oates, Bowers and the others also waited, was no more than half a mile hence. 'Hulllooo!' he shouted, but his voice seemed to hang in nothingness.

He turned again and put his arms under Willie's head. The steaming horse breath smelled disgusting, as if something had died in the nostrils.

'Come on, lad. Just one more effort.'

Gran heaved, and tugged and prodded with his ski poles, but the horse still lay in the snow, hardly moving.

That's when he heard the snap of a whip, coming from the north, and the swish of well-oiled runners being tugged by a speeding dog pack. It would be Dimitri or Meares.

Gran pulled away from the fallen animal and then raised his sticks. 'Hey!'

It was Cecil Meares. The driver pulled the dogs around and jumped off the sledge to free the animals. He thought it was the camp.

'No. Not here.'

Behind him Willie let out a long, nervous neigh.

The lead dog's ears pricked.

'Meares. No.'

Free from their traces the animals raced over, yapping and snarling. Gran skied into their path, but they bowled him aside. Their teeth were bared and their eyes blazing. The wolves within had taken over.

'Cecil, I have a horse down.'

Willie let out a hideous noise as the first dog buried itself in its belly. He began to thrash with his legs, catching one of them a good blow. It rolled away, shook its head, and rejoined the fray. There came the sound of tearing flesh and yelps of pleasure and greed.

Gran was behind them now, his skis cast aside, and he was laying into the huskies with his poles. He hit with such force one stick snapped, but the crazed dogs were lost in their frenzy, oblivious of pain.

Flowers of blood began to speck the ice and Willie raised his head and wailed in agony.

Meares was beside him now, shouting at the dogs in Russian, the only language the beasts responded to, grabbing them by their manes and flinging them over his shoulders. He began to swing his iron braking pole between the thirteen dogs and there came the sound of metal on bone. Some of them slunk away, dazed. Gran managed to position himself between dogs and horse and had his own finnesko boot torn by sharp teeth for his trouble.

'Up, up, Willie, please,' Gran pleaded.

Trailing strings of red flesh, Willie staggered to his feet. The dogs circled, furious at being denied. There was a sharp snap followed by a boom, and their ears went back. From the south came Scott and Oates, the Owner brandishing a pistol, which he fired again.

'Good Lord,' he said when he saw the garish splatters of blood staining the snow.

Oates swerved to the shivering horse, pulled off a mitten and ducked underneath the body, feeling the belly, while Willie stood panting. He mumbled comforting words as he did so.

He straightened and put on his glove once more. 'Those bastards,' he said, looking at the animals as Meares harnessed them. 'He's torn but it hasn't penetrated far. I'll treat it and bandage it at camp.' He undid some of the straps holding Willie's load and began to stack the cases in the snow. 'Leave this. I'll fetch it with Nobby later.'

'Thank you,' said Scott. 'I should never have let Willie fall behind like that. It's my fault.'

Like the others, he looked at the excavation, a swirl of depressions and trenches, mounds and ridges marking the fight. It was like a casting for a sculpture. He was sure Kathleen would find it wondrous, a three-dimensional record of turmoil, beauty out of horror. But, of course, there had been genuine terror, for man and beast. 'Are you all right, Gran?'

The Norwegian examined his leg. His boot would need repairing, but that was all. 'Yes. No damage.'

'Very good.'

Gran couldn't help thinking Scott would have been more sympathetic to one of his own men. Englishmen.

Soldier was leading Willie away, his steps marked by the spatter of blood pitting the snow crust, but Gran stopped him. 'Can I take him into camp? I shall make him some warm bran.'

'Good idea,' said Oates. 'There's a nice, tight snow wall, too.' He fell in beside the Norwegian and waited till Scott was out of earshot to speak again. 'Another lesson, Trigger.'

'What?'

'Dogs and horses don't mix.'

The pallid sun had a 'bow' around it, a glowing decoration they all knew meant bad weather ahead. The men, horses and dogs had reached seventy-nine degrees and twenty-eight and a half minutes.

The temperature was dipping to minus twenty-five and intermittent storms were plaguing them. The ponies looked terrible, bony and lifeless. The men had suffered too. Even Bowers had found his ears so cold he had exchanged the foolish green hat he favoured for something more protective. Gran had completely frozen his hands while preparing lunch and Oates had suffered frost-nipped fingers when he fed the horses.

The dogs, meanwhile, seemed to thrive on steel-springed legs. Despite being whippet-thin, their resilience surprised everyone, although their social habits, from eating their own excrement to attacking each other whenever the opportunity arose, were tiresome.

Scott decided they would depot at that point, before another blizzard took them. Oates and Gran were behind the snow wall, which protected them from the drifting surface snow. Gran was feeding the animals, while Oates changed Weary Willie's dressings, when Scott appeared to break the news of the change of depoting location. Oates was telling his favourite joke.

'So, the young lady is late for dinner and she explains to her host that the horse was to blame. That the coachman had quite a time with him. "Perhaps he was a jibber," the host says. "Oh no, he was a bugger," says the young lady. "I heard the coachman say so several times."'

Oates laughed and Gran looked puzzled. 'What's a jibber?'

'It's a . . . ah.' He caught sight of Scott. 'Hello, skipper.'

'Hello, gentlemen. I have some news.' He carefully laid out his plans. They were to deposit 2,1118 lb of stores at that very spot. Butter, fuel, biscuits, oats, fodder, sledges, skis, everything a party might need upon their return from the Pole.

'The animals are about done in, I see. They'll be glad to turn,' he said. 'You, too, no doubt.'

Oates wiped the snow blowing off the wall from his eyes. 'We are still some miles short of eighty degrees, are we not?'

'Yes. About thirty-one miles.'

'Then I say we push on, sir.'

Scott frowned. 'And you think these ponies are capable of that?'

'Yes, sir.'

Gran, knowing what Oates was considering, said: 'But not on getting back.'

Oates shot him a harsh look. Titus spoke, as he often did when trying to make a point, with great deliberateness. 'No. They wouldn't make the return. We'd have to kill them and depot them. But it would be good food for next season further out on the barrier.'

Scott looked shocked. 'My dear fellow, after bringing them all this way? I thought you cared for these ponies, Oates.'

'I do. I can't put them through the misery of a slow death on their return as well. They've suffered enough. We should get them as far as we can and kill them humanely. There will be pony meat then for the dogs and sledgers on the polar journey.'

'I have to say, Oates, you have a strange idea of animal welfare. We'll make One Ton Camp here.'

Oates spoke carefully, without emotion. 'Sir. I am afraid you'll come to regret not taking my advice.'

Scott bristled so much, snow spun off his Burberry. 'Regret or not, my decision is made. As a Christian gentleman.'

Oates bit his tongue, unable to see exactly what Christianity had to do with it. 'Very well.'

'I shall return with the dogs. So will Wilson, Meares, Cherry and Wilson. You, Bowers and Gran here will lead the ponies back. We will all rendezvous at Safety Camp. Can you manage that?'

'Sir.'

Scott turned to go. He had walked a few paces before he turned. 'Oh, and Oates.'

'Yes, skipper?'

'The tip of your nose is quite white. If you aren't careful you'll lose it.'

While Oates frantically rubbed at his face, he spoke through the moving fur of the mitten. 'I bet you a lunchtime biscuit the horses don't all make it back,' he said to Gran once Scott had left.

'Only if you swear it is one bet you are happy to lose.'

'Oh, yes,' said Oates, looking at the bags of bones he had to nurse home. 'I'd try my damndest to make sure you take the biscuit, Trigger.'

Forty-nine

Safety Camp, Great Ice Barrier, March 1911

Oates watched Weary Willie expire with a long, last shudder. He
had wanted to put him down, but Scott insisted they should nurse
him. Scott built a snow wall and tenderly fed the dying animal hot
mash. It was a night-long vigil, torture for man and beast. Several
times Oates considered slitting the animal's throat and hanging the
consequences, but Scott fussed over the pony like a nursemaid.
Oates, meanwhile, tried to keep Jimmy Pigg's strength up. The
second pony was also tired, emaciated and cold; a shivering Oates
was beginning to understand just what that felt like.

Meanwhile Meares and Wilson had set off with the dogs, aiming
to cross the four miles of sea ice for Hut Point, the old *Discovery*
base. Following in their tracks were Cherry, Bowers and Crean,
with the remaining horses. Gran had been sent to Corner Camp
to find Teddy Evans to tell him they were all rendezvousing at the
old 1902 expedition hut.

When Willie had breathed his last, Scott turned to Oates. 'It
looks as if you were right, Soldier.'

Oates said nothing. He could tell how much effort the apology –
if that was what it was – had cost the Owner. Oates felt no victory.
Yes, they should have killed and depoted the horses at eighty
degrees. Now Weary Willie would be tipped into the water and
wasted.

'We should get some sleep, Titus. You look done in. I imagine I do, too.'

Soldier nodded and moved mechanically towards the tent.

Oates had barely climbed into his bag and closed his eyes when he heard the yelling. Scott didn't need to shake him awake, but it was some minutes before he was dressed and out of the tent.

It was Crean, beaten and drawn, the big man almost in tears. His swollen eyes showed signs of snow-blindness. 'Dropped my goggles,' he explained. 'Can't see too well.'

'What's happened?' asked Oates.

Crean answered with a mumble, and Oates only caught the words 'ice' and 'floe'.

'It's Bowers. And Cherry,' said Scott, his voice loaded with fright.

'What?' Oates demanded. 'Where are they?'

'They are out on the sea ice,' Crean said. 'It's breaking up. Woke up and we'd drifted off from the shore. I had to jump from floe to floe to get here. They are still out there.'

'On the ice?' Oates asked.

Crean nodded. 'Floating offshore.'

Oates picked up whatever he thought he might need from the sledges, including ropes and ice picks. Scott grabbed provisions and more ropes. All their tiredness and frost-nip was forgotten.

As they set off for the forced march to the barrier edge, Oates asked Crean: 'The horses?'

'Guts has gone, sir.'

'Gone?' Oates repeated.

'In the night. No sign. The others are out there with them. Drifting into the Ross Sea.'

'And Wilson and Meares?' asked Scott.

'They made a faster time with the dogs and veered off south. They made landfall at The Gap. They'll get to the hut all right. But we'd best hurry if we are to save the others.'

They trudged north, with the wind against their backs, and as they closed on the barrier they could hear the familiar split and splash of bergs calving into the water. When they reached the cliff edge, an astonishing sight greeted them. Water. Miles of slab ice, dissected by wide channels and great lakes, some covered with frost mist. The floes looked like misshapen lilies on an enormous pond. The whole of the ice barrier was dis-integrating.

Worse, the sea between the floes and bergs was brash ice that was churning and rolling, like a pot brought to the boil. The glossy black triangles told them what was causing the disturbance. Killer whales. One of them broke free of the sludgy surface with a terrible blowing roar and Oates could see a long torpedo shape in the mouth. A leopard seal, still squirming as the jaws closed on it.

'Good grief, Crean,' said Scott. 'Were those brutes there when you left?'

The sailor managed a grin. 'Oh, aye, sir. Kept me jumping pretty well.'

'I see them!' said Oates.

The floe containing the tent, men and horses had drifted east and south and was nudging the bottom of the cliff. Bowers and Cherry were waving their arms, and their faint voices carried over the waters. Standing next to their tent were the three ponies, teth-ered to a line driven into the ice from the tent apex.

'Crean, stay here,' ordered Scott.

'Sir—' he began to object.

'We'll need someone to lower us down and pull us up,' said Oates, handing him a length of rope. 'Unless you want to play whale hopscotch again.'

'I will if need be, Captain Oates.'

Oates smiled. 'We know that, Tom. We need you here.'

'Sir.'

Within a few hundred yards, however, they found a spot where the ice cliff sloped down to a few feet high. The three scrambled down to the narrow littoral ice shelf at the base of the escarpment and moved along towards the men and their floe, which was no more than thirty yards across, and spinning. There were other ice blocks around it, and the pattern kept shifting as watery canals opened and closed. It was like a volatile, living jigsaw, where the pieces never quite fitted together. The sudden hissing exhalations told them the opportunist whales were still on patrol between the fragments.

'Am I glad to see you,' shouted Scott.

'Indeed, sir,' yelled Cherry in reply. 'We can't get the horses to jump across.'

'Never mind the horses, it's you I want,' said Scott.

Aware of the ice creaking beneath their feet, the three would-be rescuers moved along the shoreline so that they were level with the stranded men and ponies. Oates tied his ice axe to the end of the spare rope and threw it across. Bowers caught it and smashed it on to the ice surface. Scott, Crean and Oates heaved on the rope, but the floe refused to move any closer.

An hour passed before the lazily spinning floe finally came within leaping distance of the shore. By this time Oates's and Scott's feet were soaked through from the constant dip of melting ice. Oates could no longer feel his toes.

'Use the sledges as a bridge,' said Oates. 'And crawl across.'

'What about the horses?' Cherry said.

'I'll come out and talk them across.' If I can, Oates added silently.

Bowers lifted one of the sleds and flung it over the gap. Scott put his weight on the front runners and Cherry passed supplies over, till the most valuable provisions had been saved. Then he scampered across.

'Come on, Birdie!' Oates yelled.

'I'll stay here and help you with the horses.'

'Get off there.'

Bowers shook his head. He wasn't abandoning the animals. 'You come across, Farmer Hayseed.'

Oates crawled over the sledge bridge on all fours and dropped on to the floe. The surface was covered with an inch of water, and very slippery.

'Right, let's try Punch first,' said Oates, untying him from the tether. He tried not to look out to sea, where solid land seemed so far away and the water still teemed with predators.

Bowers took the horse's lead and looked across at Scott and Cherry. 'Eyes ahead, now, boy.'

He sprinted forward as fast as his short legs would carry him, rushing up to the edge, ready to spring, hoping the momentum would carry Punch over. The horse made three giant strides and then faltered. He skidded to a halt, and Bowers only just managed to stop. As he did so, the floe tipped. Bowers leapt backwards, his finnesko slithering. He managed to find a purchase, but poor Punch slid into the black water between land and ice.

Cherry let out a scream of warning and Oates turned in time to see a yellow and black face leering from the water at him. Close to, the white patches on the whale's body were the colour of nicotine, but the teeth gleamed bright enough.

Titus stumbled backwards and he felt the floe rock as the animal moved underneath.

Bowers was lying on his stomach, Punch's reins in one hand, the horse's head on the ice, the body swallowed by the black water. He was exhorting him to get back on.

Scott and Cherry watched helplessly as the disturbed floe began to drift away from the shore, widening the gap between the men and safety.

Oates moved to Bowers's shoulder. Together they heaved on the animal, hoping it could get its forelegs on to the ice. Hoofs thrashed ineffectually at the water. Oates felt a muscle rip in his shoulder. Punch was just too heavy, awkward and terrified.

A slick black shape broke the surface and a deadeye gave them the once-over, or so it seemed.

They felt a snag on the animal, as if someone had pulled his tail. The horse made no sound at first as his hind leg was severed. Dark blood bubbled up into the water, but Punch gave only a pathetic whinny.

Oates felt his stomach turn. 'Jesus.'

Another fin appeared and Oates released his grip and scrabbled over the ice to find his ice pick.

'What are you doing?' asked Bowers.

The poor pony's head went back, and the lips bared, showing the huge teeth. Now the noise pierced the hearts of the onlookers, a mix of unimaginable terror and pain. Only Bowers's enormous strength was keeping the head above water as Punch began to struggle.

'Shall I let him go?'

'No,' said Oates. 'They won't have him.'

The glossy black skin appeared again, water streaming off the sides. Oates pulled his arm back and brought the pointed blade of the axe down on Punch's skull. The pitiful whinnying stopped at once, replaced by a slow hissing sound as the horse went limp.

'Let him go now.'

Bowers did so and the heavy head smacked on to the ice, leaving a trail of blood, before the animal slumped into the water. At once, several of the fins circling the ice disappeared.

'Oh my Lord,' said Bowers shakily.

Oates was already with the remaining animals, trying to calm them. They were Nobby and Uncle Bill. They were remarkably calm, their panic transmitted only as a shiver through the flanks and fast breathing.

Oates looked across at the shrunken figures of Cherry, Scott and Crean and groaned. Their floe had moved further out to sea. 'We can't make the shoreline.'

'Save yourselves,' shouted Scott from the bottom of the ice cliff.

'We lose the ponies, we lose the Pole,' said Bowers.

Oates said nothing in reply. He wasn't thinking about the Pole; he was simply certain he didn't want to abandon the animals to the whales. The thought of them slowly descending to the waiting jaws was too much.

Water began to slosh over the edges of the shrinking oval of frozen water they were standing on. It was sinking.

'Come on, you two.' It was Cherry.

'Think we can get them over to that floe?' Oates asked, pointing to a neighbouring slab.

'Possibly.'

'Like Crean. Playing hopscotch. On to that one. Then the next and on to the barrier. What do you think?'

The water was up to their ankles. 'Worth a try,' said Bowers. 'I'll go first.'

Bowers untied Nobby, backed him up to the far edge and rushed forward. As he did so, an ominous fin appeared in the gap. Oates felt the ice shift beneath them, but Bowers didn't hesitate. He launched himself into thin air, stumpy legs windmilling and the pony followed. Both landed with a jarring thump on the adjacent floe.

Oates followed immediately before man or beast had time to think too hard about what they were doing. His boots scrabbled for grip and he felt a sharp pain up his leg, all the way to his old war wound. His feet slithered, went from under him, and his shoulder hit the ice with a dull crack.

'Come on, Farmer. No time for lying down.'

As Oates struggled to his feet, Bowers took Nobby across to the final floe, the one but a short step from the shore. Oates applauded, but as he took a step forward his leg buckled. Pain flashed up his thigh and into his hip. 'Oh damn,' he said. 'Not now.' He felt his leg give way again and he sat down on the ice.

Bowers, though, had jumped Nobby to the waiting Scott and Cherry and leapt back. Now, with effortless agility, his short legs pumping as he launched himself into the air, he came across to his fallen comrade. He put an arm round Oates. 'You all right there, Farmer?'

'Just my ankle,' Oates lied.

'I'll take Bill. Think you can make it over?'

'Sure I can.'

With his new-found confidence, Bowers grabbed hold of Uncle Bill's rein, lined up his jump and, screaming encouragement, sprinted forward. Bill slithered slightly as he got underway, losing momentum and, perhaps sensing he had compromised his speed, tried to stop. The hoofs locked but it was too late for him. Bowers tried to catch the skidding horse but even his formidable power was not enough. He was flicked aside like a skittle and Uncle Bill went into the freezing sea with a loud splash.

'Oh no!' shouted Oates.

Bowers executed a two-footed jump on to the other floe and

dropped prone. Oates, watching the sea, saw the swerve of a fin break the oily water.

'Birdie.'

'I can get him up.'

'Birdie.'

Bowers looked up at him. 'You'll have to do it.'

'Do what?'

Oates tossed the axe over. Bowers reached up and plucked it from the sky. 'I can't.'

'They'll have him.'

'I can't.'

'I can't watch him being eaten. Neither can you.'

Bowers began to cry, his tears turning to steam.

A grinning head appeared at the edge of the ice and Oates began to shriek and wave his arms. The creature blew a fine spray of water and submerged.

'Where?' asked Bowers.

'Put your glove on its skull. That's it. No, go left.'

'Here?' His voice was shaking.

'No. Up.'

'Here.'

'Yes. Hard as you can. Got to get through bone.'

'Oh God, oh God, oh God.'

The whale surfaced inches from Old Bill, the mouth gaping in anticipation, looking as if it would sever the animal at the neck. Bowers yelled at it, his face purple, turned, and struck home. The late sun glinted on the metal as it splintered its way into the brain. Bowers left it where it was as Uncle Bill joined his companions in the water.

The Owner was shouting from the base of the cliff. Oates stood watching the agitated water. It was as if propellers had started to turn. Particles of flesh began to bob to the surface.

There was more hollering from the shoreline.

Oates looked up at the men waving at him. Next to them was Nobby, the sole surviving pony from the floes. In all, only two horses remained, Nobby and Jimmy Pigg, back at camp. They should have marched them on and given them a dignified death at eighty-two degrees. Now, all that flesh was wasted, sacrificed to feed the greedy cetaceans.

Fizzing with anger at the profligacy, Oates found himself reaching back to the language of the cavalry barrack room. 'Fuck you, Captain Scott,' he muttered under his frozen breath. 'Fuck you.'

Fifty

Letter from Captain Oates to His Mother, March 1911

Dear Carrie,

We are at Hut Point and, I must say, feeling very glum. We have lost a lot of the horses, through no fault of mine, I hasten to add. Now, we are cut off from our base at Cape Evans by the lack of sea ice. Scott says with the gales and low temperatures it can't be long before it reappears.

So we share these old quarters – Scott, Wilson, Meares, Bowers, Cherry, Evans and Atkinson, and now we have Taylor and his party of Debenham, Wright and Taff Evans. Sixteen in all. It is what you might call cosy. And all we have to read is my Napoleon book – which has proved very popular – and a stack of *Girl's Own Paper*. We can't quite decide how they got here and, of course, nobody is owning up. There is also a *Times Atlas*, a *Who's Who* – how useful to have out on the ice – and Cherry carefully thawed out a copy of Stanley Weyman's *My Lady Rotha* left by another party. The end is missing but Cherry says this adds to

347

the excitement. There will be a competition to see who can come up with the best climax. Wilson sketches in his Windsor & Newton. Others practise their knots. As you can tell, these are exciting days.

We have plenty of seal to eat and a blubber stove: warm but greasy. Every man has a black face. Killing seals is a gruesome business, but nothing is wasted apart from the entrails. We take turns to cook. I think Debenham and Meares are the best, but they always say good things about my hoosh. Some of the others, however, who fancy themselves as cooks, rather mess up the meals by trying to produce something original.

But there is worse than the overcrowding. The *Terra Nova* had sailed west to find a place to land Victor Campbell's party. They found a spot. Already taken! The Norskies are there. Amundsen has set up his base on a piece of ice at the Bay of Whales. Just where we couldn't get through to. Campbell says it is precarious but Amundsen insisted to him that it was anchored tight to some hidden land. The Norwegian offered them a spot to set up base, but Campbell refused.

Scott is very down in the dumps. Terribly impatient to get back to Cape Evans, but there is no way by land. Cherry says it is twelve or thirteen miles, Cape Evans to Hut Point. It might just as well be a thousand while we are at the mercy of the sea. The Owner snaps at poor Gran whenever he comes near. He expected Amundsen to be at the Weddell Sea. Just in case all this is very hard to understand, I shall scribble you a rough map of our situation.

We need to head north from Hut Point to Cape Evans. Sorry, my mapmaking is no better than my arithmetic.

The point is, the main reason for gloom is that the Norwegians are a whole degree nearer the pole, around sixty miles. And

348

Amundsen has a hundred or more dogs and, so Gran says, very hard men with him. While we are very young. Although Cherry thought we should go to the Bay of Whales with guns and have it out with the Norskies once and for all. Gran went quite pale at the thought. His worst nightmare – a war between England and Norway and him having to choose sides!

I keep thinking, though, we have a few sad ponies, no motor-sledges and not enough dogs. Perhaps our best course would be to ambush them.

Two days later.

There are signs that the sea ice is re-forming. Good news. It is ridiculous to be marooned here.

I despair of Scott's planning. But then I often do and, as Bill Wilson says often enough, things usually turn out better than expected. He believes minor mishaps and mistakes come together in God's great plan. And the Owner performed marvellously on the return, says Cherry, rescuing dogs from a crevasse that Meares said he would think twice about going down. Ninety-foot descent, tied to a rope in a hole in the ice, to a precarious snow bridge where the dogs were trapped. Then he hauled them up. There is nothing wrong with his guts. That is why men like Crean and Bowers are so loyal.

You must forgive some of the snaps and snarls from me in my letters. I am just like one of the dogs. One writes to let off steam. You must not worry. When a man is having a hard time, he says hard things about other people which he would regret afterwards. I suffer, as my old colonel once said, from being easily unimpressed.

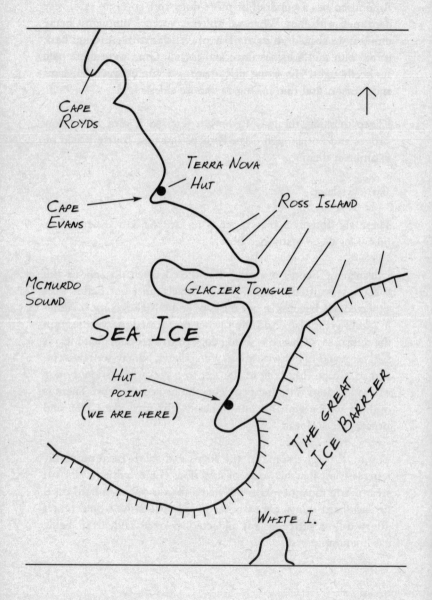

CAPE ROYDS

TERRA NOVA HUT

CAPE EVANS

ROSS ISLAND

MCMURDO SOUND

GLACIER TONGUE

SEA ICE

HUT POINT (WE ARE HERE)

THE GREAT ICE BARRIER

WHITE I.

As soon as the sea freezes – which can't be long, we hear the crack and groan of it forming at night – then we can get back to the others at Cape Evans, feed up the horses and settle down for the winter. Things will seem better when the sun comes back next season, I am sure. Love to Bryan and the girls.

Your loving son,

Laurie

Fifty-one

Cape Evans, May 1911

The sun had been gone for weeks and the *Terra Nova* even longer. Oates busied himself with the horses, making sure that each man gave his assigned pony sufficient exercise – three times a day unless there was a blizzard – and enough food. Despite initial grumbling, the men soon bonded with their charges and he had to nag less and less. Crean became very attached to Bones and Taff to Satchel; both spent more than the required time in the stables with their pony.

He improvised acetylene lighting and a heating system for the stables and, eventually, he and Cecil Meares all but moved in. Oates had fashioned himself a thick balaclava and gloves that just left his fingertips free. With a thick cable-knit sweater and two layers of underwear beneath his tatty trousers, he was, to begin with at least, warm enough in the stables, no matter what the weather.

As the winter gripped harder and the temperatures fell, he had improved on Atkinson's blubber stove, altering the air circulation so that it burned more efficiently. A newly designed fine mesh screen above the flames caught most of the greasy particulates. He could do nothing about the smell, however. Blubber was blubber.

Meares began to spend more time in the stables, ostensibly so he could look after the dogs more easily. He also found Oates's company easier than the sometimes rowdy and confrontational atmosphere in the hut. Teddy Evans and Griffith Taylor only seemed to be happy if there was a topic to argue about or expound upon. Politics and women's suffrage were popular. There were several Kier Hardies among the group, Oates discovered, and he found his own background a poor fit sometimes. The horses, however, didn't care whether he had been to university or came from a family that owned a large estate.

Although Oates knew that the Antarctic night pressed home its misery most forcefully after the first two months, he found that time passed relatively easily with Meares. Cecil and Wilfred Bruce had not got on during the journey to acquire horses and dogs, mainly because Kathleen Scott's brother had thought Meares scruffy and uncouth. Oates, who had suffered similar ridicule, found him pleasant company, happy to sit in silence but willing to talk when pushed. He no longer blamed him for his selection of ponies. Scott had insisted on white and the percentage at the market had been skewered towards dark. Meares had picked up the best of a small, bad bunch. Oates regretted acquiescing about staying behind and not travelling to Siberia. He liked to think he would have ignored the light/dark idiocy and bought the strongest on offer.

The dog-driver had travelled the world, spoke several languages and admitted to undertaking some shadowy work for the British government in Russia. He was, he hinted, a secret agent, a job which Oates thought sounded every bit as glamorous as polar explorer. He had given a talk on his adventures in Tibet, a sequence of misfortunes that ended with the murder of the expedition leader. You could have heard a pin drop in the hut while he held forth for the best part of two hours. Even Scott, who thought the dog man antisocial, had been impressed, although he offered the opinion that murdering the boss of any expedition was not to be sanctioned lightly.

That afternoon, Meares had improvised a story about a race through snowy Siberia, driving a dog team ahead of some angry Cossacks, trying to save the life of Mrs Cordingley, the wife of the British Consul in Vladivostok. She was, by his account, extremely grateful when he out-ran the sabre-waving brutes. Even Anton, whose grasp of English was still shaky, had stopped his brushing of the ponies to listen to the climax of the tale.

When he had finished, Meares poked the fire. 'Do you have a girl, Titus? At home?'

Oates shook his head. 'There is no room with my mother. Besides . . .'

'Besides what?'

Oates was glad the heat of the fire had already made him flushed. 'Besides, I'm not sure what they are for.'

Meares hooted with laughter. 'I tell you, Mrs Cordingley would have shown you. Hey, Anton, do you have a girl?'

The groom stopped what he was doing once more. 'Huh?'

Meares repeated the question in Russian.

'Ah. Yes. But she is just a leg,' he said in English.

'Just a leg?' laughed Oates. 'Well, that gets rid of some of the problems.'

Meares and Anton exchanged a couple of sentences in the groom's native tongue. 'She has one leg,' the dog driver explained. 'And he is upset you laughed. He worries about her.'

Oates pulled himself away from the fire and went over to the stall where Anton was inspecting Nobby's hoof. Christopher, the most truculent of the animals, made a lunge for him as he passed by, causing him to sidestep. A man needed the temperament of a saint to get on with Christopher; it took eight hands to get him fastened into a sledge and then he only pulled if whipped.

Oates put a hand on Anton's shoulder. 'Sorry. It was nothing. Nothing. I don't know what I would do without you.' This was no platitude. Anton, an outsider in the mostly English-speaking expedition, threw himself into his work. 'I meant no harm.'

The Russian nodded solemnly. 'I know. It just remind me.'

'What's her name?'

'Name? Elena.'

'Very nice. You'll see her soon enough.'

'I hope.'

A blast of the southerly wind hit them as Atkinson entered the stables, his cheeks reddened by the short sprint around from the hut. 'I have fresh bread and the finest New Zealand butter. Toast, anyone?'

He didn't wait for an answer, but sat down with four thick slices of bread and an improvised toasting fork. 'By the way, I checked Christopher's doings. Tapeworm. Big one.'

'Ah. Maybe that's why he's such a grouch,' suggested Oates.

'I'm sure it doesn't help. But I'll have to do all the others, so if you could collect—'

'Can we wait till we've had the toast?' asked Meares. 'Before we continue this topic.'

Atkinson had a fascination for parasites, which meant he didn't always appreciate how squeamish the subject made other people feel. His gleeful discovery of a trypanosome in a fish was met with studied indifference over one breakfast.

'How is it in there?' asked Oates, nodding towards the hut.

'Oh, chaos. Keohane got them talking about home rule for Ireland.'

'I bet the Cambridgers loved that.' This was Oates's nickname for all the university-educated scientists, even though he knew that at least one – Cherry – went to Oxford.

'Well, Taylor and Debenham were for it. Home rule, I mean.'

'Colonials, you see,' said Oates. 'Like to stir up trouble. They'll want independence for Australia next.'

'It was getting a bit heated. Bill Wilson is trying to keep the peace. It will have calmed down by the time the Owner speaks.'

'Another lecture?' Evening talks, along with Ponting's popular slide shows, had become as compulsory as Sunday Service. Oates was down to give an address on horse management that already had him waking in even colder sweats than usual.

'No. Haven't you heard in here? After dinner, the Owner's going to tell us about his polar plans.'

Conversation over supper, which as always began around six p.m., was stifled by anticipation. Scott had set up a board and easel. Whatever was on the board was covered by a blanket. As they ate the tomato soup, there was only the sound of slurping and the ring of spoons and the constant moan of wind. The silence over the fried seal liver was broken by one of Teddy Evans's frivolous stories, but few lent more than half an ear to it. All eyes strayed towards the map or chart the men assumed was under the cover.

Once dinner was done, the pipes and a bottle of port were produced and Scott invited the ratings to move some of the packing cases that divided the hut so they could see his presentation better. All drank sparingly. Scott was pleased at how relatively abstemious the shore party was, preferring to pass the time on constructive work rather than in an alcoholic stupor. Even Taff Evans had showed great control, although Oates was always trying to wheedle the 'medicinal' brandy out of Bill Wilson. That had taken on the nature of a parlour game.

As soon as dinner was over the table was upended and the legs removed to make space for the whole party. The gramophone played Nellie Melba while the seating was arranged, although gossip fuelled by anticipation drowned her out somewhat. The wall of packing cases separating officers and ranks was further dismantled.

Once he had his pipe going, Scott moved two of the blubber lamps so more light was cast on to his board. He cleared his throat and uttered the one word that killed all discourse dead in an instant. 'Gentlemen.'

He paused theatrically and sucked on the pipe.

'In case I have neglected to say it, I would just like to make it crystal clear that it is an honour and a privilege to have this group of men down here with me. I truly believe that we represent England at its best.' He looked around the room. 'Yes, Tom, and Ireland and Wales, Taff, and Scotland and the Empire.' He looked at Gran but said nothing about Norway. 'We have strength, intelligence in abundance, humour and expert knowledge. No polar expedition has ever had such a collection of scientists, so preeminent in their fields. It is a triumph to have collected such men. I am sure you all know my thoughts on the true meaning of exploring these remote places. It is knowledge and understanding.

Not merely saying you have stood on this spot or that spot.' It was, they all realised, an oblique reference to Amundsen. 'However, although the scientific programme is paramount, we would be foolish to neglect the other reason people gave us funding, equipment and their strongest sons. The South Pole.'

He flicked back the blanket, revealing a map, which showed a slice of Antarctica, with Cape Evans at the top, the Pole at the bottom, and the few known topographical features sketched in. It was Wilson's work. 'It is, as you know, seven hundred and eighty-three nautical miles from Hut Point to the Pole. For the landlubbers among you, that's the best part of one thousand, eight hundred statute miles there and back. The polar party, whoever they are, will cross on to the barrier, travel south and use the Beardmore Glacier to access the polar plateau. That, as you know, was Shackleton's route through the mountains. Don't imagine just because he did it that the glacier is a soft journey. It isn't. The Beardmore is over a hundred miles long, with blue ice and crevasses and it's tricky to negotiate. In itself, it represents one of the most hazardous sections, for man or beast. Personally, I feel that we cannot trust the dogs much beyond this point.' He indicated the foot of the glacier with the stem of his pipe, ignoring a loud tut from Cecil Meares, who had been uncharacteristically liberal with the port. 'But we'll see. We use the dogs, the horses and the remaining motor-sledges, which are now fully functioning once more, to bring food and supplies to the foot of the glacier.

'A reduced party will ascend the glacier by either man-hauling or a combination of dogs and man-hauling. At the top of the glacier, there will be two parties, which will haul the early part of the plateau. Then, for the final leg, four men and one sledge will make the last dash to ninety degrees south. I know what you are thinking. Which four? I honestly do not know and don't expect to know till the last moment. There is a lot to get through between here' – he slapped a fist over at Cape Evans – 'and here.' A jab at the polar plateau, at the spot where the quartet who would make history was to be selected. 'As for a starting date, we know the ponies suffer terribly from the cold, which means the southern party will leave a little later in the season. The end of October, or the first days of November.'

There was a stirring around the table. All knew that the dogs would be ready to leave before that date.

'This is not a race, gentlemen. We are not geared up for such a contest. We pursue the Pole in our own way and at our own pace with the tools we have brought. Now I want every man to apply himself to this scenario. All suggestions for improvement welcome. Bowers will give his lecture on sledging rations next week. And perhaps he can instruct us once and for all whether tea or cocoa is the preferable beverage out on the ice.' Supporters of each drink shouted their support.

'Brandy,' said Oates, theatrically glaring like a pirate at Wilson, who wagged a finger at him.

'And Teddy Evans is preparing a talk on sledging loads and depoting. Plus the telephone trials are going well. We expect to have a circuit between here and Hut Point shortly.' He considered what he had said for a moment and the wonder of it. 'Which really is quite remarkable.'

It was Teddy Evans who asked the one question that was on every man's mind. Teddy who took every opportunity to remind Scott that he had given up his own expedition to join Scott. Teddy who, more than anyone, found it hard to hide his itching for the Pole. 'What about the Norskies?'

'Well, as you all know, they are here. On the barrier at the Bay of Whales. Closer to the Pole. And he has dogs, which will enable him to start earlier.' A grumble, again coming from the direction of Meares. 'But, if he is heading straight south, the Transantarctic mountains bar his way. Is there another Beardmore Glacier, another way up to ten thousand feet? We don't know. If not, he is sunk. If there is . . .'

He didn't finish the thought. He didn't have to.

'I hate to say this, but it is down to fortune. The team with the best luck will win.'

'Then we'll make our luck, sir,' shouted Crean to cheers of approval and a beaming smile from Scott.

Meares leaned over to Oates, speaking just as the roar died down. 'Dogs, men, horses and tractors? I think someone should buy the skipper a shilling book on transport.'

The words carried around the hut and eyes were cast down and feet shuffled in embarrassment. Scott said nothing, just stared coldly at the dog-driver, not a trace of his grin remaining. Meares felt himself colour. One thing was for certain, thought Oates, no matter who were to be the final four for the polar rush, Cecil Meares and his dogs weren't going to be in their number.

An hour after his presentation, before nine o'clock, the table was back in place and a game of snapdragon in progress. The first men began to climb into their sleeping bags, with an accompaniment by Enrico Caruso on the gramophone. 'La Donna e mobile'. Woman is fickle. There were many who thought they could tolerate a little fickleness in exchange for company during the long dark of a polar winter.

There would be a last pipe or cigarette, hushed conversation and perhaps some reading, but for the most part the main acetylene lights were out by eleven p.m. Then men read by candlelight, but for no more than an hour, at which point the night watchman was the only one with a light burning.

They slept according to how fierce the weather howled around them and whether or not the dogs started one of their mournful group howls or if there were the snores of dreamers or Cherry sleepwalking. There were other forces at play that might disturb a man's sleep. Tensions simmered, even though the total darkness was but a few weeks old. An argument over a carelessly dropped biscuit or an imagined slight could fester for days. Friends swore they'd never speak to each other again, only to find they had forgotten the reason for their falling out within hours. And there were the worries, anxieties and quests for solutions to logistical puzzles that kept brains turning long after sleep should have shut them down. Scott and Bowers suffered most from this fatiguing syndrome.

At a little after nine-thirty that evening, Scott was writing at his table, dead pipe still clamped between his teeth, when Wilson and Cherry came and crouched next to him, their voices low. Wilson had left him alone for he knew how much addressing the men took out of him. On the surface, Scott was robust enough, but strip away the temper and grit and you had a shy, reserved man at heart. He fought that nature as much as he fought the ice, Wilson thought.

'Have you considered it?'

Scott took the pipe out of his mouth and tapped the contents of the bowl on to a metal saucer.

'I have. And I am inclined to deny you.'

Cherry started to speak but Wilson put a hand on his arm to stop him. 'Might we ask why?'

'It is a waste of our resources. The temperature has been steadily falling. Thirty degrees of frost now. And the wind. In total darkness. All for a few penguin eggs?'

Wilson wanted to retrieve an Emperor's egg, to try to fill in some of their biology. Only by going in winter could they do this. It meant crossing to Cape Crozier, the journey that had nearly done in Royds on the *Discovery* expedition. And that had been in the sledging season, not in the dead of winter.

'But it will give us a chance to test the sledges,' Wilson objected, 'and the double tent.' This was a newly improvised dual-skinned affair, designed to trap air between the layers and, so the theory went, insulate the men inside. Taff and Lashly had constructed them to Scott's specifications, but they had never been tried on the ice.

'And the sledge rations,' said Cherry. 'Bowers has worked out a way of altering the fat ratio so we will all be on a different regime. He's already made a list of requirements.'

He passed it across. Scott scanned it. There were 135 lb of Huntley & Palmer's Antarctic biscuits, 110 of Bovril pemmican, 21 of butter, 3 of salt, 4 of tea, 60 of oil, the sledges, tents, rope, crampons, ice axes, lamp box, sennegrass for the boots, scientific and sample boxes plus spare parts for the stove, toilet paper, candles and spirit for lights. The list went on for two pages and totalled 790 lb in all. Over 250 lb per man.

As Scott was reading and making non-committal grunting noises, Wilson winked at Cherry. He had explained to the younger man that figures on paper were catnip to the Owner. To him, lists, formulae and tables was a way of breaking nature and the unknown into manageable forms.

'That's a lot of oil. How long are you expecting to be away?'

'It's a hundred and forty-one miles, round trip. That provision list represents six weeks' supply, which should be plenty.'

'Well, we are having our Christmas on June the twenty-second.' This was the point of midwinter in the topsy-turvy world. 'It would have to be later than that.'

Wilson nodded. 'It's a secret, but Bowers is making a tree. From penguin feathers. So he won't want to miss the celebration.'

'No.'

'And apparently Emperors don't lay till the end of June or early July. So we were thinking, June the twenty-fifth, or something like it. We'll be back in plenty of time for the southern journey.'

Scott considered for a moment. 'Very well. Almost against my better judgement.'

'Thank you, Con.'

'Yes, thank you, sir,' said Cherry, an inflection of nerves in his voice now the winter journey was a reality. 'I'll tell Bowers.'

After he had gone, Scott said, 'For eggs, Bill.'

'Embryos, Con. If it is true that the penguin is the most primitive bird on the planet, then its embryos just might prove that feathers really do develop from scales.'

Scott was silent again, as his appreciation of science battled his innate conservatism when it came to risking his men. 'If you go, I also want you to try out the double bags.' Another innovation was the decision to put eiderdown inside the reindeer bags, which made them more comfortable, but it remained to be seen how 'icing' from perspiration would affect them.

'Of course. We'll compile a list of objectives.'

As Wilson stood, Scott said, 'Oh, and Bill.'

'Yes?'

'Bring them both back alive, won't you? And yourself.'

'I'll do my best, Con. I'll do my best.'

As the men fell asleep, Wilson went outside to watch the great vertical sheets of the aurora. Gran was already out there, binoculars clamped to his eyes.

'Hello, doctor.'

'Trigger.'

'Lovely night.'

'Yes.'

There was a silence that slowly thickened. Wilson knew the young man had something on his mind.

'You know, I once played football for Norway.'

Wilson tried to keep the surprise from his voice. He wasn't aware the Scandinavians had national sides. 'Did you?'

'Yes. Not like playing for England, but a high standard. But here, I am not used properly. In goal. Not my position.'

'You should say something.'

'I try. But they don't use me correctly,' he repeated. Wilson became aware once more of just how young Gran was. The ice had that effect; he had even forgotten that Cherry was a stripling, yet here he was taking him on a winter journey. 'Why doesn't he like me?'

'Who?'

'Scott.'

'Doesn't he?'

'Not so much. He doesn't use me properly either.'

The doctor thought about this for a while, watching the light show sparkle across the heavens. Sometimes it was like celestial semaphore, as if God was trying to talk to them. 'There is a secret to Scott,' said Wilson softly. 'That is to be busy. He hates idleness.'

'I am busy,' said Gran, unable to keep a petulant note from his voice. 'I ski, I cut ice, I skin the seal.'

'Make sure he sees you.'

'I think it is because I am Norwegian.'

'No. Not that.'

'You don't sound so sure, doctor.'

Wilson laughed. 'Well, perhaps you just remind him what is over the horizon.' He pointed east, in the direction of the Bay of Whales.

'I cannot help that.'

'Nor can he.'

'So I should stay busy?'

'Yes. And make sure the Owner sees you. I tell you, he'll soon come round.'

Gran handed Wilson the binoculars. 'I shall go and check the skis. Loudly.'

Wilson watched him go. So very young, he thought once more. He looked back at the radiance above them. What would God say to his party of three striving to Cape Crozier to recover penguin eggs? Come on and try your best? Or, Go home, you blithering fools? Wilson caught himself. Trying to know the mind of God was the first step towards madness. He turned away and went back inside to get some sleep, hoping the Norwegian boy didn't keep him awake with his energetic ski waxing.

Fifty-two

Letter from Kathleen Scott to Robert Scott

Dear Con,

The most marvellous news today. Well, yesterday now. I have to confess it is very late. Two-thirty in the morning. I had a party for my birthday. I know that seems callous with you away, but I have been so lonely without you since my return. I needed a little life around me. Fifty-two people came to the studio, which was filled with daffodils. We danced and drank and I laughed properly for the first time in ages. Guess who turned up? Nansen. He didn't stay long, said he wasn't comfortable with that many people unless he was sharing a ship with them. I think he could become a dear friend. He knows so much about what you are going through. I expect you are all tucked up for the winter now. I have tried to explain to Peter how the sun disappears for four (or is it five?) months at a time. I used balls of clay for the earth and the sun, but I fear I was not as clear as you would have been. Peter is the only authentic thing in my life without you here.

The good news I spoke of came right in the midst of the party. A telegram. From New Zealand. It simply said:

SHIP SIGHTED. ALL WELL.

So the *Terra Nova* is back and on it your letters, I hope. And I will get this and the others to you before it comes south to see you once more in your spring.

Tell Cherry-Garrard I have seen his mother, a dear thing, charming and sweet and frightfully intelligent, and his lovely sister Mildred. And I took tea with Ory Wilson, who is missing her Bill terribly. She even talked of going down to New Zealand to wait and see if he came back before next winter. I told her that would be awful, just endless waiting. I told her that if you stay on for a second winter, then Bill will too. He is nothing if not loyal, we both know that. She wept. (You don't have to tell Bill that part.)

Once I have your letters I shall go straight to your mother and we will have a veritable Antarctic orgy with her. I always had the feeling to begin with that Hannah wanted to stab me and that she certainly would if she thought I'd hurt you. I hope we are past the knifing stage now. I think Peter made all the difference.

I have an invitation to go to the opening night of Shaw's Fanny's New Play. I am not sure whom to take. Perhaps Nansen, because he likes the theatre. Then there is a flying race at Hendon the next day I would love to see. Airplanes are beginning to have a strange appeal: perhaps you should get one for your next expedition. Flying over the ice must be better than walking it.

Oh, my love, I have so much news, but all of it seems so trivial next to the cable. *SHIP SIGHTED. ALL WELL.* I cannot recall four such lovely words. I shall go to bed now and dream of them.

Fifty-three

Cape Crozier, July

'You've got it in the neck, now stick it, stick it; you've got it in the neck, now stick it, stick it.'

As he edged cautiously around the ice-strewn scree-fields of Mt Terror the words looped through Cherry's brain as they had done for much of the last three weeks. He had to fill it with something, a distraction, or he might go mad. He'd suffered endless days of blisters and cold that seeped through to the bones, seemingly turning them to columns of ice. Sometimes it was like having steel pins driven into your limbs. Minus 77; that was 109 agonising degrees of frost. Cherry hadn't thought it possible to be so frozen that your internal organs were chattering to stay warm. But they had; and it hurt. He'd cried a lot of iced tears.

He stumbled over something in the darkness and, in doing so, found the rock he was looking for. With the wind snarling at him and the clothes of unyielding lead keeping him upright, he somehow managed to bend at the waist and pick it up. As soon as he tried to straighten, the gale snapped him upright, causing him to stagger back.

The grip made his fingers burn in the mittens, a souvenir from taking his gloves off to haul on the sledge ropes. They had blistered within seconds. And that had been on the second day. They still throbbed and ached. He hugged the great lump of stone and turned back up the slopes of Mt Terrror, where, on a moderately level piece of moraine, they were building their pickling and dissecting igloo.

'*You've got it in the neck, now stick it, stick it.*'

'You all right there?'

Cherry squinted to his left. It was so cold it was impossible for him to wear his glasses for any length of time. He was forced to remove them at intervals and slip them into his jacket, hoping a little of his body heat would melt the hoar on the lenses. Without them his world was reduced to a white blur. But he could tell from the squat silhouette it was Birdie Bowers. By the look of it, he was carrying a rock twice the size of his own. Nothing was too big for this man. 'Yes, Birdie.'

'Wind's getting up.'

'Aye.' As if that would worry Birdie. He had snored through nights when Cherry was rocked with tremors from the cold.

Together they staggered over the ice-dotted gravel surface to where they had deposited the first layer of rocks for the igloo. Bill Wilson was repositioning them, making the layer as wind-proof as possible. 'How's the wound?' Cherry asked as he dropped the rock at his feet.

'Bearing up.' Wilson had splashed hot blubber from the stove into his eye, burning it quite badly. It was covered in salve and bandaged. Cherry was certain it was worse than Bill was letting on. 'It's three a.m. We should turn in.'

'I'll get a few more rocks before I do,' said Birdie. 'You two go ahead.'

A sliver of moon appeared from behind the clouds and Cherry took out his glasses and wiped the ice from them. He was in no hurry to start chipping at the frozen slab of a sleeping bag he would have to slide into. That might take thirty minutes or more alone. The wind whipped at him as he stared out from their little camp, but the grainy grey-white view was scarily magnificent. Huge knife-edged pressure ridges of ice eight hundred feet below ran north to the frozen Ross Sea. Moonlight lent the ice a ghostly gleam. It was like a half-remembered dreamscape. Yet somewhere down there were the Emperors they needed, the eggs to pickle and the adult birds to provide blubber. They had brought six tins of oil; they had used five, even after taking it down to two hot meals a day. The penguins would provide fuel. There were cliffs and a crevasse between them and the rookery, but they would have to be crossed to harvest the birds – and their eggs – if they were to survive the return journey.

'You can't do it in one night, Birdie,' said Wilson. 'Even you.'

Birdie muttered something that might have been a curse. 'I suppose you are right. We'll start again in the morning.'

'It is the morning,' said Cherry gloomily as the moon dis- appeared again and the blackness descended, masking the landscape once more. Already his breath had frosted his spectacles; he would have to take them off again soon. From out on the ice he heard the faint cry of a penguin, mocking him. How dare you come here in the darkness to steal our young? it seemed to ask. This was, thought Cherry as his body began to convulse with the cold, a very good question.

The door of the hut opened and George Simpson, the meteo- rologist, dashed in, his temperature readings clutched in his hand. He shook the snow and ice from himself like a wet dog, shed his outer layer of clothes, and went to Scott's corner. 'Minus forty-eight,' Simpson said. He had been taking readings from the thermometer boards, which were mounted away from the hut so as not to be affected by any still air or leakage of heat.

Scott sucked on his pipe and indicated his notebooks. 'You know, I have been comparing our temperatures with those taken in the Arctic by the Norwegians. Winter seems to be the same in both places. But the Arctic summer is much warmer than here.'

Simpson knew he was being invited to postulate a theory. Scott loved a meteorological discussion. He was a good listener and Simpson knew he took his opinions seriously.

Scott placed his pipe on his desk. 'Any thoughts?'

'It's the sheer expanse of unbroken ice,' said Simpson. 'As far as I can see, that is. The reflection is tremendous. Which is why the glare causes snow-blindness. I am of the persuasion that the reflection from the ice means that the sun fails to warm the atmosphere sufficiently by the time the summer solstice is reached. Which means it is a rare day when it gets much above freezing, even in summer. Thereafter, the amount of solar energy decreases, of course, as we move into autumn. The Arctic is a smaller surface, with a greater area of open water.'

'So it's reflection.'

'The albedo. Yes.'

Scott frowned, thinking for a moment. 'Is there any way to measure this?'

Simpson nodded. 'I have been working on those hydrogen balloons. They can be modified to measure received sunlight. There must be a way to estimate percentage reflection.'

'Very good. You want to draw something up for next season?'

Simpson, who relished a challenge, nodded. 'Of course, skipper. I have to re-calibrate the magnetometer, but after that I'll get right to it.'

'Excellent.' Scott put his pipe back in his mouth. 'Minus forty-eight, you say?'

'Yes.'

Scott went back to his pipe, but Simpson could tell it wasn't the temperature that concerned him, but the thought of the three men out in it, surrounded by the cold, dark night.

'I'm not going in there,' said Cherry, pointing at the ominous black hole in the face of the ice cliff. There was moon, enough to show the outline of the landscape's features, not enough to penetrate the lair-like hole before them. Cherry's imagination had already conjured up some great worm-like creature that called the tunnel home.

'We have to,' said Bowers. 'The penguins are on the other side of this ridge.' He pointed upwards. 'Unless you want to try and climb that.'

'No, I don't,' said Cherry glumly. On the way down from their plateau he had fallen so many times he had lost count. He would tally his grazes and cuts later. They had scaled steep cliffs, traversed ridge after ridge and stumbled into crevasses, all to get close to the edge of the sea. Now this enormous wall of ice barred their way. The sledge was miles back and still they had not found the penguins. There were meant be thousands of them, according to Bill, who had witnessed the colony on the *Discovery* expedition, but they had found no evidence of them other than hearing their strange metallic callings.

'I'll give it a try,' said Wilson, pointing at the hole.

'Oh, no,' replied Bowers, looping the Alpine rope around his waist. 'I'm the smallest. If I get stuck, yank me out. I'll pull on the rope three times. All right?' Bowers didn't wait for a reply, but plunged in headfirst.

'Oh God,' said Cherry, shivering again in his board-like clothes. 'Will we ever be warm again?'

'We get some penguins and we'll get the stove going at full-blast.' Wilson clapped Cherry on the back. 'I promised the Owner some Emperor's eggs and he'll have them.'

'Birdie!' Cherry yelled into the cave mouth.

They heard a muffled reply. Wilson watched the rope slip through his mitts. 'Seems to be still going.'

A few minutes later it stopped and went slack. Wilson looked at Cherry with his one good eye. Cherry took out his glasses and put them on, as if it might help him see what was happening within the ice cave. 'Birdie? You all right?'

There was no reply, just the swirl of wind around the aperture. Wilson pulled on the rope and it came easily. Soon enough, he had the free end in his hand.

'Oh,' said Cherry. 'What do we do now?'

'I'll go next,' said Wilson.

'No, wait.'

'What?'

'I'll be here by myself.'

'Right.' Wilson thought for a moment. 'Do you want to go next, then?'

'I . . .' Cherry hopped from foot to foot. 'Erm.'

'I'll go, shall I?' said Wilson gently, placing a hand on the agitated young man's shoulder.

'Yes. Good idea.'

'You hold your ice axe at the ready in case something other than me comes out.'

'Like what?' asked Cherry.

Wilson raised his arms above his head in a threatening manner. 'A carnivorous penguin?' he smirked.

'Not funny. Plays tricks on you, this light. My bloody glasses have gone again.'

Wilson tied the rope to his belt, raised a hand and was gone. Cherry heard the shuffling of his knees and elbows, but that soon faded. He was alone with the moaning of the wind and the chattering of his teeth.

'Bill?'

Again, silence. He prayed nothing would happen to Wilson. He was the reason Cherry was here. He was a family friend and his quiet tales of the *Discovery* had long inspired Cherry. Perhaps, back in front of a roaring fire in England, this would be such a story. The Great Quest For Penguin Eggs. Yes, that had a ring. Would he by that point be able to recall the throbbing in his fingers, his grumbling stomach, the judder of muscles desperate to keep warm? He hoped not. He didn't want this feeling with him for the rest of his life. He hoped his memory would kill it.

The sky had begun to haze with sheets of thin cloud, masking the stars and dimming the moon. The mountain and cliffs above him lost their silvery edge and returned to black and brooding. He pulled the rope. It came a good two feet. He pulled once more and knew there was nobody at the other end.

'Oh, Lord.' There was no point in pulling it all the way through, because there would be nobody left to pull him back should he get stuck.

He stared at the hole as he jumped up and down, flexing his limbs to try to create some give in his rigid clothes. It would be like trying to crawl while coated in cement.

'Ah well, Cherry. Here goes. Just remember, you paid a thousand pounds for this privilege.'

Cherry carefully placed his spectacles out of harm's way and levered himself into the ice hole. His ears filled with a soft roaring, as if there were surf at the far end. But that was ridiculous. Wasn't it? At minus forty, fifty or sixty, any sea would be a frozen fossil.

Soon even the pathetic light of the outside world had gone, leaving only a thick, tar-like blackness. Now and then he could see shapes in the air ahead of him, swirls, like patterns in drinking chocolate. He knew it was his eyes, trying to make sense of the dark, but the forms still disturbed him. It was as if the inky curtain was holding back restless demons.

He tried to find a rhythm of knees and elbows to push him on through. Whatever lay on the other side had to be better than this strange borehole. *You've got it in the neck, now stick it, stick it.*

Another sound came to him, a low, guttural laugh, but he wasn't sure whether it came from ahead or behind. Was he being chased?

The voice, when it crystallised, appeared to come from a spot right in front of him, inches from his nose.

'Take it easy near the exit, Cherry.'

It was Bill. His voice calm, even and soothing.

'The ice is quite sharp there.'

Ahead he could see a perfect circle of soft grey light. He was through. He was within ten feet of it when he heard the scream that made his insides turn to liquid. He clenched his sphincter, fearing he might soil himself. His instinct for survival made him slither backwards for a few inches. Then the words popped into his brain: *Now stick it.* He took a deep breath and pumped his elbows. Sure enough, as Bill had warned, some of the iced razor edges cut through his clothing, but he didn't care. He shot out on to a glacial tongue and rolled over, his fists clenched to face whatever Cape Crozier could throw at him. Looming above him were two dark shapes.

'Aaargh,' he cried.

The other two looked down at him and, whatever they saw in the half-light illuminating his face, made them both laugh. 'You bastards!' he cried.

'Now, Cherry,' said Wilson, feigning distress. 'What would Evelyn say to such language?'

'My mother would forgive me, given your behaviour. What was that scream?'

Wilson pointed over the ice to where the dark hump of a penguin lay still. 'Just a bit of encouragement to myself so I could put the axe in, Cherry. Sorry if it scared you. Here.' Bill Wilson held out his hand and Cherry took it, allowing himself to be pulled to his feet.

He examined his surroundings. Directly opposite the ice tongue was a cliff, its vertical face clear of ice and snow, and below that he could just make out the fuzzy white dress-shirts that were the breasts of the penguins. 'They are here,' he said. 'That's something.'

'Not many,' said Wilson. 'Dozens rather than thousands. I suspect the rookery is being abandoned. But there are eggs. Not every bird, one in four or five.'

'I think we need three skins and blubber. I'll skin this one, shall I?' said Bowers.

The others nodded. A male Emperor penguin might only be a shade over three feet high, but they weighed over six stone. There was no way they could manhandle the entire carcass over the ridges and cliffs, so they would have to take what fat they could attached to the bird's epidermis.

As Bowers got busy with the knife, Cherry moved towards the animals, treading carefully over the ice. They began to trumpet their bizarrely metallic alarm call. The Emperors shuffled back, to press themselves against the wall. He could tell they had incubating eggs down at their feet from the way they moved.

Cherry made a start towards the nearest animal, which tried to waddle away as rapidly as it could, but stumbled over its precious cargo. The egg rolled free. Instantly two other penguins charged for it and Cherry realised they were eggless males, looking for something to nurse. He dived like a goalkeeper, scooping up the precious oval and rolled on to his back as he slid over the ice. He held the intact egg aloft as the three angry penguins barked at him. 'One,' he cried.

'Well done, Cherry,' said Bill Wilson.

Just then his prize crumbled into ice crystals and rained down on his face. Within a second there was nothing but powder in his mitts.

Wilson came over. 'False egg, Cherry. Some of the birds that don't have the real thing use substitutes. Well done for getting it. Now find me a real one.'

Cherry spat out a mix of ice and penguin feather fragments and tried not to gag at the oily taint. 'Aye, aye.'

As he stumbled to his feet and went among the birds, ignoring their cries, Cherry felt for the poor creatures. The possession of an egg was such a powerful biological drive that clearly they would be leaving the carers bereft. On two occasions he chipped an ice-block into the rough shape of the real thing and offered it to the Emperor he had robbed. One even accepted it.

The thin light began to fade further and the wind picked up once more by the time they had three skinned birds and five genuine eggs. Cherry was given two to carry and he slipped them inside his mittens. The gloves were large enough so that he could still get his balled fists inside to keep them warm. Bowers lashed two skins to himself and carried one egg. Cherry volunteered to take the third skin, even though the smell of warm bird blubber and blood turned his stomach. Wilson also took two eggs in his mittens.

The tunnel seemed shorter on the way back, although they had to crawl through with their prizes in front of them so as not to crush them. Once on the far side, with a gale threatening, they roped themselves together. The stars were disappearing, and the way back up the cliffs, once so clear, was concealed in the shadows. Wilson began to chop steps with his ice axe. Birdie followed. Cherry, his spectacles useless once more, stumbled along as best he could.

It grew so dark he could no longer even see the footholds. 'Cut your own steps,' Wilson shouted down to Cherry as he missed his footings once more, causing the rope to jerk painfully on the other two.

'I'm trying,' he shouted up the slope. 'But it's hard with the eggs.'

'You really must learn how to use an ice axe.'

'Sorry, Bill.'

They laboured upwards in silence, apart from the sound of heavy breathing and the increasingly aggressive roar of the wind. Cherry's leggings were sliced through by rocks, as were the sleeves on his jacket. The wind now had free access to his body and punished him for it. He felt like howling in pain, but his two indefatigable companions prevented him from showing such weakness.

Now stick it, stick it.

They pulled themselves on to a wide plateau of ice and rock that looked familiar. 'Where's the sledge?' Cherry shouted up.

'I don't know,' replied Bowers, undoing the rope that attached them. 'I thought we would have seen it by now.'

Cherry felt a stab of panic and swallowed hard. It had been lashed down, but that was no guarantee it hadn't been dislodged. Without the sledge they would have no way of transporting their supplies – tent, cooker, food – home.

'We'd best sleep in the igloo tonight,' said Bill, the words snatched away as they came from his lips, his hood cracking as the wind caught it. 'I think there's a blizzard coming. Might be a snorter.'

'I see it!' shouted Bowers. 'Over there.'

As Cherry turned to look, one of his boots went from under him. He spun in the air trying to keep his balance or at least land well, and felt Bill's hand pluck at his sleeve to try to steady him, but there was too much momentum. Over the thud of his body hitting the ice and the whoosh of breath from his body, he clearly heard the sharp crack and slosh of warm liquid as the two eggs split asunder.

'For God's sake, Silas, will you keep still?'

The hut fell silent for a moment, shocked by the vehemence behind the words. The Canadian, who had been pacing the floor, stopped in mid-stride. 'First you snore all night, now clump, clump, clump.'

Silas Wright looked confused. 'Sorry, Titus.'

Oates slid off his bunk. 'Yes. Well.'

'Just thinking.'

'Well, think more quietly.' Oates pulled on a tatty jumper and went outside, back to his horses.

'Time for some slippers, Silas,' said Frank Debenham, breaking the tension. It was late afternoon, lunch well behind them, and the day's quota of sledging preparations had been carried out. They were in the lull before dinner, when the long days seemed at their most interminable. Most people were reading or making repairs, a few were doing laundry and a handful were out taking measurements.

'Is Soldier all right?' Scott asked. He had noted him becoming more taciturn as the perpetual night wore on. It always affected a few of the group; he recalled the suicidal young seaman on *Discovery*. He hoped Titus wasn't heading in that direction.

Tryggve Gran cast his book aside. 'I'll go and see.'

'Good man.'

As Gran left, Silas walked over to Scott's table. 'I was just thinking, skipper, that we could make a hole in the hut floor.'

'Is that what you were doing?' asked Atch. 'Trying to wear it away?'

Silas ignored the remark. 'My gravitational pendulum in the ice cave is growing. Crystals are forming on it, distorting the results. I think we need a secondary source of information. A control.'

'Go on,' said Scott.

'If we were to make a panel, like a trapdoor, in the floor and drill into the permafrost below it, I could suspend a pendulum down there. We could make the gravitational measurement from within the hut—'

'In the warmth, is that it, Silas?' asked Simpson, who didn't have such a luxury for his meteorological recordings. By definition, outside temperatures had to be taken outside.

'Well, it's not a bad idea,' said Scott. 'Anything that reduces the tramping around in blizzards has to be considered. It'll wait till the sun returns, will it?'

'Yes, skip.'

'Make it in the floor of Ponting's darkroom, you'll be out of everyone's way. Is that all right, Ponco?'

Ponting looked up from his book. 'Suppose so. As long as I have priority.'

'Of course,' said Scott. 'You giving the talk tonight, Silas?'

Wright shook his head. 'Nelson. Biology. On what he found in the D net trawls.'

'Excellent,' said Scott with genuine enthusiasm. 'And Frank?'

Debenham was writing up his geological notes. 'Skipper?'

'Volcanoes.'

'I haven't forgotten. Have the talk ready in a day or two.'

'Well done.' Scott checked the time. An hour remained before preparations for dinner would begin and the gramophone put on. 'Gentlemen, it is time to exercise your horses.' And perhaps find out what, exactly, was eating Captain Oates.

Cherry knew that Birdie Bowers was singing, but the roar of wind and swirl of snow filling the igloo meant he couldn't make out the words to join in. Wilson and Bowers were feet away, but there was a white-out between them. All three lay in their slab-like sleeping bags. Cherry was shivering so hard his ribs hurt. It was as if someone had been playing them like a xylophone, but using lead mallets.

The canvas roof of the igloo had gone, blown away with an almighty crack. Then the snow blocks had collapsed, allowing the wind to invade the main space. And to top it all, the tent, their precious tent, had lifted up its skirts and fled into the night.

Without the tent they simply wouldn't make it home. No shelter from the storm, no way to cook in a gale. They were going to die. And from the terrible pains wracking his body, it wasn't going to be an easy death.

Someone loomed over him. It was Bowers, trying to repack snow between the loosened blocks. 'All right in there?' Bowers asked. 'Snug?' Cherry couldn't answer. He felt ashamed that he didn't have the power and fortitude of Birdie. 'You have to speak, or I won't know you are alive. How are you?'

Bowers leaned closer to catch his reply. Birdie's face and beard were completely frosted, as if he had fallen into icing sugar. Cherry wasn't sure where to start. The feeling that icicles were being shoved into his thighs, the sickening ache in his balls, the fire consuming his feet or the rodents tearing away at his insides. 'I . . . feel . . . like . . . I am . . . going to crack in half.'

'Get up too smartish and you might. I took a reading. Minus seventy-six and over seventy miles an hour. Bill was right. It's a snorter. There.' He finished packing the snow into some of the cracks between the rocks. 'Think that'll hold?'

Cherry was aware that the gale battering his head had lessened. 'Yes. Thank you, Birdie.'

'You want my bag lining?'

'You need it.'

Birdie came close once more. He checked the young man for frostbite, but there was none. 'Haven't used it yet.'

'Oh God,' said Cherry. 'What are you made of?'

Birdie laughed. 'Want a sweet? I brought them in case we felt a bit low. And for Bill's birthday.'

'Tomorrow.'

'Yes, it is. You can have one now.'

Cherry heard a rustle of paper and felt something popped into his mouth and the flavour of mint flooded through him. 'That's delicious.'

'We'll be all right, don't you worry. I'd best go and thump Bill, make sure he is alive. Can't freeze to death on the day before your birthday.'

Cherry must have dozed off. When he awoke, the howling gale had subsided slightly, but it was still as black as the depths of hell around them. No star shone in the sky, and snow had drifted up inside the igloo. But it was certainly quieter. He could even hear Bill breathing and Bowers, damn the man, snoring.

'Bill.'

'Yes, Cherry?'

'Are you awake?'

'No, I'm talking in my sleep.'

'Sorry. I meant to ask. You have morphine?'

'I do. Are you hurt?'

Cherry just wanted to sob in reply. 'All over. I've had enough. We've no tent. My feet were burning but now I can't feel my toes. My head hurts. I'm ready. I'll only hold you up. If you are to have a chance—'

'Stop it.'

'Please, Bill.'

'The storm is abating.'

Yes, he wanted to say, but we have no tent. WE HAVE NO TENT. And God alone knew what else had been tossed away into the night. It would be nineteen or twenty days back, at least. Sleeping in the open. At the mercy of elements that didn't know the meaning of the word. It was going to be a terrible demise. 'Please, Bill. I'm the weak one. Birdie could carry you on his back if need be. I can't even see where I am going. I would just drift off, wouldn't I? With the morphine, I might even feel warm. That would be worth it. I'm not worried about dying, Bill. It's the pain. Everything aches.'

Wilson barked his reply. 'No.'

'Why not?' Petulant now, like a child at the seaside denied a stick of rock.

'I haven't stopped praying yet.'

There was pause while they listened to Bowers snore, no doubt deep in one of his food dreams.

'Bill?'

'Cherry?'

'Sorry about the eggs.'

For some reason, Wilson found this immensely funny. The richly ironic sound sent an even deeper shiver through Cherry. He knew now that Bill, too, reckoned they weren't going to make it back.

Scott ascended the ladder to the top of the hut very slowly, one cautious rung at a time, bracing his body against the wind each time it gusted. The anemometer had jammed again and needed to be freed. This was the night watchman's job and it was his turn on duty. He consoled himself that he could have his sardines on toast when he got back down.

There had been a two-day storm. The meteorological records had been frightening, with precariously low temperatures and high winds. Then the anemometer blade had jammed. Atkinson had gone out to make some readings with the portable machine, become disorientated, and was lost for hours. His face and hands were badly frostbitten, but, mercifully, he recalled little about his ordeal.

Scott made it to the apex of the roof and leaned on to it, stretching his arm to reach the damaged instrument. His face was beginning to tingle, so he knew he had little time before he was frost-nipped.

Above him the sky had cleared and there was the first shifting green curtain of the Aurora. He grabbed the blade in his mitten and gave it a shake. It made a squeaking sound and began to turn, picking up speed till it was clacking away.

Gingerly he descended the ladder and hurried back towards the entrance of the hut. As he did so, Bill Wilson's words came back to him: 'The Good Lord alone knows why the penguins have chosen the most windswept place on the planet to make their rookery.'

The most windswept place on the planet.

The wind was forty to fifty miles at sheltered Cape Evans, peaking at eighty-two mph some days. On the hills it was twenty per cent higher. What must the Crozier party be experiencing? Scott wondered as he stepped inside into the fug of the hut's enveloping warmth. Five weeks they had been gone. At what point did you begin to think the worst?

Fifty-four

Cape Evans, July 1911

Oates took the warmed blanket off Anton and laid it over the prostrate form of Jimmy Pigg. The horse was in bad way; he'd been racked with a colic and fever since the morning.

'Will he be all right?' asked Crean. He had taken him for his daily walk, but had had to bring the animal back. Jimmy was walking with legs of rubber and making the most alarming noises. That had continued throughout the day till, in the evening, he had lain down. It was Oates's job to ensure he got up again.

'Nothing you can do here, Tom,' said Oates. 'Go back inside. Have something to eat.'

'Aye.'

But he didn't move, just kept staring at the downed animal.

Strangely, Oates welcomed the crisis. Without such incidents the days seemed interminable and he could feel the long dark sucking away his resolve and confidence. He had bucked up for the midwinter party, had even got tipsy and danced with a bemused Anton. But later, when the three men had departed for Cape Crozier – he had even envied them, having a goal to strive towards – Oates had felt despair calling again.

Why? He wasn't normally prone to gloomy episodes. It could only be the lack of sun, something he had thought he wouldn't miss. Moonlight football usually cheered him, as any physical

381

competition did, but the last few times the intense cold had drilled into his old wound and he had limped from the field.

'Off you go, Tom,' Oates prompted him. 'You can have a turn later.'

Crean left and Oates began to rub at the horse with a second hot blanket. When they were seriously ill, the animals stopped whinnying or snorting. Instead, there was an ominous silence and stillness, punctuated only by the spasms that shot through the flanks.

'Make up some mash, can you, Anton,' he said. 'I'll try and feed him.'

'I get you some food, too,' said Anton.

'Very well, thank you. There you are, fella, how does that feel?' He spoke softly to the horse as he rubbed him from head to tail. 'And Anton, ask Atch for an opium tablet or two, would you?'

'Opium?'

'For the horse. Not me.'

Another six hours passed of hot blankets and small feeds laced with drugs. Crean returned with bread for toasting and sat with them, taking turns with Meares to relieve Oates now and then. It was a bedside vigil worthy of any human, thought Oates as he went outside.

He crunched over the fresh snow for a hundred yards and urinated under the stars. At least the weather had improved; he hoped the Croziers were experiencing the same calm after the storm. Oates had just adjusted his clothes when he became aware of a figure to his right. A match flared. Scott. Oates walked over to him.

'Hello, skipper.'

Scott puffed on his pipe. 'How's Jimmy?'

'The same. Well, his ears are pricking to some sounds, which is usually a good sign.'

It sounded like precious little to Scott. 'Will we lose him?'

'Not if I can help it.'

Scott grunted. 'We can't afford to lose even one, Soldier. I've overstepped the margin of safety.'

Oates said nothing.

'You all right? In yourself, I mean.'

'Bearing up.'

'Home run, now. Sun will be back soon enough. What a difference that makes. You'll see.'

I hope so, Oates thought.

'Titus!' It was Meares. 'Come quick.'

Oates and Scott trotted towards the stables, both apprehensive about what they would find. They bustled in to find Jimmy Pigg on his feet, head held high.

'Drank a bucket of water, sir,' said Tom Crean proudly.

'And he's feeding,' added Meares.

'Well done, everyone,' said Scott with feeling. He looked at his watch. 'It's two-thirty in the morning. I think we deserve some rest. You too, Titus.'

'Sir.'

The others trudged off to bed, but Oates stayed at the stove with his pipe, listening to the soft breathing of the horses, content to enjoy the transient feeling of mild elation while it lasted.

Fifty-five

Cape Evans, 1 August 1911

'Spread out,' croaked Wilson, 'so they will be able to see there are three men.'

Bowers and Cherry moved apart, their painful feet almost giving up as they came within sight of the hut, its brooding silhouette punctured by the glow of the acetylene lights leaking through the windows. The smoke from the chimney was clearly visible in the pale moonlight that illuminated the island to all but Cherry. He squinted through his ice-coated glasses, trying to make sense of the blurred image.

They were a few hundred yards away when the door opened, flooding more light into the Antarctic night.

'Good Lord!' someone shouted. 'It's the Crozier party.'

The door closed again and Wilson laughed. 'That's not quite the welcome I expected after five weeks away.'

Cherry didn't answer. He knew, once inside the hut, he would collapse. All that horror and all they had to show for the misery were the three surviving penguin eggs.

Yet he had learned something beyond science. That Bowers and Wilson were two men you needed in a tight spot. Wilson because he was imperturbable and extraordinarily calm in the face of the most horrendous adversity. Bowers because he had the staying power of an ox, albeit one with very short legs, and was of constant good cheer.

'We did it, then,' Cherry said.

'Yes,' croaked Bowers. 'And people said we were mad to try.'

Wilson's rueful laugh was laced with exhaustion. At least, thought Cherry, he had two good eyes now.

The door opened once more and shadowy figures, now dressed for the outside world, sprinted across the ice towards them, the relief obvious in their voices as they shouted their welcomes.

Oates reached Cherry first and tried to take the sledge harness over his head. 'No,' his swollen cracked lips managed to say. 'Like to make finish line.'

'Of course you would, Cherry.' Oates fell in to walk alongside him, hand pressing lightly on the young man's shoulder blade as he heaved the last stage to the hut. He could feel the sharp ridge of bone through his mittens.

Taff Evans slapped Bowers on the back, but it was the sound of flesh on metal. His clothes had turned to iron plates.

The welcoming committee accompanying them for the last few yards unleashed a barrage of questions in rapid succession. The three tried to answer as best they could, but exhaustion and starvation had blunted their powers of thought and speech. Atkinson, who would check them for scurvy and frostbite, said: 'Hold on, chaps, let's get them inside first.'

Once they did, Atkinson supervised the cutting of their clothes, careful to move along the seams in case the material could be reused. Scott watched, pipe in mouth, concern on his face. He was in his night clothes. The hut had been about to turn in.

'Tough, was it, Bill?'

Cherry laughed, a soft chuckle to himself, nudging towards hysteria, rubbing the melting ice from his lenses as he did so.

'You could say that,' said Wilson. There was disappointment in his voice for all to hear. He haltingly explained the journey, the sudden cold snap, the lack of penguins, the broken eggs and the lost tent. If Bowers hadn't found the canvas triangle and its ropes wrapped around a rock, they would have died. Then there were the blizzards on the way home. 'At one point Cherry turned his head to speak to me and his helmet froze, so he couldn't turn his head back. We had to heave harder to make him sweat so he could move his head.' He was silent for a moment and someone laughed. 'It sounds humorous now . . .'

By the time the clothes were off, they were in three piles, looking like discarded scrap metal. The men made no comment on the soiled underwear; all knew that when a blizzard trapped you in your tent, defecation was extremely tricky and embarrassing. Cherry sponged himself down and dressed in clean underwear. It felt like mink next to his skin. He eyed his bunk and, his head filling with a fog of weariness, he stumbled towards it. 'I could sleep for ten thousand years,' he said, the words coming thick and slow. 'But wake me after nine thousand for breakfast. Peaches and syrup, please.'

Scott, knowing Wilson and Bowers must be just as drained, decided a full report could wait till the next day. As Cherry snuggled down, he murmured: 'I'll tell you what, skipper, no matter what the Pole throws at us, it can't be any worse than that.'

Scott was about to answer when he realised the lad was asleep, even as his head arced down towards the pillow.

The next day, Scott observed the group, hobbling on sore feet. Their cheeriness, considering what they had been through, was remarkable. He sat down and wrote up his log, striving to recall just how damaged they had been the night before.

Wednesday, 2 August
The Crozier party returned last night after enduring five weeks of the hardest conditions on record. They look more weather-worn than anyone I have yet seen. All for three surviving eggs. Their faces were scared and wrinkled, their eyes dull, their hands whitened with constant exposure to damp and cold, yet the scars of frostbite were very few and this evil had never seriously assailed them. Atkinson says that a preliminary examination uncovered no sign of scurvy. C. Garrard's sleeping bag of reindeer and eider-down weighed 17lb when he left. Thanks to ice accumulated in it from perspiration it was 45lb when he returned. It was so stiff it couldn't be rolled up. Wilson disappointed with the number of

penguins, but we learned much about the equipment and the rations. Wilson had lost the most weight (3½ lb), C-G the least (1 lb). Their feet are exceedingly sore; it will be some time before they are quite right. Apart from Bowers, who seems as indomitable as ever.

Wilson says the gear is excellent. But one can only wonder if the fur clothing of the Esquimaux might outclass our more civilised garb. That can only be speculation.

The sun will return in three weeks, then preparations for the Pole begin in earnest. I feel we are as near perfection as experience can direct.

RFS

Fifty-six

London, September 1911

The reporter from the *Daily Mirror* was nice enough on the outside, but, as Kathleen soon discovered, he was in possession of a devious mind. The paper had certainly sent a smart one: Ronald Baker was very well turned out in a grey three-piece suit and shoes that suggested a military background. His hair was neatly oiled and his moustache trimmed, not what she expected from a man of the press.

Baker looked around the nursery he had asked to see and at young Peter drawing at his desk. Kathleen had taken the precaution of having his nanny dress him in full attire, 'proper clothes' as the woman had said approvingly. The windows were open, with a breeze ruffling the curtains. The summer had been stifling, with London perspiring all through July and August. It became impossible to imagine what cold must be like, let alone the ice-bound permanent gloom Con was experiencing.

She knew, though, that the sun must have returned after the lengthy dark. There would be spring sledging trials and the dogs and horses could run free once more. And the men. It would be blissful after the lengthy confinement. But Scott would be well aware, even out there, cut off from the outside world, that the expedition was still badly in debt. Many of the cables from New Zealand demanded money for repairs to the *Terra Nova* and cash for provisions to be taken down to resupply the party for next year. Sir Clements Markham had suggested a 'Mrs Scott and son at home await their brave husband and father's return' article in a newspaper might help raise some funds.

'Is it true you fly, Mrs Scott?'

'Fly?' she asked, stalling for time.

'Lighter-than-air machines. Aeroplanes.'

Kathleen shook her head vigorously, loosening a lock of hair. 'Oh no.'

The family had sent Con's brother-in-law to dissuade her from such a dangerous activity. She was rather amused because the last time she had seen him was at an aerodrome when he had pleaded with her not to tell his wife that he also went up on joy rides.

'There was a picture of you in a magazine in a machine, wasn't there?'

She re-pinned up the stray curl. 'Oh, I thought you meant did I fly aircraft myself. I have been up, yes. But no longer. It is a thrill, but not entirely safe. I have Peter to think of, as well as Con.'

He looked across at the boy. 'Yes, I see. And I see you are arranging a fund-raising gala at the Coliseum?'

'Yes. Mr Ponting sent some cinematographic film of the crossing and the unloading on the ice. We will show that. Lloyd George may come.' The man began to scribble on his pad. 'No, don't publish that. It is a sure way to put him off. You can mention the films. They are quite splendid by all accounts.'

'And will Mr Shackleton be there?' he asked, with exaggerated innocence.

A skirmish of letter writing had broken out between Shackleton and Sir Clements Markham in the pages of *The Times*. Markham was promoting Con, while Shackleton was suggesting that the Norwegians might beat him to the Pole.

'Mr Shackleton has been a great supporter of my husband. And vice-versa. He has an open invitation.'

Baker seemed unconvinced but wrote down her comments.

'Mrs Scott, how much money does the British Antarctic Survey need to cover its debts?'

'Well, every little helps,' she said. The figure was close to forty thousand pounds, a sum so great it made her feel giddy.

'How about four thousand pounds?'

The size of the offer took her aback. Caroline Oates had written offering two hundred pounds, and that had seemed quite a decent amount. 'The paper would pay that?'

'No, the British public would. If you have little Peter here writing a letter on behalf of his father. We could show a photograph—'

'No.'

'It would touch hearts.'

'A begging letter, is this?'

'An appeal.'

'No. Already people come up to him in the park because his picture has been shown.' She had hired a company to shoot cinematographic film of Peter, to record his growing, for Con. Someone had sold off stills from it without permission, which angered her immensely. 'He doesn't like it. It frightens him.'

'But four thousand pounds.'

'You are just guessing at that sum, Mr Baker.' She was growing angry now and began wagging a finger at him. She knew that she cut an imposing figure when aroused. 'You have no idea what could be raised. I do not want my son bandied about in the halfpenny press.'

'Mrs Scott—'

'No, that's enough. You have taken up a goodly portion of our time. If you will excuse us.'

From the way her face had furrowed and flushed, Baker knew better than to argue. He fetched his hat and coat. As the maid opened the door to show him out, he walked straight into Fridtjof Nansen, almost bouncing off the big Norwegian's chest.

When the explorer had been admitted and the front door slammed, Baker took out his pad once more. As he walked back towards the tube, he ran through variations of the headline for the story he would run. Mrs Scott Comforted by Famous

Explorer. The Scotts Besieged by Norwegians at Both Ends of the Earth. He liked that. Mrs Scott and the Ice Man. So many possibilities.

It was just a shame that he hadn't had a photographer with him. That way—

Mr Baker experienced a hard pull at his jacket and his feet left the ground. His starched collar cut into his neck and he felt himself turned through the air. Before him was the great, glowering face of Nansen.

'Mr Baker, isn't it?'

Baker could feel the hot breath on his face. People were staring. 'Sir. Could you put—'

Nansen let him drop and Baker staggered for a few steps. Then the man was up against him again, as if he were a stag rutting, about to charge. Baker retreated till he felt cast-iron railings in his back. 'Mrs Scott just told me what you are. A member of the press.' He said it as if it were the name of a plague.

'*Daily Mirror.*'

'Well, Mr Baker, I have seen remarks in some portions of the press about the fact that I accompany Mrs Scott here and there. Sly allusions, one might say. These have caused Mrs Scott's mother-in-law great pain. Do you understand?'

'Oh.' Baker was hardly concerned with Hannah Scott's traumas; he was far more dismayed that someone had scooped him by alluding to the 'friendship' between Nansen and Kathleen. 'Yes, I understand.'

'So I don't expect there to be anything in the article you are writing about our lunch to discuss the finances of the British Antarctic Expedition.' Then his voice boomed like a foghorn. 'Do I make myself clear?'

'Perfectly, Mr Nansen.'

'Professor.'

'Sorry. Professor Nansen.'

'So we have an understanding?'

Baker nodded, wanting to be as far away from this crazed Viking as possible. 'We do.'

'Very well.' He took a step back. 'Good day, Mr Baker. And give my regards to Mr Harmsworth. We were very good friends when I was ambassador.'

'I shall.' Not that someone like him ever passes the time of day with the proprietor, he thought. But he was under no illusions about what was behind the mention of the *Mirror*'s owner. 'Good day.'

Baker was aware of Nansen's eyes on him as he strode away, his legs shaking slightly as he did so. Well, no matter what the truth of the matter, he reckoned that the prickly Kathleen Scott and the thuggish, blackmailing Fridtjof Nansen more than deserved each other.

Fifty-seven

Cape Evans, September 1911

The return of the sun had not been the fillip Oates had hoped for. While others seemed revitalised by it, and his charges were certainly cheered, his own mood sank further into despair. Gran, who had been keeping a low profile over a winter in which his fellow countrymen were often disparaged, was sent by Wilson to the stables to try to gauge Soldier's mood. The blubber stove was bubbling, and Oates was smoking his pipe, looking pensive. Half the horses were out being exercised by their handlers, the remainder were unusually skittish, as if aware that their colleagues were having a good, frisky roll in the snow.

Oates looked up. 'How did the skiing lessons go?'

'Good,' said Gran, who had been tutoring the sledging parties on man-hauling with skis. 'The Owner is very pleased, I think. Teddy Evans competes hard with me. My God, he wants to go to the South so very bad. Birdie is holding out on the lessons, saying he can beat any skier on his two good legs. But he'll come round. Your turn next.'

Oates grunted. 'I wouldn't bother with me, Trigger.'

Gran crouched down, feeling the warmth of the fire redden one of his cheeks. 'What is wrong, Titus? Everyone has noticed how tetchy you have become.'

Oates reached into his pocket and brought out a crumpled piece of paper.

'What's this?'

'A cheque. To cover my costs.'

'Costs?'

'The cost of me being here so far. I want to go home.'

'Titus—'

'I'm sick of this place. Sick of the ponies. Sick of the people. Present company and one or two others excepted.'

Gran shook his head. 'But we know this well in my country. The winter glooms. It goes when the sun shines.'

'The sun is shining.' Outside was a cold but dazzling day, the ice so white it looked as if it had been bleached over the winter. The group had not yet had time to have an impact on the landscape with their comings and goings, which would soon scar it with sled tracks and blot it with animal droppings. For the moment, it was pristine.

'It takes time to chase away this feeling. But it will change.'

'I want to resign, Trigger.' He poked the fire dejectedly.

'I thought your regiment wanted you at the Pole.'

'It does. But what chance do we have with these crocks?' He indicated the ponies with a thumb. 'With the mules, perhaps. But I can't wait that long.'

Scott had asked Oates to order some new animals for the following season. He had put in a request to the Indian Office for Himalayan mules. If the Owner failed to make the Pole that season, he'd wait out another winter and try again with better livestock. Oates wasn't sure he could tolerate the place that long.

'He might do it this time around, Titus. It's a bit of a circus, very complicated, but as Uncle Bill says, you just never know. He might reach it.' Bill Wilson and the other two had recovered from what was now officially known as the Winter Journey to Cape Crozier, although Bowers called it The Eggspedition. Everyone expected the doctor to be one of the Polar party, unless something catastrophic happened to him.

'Yes, but that still might mean an extra winter in the hut if we didn't get back in time for the ship. You wouldn't catch me suffering another one of those if I can help it.'

'So you don't want to go? To the Pole?'

'Of course I bloody do. But I won't, will I?'

'Well, you have a greater chance than I do.' Thanks to his increased work load, Scott's attitude had improved towards Gran, just as Wilson had said it would. But there were limits. 'I think the Owner believes there are enough Norwegians heading for it as it is.'

Oates gave a small laugh at that, breaking the mood. Outside they heard the chugging of the motor-sledge's engine. Scott had given overall charge of those to Teddy Evans. Oates thought that more of a poisoned chalice than even the aged ponies.

'Look, Soldier, I spoke to Bill and Debenham and they both said you might well be selected. Because the Owner would like the Army represented. Would you stay then?'

'He isn't going to tell us who the four are, is he? Not till he is sure.'

'No, but, as I said, you have a better chance than most.'

'I expect you are right.'

'You know I am.' Gran thought for a moment. He was well aware that the winter blues were dispersed by light and exercise, both in short supply during the long night. 'Come on, there's football outside. The spring championship. I have been promised centre-half at last.'

'I'm fine here.'

'Have you written to your mother?' Gran asked.

'No. Debenham's been at me to do so, so I've started a journal for her to read.'

'I told you it would be good for you. A record.'

'Is it? You know I'm not one for words. It seems to make me maudlin.'

'Why?'

'It makes you confront things, doesn't it?' Gran didn't reply. 'I'm going to tell you something I've never told anyone else. It has been preying on my mind more and more—'

'The dark does that. Magnifies things. Good and bad.'

'This is both. Good and bad.' He allowed himself a small smile. 'Although why I should tell a foreigner—'

'Because I am a foreigner. An outsider. I don't judge the way the English do.'

'No, Trigger, you don't.' Oates took a deep breath as if steeling himself. He put his head in his hands and rubbed his face. 'I once, a long time ago—'

'Soldier.' They both looked up. It was Scott.

'Sir.'

Gran cursed the Owner's timing. He knew that such a moment with Oates was unlikely to come round again in a hurry.

'Bill Wilson tells me you are still down in the dumps.'

'Out of sorts.'

'Been in here too long with your ponies, I expect.'

Oates shrugged. 'Yes.'

Scott spoke with all passion he could muster. 'Soldier, I need you. You are part of the plans for the southern party. It's four hundred miles to the Beardmore. I need the horses to make it. I think you are the only man who can get them there. The ponies are in far better condition than last year, thanks to you. You are certainly the only one who can encourage Christopher to move.'

Gran nodded in agreement. Despite being treated for his worms, Christopher remained at best spirited and at worst dangerously violent. Only Oates could handle him without risking a split skull.

'What do you say? I can think of nothing left undone to deserve success. Unless you refuse me.'

Oates stood. As always any animosity he felt towards the man dissipated when faced with his determination. Scott had his faults, but lack of courage wasn't one of them. And the suggestion that he might put the entire enterprise in jeopardy was too much. 'I couldn't do that.'

Scott beamed, the smile that transformed his face from worried, grey man into the sparkling commander. 'Good man.'

'We're just going outside for some football,' said Gran.

'Splendid, Trigger. I'll come and watch once we've taken the magnetic readings.'

As Oates passed, Scott slapped him on the back and then did the same for Gran. He spent a few more minutes looking at the remaining horses. Jehu looked pained simply standing there, and he knew Oates wondered if it was even worth taking him. He reckoned they'd be shooting him by Hut Point. The horses were sadly depleted in number and in strength, and it galled him to have to rely on such animals – any animals – for success.

Outside, the tractor spluttered and died. He heard a bad-tempered Teddy Evans shouting abuse, at man or machine he couldn't tell.

As he walked out, he squinted into the unfamiliar light at the men playing football. They were watched by a small group of penguins, like dinner-jacketed fans on the terraces. His breath clouded the air in front of him, but hung there. The wind had dropped, the sky was a pale cornflower blue, streaked with translucent strings of clouds.

A distant dark line moved from left to right across the ice, just in front of Cape Barne. Cecil Meares of the foolish mouth, exercising some of the dogs, letting them run in the traces with an unloaded sledge. They moved like an express train.

Beyond them, a small sphere hovered in the sky. A balloon, released by Bowers and 'Sunny Jim' Simpson – the meteorologist whose nickname came from a popular cartoon – hovered dead still in the air, not a current to disturb it.

Turning his attention back to the ad-hoc match, Scott watched Debenham go up for a ball, miss, and come down heavily. The sound of his knee striking the ice was sharp and made him wince. Debenham lay on his front, not moving, while the others gathered round.

Atkinson came running over the ice towards Scott, concern on his face.

'What is it?'

Atch pointed with his damaged hand to the kennels. Beneath the mittens, Scott knew it still showed signs of the frostbite he had picked up when he got lost in the blizzard. He had been wandering for six hours before they found him. His fingers had puffed to the size of éclairs. His scarred foot and mangled hands meant, bar a miracle, Atch had ruled himself out of the final group for the Pole once and for all. 'One of the dogs has died, sir.'

'What of?'

'We don't know. Bill is with him now.'

'I'll be along shortly.'

As Atkinson left, Scott swore under his breath. He watched Evans and Lashly trying to coax life out of the seized tractor, the chimney coughing blue or black smoke as the engine refused to catch. Lashly was a reliable man, a good choice, but Scott felt he had erred in making Teddy his second-in-command. He was a fine navigator, but a bit of a duffer when it came to other activities. Scott corrected himself. Evans had spent the winter assiduously repairing and strengthening some of the equipment and his skiing and stamina were first rate. In his heart, Scott knew his main objection was the fact that he didn't care for Kathleen and they had clashed in New Zealand. He had to overcome that. Such sentimentality would have no place when it came to selecting the final four who would go to the Pole. Then again, Evans had also cost him Reg Skelton, with his petty squabbling about ranks. If anyone could have got the best out of the tractors, it was Reg. Perhaps he shouldn't have acquiesced quite so easily, but, like a naïve bridegroom, he'd been blinded by the size of Evans's dowry.

Meanwhile, Debenham was being carried off the field in some pain. Scott had already had words with the young Australian when he had gone off by bicycle and found himself lost on the barrier six miles away. He had scolded him for that, because he hadn't informed anyone what he was doing. It was only when they discovered bicycle and man missing that they put two and two together. And now this. Sometimes he felt like the headmaster of a minor public school, dealing with the remove. Still, he liked the colonials, they had a way of grasping the nettle of any situation, a pluck he admired. Debenham would recover. But what was ailing the dogs? Surely not some repeat of the *Discovery* fiasco?

Machines, men, dogs and ponies. They could all let him down, one way or another. It depends on luck, he had told his company. He hoped there was some of that over the horizon, too.

His calculations meant that leaving late for the Pole for a trip of 144 days and a return around March would mean *Terra Nova* and Pennell, her temporary master, might well have departed. The problem was, there were no funds for another year. He would have to ask some of the officers to forego their salaries, so money could be diverted to New Zealand.

The scheme for the Pole was simple. Sixteen in the party, gradually reducing till two teams of four were man-hauling and then, for the last dash, the final four. Strength was needed, which suggested Birdie, as long as the Crozier trip hadn't had hidden consequences. There should also be someone from the lower decks. Lashly? Crean? Taff Evans? All keen and strong. And who of the scientists? Cherry? Taylor? Debenham, if his knee healed?

'It's in the lap of the gods,' he said softly to himself, feeling a pang of an old loneliness, the weight of decisions, just like the agony of deciding whether or not to send Shackleton home.

The heavy leather football came over and landed at his feet and he hoofed it back to a chorus of cheers. They were one big happy family out there frolicking on the ice, but he could never, ever allow himself to join in with them. There always had to be a distance. Which made him a man forever alone.

He shook the feeling off. It was not a moment to succumb to melancholy. It was time to find out who the fickle gods of the ice really favoured, the English or the Norwegians.

Fifty-eight

Letter from Fridtjof Nansen to Kathleen Scott, September 1911

Norway.

My Dear Kathleen,

How wonderful to meet a woman who is so like the ones one has dreamt of, but never dared hope to meet. Your husband is a very lucky man, to have you and have you love him so much.

I was concerned about how we parted. I know you were worried about that newspaperman, but, as I predicted, nothing appeared. You said you were afraid? Was that what you feared? Or are you afraid of passion? Perhaps your passion or mine? I feel they are both there, I see it in your eyes and on your lips I have never touched. Dare I hope that I will?

But you know I would do nothing to hurt your husband and child. All this might be something to bear, to tolerate, throughout what I hope will be many years of friendship. Even that will make my life far richer than it deserves to be.

Ah, but I am in Berlin again quite soon. Will you not join me? I will tell you the hotel. You could get a room.

Please do not be shocked by the suggestion. I am Norwegian and we have different ways of expressing ourselves, not in letters or words, but in deeds. They matter to us more than any declarations.

I have enclosed a ticket to the event so you can plan the travel. We have a few months, but I pray they go by quickly. I am also thinking of your man, out on the ice, I hope you know that.

Yours truly,

Fridtjof

Kathleen received the letter on the evening that Tomkins, an ugly bore, had tried to accompany her home from the theatre. He had not taken the rejection well, and she had been forced to be rude about his breath.

It was all too much. Each week there was some fool who tried to make love to her. She felt that she had become a challenge, as if she were a widow to be wooed. Every time she showed any gaiety, they took it as a sign she was open for business. Part of her wondered if there was a wager concerning it, but the thought was too awful to contemplate.

She was relying on Fridtjof to be a good friend, but even he kept crossing the line. She liked the Norwegian, but found the letter confusing. How could he think of her in that way yet have any sympathy for Con?

Get a room, he said, but for one or two? He couldn't mean two. Could he?

Kathleen had the maid make her cocoa and retired, still disturbed. She awoke after a horrid dream of being chased over the ice by hordes of Eskimos. As they all began to sweat from the exertion, the pursuers cast off their outer garments, leaving them strewn on the ice. Underneath the furs were the braying rakes of London, in full evening dress, apart from huge fur boots. They began to chant her name. She backed away from them, and found the rotten ice cracking beneath her feet, plunging her into a freezing polynya. She sat up with a start, her heart thumping.

As she reached for the pitcher of water, she saw that the pale shape of Peter was standing in the room, naked, a teddy bear dangling from one hand.

'Daddy's not coming back,' he said slowly.

Kathleen held out her arms and he ran through the gloom of the room to her. 'Nonsense. Daddy's coming back. He has to come back.'

'I dreamed it. Daddy's not coming back.'

Kathleen pulled the little lad tight, squeezing so hard he gasped. She turned her head to one side, so that her tears fell on the pillow, rather than on to Peter's head.

Part Five

'*Great God! This is an awful place*'

Captain Robert Falcon Scott,
Diary

Fifty-nine

Essex, 1917

Gestingthorpe was a house in mourning. It was as if the colour had been sucked from the building and its grounds. Even the gardeners wore black, and the front door was still adorned with a wreath, more than five years after Oates had died.

Tryggve Gran was shown through to the drawing room. As he passed the library, he noticed a sledge was propped against the bookshelves. And there was a bust of Napoleon. 'That will be a museum in time,' the butler whispered. 'To Mr Laurie.'

A museum or shrine? Gran wondered, but said nothing.

He was shown in and Caroline Oates stood. She was dressed entirely in black, as was much of the room. He felt the sense of claustrophobia assault him. It was a mausoleum.

'Mr Gran.'

'Mrs Oates. Thank you for seeing me.'

'Not at all. I welcome anyone who knew my boy. Sit, please.'

Gran did so.

'Can I get you something?'

'No, thank you. I don't have much time. I—'

'Have you been to St Mary's? Our church.'

'No.'

'You must. There is a plaque there, from the Inniskillings. To Laurie.'

'I shall take a look, of course.'

'You know, Teddy Evans comes to see me quite frequently. Less so now he has remarried, but we have had interesting talks. He has strong views on Captain Scott. As have I.'

So there were to be no pleasantries. It was a full-frontal assault. 'He was a fine man.'

Her lips pursed. 'A fine man who killed my son. Murdered, more like.'

'Murdered?'

'I don't use the word lightly. It was murder, was it not? Or do you think manslaughter?'

He didn't intend to be caught in that trap. 'I think it was bad luck.'

'No, no, I can't accept that.'

Gran chose his words carefully. 'You can't accept bad luck happens?'

'Did Amundsen have bad luck?'

'The first time he set off for the Pole he had to turn back. Beaten by the weather. Dogs froze to death. His party suffered frostbite. There was much bad feeling. Almost a mutiny. Later, a suicide.'

'Oh.' He could tell Caroline Oates hadn't heard that. Few had. His fellow countryman was presented as the one with all the luck in his favour, his undertaking a lean, smooth-running machine.

'But Amundsen was not – is not – a man for giving up. So he went again, and this time luck was with him. Scott was the same, determined, but luck was elsewhere that season.'

'Why are you here, Mr Gran?' Her voice was laced with suspicion.

'To ask you to be careful.'

'About what?'

'About how you proceed. I know the loss of your son—'

'No. No, you don't. Teddy does. He lost his wife on the voyage home.'

'I know of that.'

'He understood.' Teddy would have been whispering in her ear, fuelling her grief and bitterness, feeding her with his own.

'Evans and Scott didn't always see eye to eye.'

She made a grunting sound. 'Neither did Scott and my son. I have read his account. Scott's, I mean. Written with one eye on history. A litany of excuses. It should have been called *It's Not My Fault*.'

'That book has made your son a hero.'

'I'd rather he were alive than a hero. I ask again, what do you want?'

Gran turned the question back on her. 'What is it that you want from all this –' he indicated the shrouded room – 'and from Teddy?'

'The truth.'

'No.' Gran smiled. 'No you don't.'

'I beg your pardon?' The tone reminded him of the Antarctic winds. He tried to ignore the piercing gaze. She was a formidable woman.

'I don't think you want the truth, not really. Not all of it. Just part. I will tell anyone about Scott's mistakes. But there are other considerations.'

'Such as?'

'Titus's diary.'

'There is no diary.'

'That's what we all thought. I was surprised when he told me he was keeping one.'

She said nothing.

'It was with his sleeping bag. I know Teddy brought it back and gave it to you.'

'Do you?'

'I know what Teddy said. That nobody had read it.'

'There is no diary to read.'

Gran wondered how she could lie so shamefacedly.

'I know there is, Mrs Oates.'

'How do you know?'

'Because I saw it. Titus, Laurie, said he would make sure it came to you should . . . anything happen.'

What little colour there had been in Caroline Oates's face drained away. What, he wondered, was in the journal?

'Mrs Oates, an official inquiry or a muck-raking book might not be a good idea.'

'If it unmasks Scott, it will be.'

'It will unmask more than that. You see, I know all about Edie.'

The sound that came from Caroline Oates's throat suggested she might be choking to death. 'You scoundrel. How do you know? Did you read his journal?'

Gran took out the parchment-like letter he had kept all those years. 'He wrote it down for me.'

'Can I see?' As she said it her eyes flicked to the fireplace. It was a fleeting glance, but it betrayed her intentions. The letter would be consumed by the flames.

Gran refolded it and placed it in his pocket. 'It was written for me.'

'You are an unscrupulous swine. How much do you want?'

Gran struggled to dispel his anger at the accusation. 'Really. I am not blackmailing you, Mrs Oates. I simply think you have to be prepared for everything to come out. For the moment, your son is a national hero. A beacon, an example. What more could you ask short of having him back? But I am not here to threaten you with exposure. The secret is safe with me.'

'Is it?'

'You have my word.'

'Then why come?'

'To deliver a request from your son. I know for a fact it was his wish that no blame be attached to Captain Scott.'

Mrs Oates recovered her composure enough to ask: 'How do you know this? How on earth could you?'

'Your son told me.'

'When?'

Gran shifted in his seat. He had never revealed this to anyone else and he felt self-conscious saying it. 'As he lay dying.'

Sixty

Hut Point, 2 November 1911

'Oh no!' The anguish in Captain Scott's voice caused every man in the Southern Party to turn and look at him. They were gathered in front of the old Discovery Hut, slowly getting colder as Ponting fussed with his camera, the photographer seemingly oblivious of the tail end of the blizzard swirling around them. 'Damn it.'

'What is it?' asked Wilson.

'The flag.' Scott took off his hat and dashed it to the floor. 'We've left the flag at Cape Evans.'

'I have a Welsh one,' said Taff Evans, causing a ripple of laughter. 'We could always plant that at the Pole.'

Scott glared, his sense of humour, never very reliable, suddenly AWOL. 'It's the flag Queen Alexandra gave us.'

'I'll go, sir,' said Bowers, ever the little red-haired terrier.

'There might be no need. Hold on, Ponco, I'll be back.' Scott retreated into the hut.

Oates looked at Meares who shrugged. 'What's a few more minutes ponting around out in the cold?' Ponting was the term used for posing for the photographer: it described a condition of slowly turning blue while Ponting adjusted his lenses.

It was more than a week since the motor-sledges had set off, dragging their loads of one and a half tons, nursed by Teddy Evans, Lashly, Day and Hooper, crawling at barely three miles an hour.

They had heard the machines coughing and spluttering long after they had disappeared into the white. Scott had intended to follow sooner with the horses, but the weather had turned grim. Now it was clearing, but every man waiting for the photograph could feel the keening wind through his clothes. 'Can you hurry up while I've still got ten fingers?' said Debenham.

'You can't rush art,' said Ponting.

Someone let out a long, rippling fart and the party dissolved into laughter and ribald comments. Ponting began to fume at the disrespect.

'How is Christopher?' Meares asked Oates.

Oates slipped off a mitten and showed his wrist. There was a series of deep red dashes across it. 'Still got those teeth.'

'I've telephoned Gran,' announced Scott as he emerged from the hut. 'He's skiing over with the flag. Be a few hours at most.'

'What a shambles,' Meares muttered.

Oates said nothing. He and Meares had griped their hardest on the journey over from Cape Evans with the animals, baffled by the logic of stretching out the party. First the motors leave, then the weak horses – Atkinson and Keohane had already set off with the worst of the crocks – then the stronger ponies would depart. They would be followed, a considerable way behind, by Meares and Dimitri with the fast-moving dogs.

'Not only that. Our journey starts with a Norskie carrying the Union Jack,' added Meares.

'That's all right,' said Oates with a grin. 'At least he's our Norskie.'

'Gentlemen,' said Ponting, 'if you will just look this way. Hold very still. And gentlemen,' Ponting looked over the camera body at them, 'if even those of you with rancid bowels could at least try and look heroic.'

They laughed at this and the shutter snapped on what appeared to be a happy band of explorers.

Gran arrived in record time, the silk flag safe in his backpack. After he had handed it over to Scott, and received his thanks, Oates took him to one side.

'Trigger, can you take this?'

It was a thick sheet of paper, folded in half, with no envelope.

'Sorry about the writing. Just scribbled it down while we were waiting for you.'

'Is it for your mother?'

Oates looked over at the caravan of men and horses, the former eager to be gone, the latter already looking half beat. 'No. She can have my journal. It's for you. Just to say thank you.'

'For?'

'Being a friend. Sticking with me when you should have just thrown me to Christopher and had done with it. And to explain something. About my black mood the other day.'

'There is no need—'

'There was something preying on my mind. It's clear to me now. I shall make amends when I return.'

'After you have seen the Pole, unless I am mistaken.'

'Ha! Perhaps. You're not a bad lad, Trigger.'

Tryggve Gran smirked. 'For a Norskie.'

'Oh, yes. I was forgetting. For a Norskie.'

The two of them shook hands, for the last time.

The weaker horses were also the most docile, and Chinaman and Jehu stood stock-still while they were harnessed to the sledges. Christopher turned into a devil the moment he saw the load he was expected to haul. Anton and Oates wrestled with him while the other horses were slipped into their traces. It was circus entertainment to them; Oates knew such behaviour out on the barrier would not be at all amusing.

Anton was caught on the shin by a hoof and cursed in Russian.

Scott came over and pulled Oates back from the skittering horse. 'Titus, I don't need you to get a kick to the head, not now. Don't take any chances.'

In the end, Oates resorted to grabbing a foreleg and bending it up. With Christopher unbalanced, Crean came over and with Cherry's help, they pulled the animal down on to the ice.

'You ungrateful monster,' said Oates to his face. Christopher rolled back his upper lip and bared his yellow teeth.

'Remind me,' mused Cherry. 'What has he to be grateful for? You are about to make him drag hundreds of pounds of provisions four hundred miles to the foot of a glacier where you will shoot him.'

Oates stroked the horse's head, but he continued to thrash. 'He should be grateful he doesn't shoot him here and now,' said Anton.

'Shush, don't listen,' said Oates. 'Nobody is going to shoot anyone. Anton, get me some rope.'

As gently as he could with such a recalcitrant beast, he hobbled the animal by tying the front leg into the bent-back position. Now it was a three-legged horse.

'Let's see you be quite so frisky with that,' said Oates as he stood up.

Christopher let out a loud neigh, thrashed about, and then levered himself to his feet. He lunged at Oates, causing him to scrabble back and fall over, made a feint for the terrified Cherry, and then sprinted off over the ice on three good legs, barging aside anyone in his path.

Oates began to laugh.

'What's so funny?' Anton asked as Christopher stopped some two hundred yards away and looked back defiantly, tossing his mane.

Oates shook his head. 'I don't know.' He looked at the other ponies, for the most part now in their traces, a sorry-looking bunch. 'But if I don't laugh, I'll cry.'

'What should we do?' asked Cherry, who did sound close to tears.

'We wait,' said Oates.

Christopher eventually became hungry and the leg binding began to chafe, so Oates was able to coax him to the sledge and harness him, with only minor damage for his trouble.

The convoy set off in the late afternoon; Scott with Snippets and Wilson with Nobby leading the plodders and Bowers, Crean, Taff Evans and Oates bringing up the rear with the more spirited

412

animals. Counting the two early departures, there were ten men, each leading a doomed pony and a heavily loaded sledge.

Ponting took some more photographs, but there was a real impatience in the team as he posed them. It was time to leave, to take the first steps south; there had been enough preamble to last a lifetime.

It was difficult for any of them to grasp the full enormity of what they were doing: heading for the Pole. Or at least, four of them were. Four out of fourteen would be selected to make that final assault. Oates, though, wasn't thinking about that. He had one overriding duty: to get his charges to the foot of the Beardmore Glacier. After that, he would see what fate offered him.

The going was good, the snow firm, and all the ponies pulled well. In spite of his continued truculence, even Christopher occasionally stopped twisting and bucking and put in a good spurt. Bowers, who had initially been sceptical about the horses, nursed and encouraged Victor every bit as attentively as Oates might have. Oates spotted him slipping the pony a biscuit from his own ration.

Not bad, he thought, for a bunch of twisted old cripples. Even as it went through his mind, he felt a twinge in his thigh, as if his body was telling him it wasn't only the horses that were damaged goods.

They were only a few miles into the march when they passed the first ominous marker. There was a black and brown patch of oil sullying the snow and two dented petrol containers had been tossed aside. A little further on was a tin, which Scott stopped to examine, causing the party to bunch up. Oates stayed well back, not trusting Christopher. It was Cherry who crunched over the snow and told him what was inscribed on the metal. A message from Evans. 'The big end has gone on one of the tractors.'

'What's a big end?' asked Oates, as Christopher tried to free his head for a bite at the young Cherry.

'I don't know, but it's pretty vital judging from the Owner's expression. There is a dot in the snow over there.'

He pointed due south. Oates squinted through his goggles, but could make out very little. 'What is it?'

'One of the motor-sledges, Bill Wilson reckons.'

Oates knew the mechanic Day would have worked his fingers to the bone to save it. It wasn't an idle expression. He'd seen him strip great rolls of skin from his hands as he fiddled with nuts, bolts and wires. He wouldn't have abandoned a motor-sledge unless there wasn't another yard to be had from it. 'How far have we come?'

'On to the barrier? Four miles.'

Anger flashed through Oates. 'Three motors at a thousand pounds each. Nineteen ponies at five pound. Thirty-two dogs at thirty shillings. I tell you, Cherry, if Scott fails to get to the Pole he jolly well deserves it.'

Cherry, shocked into silence, walked back to his sledge, hoping that Soldier was wrong and it was still his dark-fed depression speaking.

The next day, they came across the second machine, surrounded by a halo of burned oil where it had spilled its guts in spectacular fashion. Scott's face told Oates all he needed to know. He'd witnessed other commanders panic as misfortunes piled up. He prayed Scott wasn't one of those. Somewhere ahead the four tractor-men had switched to man-hauling, with still the best part of the four hundred miles to go to the Beardmore.

Looking at the forlorn machine, its useless tracks already half covered with drifting snow, Oates realised there was something else he hadn't considered. Unlike a horse or a dog, when a lump of metal broke down, you couldn't even eat it.

Sixty-one

15 November: One Ton Depot

Both men and animals welcomed the rest stop at the 'One Ton', the depot of food and fuel they had laid the previous season, just short of eighty degrees. Fourteen long days of fighting blizzards, soft snow and headwinds meant that every night they were, in Oates's words, 'dead cooked'. He noticed something else, too. His feet sweated in the fur boots far more than he expected. Unless he was careful, the moisture froze at night. He had experimented with different sock and insulating hay combinations, but couldn't get it right. Too swaddled and they perspired. Too little insulation and he risked frostbite in the deep snow.

While the others fired up the stoves in their tents, Oates set about building yet another snow wall to protect his charges before feeding them. The horses stood in a line, stock-still. Green waxed covers lay over them, but the exposed sections of their skin glistened with iced sweat. They were shivering and hungry. Christopher would be fed first, because he would create a terrible fuss if denied. The horse confounded Oates. Every day it was a struggle to make him move, but he refused to stop for lunch, instinctively knowing when the day's march was finally over. Oates had not had a midday break for the best part of two weeks now.

'Need a hand, Soldier?'

Oates looked up. It was Scott. 'I am fine, sir. You should eat.'

'Bill's cooking.' He picked up one of the blocks Oates had cut and carried it across to the foundations that had already been laid. 'These have been horrid marches, haven't they? But they are doing well, aren't they? The horses.'

Not as well as Meares and his dogs, Oates thought. At every camp the huskies pulled in looking fresh and eager after their later start. Scott had told Meares to set out even later each day so as not to out-run them. Oates knew Cecil resented cooling his – and his animals' – heels like that. He never hesitated to point out that the horses and their handlers were comparatively beat. They hadn't even caught up with Evans and his team, who were still up ahead, man-hauling towards the Beardmore. Had they been using dog teams, they would have scooped them up by now.

'Better than the tractors,' said Oates, tactfully.

'Yes, well. But to have got the motors here and working is a feat in itself. One day, they'll come good, you'll see.'

Oates didn't want to be drawn into that argument. Surely they hadn't come to blaze a trail for someone else? 'You know, the ponies are losing condition, skipper. Jehu and Chinaman particularly.'

Scott glanced over at the nearest pony. The wind lifted its cover. Sure enough, the blown snow was clinging to the vertical spars of bone that were its ribs.

'There's something else.'

Scott sighed. 'There always is.'

'They are burning a fierce amount of energy breasting through the snow. To keep them in condition, I have had to up the fodder. We are going to be short before we reach the glacier.'

Scott looked to argue, but held it in. Oates had already heard him disagreeing with Bowers about the sledge loadings and carping with Cherry about his handling of his horse. The compendium of delays and setbacks was testing his temperament. 'I think they will keep it up.'

'No,' said Oates firmly. 'You don't understand. We'll lose them all if we divide the food equally and try to get each and every one there. I know Bowers wants to ditch some fodder to lighten their loads. Perhaps he's right. And then we'll have to start killing the weaker ones to make sure there is enough fodder for the stronger.'

Scott blanched. 'Already?'

Oates began cutting another block for the snow wall.

'Already?' Scott repeated.

'Soon. There is no room for sentimentality now.'

Scott knew he was referring to their argument at the same spot months previously, when Oates had been for killing and depoting the ponies closer to the Beardmore. Scott had tried to get them back alive. And he was to be blamed for that? Since when was trying to make the best use of a creature a weakness? 'Do your best, Soldier,' he said brusquely.

Scott turned into the flurry and walked back towards his tent. So much for lending a hand, Oates thought, as he staggered over with the new ice-brick.

A few minutes later, Taff Evans yelled in his ear. 'Skipper said we should help.' With Taff and Crean cutting and hauling the wall was built in twenty minutes, and the horses fed within the next quarter of an hour. As he squelched across for his hoosh, Oates noticed once again that his feet inside the finnesko were soaking wet.

'Come on, Jehu. Come on, fella. I know you're hungry, but I can't waste fodder on you. Not now. All right, one last biscuit. You've earned that. Steady there. I know. You don't have to show me how strong you are. I know you have a few days left, but we have to keep the others' strength up. Those snow-drifts, they are a bugger, aren't they? Up to your chest. And not just the horses—'

'Are you all right, Titus?'

'Yes, Atch. Best it's me. Isn't it, Jehu? Don't worry, Christopher won't be far behind. I know he deserves it, but he's still pulling all day without a break. Like Taff says, he has the devil up his arse, doesn't he? I reckon Chinaman next, then either Christopher or Victor. Although Victor will break Birdie's heart, I think. Never seen a man become a horse-lover so quickly. Over here, come on. Away from the others. Has to be done. You'll go to a good cause, and not just your colleagues. I tell you, Day and Evans

417

and those tractor-boys, have you seen them? Day is thinner than a pencil. All that man-hauling. Didn't expect it to start quite so early, y'see. So you are going to have to feed him up. It's worrying, because he's been on pemmican. Same as us. But it's the hauling. Worse fucking thing he has ever done, he said. Boring as hell. He says they ran out of conversation on day three! Well, much the same here, I suppose. Marches are getting quieter, have you noticed? Nobody is talking about Tennyson much any more. Day says he doesn't fancy the thought of hauling all the way to the Pole. Teddy Evans won't complain, though. Left a little here, lad. If the Norskies are going like Meares and Dimitri, though, God help Captain Scott. You know, there is a bit of record here. Just a little, but we can take some comfort, I suppose. Well, the Owner will. He's got Shackleton at his back, and the Norskies at his front to drive him on. But he reckons we are about fifteen miles further on than when Shackleton had to kill his first horse. I know, it's not much consolation, is it? But we are ahead of Sir Ernest and that counts for a lot in some quarters. I'm not sure now whether I want the Pole. I've forgotten what it is like to have warm feet. I suspect you have, too. Cold hoofs. It's miserable, isn't it? I'll get your friends, some of them anyway, to the glacier, then it's job done. I'll go back. Make sure I catch *Terra Nova*. Perhaps do some studying for major on the way back. Oh, all right. Lots of studying. Major Oates. Sounds good, doesn't it? Pick up your hoofs here. Bit of a drift. I reckon we are far enough away now. On the other hand, it would be good for the army to be there, wouldn't it? The Inniskillings represented at the Pole. Well, we aren't even at the glacier yet. Just come here. Steady. Goodbye, fella, and thanks.'

My Beloved Kathleen,

It is 9 December. The fourth day of a wet blizzard that has kept us in our tents. All, except for Oates, who goes outside into the blankness of the snow to feed the remaining ponies. He shot Christopher before the storm hit. The bullet entered the skull, but the beast didn't die. It stampeded away from him into camp. Nearly trampled poor Crean before we got another shot in it. I have been troubled by the death of the ponies. Jehu had plenty of fat on him, so was not as far gone as we thought. But I was hardly disturbed by the shooting of Christopher, given the pranks he has performed.

The enforced delay has meant we have consumed food meant for the Summit ration, food we had designated for the plateau. We will have to make it up with pony hoosh.

I am not sure what we would have done without Oates. The temperature is +32 or +33F, even with the blizzard, and the movement of the horses makes for much slush, so he is getting very wet and is feeling the cold more than most of us. He has already suffered frostbite on his nose, as has Meares. He gets little relief inside the tent, with its dripping socks and sodden bamboo. Everything is chill and damp, and the only noise is the patter of snow and the crack of canvas. Bill Wilson keeps the spirits up as best he can.

I have sent Day and Hooper back to Hut Point with a couple of the dogs. Both are pretty much done in. We named one of the depots, the one below One Ton Camp, Mt Hooper. He seemed quite pleased to have something called after him en route. Teddy Evans is putting a brave face on it, but he too has been dragging a sledge for a month now. Man-hauling isn't for everyone.

I am going to tell you something I should have told you in New Zealand, but I didn't want to worry you nor think I was blaming your brother. I think the horses were very poorly selected. They have struggled the whole time. We have to beat them through the deeper drifts now, which is cruel but necessary. If it wasn't for the Soldier they would have been as much use as the tractors. (Five years I wasted on those machines and I could barely get five miles out of them in the end.) So, Oates was right about

419

the horses. Not sure I can find the words to tell him, though. Mind you, he won't admit that the snowshoes actually work; I wish we had brought more, because they tend to break after a few hours.

I have just been outside. The wind is dropping and shifting to the North. Perhaps tomorrow we can carry on. There is no food left for the ponies, but Oates thinks he can work them as far as the barrier as long as the going improves. It is a terrible business. Thank God for Soldier.

Birdie Bowers cut the hoofs off Victor after Oates had despatched him. He has buried them in the snow. He says he will retrieve them on his return journey; he wants something to remember his old friend by. And people accuse me of sentimentality towards animals!

I should try and sleep now if the noise will allow, because we will need all our strength and good fortune for tomorrow. I pray this is not a widespread atmospheric disturbance across the whole region and is just localised trouble. To get such a blizzard in December can only be rotten luck. Let us also hope we have not chosen a bad season for our efforts. My love, as always, to both of you. At least I know you are safe and well at home with Peter.

Sixty-two

The Bechstein Hall, Wigmore Street, London

The lecture was preceded by a piano recital. The builders and proprietors of the small but acoustically perfect Bechstein Hall on Wigmore Street also owned the piano shop next door, and took every opportunity to display their superior German instruments.

Kathleen Scott sat at the rear, on the raked section of the stalls, and listened to Artur Schnabel play a piece by Schubert and a rather taxing one by Beethoven. When he had finished and the applause had died, he stood and announced in heavily accented English: 'Ladies and gentlemen, I feel sorry for you. I think sometimes I am the only person in the room who enjoys the Beethoven's Diabelli Variations. I get paid, you pay for tickets and you suffer.'

'Never!' shouted someone from the balcony. The audience tittered.

'Thank you. And I would like to thank the Bechstein Company for the use of their exemplary piano. If any of you should wish to purchase one of these marvellous instruments . . .' He paused and smiled to show that his salesmanship was ironic. 'Then a representative of the company will be in the foyer after the talk. But I am aware that you are not here for my music. There are thirty-three variations in all. I played but seven, so as not to keep you from our distinguished guest. If you want to hear the others, I am at the Albert Hall in two days' time.' There was scattered clapping – possibly, thought Kathleen, because some were relieved that they had been spared the other twenty-six. 'Now, to the evening's main attraction, as they like to say in Music Hall. I first met him in Christiana a decade ago. He is my very good friend, the greatest explorer of his age –'

Kathleen felt herself squirm. Surely that was yet to be seen.

'Professor Fridtjof Nansen.'

Nansen emerged from a door at the rear of the stage and she was conscious of how his bulk filled the entire space. It was as if a polar bear had emerged, loping across to the lectern, which seemed dwarfed by his great hands as he gripped it. The Norwegian surveyed the crowd, nodding to accept the applause.

'Thank you very much for coming out on this cold November night. Yes, even I feel the cold in London.' He let the polite laughter die. 'My Lords, ladies and gentlemen, before I begin my illustrated lecture, I would like to introduce a very great gentleman indeed. A king of polar exploration. I am sure he won't mind standing. Please. Do not be shy. I give you, Sir Ernest Shackleton.'

Kathleen felt her throat constrict. She had had no idea he would be there. As the Irishman stood, there came foot stamping and fevered clapping. Nansen beamed as Shackleton crossed to the low stage and the men shook hands. The cheers reverberated around the ceiling.

'Sir Ernest, like myself, is keeping a keen eye on events at the South Pole. I want to say now, publicly, that I wish my countryman had taken a different course of action.' There was less enthusiastic clapping. The audience didn't like to be reminded of Amundsen's treacherous change of tack. 'Just to illustrate that we explorers of the ice are one large family, there is someone else here I would like you to acknowledge. My—'

Kathleen didn't hear the rest above the roaring in her ears. How could he do this? For her to be recognised from the stage by a Norwegian, of all people. Had he no sense of decorum? What would Hannah Scott make of it? She regretted sneaking in; how could she have been so naïve?

If anything, the roars for her were louder than for Shackleton and, in the end, she had to half rise from her seat before they would stop. It was a good thirty minutes before her reddened cheeks stopped glowing with anger and chagrin and she felt composed enough to slip away without drawing too much attention to herself.

'I have ruined everything.' Nansen sat at the lunch table, his face hangdog.

'No, Fridtjof. It's just that I have to be so careful. The public watch my every move.'

He reached into his pocket and placed an envelope before her.

'What's this?'

'Two hundred pounds. For *Terra Nova*.'

'No, I couldn't take that—'

'It's not from me. It's from the talk last night. At the end, I asked the public to be as generous as possible. Shackleton backed me to the hilt.' He smiled. 'Of course, you weren't there.'

'You saw me leave.'

He nodded.

'I'm sorry, I had no choice.'

'And you have heard all my stories and jokes before.'

'No.' She laughed, thinking of his sometimes clumsy English. 'Well, yes, I have. But that isn't the reason. I have already explained.'

'So why did you come in the first place?'

'Ah, here we are. Thank you, Bellamy.'

The soup had arrived and they talked about where Con might be for a while, but Nansen was too wily to be diverted. He waited till Bellamy had left before he retraced his steps. 'So, why did you come? You know the lecture. You have said we should be discreet.'

She took a last sip of the soup and put down her spoon. 'I missed you.'

'A-ha.' He wagged a finger. 'Now, I think we have the truth.'

'The truth is I can be surrounded by people and still be lonely.'

ROBERT RYAN

'You know, before I got caught by the ice, I studied anatomy. Chiefly the brain.'

'The brain? How fascinating. What did you learn?'

'About anatomy, lots. An intriguing organ. But, in terms of psychology, or emotions, motivations, feelings, nothing. Nothing. You dissect the heart and you say, yes, I see, I understand. The kidneys, too. Even the liver, under the microscope, releases its secret. But the brain? Why do we feel lonely or sad or happy? Why do some people nourish us, just by being in the same room, while others drive us to melancholy? We don't know. And I hope we never do.' He reached for his glass of sherry. 'Let us toast the mystery of humans.'

They clinked glasses.

'I think some people are like the sun, able to give off invisible rays that warm,' Kathleen said. 'I think you have that power.'

'And your husband?'

She didn't answer. She was becoming frightened of how ethereal he felt of late, a ghost out on the ice, as insubstantial as the crystals that sometimes swirled around him. Only by staring at little Peter could she conjure him up. It was hard having a man who was at the bottom of the world, too far for any of his warming rays to reach her.

The soup was cleared away and Nansen leaned forward, his eyes wide and voice low. 'So, Kathleen. You missed most of my lecture last night. I had a new joke.'

'Shame.'

'Will you come to Berlin with me in the New Year? January?'

'Do you like whiting, Professor?'

'I do.'

'I get these at Johnson's.'

'Lovely. Thank you.

'And a white wine? Hock?'

'If you'll join me.'

Bellamy fetched a bottle and, once it was approved, poured the wine. 'Tell cook I'll ring when we have finished this course,' Kathleen said as he left. 'Come back then.'

'Very good, madam.'

'So. Where were we?' she asked.

'We were in Berlin.'

'Not quite.' Her cheek dimpled as she smiled. 'You were in Berlin.'

'Will you come?'

'Yes, Professor,' Kathleen said slowly. 'I believe I will.'

Sixty-three

The Beardmore Glacier, 12 December 1911

Bill Wilson held on to Nobby while Oates loaded the revolver. Both men were blinking back tears. It wasn't getting any easier.

'How are the hands, Titus?'

'Fine.' He had to take his mittens off to use the revolver and Wilson could see the skin was white and wrinkled. Although they were cold, his hands hadn't suffered like his nose, which was often hard to the touch by the end of the day and required much massaging in the tent. His leg was aching, too, the old wound flaring hot now and then, and his hip throbbed at night. 'How do you feel?' he asked Wilson.

'Oh, you know.' He looked over his shoulder.

A few hundred yards away, Bowers was swinging the thermometer over his head. Next to him the tents were being erected. Crean and Lashly were waiting to skin the horses and form the depot, and to the south was the Beardmore. He hadn't been to look at it yet, concentrating on the job in hand. They had covered eleven miles in eleven hours on the last march through that strange, wet snow, whipping the horses every step of the way, it seemed. Oates was tired.

'I worry about the skipper,' said Wilson. 'When I manage to read, I see him sitting, fretting, chewing his lip. How many miles today? Tomorrow? Are we depoting enough? Are the depots close enough? He can't relax.'

'Hold Nobby steady. We don't want another Christopher.'

'Have you been keeping count?'

'Of what?'

'Camps. This is camp thirty-one. You know, Nobby and Jimmy are the last survivors of the original depoting journey.' Wilson looked wistful, his gaze drawn to the ice beneath his finnesko boots. 'Nobby escaped the killer whales—'

The shot made Wilson jump. Nobby gave a small exhalation and folded down on to the ground. Both men stepped out of the way and felt the impact through their feet. A surprisingly small amount of blood trickled from the wounded head, hot and smoking.

'Dear Lord,' said Wilson. 'What a shambles.'

Oates nodded, but kept his counsel. He had to get through this and his work was done. He cupped his mouth with his mittens and shouted over to Silas Wright at the pony string. 'Next.'

After the last pony had been shot, Oates walked with Wilson and Bowers to take a better look at the Beardmore. It was snowing again, but without the driving force of the wind, the flakes swirled gently around them and visibility was better than they expected.

'Thank God that is done with,' said Wilson. 'We can do the hard work ourselves now.'

'Show those Norskies how it should be done,' added Bowers. 'That the British are not as degenerate as they think.'

Oates stopped, sensing the snowfall was diminishing. Within ten minutes it had ceased altogether and the three men wiped their goggles and peered upwards.

'My God,' said Bowers.

They were staring up at a wide channel of ice, a frozen roadway, with saw-toothed mountains where the hedgerows should be. The gateway to this express path was framed by a trio of huge granite columns on the left and, far away to the right, Mt Hope, which really had lived up to its name. Whenever the storm abated they had seen its distant shape, offering hope of a change of scenery, something from the monotony of the barrier. Now Oates could see what this change would be, he wasn't quite so certain it was an unalloyed joy.

'How can it be just ice and wind?' he asked himself softly.

Scott's voice came from behind them. 'Fourteen miles wide, a hundred and twenty miles long. It rises to ten thousand feet. At the end of it is the Polar Plateau. We have to thank Shackleton for showing us this way.'

'And warning us of its crevasses,' added Wilson.

'Which is why we'll keep away from the mountains,' said Scott. 'And there is a lot more snow than when Shackle was here. He describes blue ice from here on up.' They all looked at the deep drifts the storm had deposited. Scott had hoped he would have had some horses in hand for the initial ascent, but the blizzard had robbed him of all margin.

He turned to Oates. 'You did wonderfully well to get us here, Soldier.'

'You have. I congratulate you,' added Wilson.

'And I thank you, Titus,' said Scott with feeling. He took off his mitten and held out his hand. 'We'll take the dogs up a little way, eh, Bill?'

Wilson looked puzzled. 'If you say so, Con. Meares claims he is going back on *Terra Nova*.'

'Yes. Well, we'll see about that.'

Oates looked up at the glacier, and felt butterflies in his stomach at the majesty of it. And not a little fear. They had completed stage one. Stage two was the Beardmore. And the final leg was the plateau. In regular land-miles, which he tended to think in, unlike Scott, they had come four hundred miles. There were still five hundred to go to the Pole. It was a daunting thought.

Yet he felt pleased that he had at least done his duty. As he took Scott's hand, he experienced a strange sensation, like an infusion of calm into his bloodstream. All the animosity he had felt towards the man dissipated like the falling snowflakes. He now knew that half his own mood swings had been caused by the worry that he wouldn't get the animals this far, that he wouldn't fulfil his part of the contract. That he would let Scott down.

'We go on,' said Oates, nodding at the glacier.

'We go up,' agreed Scott. 'And from this point I'd like you in my sledge team, Titus.'

Oates smiled and nodded. For some reason the Soldier couldn't quite fathom, he felt strangely pleased.

Three groups of four began their ascent of the glacier on 10 December. Scott, Wilson, Oates and Taff Evans; Teddy Evans, Wright, Lashly and Atch; and Bowers, Cherry, and the Irish duo of Crean and Keohane. The horses were dead and buried in the snow. Scott told Meares that the dogs, having gorged on pony flesh, were to go on a little further up the glacier, pulling eight hundred pounds of supplies between them. Meares was not happy. He had expected to turn his huskies for home well before that point, and his food margin for the dogs on the return trip was, therefore, not generous.

Oates had never experienced man-hauling in anger before. He found the harness uncomfortable. He felt, in fact, like a beast of burden. But Scott's enthusiasm was infectious and for the first few miles it seemed to Oates that the load felt less than the 170 lb they were pulling. He soon got the rhythm of the skis and silently thanked Gran for his nagging. Oop the Fut, he recalled, and laughed to himself. Taff Evans had also improved and stiffened the ski boots, so there was less strain on the Achilles tendon, for which Oates made a mental note to thank him.

The snow deepened, though, and he found the sledge snagging all too easily. Now, after every stop, they had to jerk the runners free, with a one-two-heave. It sometimes took ten or twelve jerks, and left his spine and hip plagued by a dull ache. But Scott, Wilson and the burly Taff were pulling like locomotives, so he made sure he did his part.

The momentum was hard to keep up. If, on a steep section, they slowed, the sledge began to sink, till it became a snow-plough. They sweated so hard they were working in singlets. When they made camp on the first night, all were ravenously hungry. After they had eaten, Oates went out for a pipe, leaving

Scott and Wilson to their fretting. Taff took himself off to Crean's tent, knowing the officers would talk more freely without one of the men present.

Oates walked over to where Meares and Dimitri had settled the dogs, which were gorging on more pony. The covering now was a good twelve or fourteen inches deep, and his feet throbbed, as if the bones themselves had been bruised as he trudged through it. 'Titus, how goes it with the Owner?'

'He keeps a very neat tent.'

'I'll wager he does. If only his mind was so tidy.'

'Ssshh.'

'Oh, the captain is your new chum, is he?'

'Hardly,' said Oates, well aware of what the dog-man thought of the Owner. 'But that isn't the issue, is it? It's making the Pole. And I am confident we can do that, at least.'

Meares twisted his upper lip into a sneer. 'Making it isn't the problem.'

'What do you mean?'

'It's the same dilemma we face. Me and my dogs, I mean. Food. I have to turn for home soon. And later than I planned for. Over four hundred miles, with just what we can carry for man and dog. We've come on a lot further than intended with the dogs, according to his crackpot plans. Yet I mustn't disturb your depots if I can help it. And I haven't eaten tonight because it will take away from the plateau rations.'

'That's ridiculous. We have far more food than Shackleton had,' Oates reminded him.

Meares laughed and some of the dogs looked up, alarmed, perhaps, by the bitterness of it. 'Shackleton didn't reach even the Pole.'

'We will.'

'We?'

'Scott and whoever he takes,' Oates corrected.

'Look, Titus, don't be blinded into doing something you don't believe in. Scott, for all his infuriating ways, has an odd magnetism. Resist it. You could come back with me. With the dogs we can certainly catch *Terra Nova* before she sails. Back to the army, that's what you said.'

Oates felt the tug of a momentary temptation. 'No. Not yet.'

'Why?'

He pointed up the glacier. 'Three parties of four. That's what we have banked on. I'm with the strongest. I leave them, they'll take one from the other group, perhaps. That weakens it. You've seen some of them.'

'Aye. Teddy Evans only pulls when someone is watching,' agreed Meares. He meant Scott, who stopped sometimes to assess the progress and attitude of the other teams. That was when Evans really put his back into it.

'He and Lashly have been man-hauling more than any of us. Seven weeks, since Corner Camp. I think Teddy is beat.'

'Yet he won't admit it.'

'Because he still wants the Pole,' said Oates.

'The Pole, the Pole.' Meares shook his head. 'Such stubbornness can be the death of a man.'

Somewhere in the mountains they heard the growl of an avalanche, an ominous full stop to the sentence.

'I'm going back to New Zealand, Soldier.'

'You'll be missed next season.'

'By you perhaps.'

'By all of us. Yes, the Owner too. We'll need your skill.'

Meares laughed. 'My skill has hardly been appreciated so far. The look Scott gave me whenever I passed him said it all. He resents being reminded that dogs pull, horses and men flounder. Change your mind?'

'No, Cecil. Safe home.'

'And safe Pole, Titus.'

Kathleen – Just a tiny note as the dogs are departing. We have made a new deposit of food. Lower Glacier Depot. Around here Shackleton had blue ice; we have deep, sticky snow. An extraordinary difference in fortune. Now with the dogs gone, we have redistributed and pull 200 lb per sledge. Skis are the thing but not everyone has prepared for that and some prefer snowshoes. It is tiresome. I am fit and well and hauling as well as any man in the group. Oates is a tower of strength, and Bill and Taff do their part. We are behind Shackleton, though, which is galling. That blasted storm that pinned us down is to blame. So, things are not as rosy as they might be, but we keep our spirits up and say our luck must turn.

'The man is a bloody fool.'

The words stung Scott like a slap across the face.

'And dangerous to boot.'

The voices were muffled and it was some time before Scott could make out who was speaking. The men often treated canvas walls as if they were brick, unaware of how far words carried beyond them and on to the ice. It was a fine warm evening, the silver fog of the day having finally dissipated. Scott had come out of his own tent to take a pipe, prior to telling Cherry of his decision. He had certainly brought no intention of eavesdropping, but he found himself unable to move away.

'Keep your voice down.' It was Atkinson.

'I don't care who hears. I should be going on.'

'We all should.'

'I'll tell him what we think, then.'

'It'll do no good, he's made his mind up.'

'What mind?'

Scott bit down on the stem of his pipe, threatening to snap it. How dare they?

'You are just upset.'

'Of course I am bloody upset.'

'It's cruel, isn't it? To keep us hanging on. Not knowing till the last minute who will go on and who will turn back.'

'Scott is a bloody fool.' Ah, it was Wright who was cursing him.

'Ssshh.'

'And another thing. Teddy bloody Evans to go? Teddy Evans and not me?'

'Personally, I wouldn't take Taff Evans either. Full of hot air.'

That was too much, maligning one of the hardest workers in

432

the party. Scott had heard enough, had suffered enough; he moved away before he succumbed to the urge to enter the tent and give them a piece of the mind he apparently didn't possess.

Scott thought Cherry-Garrard was going to cry, but it was difficult to tell because every man's eyes had been red and raw for days. He felt wretched, but the plan had to be adhered to. They had made the summit of the glacier without mishap or loss, although more slowly than he had hoped, and plagued by exhaustion and thirst. He had been forced to stop Oates and some others eating snow, warning them that it would chill their core and they would die of hypothermia. But it consumed so much fuel to melt the ice they would drink, he had been forced to limit it. So, four had to turn back as planned.

Scott sat in the tent with Cherry, explaining his reasoning for the young man's deselection.

'I know it's a blow.'

'Well, sir, it is. But it had to fall on someone.'

'How are the eyes?'

'Better, thank you.' They had all suffered at least some snow blindness. Given the exertion of hauling up the glacier, their goggles had fogged, which meant they could not spot crevasses. Taking the goggles off had caused glare damage. 'The cocaine helped. And the tea leaves.' The dregs of a good brew helped soothe burning eyes.

'We did it, Cherry. Stage two gone.'

'Have I let you down, sir?'

Scott reached over and patted Cherry's knee. The lad was like an anxious puppy sometimes. 'No, no, don't be ridiculous. I am sure you are disappointed.'

'I am.'

'So is Silas. He called me a fool. Actually, I think it was a bloody fool.'

Cherry was shocked at Silas Wright's behaviour. 'Sir?'

'Oh, not so I'd hear. But the walls of the tents are hardly sound proofed unless there is a blizzard.'

433

Cherry laughed. He could imagine the Canadian letting off steam; he thought Teddy Evans a poseur, and he himself was as fit as any man in the team. 'Who else will return?'

'Keohane and Atch.'

'Oh.'

'You were expecting someone else?'

Evans and Lashly, he almost said. 'No, I suppose not.'

'I know Wright is upset, but tell him there is good reasoning. He is a fine navigator. You'll need him to get home.'

'Of course, skipper.'

'But we also need another day of your efforts, Cherry. To get over the crevasses.' Where the glacier flowed off the plateau, the strain on the ice produced a web of huge cracks; they were facing the last of them.

Cherry fought hard to keep a waver from his voice. 'Whatever you require, sir.'

'Don't take it too hard. This is a bad enough business as it is.'

'I won't. I am sure you have chosen well.' Cherry tried his best to sound bright. 'Is there any message for anyone?'

'For you. I want the dogs brought out to resupply One Ton Camp for our return. Just in case the returning parties have depleted it. Don't risk them any further. Tell Meares. And if Meares has left on *Terra Nova*, as the bugger is threatening to, tell Dimitri. One Ton Camp, on or around March the twenty-seventh. Don't forget.'

'I won't. I'm sure they will find you there.'

'Count on it.'

After Scott had left, Wilson slipped in, while Cherry was sorting through his gear. The young man was upset, but in his heart he knew the Owner was right. He didn't have the pull for the Pole.

'Sorry to lose you, Cherry,' Wilson said.

Cherry bit his lower lip. He was aware Wilson had probably had a say in the decision. 'Thank you.'

'I won't be far behind.'

'Spare finnesko,' said Cherry, lifting up the boots. He was trying

434

not to meet Wilson's gaze, unless he saw the slick of moisture in his own.

'Birdie would welcome some. His are pretty poor.'

Cherry laid them to one side. 'What do you mean, you won't be far behind?'

'I doubt I'll make the final group. Pretty tired after the other day.' They had pulled up the treacherous incline of the glacier for nine and a half hours and made three miles.

'Who isn't? Even Birdie says it is the most back-breaking work he has ever done. Your sledge group is by far the strongest. The Owner sets a hot pace.'

'Remember the tortoise and hare, young man.'

'Neither of whom had to run through four-foot drifts and then this ice.'

Wilson smiled. The soggy snow had seemed hard enough; the blue ice with its unforgiving surface, need for crampons and hidden crevasses was even worse.

'Why did you come back, Bill? Out on the ice again, with a new wife at home?'

Wilson sighed. 'I was getting too soft.'

'Meaning?'

'I grew to like hotel dinners and preferred hot water to cold.'

Cherry laughed. 'Oh, for a hotel dinner and some hot water.'

'Yes. I think I am ready for it now.' Wilson smiled. 'But also for him. Scott. I came south for him.'

'He needs you.'

'No, he would have come anyway.'

That wasn't what Cherry meant, but he let it go. No use explaining that, without Wilson to soften the mood swings and peevishness he suffered from, Scott would not be half the leader he was.

Cherry produced a small package from his belongings. 'Will you give some baccy to the Owner?'

'You can give it to him yourself.'

'As a present. On Christmas Day. Just wait the five days. To show there are no hard feelings.'

'He'll know that.' Wilson reached over and took it. 'But he'll appreciate the gesture. Will you take a letter for my wife?'

'Of course.'

Wilson touched the young man's arm. 'He saw you pulling your guts out, Cherry.'

A bubble of frustration burst within Cherry. If only he knew what Teddy Evans said, preaching sedition sometimes, and the half-effort he often put in, surely he would have been the one sent back. 'Then why—'

'It's a matter of priority. And age. You are young, Cherry. If we don't make it this season, who knows? Maybe you'll make it next.'

'Who do you think he'll choose for the last push?'

It was the question on everyone's cracked and blistered lips. It was no secret that Scott frequently consulted Wilson about the men's fitness and their potential.

'There will be someone from the lower decks, I'm sure. Evans?'

Wilson shrugged. 'It's a possibility.'

'Atch says Evans is a windbag. Talks a big story.'

'Atch is entitled to his opinion. It isn't his decision.'

'Will the Owner choose Titus, then?'

'Well, he's got to be in the running. Nothing wrong with him as far as I can see.'

Cherry thought that Wilson could not have been looking very hard, but knowing it would sound like sour grapes, went back to sorting through his equipment for gifts for the lucky eight who would go on.

'I see. Well, good luck, Bill. I hope it's better than our journey together.'

'It could hardly be worse.'

Cherry laughed; that much was true. 'Here. You should take this. For old times' sake.' He handed over his copy of Tennyson's *In Memoriam*, which Wilson was fond of. 'You are a good friend. I value that more than anything. Along with Birdie. Knowing you two means a lot more to me than reaching the Pole.'

'That's kind of you.' He reached across to take the volume. 'Sure?'

'Positive.'

Wilson weighed the green leatherbound book in his hand. It, too, was like an old friend. 'Thank you, Cherry. I'll make sure you get it back.'

After the communal meal of pemmican and biscuits, Oates had a rare moment of privacy in the tent. Scott and Wilson were out consoling those who were to be sent back and Taff Evans was working on honing and straightening the ski runners on the sledges.

Firstly, he positioned himself so that his hip stopped giving him trouble with its damnable twinges. He was forced to sit slightly twisted. He was all too aware that the one short leg meant he had a cock-eyed stance in the traces, but, fortunately, nobody noticed it. All pulled as best they could, some favouring one leg or one shoulder, but then every other man had two equal limbs. Who would have thought a Boer bullet would come home to roost in such a way?

Slowly, he undid the bindings of his boots and eased them off, gasping as he did so. A strange odour came up at him: wet hay, sweaty feet, damp socks and something else, slightly sickly. The hard ice had left his soles feeling unbelievably tender, and he grimaced as he took off the socks and hung them up.

His feet were like big, pale fish, something that had been brought up from the depths. For the most part they were numb with cold, except where they ached, and his tendons felt as though they had been stretched four inches. He brought his left foot up and began to massage the spongy skin and the stabs of pain made him weep. He looked down at the extremity closely. The big toe had a worrying sheen to it. In the strange half-light of the tent, it looked as if it was turning black.

Oates quickly pulled on a semi-dry sock when Taff Evans came in through the entrance tube, his bulk filling the tent. He was cursing as he tied up the stays that closed the opening.

'You all right, Taff?'

'Aye, sir,' Evans said. 'Grazed my knuckles on the runners.'

He removed his mitten and Oates saw a line of raw skin across the back of his hand, the blood not yet clotted.

'You should let Bill look at that.'

'No need. It isn't the first time I've cut m'self on one of those damned sledges and I'll wager it won't be the last.'

It was Lashly who started to sing the carols as they hauled on Christmas Day. Scott's group heard them intermittently, whenever the headwind faltered. The glacier was behind them, and they had passed through ten thousand feet and were descending ever so slightly. Of course, they could only guess at that because Birdie had broken their only hypsometer. Scott regretted bawling him out now. They should have brought a spare, but that was as much Scott's responsibility as it was Bowers's. He apologised later, which at least stopped the little man skulking around with a face like a deflated football.

'Away in a manger –' Lashly began. He was bringing up the rear with Teddy Evans, Crean and Birdie Bowers.

Despite the thin air and the laboured breathing it brought, they were making good progress in bright sunshine. Scott was already devising the Christmas dinner they would have when they halted. Pony hoosh at full whack – and damn the extra oil the primus consumed at altitude – with ground biscuit, plum duff, cocoa, crystallised ginger. He laughed to himself when he remembered Shackleton's Christmas surprise. Odd, the closer he got to the Irishman's Furthest South, the more warmly he thought about him. It had been all about beating his figures; now he was on the verge of doing so, the old animosity had dissipated. Perhaps, one day, they could be friends again. After all, it wasn't Shackle's idea he should receive a knighthood, despite his falling short. It was thrust upon him. And no sane man would turn one down.

Oates was lost in the mindless repetition. Shush, shush, breathe, shush, shush, breathe. The soft noise of the gliding skis contrasting with the harshness of the air being forced into burning lungs. There was a rasping, squeaking noise, followed by a dry sound, like leaves rustling, with each intake. Shush, shush, breathe. But the next snatch of lusty singing penetrated even his head.

'Once in Royal David's –'

'Where does he get the wind from?' Oates muttered.

'It's Lashly's birthday, sir,' yelled Taff Evans.

'Ah.' That made him forty-four. A year older than Scott.

'– cattle shed –'

'Old enough to know better than to waste his breath,' suggested Oates.

'Sir,' laughed Evans.

'We should take off some layers soon,' said Wilson to Scott. 'Sweating rather a lot.'

The temperature was still rising. Scott didn't want a long halt; they had covered fourteen miles on Christmas Eve. He was set to beat that so they all earned their plum duff. 'All right. Give the others a chance to catch up.' He raised an arm. 'Halt.'

They slithered to a standstill and the pains began as muscles started to protest at what they had been put through. There was a strange rhythm and an odd gait to man-hauling that, once you found it, was capable of being maintained for hours. It was when a man stopped he truly appreciated just what an unnatural strain the whole process was, how tiring it was, and what damage it inflicted.

'Everyone all right?' Scott asked.

Oates lifted the harness over his head and turned away to hide the spasm of pain shooting up his leg. He had looked at his bullet wound and the old scar seemed intact, although it had some soft patches where the old surface had dissolved. Weeks of damp, dirty clothes had not helped.

They all turned and watched Teddy Evans's party lumber towards them, with Lashly in the lead, singing, the others behind, their arms and legs pumping over the smooth surface. Scott had taken the humped sastrugi in his stride, but they were finding them hard and had moved slightly to the east on to a smoother surface.

'God rest ye merry –'

439

'Well, someone is happy,' said Oates as he reached into his tunic for a half-biscuit he had been saving.

It was at that moment that the earth swallowed William Lashly, aged forty-four.

Sixty-four

Cape Geology, 25 December

Tryggve Gran woke up with a start, thinking he was suffocating. He found his mouth filled with reindeer hairs from his sleeping bag. Yet it wasn't only that which had caused his choking. His airways were constricted by fear. He was scared, apprehensive. Something had pumped ice into his veins, even though he was warm and snug in the shelter they had built at Granite Bay.

As he pulled the last hairs from his lips, he looked around the hut. The others were still asleep, although Taylor was mumbling. His fingers were bad, and causing him great pain, even though there was no obvious cause. The Irishman Forde and the Australian Debenham snored on.

Gran slid out of the bag and pulled on his outer clothes and boots. It was only just gone six, but it was also a few days after midsummer. The sun would be high. He left the gloomy hut and walked out on to the mix of ice and rock that led down to the sluggish sea and the remains of the frozen spray icicles. It was another day tinged with the mist that rolled down from the mountains. However, in the far distance, across McMurdo Sound, he could just make out Erebus. The Antarctic sun was relatively strong at this time of year, and he was sure the fog would lift and give them another glorious day. They had eggs and seal steak to consume for the Christmas celebration. But Gran knew he had drawn

441

the short straw and would have to cook up the seal pemmican for their forthcoming cartographical and geological journeys. It was a filthy job, which made a man smell rancid. Still, none of them reeked of spring flowers.

The mist parted enough for him to see the ice sheets to the north, where the pack had stubbornly refused to retreat before the summer temperatures. Behind him was the building they had named Granite Hut after Jules Verne and *Mysterious Island*. Beyond it rose the glaciers and mountains they would christen over the next few days. They were majestic and terrifying, but he half hoped that by the end of their trip Debenham, the chief cartographer, might have named one of them after a certain young Norwegian.

Gran reached inside his jacket and produced a cigar, a gift from Forde. A strange Christmas breakfast, but this was a strange Christmas. This was his second in Antarctica, if he included the previous year on the ship, when it was held firm by the ice pack. It seemed more than twelve months ago, and he recalled that they had celebrated that whole day and the next one, too, for the twenty-sixth had been Debenham's birthday. Gran had a pack of cigarettes with him which he would give to Frank the next day. The Australian enjoyed a smoke and Gran liked the easygoing Australian.

It felt strange that the band of men from the *Terra Nova*'s wardroom and mess were now scattered over hundreds of miles. Some were still moving south on the plateau, others would be heading back down the glacier or be on the barrier already. Another group under Atkinson was at Cape Evans, in the hut. Campbell's party was somewhere to the north, having been landed at a new site by *Terra Nova* after discovering Amundsen had claimed the Bay of Whales. That Northern Party would be picked up by the ship when it returned from New Zealand. And then there was their own small expedition, charged with mapping the western edge of McMurdo Sound. When they had discovered that Amundsen was on the ice, Teddy Evans had suggested that this group be rolled into the polar party to give strength in numbers. Scott had disagreed and Evans had sulked. But Gran knew Scott was right. It wasn't more men and mouths to feed the Owner needed. It was more dogs.

'Happy Christmas, Trigger.'

Taylor was squeaking towards him.

'Happy Christmas.'

'Any more dreams?'

Gran thought it best not to share the sense of foreboding that had woken him. He had been foolish enough to tell his colleagues that, while dozing on 15 December, he had seen the image of a telegram. It floated on to the wall of the tent, as if projected. It had said: 'Amundsen reached Pole, December 14th.' The others had laughed, said it was wishful thinking by a Norskie, but he had written it down and noted time and date just in case it was a premonition.

'How are the fingers?'

Taylor took off his mitt. 'Bloody sore.'

Gran examined them. Two had swollen up like plump salamis. He felt his pulse.

'I thought Debenham was the medic.'

Gran laughed. 'Good with maps. I think he knows as much as Dr Wilson can write on a postage stamp. I am going to put my arm inside your jacket.'

Gran felt under the armpits, but there was no sign of swelling. He squeezed the fingers that weren't swollen. Then touched the two bloated digits. Taylor yelped.

'There is no blood poisoning. Yet. I'll have to lance those two,' said Gran.

He grimaced at the thought. 'Oh, very happy Christmas.'

For some reason, this made them both think of the polar party, hauling south as fast as they could. 'They will be four by now, I suppose. I wonder who he has selected.'

Gran shook his head, not wanting to speculate. His eyes were drawn to the hazed south. 'God Bless Captain Scott.'

Taylor nodded, his throbbing fingers forgotten. 'Yes, God bless Captain Scott. He may not be perfect, but I tell you, none of us could do what he's done. Not one. Merry Christmas, boys, wherever you are. And Happy Birthday, Bill Lashly.'

Sixty-five

I have a family!

The objection – thought, rather than shouted – filled Stoker Lashly's head as the snow crumpled beneath his feet and the shiny-lipped jaws of the crevasse opened up to swallow him.

'I have a family and nearly my time! A full pension!'

His stomach forced its way up into his throat as he fell into the abyss, accompanied by a glittering shower of ice.

'It's my birthday!'

The shimmering blue of the cavern's side flashed by him and he closed his eyes, resigned to the fatal impact, when he felt the traces bite under his shoulders. He jerked to a halt with a force that squeezed every last breath from him. He was arrested for less than a second before he began a slower descent as his colleagues and the sledge were dragged down after him. If the fall didn't kill him, three bodies and several hundred pounds of supplies landing on his cranium would.

Then he stopped again, the downward progress halted.

He began to spin in the traces and dared open his eyes. Above him he could see the skeletal form of the sledge, bridging the gash of the opening. A steady rain of ice particles fell on him.

'Lashly!'

The voice from above seemed to fill the cave.

'Are you all right?'

'I think so.' Lashly looked around. His skis were still on his feet

444

and his poles around his wrist. He used the latter to estimate the scale of the hole that had taken him. The cyan cavern was about fifty feet deep and about eight wide. He could see the bottom, pearlescent in what little light was penetrating down there. The surface crack was about a hundred feet across. Scott could only just have missed it.

'We're just going to wedge the sledge. The others are coming over. We'll haul you up.'

He wasn't the first man to go down a crevasse. Most had experienced the terror of a snow bridge collapsing under their feet and nearly all had fallen some distance. Teddy Evans and Atkinson had gone in by the whole length of their traces at the top of the glacier and survived. He could do the same, God willing.

Lashly became aware of just how chilly it was. The skin on his face began to tingle. The glistening walls around him were acting like a giant icehouse. If they didn't hurry he'd have as much circulation as a Billingsgate cod.

'Ready now?'

Damn idiots. What was he if he wasn't ready, dangling there like a corpse on a gibbet? 'Oh, aye. Just wait a second. Right, there you are. Ready.'

It was hardly a smooth elevator ride to the surface as he rose in a series of jerks that squashed his ribs and snapped his neck with each pull.

'Nearly there.'

As he reached the lip, hands grabbed the sledge straps and his clothing and he was yanked out to find himself standing upright. Tom Crean pulled off his harness and then slapped him on his painful shoulders. 'Happy Birthday, William.'

For some reason everyone found this funny.

'Sledgemeter is broken,' said Teddy Evans. 'You great oaf, Lashly.'

Crean was about to say it was hardly the stoker's fault, when he heard the Owner's voice.

Scott pushed his way through and asked, 'Lashly, are you all right?'

'Few bruises.'

'Nothing broken?'

'No.'

'So all right to continue?'

The stoker shrugged his shoulders and spun his arms. Apart from a few clicks and pops, all seemed well. 'Aye, skipper.'

Scott touched the stoker's cheek and rubbed at a pale spot of skin. 'You watch that. The wind'll do more damage yet.'

Lashly took off his mitten and touched his face. Like all similar patches, it was scaly to the touch, where it wasn't covered in his red hair. 'I will.'

'Right, we lengthen the traces for the lead hauler,' he announced. This meant that if anyone fell through, there was time for the others to react. 'And Lashly.'

'Sir?'

'An extra spoon of chocolate hoosh for you this evening.'

Water, cocoa, sugar, biscuits, raisins, all thickened with arrowroot: the very thought of chocolate hoosh made everyone's saliva flow. 'Thank you, sir.'

Scott clapped his hands together. 'So, lads, how about we aim for fifteen miles for Christmas Day?'

As quickly as it had appeared, the saliva suddenly dried in every man's mouth.

For the next few days the wind from the south never stopped. It was forever pushing at them. Even when the sun shone and the surface was smooth under the runners and skis and they stripped off their outer jackets, it tried to halt them in their tracks. It was as if a giant fan existed just over the horizon, pushing the air towards them, drying lips and eyes. Even at camp, with its constant moan and snatching at the tent and the whiplash of canvas, it drove them to distraction.

On New Year's Eve, Scott called a halt after a half-day in which seven laborious miles had been covered. They had caught up with Shackleton's figures – a cause for celebration – but Scott had been worried by the performance of the sledges. Crean and Taff Evans set about sawing them down to ten feet and reconfiguring them.

It would save weight and make them more manoeuvrable. However, they couldn't fix the damaged sledgemeter on Teddy Evans's sledge.

That night the five officers – Scott, Wilson, Oates, Bowers and Teddy Evans – shared a tent and not only did it seem more snug, the wind was muffled too. After supper they took to their bags, while Scott summarised their progress so far. He was full of praise for Crean and Evans and their efforts on the sledges. If they all pulled true, he was hoping for up to twenty-five miles per march.

Nobody groaned, but all felt like doing so. They had managed between fourteen and seventeen miles a day, although it was true that sledge problems and bad surfaces – including crevasses – had caused them to tarry. But twenty-five, a third more than their best recent day, felt as if it was asking a lot. Except nobody had any doubt that if there were four Captain Scotts per sled, it would be achieved. Shove, shove, shove, Cherry had observed about him, and he was right.

Evans, though, was only half listening. Scott had made his group jettison their skis, ostensibly to save weight. Man-hauling on foot had taken the last of his reserves and he had trouble keeping his eyes open. Oates wondered if this was why Scott had done it, to make it clear just how depleted he was. Everyone in the tent knew that Scott's party would go forward, although Oates was sure Crean or Bowers would take his place. He hadn't been able to disguise totally his limp, despite not wanting to show weakness.

'Hell of a thing.'

'What is?' Scott asked.

Oates was not aware he'd spoken. 'What's that?'

'What is a hell of a thing?'

'Sorry. I was thinking about the Boers.'

'What about them?' asked Wilson.

Oates pulled the sleeping bag up to his neck, moving his feet to try to get them warm. 'Nothing.'

'Come on, Farmer Hayseed,' said Bowers. 'You tell us little bits about them and what you did and then stop. It's about time you told us about the army. Nobody here knows anything but the Navy. Dr Wilson not even that. Tell us about the cavalry.'

So, to his own surprise, he did. He spoke about South Africa, Gestingthorpe, Eton and Ireland, then the respective merits of Napoleon and Wellington, then back to his youth in Essex, till he ran out of words. When he had finished he said: 'I think I deserve a brandy after that.'

Wilson laughed and rolled over. 'Sorry, the supply is purely medicinal. But thank you for an entertaining evening.'

Scott patted him on the leg. 'Yes, thank you. You've quite come out of your shell, Soldier. Well done. And happy New Year.'

Oates pushed himself down into the bag, cursing his freezing feet and numb hands but, for some unfathomable reason, enjoying a warm glow of contentment inside. As he drifted off to sleep, he composed the next note he would scribble to his mother if he were lucky enough to be in the final party.

> I am afraid the letters I wrote you from the hut were full of grumbles but I was very anxious about starting off with those ponies. But now I am part of this last push, I am full of hope. I might even be selected for the Pole. Imagine that! We have plenty of food and as soon as we start back we have good depots. Some of us shall get to the Pole all right.

'That's a bad cough you've got there, Crean.'

The seaman looked up at Scott. It was 3 January; time for the parties to split from each other. They were 150 miles or so from the Pole. It was now they had to gather themselves for the final sprint.

Crean did have a bad cough. The same cough he'd had every morning since he started smoking a pipe. 'I understand a half-sung song, sir.' And, despite his inner turmoil, he smiled.

'Thank you, Crean. I knew you'd take it well.'

Crean didn't take it so well inside. He was tough, fit and loyal. Fitter than most. And he was intact. Taff Evans had cut his hand badly when they were sawing down the sledges. He'd kept it from Scott, lest it influenced his decision, but it was going to make some of the manual work harder for him.

But Crean was loyal to Taff, too. So he kept quiet. He waited till Scott had left the tent before he punched the floor till his knuckles ached. Then he let himself weep with anger and disappointment.

Next Scott took Teddy Evans to one side. They stood with their back to the wind. Scott found it difficult to say the words. In the end, Evans did it for him.

'I'm not going, am I?'

'No, Teddy. You are slowing us down.'

'You made us depot our skis.'

'You weren't using them properly. It saved you a hundred pounds, Teddy. That was why. Anyway, I had made my mind up before then.'

'Back in New Zealand, no doubt.'

Scott shook his head. 'Don't be ridiculous. You have hauled longer than anyone, Teddy. You've pushed yourself to the limit and beyond.'

'I could make the Pole. It can't be more than a fortnight, if the weather holds.'

'I know you could make it. That's not the trick just now, is it? It's getting back to tell the tale. We've demonstrated my team has the speed and the stamina. We exchanged sleds and we were still the quicker.'

'You promised me, skipper.'

Scott thought Evans might cry. 'There were no promises, Teddy.'

Evans rubbed his aching eyes. 'You'll take all of them?'

'Yes. Wilson, Taff, Oates. A scientist, a seaman, a soldier and myself.'

Evans dipped his head and Scott heard his teeth grind. 'Very well.'

'And, Teddy, I think you should go back on the *Terra Nova*.'

Evans's head whipped up. 'Why?'

'To sort things out for next season. There is much expedition business in Lyttleton. Fending off creditors for one, no doubt. Sourcing fresh animals.'

Evans narrowed his eyes. 'You want rid of me?'

449

'No, that's not it.'

The anger flooded back into him. 'Like Shackleton. You want rid of me.'

Scott overcame his usual embarrassment at such confrontations and spoke firmly, and to Evans's face. 'I am no fool, Teddy. I know what you have been saying. You aren't happy with my leadership. Fine. But I don't want a second-in-command back at the hut questioning my orders or motives. Do you understand?'

Evans remained quiet. He had certainly been grumbling about Scott's planning and imperious attitude, but only in private. Had someone betrayed him?

'I have written a commendation for you, should you decide to return to England. But I hope you'll come back south next season on the ship.'

'Sir.' The word was pushed out with great reluctance.

'And one more thing. Could you spare me Bowers?'

Evans look shocked. 'Birdie? Five?'

'Yes.'

'But we cached for four. Everything is worked for four to the Pole. The returning party will have to try and divide the depoted food into five and three. And you only have supplies for four.'

'But the man pulls like a train. What we lose in rations we gain in speed. And he can navigate and has the eyesight of a hawk.'

'And the tent routine?' Evans asked.

'We slept five the other night. It was much warmer.'

'One night is hardly the same as rubbing up for months. And we know how you like a shipshape tent.'

Scott ignored this. Evans was notoriously slipshod and untidy on the ice. 'I hope you don't mind.'

'Will he, though? He has no skis.'

A flicker of irritation crossed Scott's features. 'If anyone can manage, it's Birdie.'

'So I have to pull back with just three. And only I can navigate. What if anything happens to me?'

'Don't let it. I know the broken sledgemeter is a nuisance, but you are the only man here I would trust to get back that distance without one.' That much was certainly true. 'Only you, Teddy.'

He gave a rueful laugh. 'You know how to soften a blow.'

'It's not that. It's the truth.'

'Five. You are sure?'

'I have considered it carefully. If we are going to make it, we have to be whip-fast.'

Now it was done, the decision made against him, Teddy Evans felt a strange sense of calm come over him. Was it relief? Had he ever really wanted the Pole that badly? Or was it exhaustion? He couldn't tell. 'In which case, please take Birdie with my best wishes.'

That night, as they ate their pemmican in strained silence, Teddy Evans gave Birdie Bowers a small silk flag. 'It's from Mrs Evans. I told her it would fly at the Pole. I had expected to be there to see it.'

'It'll fly there, sir, don't you worry. And I'll take a photograph for Mrs Evans.'

'You will make it, won't you, Birdie?'

The little man nodded. 'Make it or die trying.'

'Don't say that, Birdie.'

Bowers laughed at the superstition in Evans's voice. 'Then I will see you back at Cape Evans.'

'Be certain of it.'

They separated the next day, once Evans, Lashly and Crean were sure the Scott sled was pulling well and the strange combination of four on skis and one walking would work. It did, thanks to Birdie Bowers's prodigious efforts to keep pace with the skiers. A lesser man might have stumbled, but Birdie set his jaw, leaned into the traces, and tramped and pulled, as Wilson put it, for all he was worth and about ten per cent more. When they stopped to make their goodbyes, Crean cried once more, but Lashly and Evans put a brave face on it.

Lashly took Taff Evans to one side and slipped him a few squares of chocolate. 'I'll tell you one thing, Taff.'

'What's that?'

'Sharing a tent with four officers?'

'Three and the doctor. And Titus ain't Navy. But what about it?'

'We get another blizzard like that last one, you'll find out whether their shit really does smell the same as ours.'

Lashly dissolved into guffaws, but Taff wasn't smiling. He really hadn't considered the lavatory etiquette of being tent-bound with the Owner. All dignity went at times of need and he had shared with officers before, even with Scott, but never had to face up to being unable to step outside to do his business. It had happened just before the Beardmore, but he hadn't been with Scott then. 'We'll manage,' he said glumly. 'We've all got but one arsehole. Even you. And sometimes you speak out of it.'

'Oh, now, Taff, don't go off like that. It's only jealousy speaking.'

Taff brightened at this. 'I suppose it is. You'll wish me luck, then?'

''Course I will, Taff. And I'll be drinkin' at your place one day.'

'That you will.'

'I expect a free pint, mind.'

'We'll see about that.'

A few yards away, Oates slapped Evans on the back and said: 'Quite a slog back, Teddy, but at least you'll have Christopher waiting for you to eat. Say hello to the old bugger from me.'

'Don't worry about us. You get to that pole.'

Scott handed Teddy Evans the letter he had written to Kathleen. 'Can you give that to *Terra Nova*, Teddy? It simply says we are in a good position with a fine party.'

'Yes, of course.'

'And Teddy, I told Cherry to make sure the dogs come to One Ton Camp in March. The twenty-seventh. I would like to change that. Best make it Mt Hooper, which should be restocked with whatever you take, and perhaps as far as eighty-two degrees. And a week earlier than I suggested. Just in case.'

'Aye, skipper.'

'Mt Hooper, then south, eighty-one or eighty-two, depending on conditions, although no further. Tell Meares.'

'Meares will have gone by then. He's back on *Terra Nova*, too.'

'Oh. Yes.' How could he have forgotten that? 'Dimitri, then, and Atch or Wright. A good navigator. You won't forget?'

'Stand on me, skipper.'

'Need it in writing?'

Teddy Evans tapped his temple. 'Up here, sir.'

With the wind tugging at their clothes, their faces masked by windbreaks and goggles, the two groups shook hands one last time.

Scott reckoned that his team watching the Last Returning Party turn north for home would be a terrible mistake for morale, so he pushed on. They had travelled a few hundred yards when they heard the hip-hip of three cheers and he felt his eyes burning from more than snow-glare. His goggles fogged. He suspected the others' did too.

After a mile or so, Oates glanced back and saw the three men waiting in line despite the wind in their faces, intent on watching till the polar party shrank to nothing and were swallowed by the whiteness of the plateau. At least when they turned it would be at their backs, he thought, pushing them back to safety. Scott's team had another thirteen or fourteen days before they had that luxury.

At first they made good speed, over a smooth surface, but then they hit the type of snow that baffled Scott. It was more like gritty sand, and refused to let the skis or runners glide, acting more like starch paste than a lubricant. They managed twelve and a half miles, a good tally given the conditions. By the time they camped, though, the hated wind had dropped and the temperature had risen, and the five men were able to stand around outside in comfort, smoking and gabbling with the nervous talk of the overexcited. The last of the partings was done, and it gave all of them a heady sense of liberation.

After the euphoria faded slightly, they went back to work. Oates and Wilson set about unpacking the stove and pannikins. Taff worked on dividing the rations for five. Bowers used the swing thermometer. Scott excused himself; he had much to write.

'Sir,' said Bowers to Scott as he stepped towards the tent.

'Yes, Birdie.'

'I just want to say thank you.'

'What for?'

'Bringing me.'

'Without skis? I'm sorry about that.'

'I'd walk barefoot to be with you there, sir,' said the little man. Scott believed him.

'What do you think our chances, Birdie?'

'If God be with us, who can be against us?'

Scott smiled. Both Wilson and Bowers were convinced they had God on their side. Who was cheering on Amundsen, then? he wondered.

The thought punctured his mood, and he imagined he could hear the ghostly yapping of dogs somewhere on the plateau. The howling echoed off the distant mountains. When he cocked his head the better to catch it, the noise had disappeared. An illusion; the wind perhaps. There had been no signs of the Norwegians, so whichever way they had come, it hadn't been the Beardmore. And who was to say there was another stairway to the plateau like that one?

God could, indeed, be on their side.

Scott excused himself and went into the tent to write up his journal.

I wonder what is in store for us. At present everything seems to be going with extraordinary smoothness, and one can scarcely believe that obstacles will not present themselves to make our task more difficult.

Wilson entered and began to set up the primus stove. In all the excitement, they were late with dinner. 'Everyone seems in good spirits.'

Scott, writing, was only lending half an ear. 'Yes.'

'Oates has lost his pipe. Reckons he dropped it saying goodbye to Teddy and the others.'

'Shame.'

'You know, Taff cut his hand when he was sawing those sledges down.'

'Hhhmm.'

'Won't let me look at it.'

'He's a big strong lad.'

'I suppose. Hoosh?'

'Sorry?'

'Dinner? How about hoosh for a change?'

'Why not?' asked Scott, with a grin.

'Good choice, if I may say so.'

By the time they had eaten, Scott's words had come back to haunt him. *One can scarcely believe that obstacles will not present themselves to make our task more difficult.*

At close to ten thousand feet, the food was difficult enough to heat through properly at the best of times. Once Wilson had made his hoosh and Scott had checked the total cooking time, a niggling fact occurred to him. At that altitude, it took a lot longer to melt ice and prepare food for five than it did for four. Which meant they consumed considerably more fuel. They would need every ounce of Taff's and Bowers's considerable strength to keep ahead of that curve, he thought glumly.

Sixty-six

Entry in Kathleen Scott's Diary

I wonder what is in your log? I would love to be able to read it, to hear what you are experiencing. And when the ship arrives, and you come back from your adventure in the South, you will find my journal with my last entry in October and therefore so, so out of date. Such a gap between the doing and the reading of it. In those pages I said that we were lucky dogs, you and I. Now I am not so sure. The separation is hard for Peter and me. I have been keeping track of where you might be. It is January. About now you must be turning around. Oh dear, if I could only know how you have fared. The waiting would be a lot less agony. I wonder if you thought of me on New Year's Eve – I went lonely to bed quite forgetting it was New Year's Eve, but I woke up in the night hearing, I thought, three loud taps. I lit the light and found it was exactly midnight. I lay and thought about you so perhaps it was you who woke me – oh darling, I do so love you and so hope you haven't forgotten me. Oh, I so hope you are turning around, back towards me.

Sixty-seven

The only constant of the next few days was pain, thought Oates. Every pressure sent a jagged lance of agony from the ball of his foot. No matter how much padding he put in the boot, it was as if the flesh had been stripped from his soles and he was skiing on the uncovered bone. The leg, too, was giving him some trouble, the wound burning like fire or sometimes turning down to a dull but constant ache. Trying to favour the right meant his hips and lower back hurt.

Antarctica also seemed to have waited till all support had gone before launching an attack on them. 'Just like the Boers,' he muttered to himself. Now, at their most vulnerable, the plateau began to hamper their progress. First came more of that strange, sticky snow, then the sastrugi began to switch and turn, becoming cross hatched in places, so it was difficult to get any sort of rhythm going. The confusing, undulating surface meant Bowers slithered and stumbled in the traces.

'Halt!'

Scott raised an arm and they stopped. Now came the agony of muscles cramping and burning. It was too early for lunch, so Oates wondered why he had arrested their painful progress.

'I think,' said Scott through his wind-chapped lips, 'we should try without the skis. These sastrugi are not good.' He bent down and snapped off one of the fish-hooked tops. 'We are in danger of breaking one of the skis.'

'Now we'll see who pulls the best,' says Bowers, pleased they would all be on an equal footing.

They strapped their skis to the sledge and as they did so, Taff Evans suddenly let out an exclamation.

'What is it?'

'There's a sleeping bag missing,' he said.

'What?'

'There're only four, skipper.' Taff looked as if he were about to cry, even though it wasn't he who had strapped them on. 'Only four.' His lower lip began to quiver.

'Oh, for God's sake. Who—'

Scott stopped himself when Wilson put a hand on his shoulder. 'It doesn't matter who. Only how. As in, how long ago do we think it fell off?'

Nobody could say. Wilson volunteered to return and search for the lost item and Oates went with him.

'Are you all right, Soldier?' Wilson asked as they shushed back over their tracks, making good time with a following wind and no sledge.

'Well enough, Bill.'

'I never knew the bullet wound was quite so bad till that night in the tent. Shattered the bone, you said. Does it trouble you?'

'Not really.'

'I'll take that as a yes. I wish I'd known.'

'Would you have stopped me coming?'

Wilson said nothing.

'Is PO all right?'

'Taff? He's pulling as well as ever.'

That wasn't what he meant. Oates could recall being so tired he wanted to sob, but it hadn't happened on this trip. Not yet. But he sometimes saw that moment in Taff's trembling lip, a look of total despondency. They skied on in silence.

'There it is,' said Wilson.

It cost them less than an hour in all before they had returned and were ready to move the sledge on foot, having stowed the skis once more. The increased effort made Oates sweat in his clothes.

He had to lean forward at a steeper angle, and the sinking of the boots made for a much tougher march. Nobody spoke; each just found their own way of tugging. The slog caused his old wound to grumble even more.

The others, so they said, thought about food while they hauled. Oates dreamed of warmth. He had forgotten what it felt like for all of his body to be at normal temperature. Something – feet, hands, face – always seemed to be frozen, even in the tent. He often imagined the drawing room of Gestingthorpe with the eternal fire, never extinguished, always stoked by Gilbert. It was a challenge to remember how it felt to be toast-warm, to sweat fluid that didn't start to chill within seconds. To feel safe and content.

'Halt.'

The men stumbled to a stop.

'We camp.'

Already? thought Oates.

The hoosh was thick with biscuit that night, and as they ate, Scott announced that they had passed Shackleton's Furthest South. They all gave a ragged cheer. Even the wind gave a hoot, it seemed.

'How far to go?' asked Taff Evans wearily. 'In time, I mean, not miles.'

'A week, if we can stay in double figures,' replied Scott, still glowing from having surpassed his old friend and rival. 'But I fear we must go back to the skis. Is that all right, Birdie?'

Bowers nodded. The constant sinking of his legs in the drifts made for terrible cramps and aches, but he would plough on. Oh, for a firmer crust. 'Of course, sir.'

'We'll have to make one more dump and we can lighten the sledge for the last day or two's march.'

The men began the difficult manoeuvre of settling into position for the meal without encroaching on anyone else's space. Elbows were lethal weapons in such tight surroundings. If they were all the size of Bowers, it would be no problem, thought Oates, but he and Taff felt like giants. It was worse when they slept, because someone inevitably pushed against the walls, letting cold air or snow in as the side parted from the groundsheet.

'Ow.' Taff said it involuntarily as he gripped his spoon awkwardly.

'Can I see that hand, Taff?' asked Wilson.

'Nothing, sir.'

'Nevertheless, PO.'

'Do as he says, petty officer,' said Scott firmly.

Taff reluctantly unwrapped the dirty bandage covering his wound and held his hand out. All could see the crimson gash across the palm, its edges blackened and puckered.

'For God's sake, Taff, that needs a decent dressing.'

'Had worse.'

'I don't doubt it. At sea level. Not in this cold. I'll bandage it before we set off.'

'As you wish, Dr Wilson.'

They ate on for a while, lost in their thoughts.

'What'll you do when you get back, Taff?' asked Birdie, trying to lighten the seaman's mood. He appreciated it must be hard being the only rating in a tent full of officers.

'Me? I'll open a pub. The South Pole.'

They all laughed. 'What?' he asked, baffled by the response.

'The trick to owning a public house, PO,' said Scott softly, 'is to make sure there is some ale left over for the public to buy.'

This time Taff joined in the laughter. 'You can josh me all you like. I don't think you understand. A Welshman at the South Pole. I'll be famous, man. Famous.'

'What about you, Soldier?' asked Wilson.

'Back to the army.'

'Pah,' said Wilson. 'You can't just go back to the ordinary army after this.'

'Watch me.'

'Is there no other ambition?' Wilson asked.

There's one, Oates thought. There is a little girl I'd like to find. But he shook his head. 'To win the Military Cup, perhaps.'

'No sweetheart?' the doctor pressed.

'The only woman I have ever loved is my mother.'

'Here, here!' shouted Bowers.

Scott thought of Hannah and raised his pannikin of cocoa. 'To mothers.'

'To mothers!'

For the next few days, the surface was bad and the sun misted over so comprehensively it could hardly be distinguished. They managed between six and ten miles a day, leaving frequent marker cairns to help them navigate on their return. When they camped on 12 January, nobody could get warm; all shivered in their bags, apart from Bowers. He sat half out of his, writing up his sitings and checking and rechecking the food stocks and depoting arrangements, which he confirmed were still very satisfactory. 'No reason why we shouldn't make it,' he concluded. 'None at all.'

'If God will just send us some better weather,' said Oates.

'And smoother surfaces,' Scott added.

Bowers and Wilson, the two most religious men, said nothing.

Scott noted down that Oates seemed to have the most trouble of all with the chill, his teeth chattering. Taff Evans, uncharacteristically, complained of cold feet. Scott, too, found his hands shaking, even with a warm pannikin in them. He checked the temperature, but it wasn't particularly low, around minus eleven. This was fifteen or more degrees warmer than they had been experiencing at night, and with little wind. So why were they so frozen? *Must be a damp in the air*, he wrote in his dairy. And then he prayed that's all it was.

Sixty-eight

The Beardmore Glacier

Tom Crean thought he had never heard an officer apologise quite so profusely. Not one like Teddy Evans at any rate. Lashly, too, raised his snow-frosted eyebrows to show his surprise.

'Let you down. Sorry,' said Evans. 'I really am. Don't know what I was thinking.'

The three of them, still in harness, were standing at the top of an icefall; below them was the glacier. They had come too far across to the West and were now facing the most heavily crevassed section of the Beardmore, the one Shackleton had warned them about. There was little they could make out through the silvery mist that swirled across the ice. Where it did part they could see the tell-tale blue glint of canyons. Cherry had called the ones they had experienced on the ascent 'as big as Regent Street'. In which case, they were facing canyons the size of a small town. Derry, perhaps, thought Crean.

'We could go back around,' Evans said, pointing with his pole. They had detoured to miss another set of fissures and had clearly chosen the wrong way. It would lose them another day to go back. They had been hauling for a week since they left the polar party and it had been hellish, especially for Crean, who had suffered an instant attack of snowblindess.

Evans sounded weary. His eyes were going, just as Crean's were

462

getting better. Goggles didn't seem to help. He had complained of pains behind his knees, too.

'They should have reached the Pole by now,' said Crean absent-mindedly.

'Yes,' said Lashly. 'In better shape than we are, I hope.'

Pulling with just three men was bone-breaking, far harder than they had imagined. All of them had damaged muscles and tendons, and they were still a long way from home. 'Unless that blizzard hit them too.' A squall had cost them a day in the tent.

'Well,' said Crean, 'I vote we go down.'

'We have no crampons,' said Evans tetchily. 'We wouldn't last fifty yards. We'll have to go back.'

'There isn't enough food allowance,' said Lashly. 'But, Tom, I'm not sure we should try and ski down.'

'I'm not suggesting we ski down. I'm suggesting we go down on that.'

Evans began to laugh; a high girlish sound, thought Tom.

'You are joking,' said Lashly, following where the ski pole was pointing. 'On the sledge?'

'It's been snowing. There'll be bridges.'

'Shackleton said some of the crevasses were two hundred feet across. What kind of bridge are you expecting?'

'The Norskies do it. What have we got to lose?'

'Our lives,' suggested Lashly.

'Oh, those,' said Tom blithely. When Evans wasn't looking he made some signals to Lashly about his officer. But he couldn't convey what he was really thinking. Pains behind the knees. One of the symptoms of scurvy. If that had struck them, there would be no spare days to lose.

'Very well,' said Lashly. 'But if I die in the trying, I'll never forgive you. Sir? All right with you?'

Evans looked panicked at the thought, but could conjure up no reasonable alternative. 'Very well. If we must.'

They unharnessed and stowed the traces. The skis were strapped on the sledge, but Crean suggested they keep the poles for steering. The load was redistributed to make three places for them to sit.

Then they hauled the sledge to the lip of the icefall. Crean sat astride at the front, Evans in the middle, Lashly bringing up the rear.

'Now, William,' instructed Crean. 'You push and don't forget to jump on.'

Evans looked down at the rolling fog bank, and the shapes moving within it. He imagined the vast, waiting apertures, ready to take them like pike taking a gnat. 'You know, I think we ought to go around after—'

He never finished the sentence. Lashly gave one shove and, as if to show what it could do on a decent surface, the sledge accelerated away. Lashly managed to get on the back, but only by flinging himself diagonally over the rear section and clinging on for dear life.

Evans screamed.

At the front Crean saw the mist part to present the first opening in the ice. It was rushing towards him. There was no bridge spanning it.

'Oh, shit, hold on there, boys.'

The runners left the ice as the void opened up beneath them. The cold of the cavern seemed to suck the heat from them. Then they landed with a thump on the other side. The sledge began to oscillate from side to side, as if it were going to tip. Crean poked with one of his poles and it steadied.

The bank of fog thinned and Crean was sorry it had. He could see now what lay ahead. A stretch of fissures ripped in the ice sheet, like knife slashes.

The next crevasse was huge, large enough to lose St Paul's in, but it had three snow bridges across it. Crean steered for the wider one on the left, but the sledge's forward momentum was too much for the turn. The three of them swished on to the thinner central span, sending up an arc of fresh snow. They all heard it creak and shift beneath them. Evans screamed again.

Then they were across, rattling over pressure ridges, with their teeth clashing and vision blurred. Smaller pockets in the ice seemed to rush up at Crean and he closed his aching eyes for a second. The speed of the sledge sent them across the cracks unharmed.

Three more crevasses flashed by, each two hundred feet wide, each with a bridge in the centre, but nothingness looming on either side. Now the sledge was at maximum velocity and beginning to slither to one side, as if the rear was trying to overtake the front. Crean put out a pole to correct it and it was snatched away, bending his fingers back. The sledge continued to crab, running sideways over another snow bridge until Crean realised the whole contraption was about to spin around. Soon they would be coming down the mountain backwards.

'To port side!' he yelled.

'What?' Evans shouted.

Crean leaned his weight over the left runner, digging it in and slowing them on that side. Unfortunately, it sank further than he intended, snagged and they pirouetted through 180 degrees before crashing into a snow bank, throwing them all off on to the ice.

Nobody spoke for a while; they were busy trying to catch their breath, slow their hearts and checking that nothing was broken. Then Crean stood, unfolding stiffly as he did so, and looked back at the way they had come. They had shot down in six minutes what might have taken a whole day, across an icefall and some of the worst crevasses the Beardmore could throw at them.

He laughed, feeling giddy with relief, and looked down at his winded companions. 'Next time,' Crean said, 'someone else can go in front.'

Sixty-nine

The Polar Plateau

It was Bowers who noticed it first. The others were all lost in their thoughts and the drudgery of hauling over the sastrugi. Wilson was daydreaming about Ory. Scott was trying to picture how Peter would have grown and changed by the time he saw him again. Taff was concerned about the pains shooting up his forearm and Oates was dwelling on the irony of being racked with thirst with a world of frozen water around them.

They had covered seven and a half miles that morning, before a brief stop for lunch. Sightings told them they were at eighty-nine degrees, forty-two minutes. 'The Pole will be in view tomorrow,' Scott had promised and they all dared hope that would be the case. They would reach it in a sorrier state than they had wished. They were convinced, though, that their spirits would lift once they stood at ninety degrees south.

'Skipper,' Bowers said. 'Over there.'

'Halt.'

Oates thought for a blissful moment another afternoon had slipped by, but he realised they had only been hauling for a little over an hour. 'What is it?'

'There.' Bowers pointed into the featureless whiteness, slightly to the right of where they were heading. Oates had long learned that spots on his retina played tricks with his vision. He could see nothing. Birdie was the one with the eyes.

'What is it?' asked Wilson.

'Not sure. You see it, skipper?'

'What are you thinking, Birdie?'

'I thought it looked like a cairn.'

'A man-made cairn?' asked Oates, knowing full well there was no other sort.

'Now I am not so sure. It could be a large sastrugi.'

'It could,' said Scott.

'Or we've come round in a circle and it's one of ours,' suggested Oates.

'That's not helpful,' snapped Scott. 'It could be a mirage. It wouldn't be the first time we've been fooled.'

'We should take a look, then,' added Taff glumly. 'Just to be on the safe side.'

Thirty minutes later, every man felt the blow at the same time. Whatever it was, it was black. Black. Not the colour of the Antarctic, at least not the plateau, where no rocks poked through the vast covering of ice. Black. The sign of man. The colour of defeat.

It was a wooden sledge bearer, with a large black flag tied to it. As they pulled nearer, each step wearier than the last, they could see other signs. Sledge tracks and dog paws. Lots and lots of dogs' tracks and canine excrement soiling the snow.

When they shrugged their harnesses, Taff undid his boot bindings and fell to his knees, as if praying to an idol. Wilson put a hand on Scott's shoulder and the Owner's mitt came up to touch it.

Oates felt very little, except the sensation that he had known it would come to this all along. Since when? Since he saw the horses on Quail Island, perhaps, or the chaotic caravan of motor-sledges, dogs, skis and feet that Scott had assembled. Or when the blizzard cost them all that time on the barrier? He wasn't sure, but he couldn't feign shock. He could only express resignation. 'Looks

467

like he chose well,' he muttered, scratching at the swirl of paw marks with the toe of his boot.

'I'd keep that thought to y'self,' muttered Bowers.

Oates bent down and came up with a brown stub. He held it to his nose. He saw the look on Birdie's face and chortled. 'Don't worry. It's a cigar butt. I think they had themselves a small celebration.'

Taff had begun to sob, his forehead pressed to the icy surface. Wilson pulled him up into a sitting position. 'What of my pub now?' he howled. 'Those bloody Norskies. What of my money?'

'Taff,' said Wilson with some kindness. 'Pull yourself together, man.'

Oates examined the black flag and noticed that the material had frayed and faded somewhat. He didn't voice the thought, but it had been up some time, weeks, rather than hours or days. They hadn't just been beaten. They had been trounced, thrashed, routed.

Wilson came over and fingered the treacherous pennant. 'It's a little careworn.'

'I was thinking the same thing.' The Owner was walking in a circle, head down, deep in troubled thought. 'We have to be strong. For Con.'

Oates found himself nodding. If he had anger within, he was too tired and aching to summon it.

Minutes passed while each man dealt with the disappointment in his own way.

'Hold it!'

Bowers took a photograph. Oates imagined it would show a rather unhappy group. Scott was standing away from the others, and was still staring south, although he had stopped pacing. His shoulders were slumped, and there was a wisp of steam around his hood. They let him be and made camp some distance away from the Norwegian's dark banner, freezing their fingers erecting the tent.

Once it was up, Wilson walked out and stood a pace behind Scott. He pulled some ice from his beard. 'Sorry, Con.'

Scott spun about. 'You are sorry? No, no, it is I who must apologise. I have brought you here with the promise of glory—'

468

Wilson stopped him. 'We didn't do it for glory.'

'Taff did.'

'Taff is not himself. We did it for you, Con.'

'And I've let you down. Forestalled.'

'We aren't there yet.' The flag was not the Pole, just an outer marker.

'No. But they have been boxing the Pole, haven't they? This is where they took one of the sightings to make sure they were correct.'

'I imagine that is so,' said Wilson. He felt like crying, too, not for himself, but for what Scott must be going through. He knew his recriminations would be deep and wide ranging and the object of his anger would be Captain Scott himself. 'I think we must not let our brains overheat right now, Con.'

Scott looked around at the terrible bleakness that echoed perfectly the emptiness in his soul. 'Great God, this is an awful place. And to have laboured here without priority.' He shook his head.

'We might as well stand on it, though, Con. We deserve Ninety Degrees.'

'Yes. You are right. Tomorrow, we five will at least stand at the Pole.'

Scott wiped a mitten over his eyes and composed himself. Within a few moments, he had his bravest face on. He went to try to motivate his tired, cold men who had stuck with the Owner, only for him to reward them with pain, heartache and fury.

The Pole didn't want them. The next day it blew even harder into their faces, ripping Bowers's cheeks raw and chilling Taff's hands so savagely they had to stop for an early lunch. The temperature sat around twenty below and the dragging seemed harder than ever. Even so, Scott tried not to let the misery of disappointment slow their pace, and they managed fourteen miles. Although they passed two small cairns, mocking them as they hauled by them, there were no further signs of their rivals when they camped.

So it wasn't the day following the discovery of the flag but the day after – 18 January – that they found the tent that confirmed their defeat. It was a neat, simple affair, with a single bamboo pole. A small Norwegian flag fluttered above the apex. Below it, lest there be any doubt about the tent's provenance, was a pennant with the word '*Fram*'. Again, the whole area was marked by dog tracks.

Scott dipped inside and came out with a note, which he read: 'Roald Amundsen. Olav Olavson Bjaaland. Hilmer Hanssen. Sverre H. Hassel. Oscar Wisting. Dated the sixteenth of December 1911.'

Bowers let out a groan. Taff Evans began to curse, till Wilson stopped him.

Weeks, Oates thought, not days. It was dated 16 December, but clearly they had been in the vicinity for some time before the letter was written. He and Wilson had been right, they had been beaten by a whole month. Not a whisker, not a tiny margin, but a huge chasm. A month! It looked as if the Norwegians had their heads screwed on when it came to dogs.

There was silence for a few minutes as they tried to come to terms with another disappointment. Their ears filled with the howl of wind, the snap of cloth and the roaring of blood. Five had certainly made it to the Pole first. Just the wrong five.

A month, Oates thought again. They had been and gone, were probably almost home now. Warm. And safe.

Scott cleared his throat. Oates couldn't meet his eyes for fear of what they might see there. It wasn't a race, he'd always said. But even so, whatever it was, they'd come second.

'He has also left a letter for the King of Norway in case he failed on the return to the Fram.'

'So we are bloody postmen now, are we?' Taff asked, sitting down on the ice and banging the ground with a fist.

'Be brave, gentlemen. Even now we aren't sure we are at the Pole yet,' Scott reminded them.

'At least we will make it by good British man-hauling. The nobler way,' said Bowers. 'Not the soft option like these Norskies.'

Scott smiled at the plucky little man.

They marched the six miles till they were sure they were within half a mile of the actual Pole and camped. Shivering with cold, they built a cairn and placed the Union Jack on it and took their photographs. None could raise much of a smile for the camera. Even Bowers looked forlorn and admitted his face was terribly sore. Scott applied Vaseline and they took one more set of images.

'Where's the glory?' Taff kept muttering, as if he had expected to find something tangible by that name at ninety degrees south. 'Where's the fucking glory?'

'That's enough, PO,' Scott snapped. Taff turned to muttering his question under his breath.

More sightings were taken and the five then trudged the remaining half-mile and left the flag on a piece of spare sledge wood, as close to the Pole as they could fix it. The Union Jack looked a poor, slighted thing.

'Here ends our daydreams,' said Scott to Wilson, watching the flag snap back and forth as the wind caught it. 'Now we have to haul without the fuel of victory to urge us on. Sole author I, sole cause.'

Wilson could almost see the old gloom clouding Scott's eyes. 'We've done what we set out to, Con, remember that. It was never our intention to race anyone.' He reached into his tunic and handed him a sad, bent cigarette and, after a few poor attempts, lit it.

Scott coughed. 'My God, what a queer taste. Where did you get this?'

'Had it all along. It's taken on some of the reindeer, the paraffin and our sweat.'

'Lovely. I'll settle for a square of chocolate when we get back to the tent. Here, hand it round.'

Wilson took the cigarette and puffed on it. It wasn't so bad, he thought. He walked across and handed it to Oates, making a mental note to examine Soldier's face back at the tent. The end of his nose looked white and there was a bloom under his right eye. Frost-nips and bites were beginning to afflict them all. Oates was also standing at a peculiar angle, leaning on the leg that sported his old wound. It suddenly seemed a lot shorter than the other.

Wilson turned back to Scott, trying to sound positive. 'Now for the run home. At least Bowers can pick up his skis.'

Scott stared north, where ice crystals fogged the world once more. The best part of eight hundred geographical miles away, with the Beardmore and the barrier between them, was Hut Point. And they would be hauling all the way. Although, he reminded himself, Teddy Evans would tell Meares or Dimitri to come south, beyond One Ton Camp, to meet them which would give them an extra margin. One Ton itself was six hundred miles distant, which sounded more manageable than eight. But if the weather intended to be as uncooperative as it had been so far, it was a slimmer margin than he had planned for. What he really needed was a mild autumn out on the barrier and a good pulling surface.

All that way, thought Wilson, with the weight of defeat pressing on their shoulders, making each step heavier than the last. It would require every ounce of Scott's tenacity, all of Bowers's strength, Taff's pig-headedness and Oates's determination to do right by his regiment, to drive them on. What would they say back home? Ory wouldn't care less, as long as he returned, he was sure. But Kathleen? Markham? The British Public? How would they react to the bitter blow?

They both watched Bowers, diligent to the end, take out the sling thermometer and whirl it around his head for a reading.

When Scott finally spoke it sent a bigger shiver through Wilson than the cutting wind ever had. 'Yes, the run home.' His words came as a tremulous whisper. 'I wonder if we can do it, Bill.'

Part Six

'I am just going outside . . .'

Seventy

January 1912, Berlin

The message waiting in his room at the Adlon caused Fridtjof Nansen's heart to race wildly. Thanks to a small bribe, he had already examined the hotel register and there was no Mrs Scott checked in or due to arrive. There had been a Miss Bruce, Kathleen's maiden name, but a few marks for a description had established she was a spinster in her seventies. Unless being a mistress of disguise was among her many talents, it looked as if Mrs Scott was not coming to Berlin.

He consoled himself with a tour of the Persian exhibits at the partially completed Pergamon Museum. Berlin was cold, an east wind threatening snow, and the light went early, as did his spirits. When he returned to the hotel an envelope had been pushed under his door. It was very simple: *Please come this evening at six o'clock.*

This was followed by an address in Charlottenburg and then her initials. K.S. Had she taken another hotel, for discretion's sake, or was this an apartment she was renting? He hoped the latter. Nansen checked his fob watch. It was four. Two hours to kill. He would ask the front desk to source him some flowers, bathe, dress, then take a fortifying schnapps before crossing the Tiergarten for the rendezvous.

Knowing that Berliners demanded punctuality, he was a minute or so early when he yanked the doorbell of the private home.

A Jewish maid opened the door, and he offered his card. 'I am expected.'

'Professor Nansen!' The voice that boomed down the dark entrance hall was richly American. Its owner was a tall handsome man in his thirties, dressed in a velvet suit. 'I have heard so much about you. Come in, come in.'

Somewhat confused, Nansen stepped inside, handed the maid the extravagant bouquet and shrugged off his coat.

'I am John Harrison. My wife will be down shortly. Kathleen is all ready for you.'

'Is she?'

'Yes. I thought we'd have dinner afterwards.'

'As you wish.'

'Lovely flowers.'

Nansen exchanged the bouquet for his topcoat and his hat, and allowed himself to be guided along the corridor, past a profusion of thick-leaved plants.

'We are just renting this place. Not my taste at all. Far too fussy, don't you agree?'

Nansen made a noncommittal grunt.

'We've put you out back. There is a paraffin heater, but I'll send some brandy across. Although I would imagine you won't be taking your clothes off. But you never know with Kathleen.'

Nansen answered robotically. 'No.'

'Your talk is tomorrow, isn't it?'

'Yes.'

'We all have tickets. Maddie, that's my wife. Harrington Mann, the artist. You heard of him? No? Very good. He's painting Maddie's portrait. And Kathleen, of course. Through here.'

They walked into the kitchen, past the cook, who curtsied, and out of a rear door. The cold night hit him as he stepped into the rear garden, but it was only four paces to the conservatory, where the lights blazed.

'I'll leave you to it. Late dinner. Eight-thirty. Take your time. Go on, Kathleen's in there waiting.'

He stepped into the large glass building. It was double-height, lined with racks for holding pots and seed trays, although these were mostly empty. Kathleen was standing at the far end, next to the fumy paraffin heater and a large wooden table with a few bent-cane chairs.

'Ah, Fridtjof. Wonderful. You got my message?' she asked redundantly. Why else would he be here?

'I did.'

She strode across, stood on tiptoe and pecked him on the cheek. She smelled of turpentine. 'Are those for me? How kind.' She took them from him. 'This place could do with some flowers. It's rented and does not come with a gardener. So all this space goes to waste. I shall find a vase.'

She was dressed in a brown smock that reached down to her knees. Her hair was pinned up and she wore no make-up. It was rather a more quotidian appearance than he had hoped for.

'Kathleen, who are these people?'

She rummaged under the shelving, found a grubby crystal vase, then rinsed and filled it from the butler's sink in the corner. 'The Harrisons? Patrons of the arts. They've been wonderful. We've been skating, flying – there is a wonderful aerodrome here – and dancing. Although I am disappointed with the calibre of German officers. Hardly a duelling scar between them. They were all young and spotty. Perhaps we'll dance after your talk; that would be fun, wouldn't it? I have to keep busy, you know. If I stop I dwell. And if I dwell . . .' There was a catch in her throat. 'Do you think he has turned around yet?'

It was a second before he realised she meant her husband. 'I am sure of it.'

She finished arranging the flowers and stepped back to admire her work. 'So am I. I can feel it. Every day brings him closer to home.' She beamed at him, a smile he thought slightly demented in its intensity. 'Can you bear to take your jacket off? Then we'll begin.'

'Begin?'

She reached under the table and produced a shallow enamel bowl containing a large globe of wet, glistening clay that she

477

dumped on to the top. 'Yes. On your head. Just a preliminary shape. But I'd like to have the whole thing finished by the time Con gets back. I can show him and explain about all the wonderful times we had and how you were one of the ones who stopped me going insane with loneliness.'

'My head?'

'The sculpture? Remember? We talked about it in Fefor.'

Nansen, despite his disappointment, began to laugh. 'I see.'

She narrowed her eyes at him. 'I hope you weren't expecting something else.'

'No, of course not.' He placed his jacket on the back of one of the chairs and sat.

She came over and pulled his collar down a little. 'You have a lovely neck.'

'So do you, Kathleen.'

He reached up to touch her, but she pushed his arm down and tutted. 'Don't make love to me like that. I am not in the mood.'

'Will you ever be?'

'I have been thinking on that, Fridtjof. Wondering if you would be so interested in me if my husband was a mere commander of a Dreadnought? If he had never even heard of Antarctica? Would I be quite such a prize?'

Nansen didn't answer.

She spoke softly as she rotated his head with the palms of her hands. 'Imagine if he has been beaten to the Pole by a Norwegian.'

Nansen decided he had nothing to lose by being honest. 'As I fear he might well have been.'

'There. Perfect. Stay still.' She stepped away and walked over to the clay. She almost whispered her next sentence. 'Then it is up to me to make sure that is the only disappointment he suffers at the hands of your country, isn't it?' She raised her voice. 'Ah, here comes the brandy.'

Nansen watched the maid approach with the tray of decanter and glasses. She smiled at him and he managed to send one back, trying not to look too hangdog. He spoke to the maid in German. 'Best make mine a large one.'

Seventy-one

The Great Ice Barrier

'Leave me to die. Save yourselves. I am finished. There is no way I can go on. Just leave me. That is an order.'

'No, we've been thinking. There has to be another way.'

'Best make it quick, then.'

'No, not that.'

Lashly bent down close to Teddy Evans, so his ruined eyes could at least make out his shape. They were on the barrier now, not far from home, but Teddy Evans had collapsed totally. He was lying on the sledge, having been dragged for the past few days. The extra effort had nearly worn out Crean and Lashly completely. They had even dumped their skis to save weight, which they now bitterly regretted.

'You should have left me when I fainted.'

'Aye, m'be,' said Lashly. 'But we didn't.' He looked up at Crean. 'What do you think, Tom?'

'I can do it.'

'Do what?' asked Evans sharply and then groaned. His knees had swollen to grapefruits, and were paining him even when he was resting. His gums were swollen and bleeding and his body was covered with purple blotches. He was a very sick man. 'Just leave me.'

'I am going to stay with you, sir, keep you company. Tom is going to walk to Hut Point to get help.'

'Walk? How far is that?'

'Thirty miles, I reckon,' said Crean. 'And it's a fine day.'

It was indeed, a beautiful day, its radiance a taunt after the blizzards that had confined them to their tent, forcing them to consume their food and fuel till they virtually had neither left.

'We'll make our way, slow as you like, to Corner Camp. There might be some provisions there. Either way, we'll wait for Tom and the dogs to come and get us.'

Evans nodded. 'You are good men.'

'Just doing our duty.' There had been many arguments on the return; Evans had wanted to use as much food and fuel from the dumps as they required. Lashly and Crean were more circumspect, thinking of the polar party. Crean was disappointed in the condition Evans had left some of the depots. He should have taken more care.

The next sentence from Evans was unintelligible, and Lashly realised the officer had fallen asleep and was mumbling. He stood up. 'Well, Tom, if you are certain. I don't mind giving it a crack.'

'I'd rather you stayed,' said Crean. 'I am not one for sitting around. And there's your foot.' Lashly had several frostbitten toes he was nursing, hoping not to lose them.

'Well, here you are.' The stoker handed over the food he had put together, a biscuit they had recovered from one of the motor-sledges, which smelled as if it was tainted with petrol, and some chocolate. 'Don't gorge it all at once. And take the water.'

'No. Mr Evans'll need that.'

They shook hands. 'Good luck, Tom.'

'I'll be back before you know it.'

He watched Tom Crean stride off, bold and resolute. When he had disappeared, he roused Evans and managed to get him to his feet. 'About a mile to Corner Camp, sir. But I can't haul you. Haven't the wind. Or the feet.'

Evans stood swaying, but when Lashly put a strap over his shoulder and into his hands he began to trudge forward, pulling the sledge. Lashly sang for a while, then said, 'I hope the polar party have it better than us. Don't you, sir? Still, at least there are five of them pulling. Five is a good number. Three is a devil of a hard work. Look, I can see the flag. Corner Camp. Let's give it a last shove.'

Teddy Evans didn't respond and it was another hour before they made it to the cairn that marked the camp. There was precious little food to be had, save for some treacle, originally for the ponies, and a slab of butter. Lieutenant Evans collapsed again, lying on the sledge. Lashly was forced to move him to unpack the equipment for camp.

As he was setting up the tent, he found the note from Mr Day. It was a warning to anyone travelling to Hut Point. 'Large, treacherous crevasses have opened up on the barrier between Corner Camp and the sea ice, especially around White Island. Anyone travelling should take a detour to the East to avoid them.'

Lashly peered off into the distance. It was too late to warn him now. Only a Higher Power could decide whether Tom Crean would make it or not.

Seventy-two

The Beardmore Glacier

'The biscuit tin is short!'

'What?'

Scott was on his knees next to the excavated hole that revealed the buried supplies. He head snapped round and he glared at Bowers. 'The tin is short.'

They were at Upper Glacier Depot. It was 7 February, and once again they had suffered infuriating blizzards and falls of those strange ice crystals that ruined the dragging surface. And now, the depot was short.

'Someone must have eaten extra biscuits on the way back,' said Bowers.

'Who would do that?' Scott demanded. 'They all had orders to leave us enough food. Who would be immoral and insubordinate enough to do that? Are you sure it was properly packed?'

Bowers looked stung by the accusation. He had been in charge of the caching of supplies and felt any shortfall or problem to be a personal affront. 'Yes, skipper.'

'Con,' said Wilson, who knew it was no good fretting over riffled biscuits, trying to inject a sense of calm. 'We should put up the tent. Look at Taff.'

Taff Evans was standing next to the sledge, slack jawed. He had fallen down that morning, narrowly avoiding a crevasse, but

482

had struck his head quite hard on the ice. His already dull demeanour had become worse. It was partly a blessing, because Wilson didn't have to explain he was going to lose a good portion of his nose and several fingers. The nails had fallen off and underneath each was a mass of pus. The cut from the sledge was suppurating, poisoning everything around it.

'Come on, Taff, lend a hand.' It was Oates, starting to unpack the sledge. 'God's sake, man. Have you lost your guts completely?'

The attempt to shock him out of his stupor failed. Evans continued to move like a man disconnected from the world. They were all losing condition, thought Oates, just like the ponies had. Wilson had been snowblind and pulled a tendon so badly he couldn't haul. Oates was becoming frostbitten more and more easily and Scott had fallen and damaged his shoulder. Pulling in the harness was agony for him, which was why he was sharp with Bowers. Birdie remained unscathed; he was glad to be back on skis, which they had collected en route. Oates had also found his pipe, a small, cheery miracle.

'Note here from Teddy,' said Scott, unfurling a piece of paper. 'Made it safely, going well.' He sat back on his haunches. 'At least we are off that damned plateau. Thought we were in a bit of a fix there for a while.'

'Only when we were lost, surely,' said Wilson. A white-out had obliterated their outward tracks in places, making it difficult to locate the cairns. They had found some of the depots more by luck than judgement. If it hadn't been for Bowers's extraordinary vision, they would have missed some of the food supplies altogether.

Scott laughed. 'True. Only when we were lost.' He lowered his voice. 'We should have noted the bearings on our depots on the outward journey or laid more marker flags.'

It was a rare admission of such a basic error by Scott, and Wilson felt a sense of foreboding at the words. It was not a moment for defeatism. 'We'll know next time, Con.'

'At least we beat Shackleton this time out.'

'Yes. You've done that.'

Wilson glanced across to Bowers, who was now helping Oates and a less-than-useful petty officer Evans erect the tent. Evans was shuffling, his gait clumsy, and he was finding it hard to manipulate ropes and stays with his tortured hands.

'I doubt that tin is Birdie's fault,' Wilson said quietly.

'I know,' admitted Scott. It could have been Meares or Teddy or any of the others who had turned back who had been thoughtless. 'I should not speak in haste. Look –' he pointed across the ice to an exposed sandstone cliff – 'what about we spend a few hours getting geological samples after lunch?'

Wilson brightened. 'If you think we can spare the time.'

'Give us something else to do. Good for morale. And remember, we came for science, not the race. After lunch, I'll send Birdie off to gather some geological samples. He's a bit rusty on his skis, give him practice.'

Scott pulled one of the fuel tins from the cache and shook it. Wilson heard the slosh of the paraffin, echoing more loudly than it should have.

'Half empty,' Scott said. 'Teddy Evans?'

'I'd like to think he'd be parsimonious with our stocks.'

'Creep?'

'If it is, we can do without that.' Paraffin 'crept' at low temperatures, evaporating out of the tin. It had happened on the *Discovery* trip; they had hoped new, tighter bungs would have solved the problem.

Scott heard a cry and looked up. Evans was on his knees, cradling his cut hand. 'How bad is PO?' he asked Wilson. 'Be honest, Bill.'

'Bad.'

'Stupid, stupid man. He's slowing us, you know.'

Wilson spoke carefully. He knew Scott was holding himself back by an effort of will. He wanted to lash out at everybody and everything: Evans, Shackleton, the weather, even God. 'I think the fuel is more of a problem than Taff at the moment,' he said.

'You might be right. Let's see, should be another, here.' Scott let out a small whoop of joy. 'A-ha. This one seems pretty full.' He stood, his arms full of supplies, his mood lifted. 'Oh, and Bill.'

'Con?'

'Don't mention the creep to the others just yet. Especially Bowers, he'll take it hard.' Wilson couldn't imagine Scott believed a word of his next sentence. 'It might just be one faulty can.'

'Of course not, Con.'

'We have to stop. Skipper, we have to stop. Skipper!'

Scott reluctantly raised a hand and the four men halted, slumping in the traces.

'What is it now?' he demanded of Wilson.

'Look.'

He followed Wilson's outstretched arm. Taff Evans was standing several hundred yards behind, hands limp at his sides. Evans was no longer in the traces. He had lost the power to pull at all, much to Scott's surprise. After the scare of being lost in the crevasses, they were almost clear of the Beardmore. Scott felt that there could be no worse time ahead than the twelve hours wasted when they wandered off track, and the desperate attempt to find the mid-glacier depot. Surely, even though the hauling surface was far from good, they must be over the worst of it. But now Taff seemed all in.

Scott unhitched his harness and trudged back to Taff, who remained rooted to the spot. 'What is it now, PO?' It was difficult not to sound short, but he was costing them valuable time.

'Skis.'

He pointed at his feet. The bindings were undone.

'What about them?'

'Keep coming off. Need to adjust.'

'I'll do it.' Scott bent down, but Evans slapped him on the back, yelping as he did so. 'I can do it, sir.'

'Are you all right, Taff?'

'Never better, sir.'

'Well that's not quite true, is it?'

'I'll be fine. You go on ahead. I'll catch up.'

'We'll wait.'

'You go on.'

Scott walked back to the others and said, 'We'll pull slowly.

He'll catch up.' His tone brooked no argument. 'Ready? One-two-three-heave, one-two-three-heave – 'After five hard jerks the sledge pulled free and they carried on at a reduced pace. Every few hundred yards one of them glanced back. The hulk of Taff was clearly visible, shuffling after them till the snow began to fall, and he disappeared into the swirl.

They camped for lunch shortly afterwards, waiting for him to arrive.

'I don't know what we are going to do if he doesn't improve,' said Oates. 'We can't pull him on the sledge. Not him and those rocks of yours.'

'He was better after a good sleep,' said Wilson. 'A decent feed at Shambles will help him.' Shambles, or Pony, Camp was where five of the animals had been buried.

'I dream about those ponies all day long,' admitted Birdie. 'I fear I may gorge myself when we get back to the hut.'

'I'm looking forward to eating Christopher,' said Oates. 'A little recompense for all the misery he caused me.'

'This is a fern, I think.' Wilson was examining one of the rocks they had collected. They had about 35 lb in all and Oates often complained about the extra weight, but some of them were quite exquisite and Wilson always dissuaded Soldier from ditching them. 'Very delicate. I bet the Norwegians haven't anything like this, to prove it wasn't always a cold, lifeless place.'

Oates laughed. 'It's not what it used to be that worries me. It's what it is today. Shouldn't Taff have made it by now?'

'He'll be following our tracks,' said Bowers.

'Unless they have been drifted over.' Although Amundsen's tracks had remained tauntingly clear at the Pole, the winds they had experienced since often caused a rolling ground-mist of ice crystals that obscured all traces of their own passage.

'I'll take a look,' said Scott wearily.

It had stopped snowing and visibility had improved, but there was no sign of Taff Evans. Scott ducked back into the tent. 'Not a whisker. Come on, we'd best take a look. Leave the sledge. We'll ski.'

They found him on his hands and knees, sobbing. The skis had been lost altogether. He had cast off his mittens and inner gloves, and his hands were sickening to look at. They glistened black, as if they were made of coal. Strings of saliva hung from his lips. He was whimpering, his mouth working but no words coming.

'Oh God, Taff,' said Oates. He took off his skis, sat down next to him, and pulled him on to his lap. He looked up at the others. 'He's in no fit condition to take another pace. Go and get the sledge. I'll stay with him.'

'Can he stand?' asked Scott. 'PO, can you stand?'

'No, he bloody well can't stand,' Oates snapped. 'I am not going to ask him. Please get the sledge. He deserves it.'

Scott's frustration exploded over his face. 'For crying out loud, Taff. You're the strongest of us.'

The exhausted Evans said nothing, just shook his head.

'Get the fucking sledge, will you,' said Oates.

Scott looked taken aback by the reappearance of lower-deck language. His cracked lips pursed in irritation. 'Very well. Gentlemen, if you will.'

Oates watched the three of them trudge off.

'Oh, Taff, what have we done to you?'

The Welshman roused and twisted his head to look at Oates. His eyes were slick with tears and the evaporation fogged his eyes. He attempted to mutter an apology, but the words were slurred and his tongue thick. It was like an old, debilitated man trying to speak.

Oates took off a mitten and stroked Taff's face with his fingers. Through his own numb skin, he could feel the cheeks were hard and scaly. A crater had appeared where the tip of his nose should have been, its colour a queasy yellow and purple. He was like a great strong ox pushed beyond his limits, Oates thought. He'd collapsed just as poor Mr Daniels had at Punchestown. How long ago Ireland seemed now. And to think people there complained about that climate.

Like Mr Daniels, he thought again. Perhaps, if he had a bolt-gun, it would be time for another mercy killing.

'Sorry,' the big man finally said, his face wet with congealing tears.

'Don't be daft. Take no notice of the skipper. He's just worried about you. Our luck is running low. Like the fuel. And look at the size of you. Big man on the same rations as Birdie. Don't know if that's right.' He brushed some of the rime from the Welshman's forehead. 'I'll let you into a secret, Taff. My feet look like your hands. Hurt like billy-o. Not sure I have that many miles in me, either.' Oates felt a sob burst from his throat, taking him by surprise. It took a second to regain his self-control. 'I wonder if you can still ride to hounds with no toes?'

Oates continued to talk to Taff, mainly of horses and hounds, for the next thirty minutes, when the sledgers finally reappeared. They got Taff back to the tent, where he died at twelve-thirty a.m. in the morning without saying another word.

Seventy-three

The door to Hut Point burst open and Tom Crean staggered in, the weather snapping at his heels. He looked around to see who was in and, for a second, he thought it was empty. He felt his first real moment of panic. Then he saw Atkinson at the corner table, head in his arms, dozing.

Atkinson looked up from the table and jumped to his feet, pulling Crean inside and sitting him down. He looked awful, his face gaunt, his eyes red rimmed. Frost-nip scarred his face like smallpox.

'Dimitri!'

The dog-driver emerged from one of the bunks, rubbing his eyes. He saw Crean and his head cleared at once. He fetched a tot of brandy and laid it before the seaman. Crean slugged it back and shuddered. 'Another please.'

'That'll do for now, Tom,' said Atkinson. 'Maybe later. Don't want to overdo it.'

'Aye, sir.'

'You are lucky we're here. We were just getting some rest before we go out to the barrier with more supplies for One Ton Camp and to wait for the polar party. Where are the others?'

'Corner Camp.'

'Who is there?'

'Stoker Lashly and Lieutenant Evans.'

Just two. They must have lost a man, thought Atkinson, knowing

489

the returning parties were to be four-handed. 'How did you get here?'

'Walked, sir.'

'From Corner Camp?' It was thirty miles and this man was a near-skeleton.

'Aye. Took me twenty-four hours to get to the edge of the barrier. Weather closed in a little, I think there is a blizzard at my tail, and I fell a few times trying to get through the Gap. Hurt my back on the rocks.'

'I'll take a look.'

'No, sir, Mr Evans is out there and he is sorely ill. The scurvy, I think. He comes in and out of consciousness. And he's snowblind.'

'I don't think your own eyes are too bright, Tom.'

'They are sore, all right, sir. I had no goggles. Lost them on our sledge down the Beardmore.'

'You did what? No, tell me later. Have you eaten?'

'I walked for twelve hours and then had some chocolate and one of my biscuits. I ate the other two squares a few hours ago.'

Atkinson gasped at this and put a hand on his shoulder. 'You have done something remarkable.'

'Oh, there was no choice, sir. Lashly and I agreed it was our last best hope.'

Atkinson shook his head. For a man in his condition to make that hike was incredible, even if Crean couldn't see it. 'We have some porridge. Dimitri, would you mind?'

Crean began to protest. 'Mr Evans, sir—'

'Yes, we'll go as soon as we make sure you are all right for us to leave you.'

'I'll come with you.'

'No. You'll rest. Now tell me everything. Slowly. When did you last see the polar party?'

Crean went through the final few days on the plateau with Scott, and the eventual splitting of the party, pausing only when Atkinson quizzed him to be certain he had heard right. That Scott had taken five men to the Pole.

'Yes. Said I had a bad cough. As if that was anything. I think maybe I just showed the cough wouldn't have stopped me getting to the Pole, now, haven't I?'

'I think you have proved more than that, Tom.'

A bowl of thick porridge was put before Crean and he spooned it up. 'Lovely.'

Atkinson set about gathering some medical supplies and emergency rations for the journey to Corner Camp, while Dimitri went to harness up the dogs. They could make it to Evans and Lashly in a few hours with the huskies.

'Sir –' muttered Crean. He stood up, knocking the chair over, and rushed to the door, where he vomited the porridge across the slush.

'It's all right,' Atkinson said. 'Often happens. You must be half starved.'

'I think it was the brandy, sir.'

'I am sure it was.'

'Never happened before, sir.'

Atkinson helped Crean to one of the bunks and told him they would be back with the other two shortly and that he could get some sleep. The doctor struggled into his sledging gear and went out into a stiffening wind to fetch his skis.

He was already calculating what had to be done. It sounded as if Evans would have to be sledged over to the *Terra Nova*, which had finally arrived from New Zealand, and be sent home, along with Meares, who had opted to ship out. At some point, though, Atkinson would have to find time and resources to send the dogs south for Scott. But his first duty was to the sick Evans.

The huskies were in the traces and yapping, keen to be off, but Dimitri was looking grim.

'What is it?'

He pointed across the ice to where thick clouds were rolling in and the atmosphere danced and flexed with a strange disturbance. Already Atkinson could feel the icy sting of an advanced guard of the blizzard that had been on Crean's tail. 'Damn.'

'We best wait and see if it blows itself out.'

'Agreed.'

491

'And I was just thinking, doctor. If a strong man like Crean is that bad . . .'

Atkinson nodded; he had been plagued by the same thought. 'I know. How are the polar party getting along?'

Seventy-four

Christopher, as untrustworthy and spiteful as ever, had one last trick to pull. As they dug into the spot where he had been interred, a sickening smell rose up to greet the four exhausted men.

Oates, though, had to laugh with something like admiration. 'He's rotten. Look.' He poked into spongy flesh. 'The only horse that could spoil in an ice locker.'

The other horses had been fine. They had exhumed one shortly after they had made a cairn over the body of Taff Evans. And there had been tasty, thick pony hoosh at Shambles Camp. It was a shame they didn't have the energy to haul a whole carcass with them.

Not that they would have much fuel to cook it with. They were at the Southern Barrier Depot and Christopher wasn't the only bad news. The oil for the primus had 'crept' here as well, and they faced a real shortage. The wind had dropped, which meant the sail they had rigged up was useless. Wilson was snowblind. Oates could not hide his hobbles now, nor the pain he was in.

'There is more fuel at the next depot,' said Scott as brightly as he could manage. 'A gallon. We'll make the most of what we have here.'

They pitched tent for the night and huddled together as the temperatures dropped to minus 40. There was enough fuel for a reasonably hot hoosh using the pony meat they had taken from the last depot. Scott tried to update his diary, but his numb hands would not co-operate. It was easier to write at lunchtime, he

493

decided. Bowers had ceased his diary-keeping back in January. Wilson had stopped sketching after the ascent of the Beardmore and his entries in his diary were getting shorter and shorter. There was never much variation, he said. Cold, hungry, miserable. Wind, no wind; going good, going poor.

'I know things seem grim,' said Scott, 'but we must meet the dogs at some point. Meares will have depoted enough dog biscuit at One Ton for them to come south to meet us.'

'How far do you think they will come?'

'I told Evans to come to eighty-one or eighty-two. I hope they push on to that. They'll have the dog rations to make Mt Hooper at the very least.' That particular depot was sixty-five miles closer than One Ton.

'Hear, hear,' said Wilson. He raised his lukewarm tea. 'To the dogs.'

Nobody responded.

'How far to the next depot?' asked Oates.

'A shade under seventy miles,' Scott said.

Oates imagined seven more days of white-hot pain from his feet. It would be at least that; they were lucky if they got into double figures now. They had spread the depots out too far for the cripples they had become to make the distance with ease.

'I don't mind admitting I am cold tonight,' said Birdie, shivering in his bag.

'The temperatures can't last,' said Scott. 'Not at this time of year. Shackleton didn't have this weather.'

'I think we have shown Sir Ernest a clean pair of heels, despite everything.'

'Aye, Birdie,' Scott smiled, 'that we have. And without his luck, too. He had no snow on the Beardmore, no blizzards . . .'

Bowers's mind had drifted. He knew that it hadn't been all beer and skittles for Shackleton, no matter what the Owner thought. 'What I wouldn't give for a bowl of mulligatawny.'

As the others settled down, Scott looked at his figures. They had ten days' food; but the fuel to cook it was desperately short. He would have to eke that out.

He forced his frozen fingers to write one more line in his journal:
We may find ourselves in safety at the next depot; but there is a horrid element of doubt.

It took them the best part of two hours to get into their gear the next morning. Once again, nothing had dried in the night, when the temperature had almost reached fifty below. Socks and boots were caked in ice, which only thawed in body heat. It meant extremities chilled down far too quickly, making them instantly vulnerable to frostbite.

Oates tended to dress with his back to the others. He didn't want anyone to see his feet. He could do little about the smell that rose up to greet him, but the others, deep in their own agonies, hardly seemed to notice.

As he pulled on his icy socks, a fresh pain shot up his leg and seemed to play about the old wound. That was weeping now, a watery yellow pus. His feet were considerably swollen, and pulling the finnesko over them was even worse than the socks. Tears formed in his eyes. It was the only time his hunger pangs seemed to fade.

His finnesko boots were almost done, the soles shredded, the sides split from the effort of pulling them over his bloated limbs. He had one fresh pair left, but he would delay using them till the last possible moment. They would have to see him home.

'Home,' he said out loud, relishing the impossible word.

'With God's help,' muttered Wilson.

After they had struck camp and reloaded the sledge, Scott announced the order. 'Birdie and Bill to take the front if that is all right. Soldier and I will bring up the rear.'

That was fine by Oates. The lead positions caused the most strain on the eyes, as the vanguard searched for cairns or the old tracks in the snow. All of them had suffered blindness because of it.

Scott bent down and took a handful of surface, letting it run off his mitten. It was powdery. 'And skis, I think.'

The ski boots were also showing signs of wear; Oates didn't think his had many days' use left. Then he would be down to slogging on foot, as Bowers had once been. That was like walking over a bed of needle-sharp nails. Skiing was only similar to traversing red-hot coals.

They erected the sail they had fashioned, but did not unfurl it. Scott would wait and see how helpful the wind was going to be. Some days the wind pushed from the South, in which case it gave them a great boost; at other times it veered and came from unhelpful directions or dropped completely.

Once the fiddly work was done, cold hands were put into chill mittens and rubbed together to try to bring some life back. Then it was into the hated harnesses. Even before they pulled, Oates's back, leg and shoulders began to protest, as if balking at the memory.

'One, two, three, heave. Heave. Heave.'

Now the pain was real, heartfelt. The sky was clear, the sun bright, but there was little warmth in it. The air was bitterly cold, the slightest breeze stabbing at any exposed skin. Ice began to form on his straggly beard. They had all stopped trimming their facial hair now, too beaten by the effort after a long day.

The surface beneath the sledge runners was again poor. For a reason Scott couldn't fathom, once the thermometer dropped below minus 25, the ice changed texture, becoming more like gravel than smooth ice.

'The glide has gone again, Titus,' said Scott between gritted teeth.

'I've noticed,' said Oates ruefully. His hip felt as if someone had driven a sword into it.

'Minus forty-eight last night,' said Scott.

'It felt like it.'

He dropped his voice. 'I've got us in a bit of a pickle, Soldier, haven't I?'

Oates didn't reply. There was little to add. They were in a fix all right, but it was a waste of energy apportioning blame. After a few minutes, Oates said: 'Nobody made me come.'

'I'm glad you did.'

'What are our chances?'

'If there are no more setbacks, good. If we make a decent fist of marching for the next few days, we can open up the food a little.

Still some pony left. That will get us to Middle Barrier. And if Teddy Evans makes sure the dogs come to us, we'll be fine, Titus. We'll be fine.'

They were into the rhythm now, their breath coming hard; they lapsed into silence, thinking alternately about food and the dogs surely heading their way.

It was hard not to stare at mealtime. Oates had to force himself to look away as Scott divided the rations. With his stomach groaning and twisting, it took all of his effort not to count every crumb. He could see the others drawn into the act of division as well, like moths mesmerised by a flame. Scott's hand shook with more than cold as he dished out the portions.

Whatever poor conversation they managed while setting up camp always faltered prior to a meal, as if hunger had consumed all thoughts. The only sound was the hiss of the stove, the only thing worth watching the slow bubble of the hoosh; the smell, once so nauseating, flooding the nostrils, saliva flowing in anticipation.

'Soldier.'

Scott handed over the pannikin and Oates took it. His hand gripped the spoon, but a great effort of will stopped him digging in before the others.

'Birdie.'

'Thank you, sir.'

'And Bill.'

'Left yourself a bit short,' said Wilson, nodding to the amount of hoosh left for Scott.

'Have I?' Scott looked puzzled. 'Well, I'm sure I had a greater helping last night.'

'I think not, sir,' said Birdie as he reached over to try to spoon some back.

'Don't be ridiculous, lieutenant,' Scott snapped.

Bowers looked taken aback. For a moment Oates thought he might cry. 'All in this together, sir. Fair dos, I think.'

'Yes. Sorry, Birdie. I'll give myself extra at breakfast.'

'Very good, sir.'

497

Now came the greedy scrape of metal on metal and the smacking of lips. To stop himself bolting, Oates said: 'He should be back by now, shouldn't he?'

'Teddy?' Scott nodded. 'Yes. I expect he is.'

The thought of Teddy Evans organising their relief cheered them all immensely.

Seventy-five

Hut Point

Teddy Evans was delirious. He could make out that people were speaking, and often about him, but the words brought no sense to him. They were just noise in his ears. He opened one eye. Atkinson and Cherry were engaged in conversation, with Atch looking animated. Atch caught sight of Evans stirring and came across to his bunk. He knelt, so his head was close to Teddy's ear.

'There you are, Teddy. Had us worried there for a while.'

'Lashly?'

'At Cape Evans. As is Tom Crean. Both on the mend. I thought we'd best keep you here till you are a little stronger, then I'll move you across. Think you could manage some soup or porridge?'

A thought flashed into Evans's mind. 'Dogs?'

'Yes, I was just talking to Cherry about that, don't worry, it's all taken care of. Now, what could you eat?'

Evans closed his eyes. There was something he meant to say about dogs. What was it? 'All taken care of?'

'Yes. All in hand, old chap. Just concentrate on yourself.'

Atkinson stood and looked down at the scurvy-damaged face.

'I can't leave him,' he said to Cherry. 'You'll have to go south with Dimitri.'

Cherry suddenly looked like the young lad he was. 'Me? I've never driven dogs before. Not properly.'

499

'There's nobody else.'

'What about Silas?'

'Wright's got the whole scientific programme to shoulder. Look, if the polar party are making decent time they might even be at One Ton Camp now. And it's been depleted over the season by everyone helping themselves. It must be restocked. Dimitri can give you lessons in driving and make sure he goes in the lead. All you have to do is follow.'

Cherry stuttered with nerves at the thought of dog-driving in a white-out. 'Atch, you know I can't navigate worth a fig –'

The doctor pointed to the man in the bunk. 'I don't think you can look after Teddy Evans properly either. As I say, with Sunny Jim going back . . . ' – he was referring to Simpson, their weather man, who had been recalled to India – 'Wright has to do his meteorological work at Cape Evans. Imagine what the Owner will say if he finds gaps in that data? And everyone else is scattered to the four winds. And it isn't hard to navigate to One Ton. It's only after that it becomes tricky. Really, Cherry. It won't do.'

Cherry took off his glasses and cleaned them on his jumper. As he had found during his blind stumble from Cape Crozier, normal sledging with spectacles was not easy. It was harder at the speeds the dogs could manage. He would have trouble spotting the cairns. 'Very well. I'll do my best.'

Atkinson put a hand on his shoulder. 'I know you will.'

'So, One Ton Camp.'

'Yes. Take three weeks' worth of food for you and the dogs. And enough full rations for the polar party.'

'What if he has already been there?'

'Use your judgement. But don't risk the dogs by haring off on a wild-goose chase.'

'How long do I wait?'

Atkinson shrugged. 'You'll have to be the judge of that, too. But don't go further south than One Ton. Scott was quite clear on that because he wants the dogs in good condition for next season. There's no dog food at that depot. If you go south, you'll have to start killing huskies.'

Cherry shuddered at that thought. 'So I should leave soon?'

'As soon as Dimitri gets here.' The dog man had been trying to feed up the animals, which were still exhausted from their trip to the glacier, and he had returned to Cape Evans for fresh supplies for them. It was asking a lot of them to go out again; it was a two-week return trip to One Ton, plus waiting time if Scott wasn't there.

Cherry sighed. He still had misgivings, but with Victor Campbell far to the north and not yet returned, Scott down in the south and Teddy Evans incapacitated, Atch was the team leader now. He had to obey his orders. 'I'll put my gear together.'

'And remember, Cherry. Don't risk the dogs further south than One Ton or we'll be sunk.'

'There is something else you should see,' said Oates.

The remaining four were in the tent once more, having consumed a decent pony hoosh and cocoa. But the food had not settled stomachs or tempers. There had been a gallon of fuel cached at Middle Barrier. Three quarters of it had evaporated. So they had food, but little to heat it with. It was another sixty-five miles to the next depot, Mt Hooper, which should have been resupplied by the dog teams. Only with the most rigid economy would the paraffin last. And if there had been creep at Hooper, it was another sixty-five to One Ton. But the dogs would come to Mt Hooper, he reminded himself. Teddy Evans would see to that.

As well as the paraffin worries, the surfaces they had encountered had been atrocious, clogging the skis, forcing them to walk. They had encountered strange, large crystals that seemed to grip the sledge runners even harder than the sand-like snow. The pulling was brutal and exhausting and yet they logged only five and a half miles. And now, Oates, apparently, had a third problem to disclose.

'What is it, Titus?' Wilson asked.

Oates slid off his sodden sock and Birdie gasped at the sight. The foot was a bloated, marbled white, apart from a large red sore covering the bridge, and the sooty toes. 'Oh my Lord, Farmer. How long has it been this bad?'

'A while now.'

Wilson tutted. 'I can't believe you've walked on them. Let me see the other one.'

'Oh, the other one's worse.'

Wilson eased off the second sock, and, indeed, the foot was even more balloon-like. The skin on this one was blackened yet shiny where it had stretched. There was a rank smell. Wilson rolled up the trouser leg and saw the red ring, where dead flesh ended and living began. Titus Oates's feet were rotting on his body.

'I'll put some cream on them,' he said.

Oates laughed at the panacea. 'Can you ride to hounds with no feet?'

'Hasn't come to that, Soldier,' said Scott.

Wilson frowned as he examined the feet further. 'I'll dry them as best I can first. It might hurt. I have some morphia, if you wish.'

'Yes. And how about a little brandy?' Oates asked.

Wilson nodded. 'Purely medicinal.'

'Of course, doctor. Purely medicinal.'

Wilson found the flask and poured a measure. He handed him not more than a thimble full while he prepared the injection, but Oates cherished every drop.

'Titus, you might want to cut your sleeping bag open at the base.'

'Why?'

'The feet will only hurt when they warm up.'

'I've noticed that.'

'Keep them chilled till we can do something about them.'

'Right-o,' said Oates with a forced gaiety.

Wilson clapped him on the shoulder and moved away, hiding the concern eating at his stomach.

Later that night, with the thermometer plunging and a vile wind tugging at the tent, Scott rolled close to Wilson.

'Your own feet aren't too good, Bill. You must take care of yourself, too.'

'I will, Con.'

'Why are we losing condition so quickly? You are skin and bone.'

'I don't know, Con, I really don't. Could it have been the altitude?'

'Perhaps.' He thought for a moment. Shackleton, too, had starved on his return. 'What about Soldier's feet? Are they as bad as they look and smell?'

Wilson looked over but Oates was, as far as he could make out, asleep. 'Worse, Con. It's gangrene.'

The storm blasted into the tent when Dimitri crawled inside. He rapidly sealed the entrance again and accepted the hot tea from Cherry. 'Thank you.'

Cherry wiped the last of the moisture from his glasses. At least while he cooked the kaleidoscope of ice crystals on his lenses melted. As he had expected, his frozen spectacles had bedevilled his attempts at navigation. 'How is it out there?'

'As you say, thick as a hedge,' said Dimitri. He took a sip of the drink, shivering hard. The cold was getting to him. They had no minimum thermometer, so could only guess at night-time temperatures. But Cherry had seen the mercury at -38 the night before, just as he was turning in at around eight. It had probably dipped well below that. 'Cherry, the dogs are suffering.'

'I can imagine.'

'They are losing their coats. Stareek has stopped eating. I think Cigan is close to finished. We should go back.'

'The polar party are out there somewhere,' he reminded Dimitri. 'Possibly in the same conditions.'

Dimitri nodded. 'We have had a blizzard for four days now. They must have had it too. If they are on the barrier.'

It was inconceivable they were still on the Beardmore. 'They will be by now, surely.'

'Yes. So they are not moving. Not coming. Just laid up, sensible. Or perhaps they have passed us already. It's possible. But no matter what, we must leave ourselves eight days' food in reserve to get us back.'

Cherry did a quick calculation. They had arrived at One Ton on 4 March, but the conditions were such they had used more human and dog rations than planned. 'We have to turn for home on the tenth.'

'Day after tomorrow.'

Cherry was concerned about the five men out there, although he consoled himself with the thought that the chances were they were holed up, not too far away. He was well aware they were well provisioned with food and paraffin, and with the likes of Evans and Birdie pulling – and Wilson's calm head – they would easily make the sixty or seventy miles between depots.

He had shared that terrible winter journey with Wilson and Bowers, forging a bond that could never be broken. Cherry knew they weren't quitters. And Scott had always said they had planned everything so that they didn't need the dogs beyond resupplying One Ton Camp. Still, he was relieved it wasn't him struggling to make it home.

No matter how much he would like to wait and see his old comrades, he had no choice but to agree with Dimitri. There had been no biscuits for the animals cached at One Ton. As Atch had warned, if he went further south, they'd have to kill some dogs to feed the others. Cherry could just imagine the wigging Scott would give him about that next season. Still, he found himself kneading his hands, his stomach sick with his indecision. 'We go back even if they don't show?'

Dimitri nodded. The tea had barely warmed him and he began to cough, the pannikin falling from his hands. His right side was becoming numb, and it was hard to grip anything. It wasn't only the dogs that were going downhill, he knew; his chest hurt, his arm was partially paralysed, and his fingers were disintegrating. 'Even if they don't show.'

There were so many different kinds of pain, Oates felt that he was a walking compendium. Hot, cold, shooting, throbbing, electrical, grinding. It had invaded his head, too, a great regimental drum thumping away, so severe he had to close his eyes. It was there even during the fitful sleep, there when Oates woke in the morning to that bitter, bitter cold.

He could see the impatience in the others as he took nearly two hours to get dressed, his stiff, bloated limbs refusing to speed up, his feet stabbing with every move. They tried their best to hide their irritation, especially Wilson, but by the time he had pulled on his socks and finnesko – he had been forced to slit the new ones so he could get his ballooned feet into them – the meagre warmth of breakfast had gone. They would start cold, endure more cold, and then camp cold. The pemmican was eaten barely warmed; the tiny amount of remaining fuel was used to melt ice for tea or cocoa, drunk tepid.

And now he couldn't pull his ski boots on. All he could do was hobble alongside the sledge, head down, listening to the others strain like spent nags. Mt Hooper had proved another disaster. Someone had riffled the supplies on their way back and the fuel was a trickle. There had been no resupply of the meagre depot. 'A terrible jumble,' Scott had said.

Oates doubted they were making one mile an hour, no more than six miles in a day. They were fifty-five miles from One Ton, with a week's supply of food left at most. Even Oates's poor arithmetic told him they were going to be twelve or thirteen miles short. Why were they going on?

Scott turned and looked at the stumbling figure behind the sledge. He was walking with a pronounced limp, favouring the leg with the old bullet wound. Soldier was in worse shape than any of his ponies had been at the end.

'Bill,' asked Scott as they trudged on, 'what we discussed after breakfast?'

Wilson shook his head vigorously. 'As I said then. I am against it.'

'You are for suffering, then?'

'It is unChristian.'

Scott didn't speak for a few minutes, rehearsing his argument as they tramped on. 'Longinus?' he finally asked.

Wilson turned to look at Scott. The Owner's face was thin, and disfigured by sores and blisters, but the expression was still dogged and determined. '*The Spear of Destiny*?'

'Yes, did Longinus not shorten our Lord's suffering on the cross with a lance? Was that not a noble thing for a Roman to do?'

Wilson didn't feel he had the intellect left for an exhaustive answer. When he tried to think, food invaded his thoughts. He was beginning to suffer from phantom aromas. That day, he could smell roasting grouse. 'Jesus was already dead.'

'Surely it was a way of making sure he suffered no more,' insisted Scott. 'Or else, why bother?'

'Possibly.' Wilson looked ahead at the monochromatic canvas of the barrier, his eyes searching in vain for some feature to latch on to, a point of interest, a shadow, but there was only a blank dumbness. Strange, he had thought black the colour of Godlessness. Now he knew otherwise. 'Perhaps Melville was right.'

'What's that?'

'Nothing.'

'So, Bill, how many tablets do you have?'

Wilson caught the whiff of grouse again, and felt saliva flow and his stomach rumble. 'About a hundred and twenty, all told.'

'Thirty each,' said Scott.

'Yes.'

Scott looked back at Oates, his feet dragging through the woolly snow crystals. It was too much effort for him to lift them now.

'His nose is frostbitten.'

'I saw.'

'Poor Soldier. He knows he's a hindrance.'

'He's a fighter, Con. He asked me what his chances are this morning.'

'What did you say to that?'

Wilson couldn't speak for a while, his wind gone. When they had some assistance in the sail and his breath returned he said: 'I told him I didn't know. That it was in God's hands. But he knows the truth. As we all do.'

'If we were fit, we'd make it, Bill.'

'I know that, Con. Such luck we've had. Such luck.'

'Oh for Shackleton's Irish fortune.' Scott watched Birdie's back for a while, the tired plod of his short legs. He had stopped speaking now; he and Oates were silent most of the time, lost in their gloomy thoughts. 'Bill, I think you should issue it. Let each man decide.'

'Under protest.'

'Protest noted, Bill.'

'Very well, Con. I'll give the opium tablets out as soon as we have pitched tent.'

Seventy-six

London, March 1912

The First Sea Lord, Admiral Sir Francis Charles Bridgeman, requested he be sat next to Mrs Scott at the luncheon. The admiral was to step down from his position and it was one of a series of dinners at the Greenwich Naval College in his honour. Kathleen had been brought downriver by launch; she was sorry Peter could not be there to see the wonderful buildings and the pageantry of the welcome. But he had been suffering a strange fever for a week now, and she was concerned the chill of the Thames in winter might make it worse.

'Are you worried?' Sir Francis asked after they had sat down. 'That there is no news.'

'Worried? Not a scrap. I would not expect any, not till *Terra Nova* docks in New Zealand, and that could be weeks yet. In fact, last year Bill Wilson wrote to his wife saying they might even miss the ship.'

'Really? Harry Pennell would leave before word of their success reached the ship?'

'Yes. If they are late back, rather than risk *Terra Nova* being frozen in for the winter. So, I don't think there is much to worry about.'

'Your husband is a fine man, Mrs Scott.'

'I know it.'

'And no word from the Norwegian?'

She thought, for a second, he meant Nansen. They had written to each other since Berlin, his letters keeping her amused. He liked to proclaim his love in flowery terms, but he had accepted that nothing physical would happen between them. He was an adorable man in many ways. She sometimes felt guilty about liking him so much. But was it so very old fashioned for two people to simply enjoy each other's company? 'Oh, Amundsen. No. Nothing.'

It was over coffee that the news arrived, passed from waiter to guest, till the room buzzed.

'What is it?' Sir Francis asked his neighbour, a young lieutenant.

'Well, Chinese whispers, really. It seems Amundsen is in Hobart.'

'Tasmania?'

'Yes,' said the lieutenant. 'He says categorically Scott reached the Pole. Well done, Mrs Scott.'

'Bravo,' said Sir Francis.

She felt a giddy flush of relief before the first doubts set in. 'But he could only know that if Con got there first, and he second, surely.'

'I s'pose,' said Sir Francis.

'Then surely we would have heard from Con by now.'

'True.'

Kathleen shook her head, determined not to be swept up by conjecture or bowled over by false hope. 'There's something not quite right.'

'You think so? Don't fret,' advised Sir Francis. 'You know how unreliable cables can be.'

'Yes. But nonetheless.' She stood and Sir Francis got to his feet. 'If you will excuse me. I think I should be with Peter.'

There were reporters at the door, shouting at her, vying for an exclusive, and once she was inside they continued to hammer at the windows.

She ordered the drapes pulled, the telephone unplugged, and retreated upstairs. Peter was in bed, looking stronger. His forehead felt cooler and she took his temperature. Ninety-nine degrees.

'Is Daddy home?'

'No, not yet.'

'Who are those people downstairs?'

'Just some over-excited reporters.'

'Is he in the papers?'

'He will be, Peter. He will be.'

The cable from Nansen arrived in the evening, confirming her suspicions.

AMUNDSEN MADE POLE. NO SIGN OF SCOTT SINCE JANUARY. ONE HUNDRED AND FIFTY MILES FROM POLE. MY THOUGHTS WITH YOU.

Of course, Nansen would be one of the first on the planet to hear any despatch about the Pole. The sighting must have meant *Terra Nova* had come north again with the news about him being 150 miles away.

She closed her eyes, imagining how crushing a disappointment it would be for Con to find the Norwegians had primacy. But he would bounce back, she was sure. One hundred and fifty miles short in January? That was very late in the season. He was certain to have missed *Terra Nova*, which meant another winter on the ice. She sent a reply to Nansen for protocol's sake, one she didn't really feel. *Hurray for Norway anyway.*

Kathleen read to Peter at bedtime, a chapter from Walter Scott, whom the boy always insisted must be a relative.

'Is Amundsen a good man?' he asked when she told him the news about the Pole.

'Yes. I think he probably is.'

'I think both Amundsen and Daddy made the Pole. Daddy has stopped working now.'

'What do you mean?'

'He is resting.'

'Yes, I'm sure he is. Goodnight.'

510

Peter's strange turn of phrase alarmed Kathleen. She tucked him up and went downstairs to consult her diary and make arrangements. It was a long way off yet, but she had decided that she would travel to New Zealand, via America, and be there to meet Captain Scott when he returned from the Pole the following year.

Seventy-seven

17 March 1912

The white-hot stabbing in his legs caused Oates to cry out as he woke up. It had been so bad on the last march he had bitten into his hand; the teeth marks were clearly visible. Nothing about him was healing, apparently. As Wilson had suggested, he had cut the bottom out of his sleeping bag to keep his frostbitten feet exposed, so that they would not thaw. But the morning temperature was high enough to cause him bursts of agony around his ankles and what was left of his toes.

He looked around at the three grey, gaunt faces and the red, sunken eyes that stared back at him. The spectral green light of the tent, once so comforting, made them look jaundiced. Blisters were tracked across their faces and lips were swollen, scabbed and fissured. An ice rime from their freezing breath deposited crystals over their face and hair. Their vocal faculties, the external machinery for speech – lips, jaws and tongues – had all been damaged. Each man spoke as if he had been born with an impediment.

Oates cleared the frost from his mouth. 'Sorry. I thought. I might not wake at all. Hoped.' The words came thick and slow, such was the effort to form them. Sentences were punctuated with short gasps for breath. 'I bet you hoped so. Too.'

'Nonsense. A few more days' effort, Soldier,' said Scott. 'Soon as the blizzard goes, we march on.'

'You go on. I haven't another march left in me.'

'You must have.'

'No. None.' He pulled a leg from the bag and rolled down the sock, just to show how the necrosis had progressed up his calf. The others held their breath and glanced away till it was covered again.

Scott looked over at Wilson and nodded. It was time.

Wilson carefully opened his medical bag and extracted the four tubes. He had already counted them out, so each man had enough to end his suffering if he wished.

They all knew what lay in store now. They were cooking their final supplies with a tiny spirit lamp and a blizzard had surrounded the tent once more. The outside world was a howling maelstrom. Starvation was looming.

'Just in case,' said Wilson as he passed the phial to Oates.

Soldier put up his hands, black and swollen like his feet. 'Can't even do that without help. You should have left me.'

He had offered to stay on the ice in his sleeping bag while the others marched on. Scott had all but dragged him the next few miles to camp. 'We couldn't do that,' said Bowers with some difficulty. 'Nobody gets left behind.'

'What about Taff?' Oates asked. 'We left him behind when his skis gave trouble.'

There was a guilty silence. They had indeed carried on without him for a short while before pitching camp, before returning for him.

'Taff had gone in the head,' said Bowers eventually. 'You know that.'

Oates looked at the three men, from one to the other. None was in good condition, but he was the worst by some margin. His feet and hands useless, his brain as slow as a one year old's, although not as demented as Taff's had been. His body was worse, though. To his shame, Wilson had spoon-fed him the previous night, even though the doctor was in serious pain from his feet and a torn tendon himself.

'Do you need help with them, Soldier?' asked Scott, picking up his own tube of pills.

'Con,' Wilson objected.

'No, skipper, I don't need help.'

Oates lunged forward and managed to get on to all fours. The pressure on his bones caused him agony and his breath came in short gasps.

'What are you doing?' Scott asked.

'Just going. Outside.'

'It's minus forty,' said Wilson, thinking Titus was answering a call of nature. 'Perhaps less. Do it in your britches. Or I'll give you a hand. There's a blizzard, man.'

Oates laughed. 'Then I may be some time.'

'No, Soldier. It's too late for that. It'll make no difference, Titus,' said Bowers, stirring himself, as if he only just realised what was about to happen. 'Not to us. Don't do it for us.'

'Let me do it. For myself.' He hesitated. 'Do you think my regiment . . . will be proud of me?'

'I do,' said Scott.

'Bound to be. To have a man at the Pole, the first army man at ninety degrees south,' said Wilson.

'I'll just go outside,' he repeated.

He crawled forward towards the exit.

'Soldier.' Bowers sat up his bag, as if to lunge and grab him. 'No.'

'Let him be, Birdie,' Scott said. 'Let him be. Soldier. You were right, you know. All along. About—'

'Don't tell me that. Don't. Not now.' He knew what Scott was about to say: they should have pressed on and depoted the horses further south at eighty degrees on the original journey to set up One Ton Camp. Had they done so, they would in all probability be sitting next to it at that very moment. If they had just pressed on for thirty miles with Nobby and Guts and the others. It sounded no distance at all. At one time he could have run that. Thirty miles. In that storm, with his feet, it might as well be thirty thousand.

'Tell my mother I love her. And my sisters. And that I am sorry.'

'Titus—' Bill Wilson began.

Before anyone could stop him, Oates had untied the flap and was through the opening and into the storm. It was the fastest he had moved in days, as if he had been saving one last burst of energy.

514

He hadn't even taken his boots. The wind invaded the tent, bringing large flakes of snow with it. Scott reached across and pulled the ties to close the flap.

'There goes a very gallant gentleman.'

'Bugger,' said Bowers to himself and began to mumble a prayer for the gallant gentleman's soul. This segued into a low sobbing.

Wilson shuffled towards the door but Scott said, 'No, he's gone. You'll be lost yourself.'

'And tomorrow?' asked Wilson, staring at the vibrating entrance. 'What then, Con? Do we look for him? Say something?'

'We push on,' said Scott slowly, shaking his head. 'Titus has given us that chance. We should take it.'

Tom Crean cracked open a bottle of beer and handed it to Tryggve Gran.

'What's this for?'

'It's St Patrick's Day. Lunch, a beer and a walk on the ice.' The sea ice had thickened around Cape Evans; soon they would be able to exercise the dogs across it. *Terra Nova* had gone, with Meares and Teddy Evans. It had intended to pick up Campbell and the Northern party en route and return them, or signal their relief, but there was no sign, which was worrying. Had the ice beaten the ship back? Was Campbell stranded?

Nor was there any evidence of the polar party, but nobody had expressed too much concern. Not yet. Cherry had depoted enough food for them at One Ton Camp; they could sit anything out there. 'Perhaps get us some seals,' continued Crean. 'What do you say?'

'St Patrick?'

'Patron saint of Ireland.'

Gran looked at the date. 'March the seventeenth?'

'Every year, Trigger. Cheers.'

'*Prost*.' Gran raised the bottle and chinked it against Crean's. 'You know, it's the Soldier's birthday. Thirty-two, I think.'

'Is it?' said Tom. 'Then happy birthday, Titus Oates.'

* * *

One step, two step, three. Enough to be clear of the tent. God, it is so cold, so very, very cold. Another two steps. Can't quite straighten now. Funny, feet have stopped hurting. Another step. Come on, Titus, you can do better than that. You should have listened to me, Scott. Shouldn't you? No, don't die with recriminations. You are not without blame. You should have used snowshoes on the ponies more readily. And a horse soldier with a gammy leg had no business out there anyway. Can't blame Scott for every little thing. Brave man. A trooper. A lesser man might have lain down at the Pole in front of that damned Norwegian flag. Not Scott. He tried to get them home, that much was certain. And didn't abandon the weak. Perhaps a little hard on Taff; shouldn't have left him that day to fix his skis. But he himself had gone along with it without protest. So it was all their faults, really.

Why were they dying? Scott had a mix of bad luck, a bit of stubbornness, a smattering of foolish ideas. But the bits added up, didn't they? The horses, the motor-sledges, the fuel creep, the extended cooking time, winter coming ridiculously early, no dogs at Hooper. Drip, drip, drip.

If only Scott had listened to him about One Ton. What a price to pay for some nags that were doomed to die anyway.

In the end, does it really matter where a man died? Once you accepted your time was finite, when that terrible clarity of the waiting oblivion shone through all the guff and wishful thinking about after-lives, then whether you were snuffed out at age twenty, thirty or seventy hardly mattered. Except to those left behind.

Oh, Carrie, I am sorry for the sadness it will cause you.

Even the shivering hurts now, muscles banging against bone. Can't be long.

It would have been nice to find Edie. He wondered what she had called the baby? Was it a boy or a girl? That's all he wanted to know. That and where he could send a little money. The least he could do.

Why aren't I dead yet?

Pull off the jumper. Christ, that's—

Get up. Come on, not far enough away yet. Don't want them

wasting time making a cairn or saying some empty words. Wilson's God doesn't live out here, he won't be listening. Poor Bill. Poor Birdie. And, yes, poor Captain Scott. Oh, and poor Taff. Forgotten so soon. Mustn't remember him at the end, the broken man, but the other fellow. The proud Welshman, the happy drunkard, the tireless companion.

Get up, Titus. One, two, three. Hup. There. Now, which way is the tent? This way. No, must be over there, so I walk this way. Oh Christ, who is that? No, go back. Go back. Don't come and get me. Stupid. Oh, it's you. How did you get here? Good to see you. Yes, I think it must be my birthday. I'm just going to sit down. Take my shirt off. Can you help with the buttons? Thank you. It cheers me to see you, old friend. We've come a long way, haven't we? A long, long way down. And isn't that odd? A queer thing. Now you are here. I feel much warmer. Much warmer.

Seventy-eight

March 1912

To my widow

Dearest Darling – We are in a very tight corner and I have doubts of pulling through – In our short lunch hours I take advantage of a very small measure of warmth to write letters preparatory a possible end – the longest is naturally to you on whom my thoughts mostly dwell waking or sleeping. If anything happens to me I shall like you to know how much you have meant to me and that pleasant recollections are with me as I depart – I should like you to take what comfort you can from these facts also – I shall not have suffered any pain but leave the world fresh from harness and full of good health and vigour – this is dictated already, when provisions come to an end we simply stop where we are within easy distance of another depot.

[break]

We have gone downhill a good deal since I wrote the above. Poor Titus Oates has gone – he was in a bad state – the rest of us keep going and imagine we have a chance to get through but the cold weather doesn't let up at all – we are now only twenty miles from a depot but we have very little food or fuel.

Well, dear heart, I want you to take the whole thing very sensibly as I am sure you will – the boy will be your comfort. I had looked forward to helping you to bring him up but it is a satisfaction to feel that he is safe with you.

I must write a little letter for the boy if time can be found to be read when he grows up – dearest, that you know cherish no sentimental rubbish about remarriage – when the right man comes to help you in life you ought to be your happy self again – I hope I shall be a good memory, certainly the end is nothing for you to be ashamed of and I like to think that the boy will have a good start in parentage of which he may be proud.

Dear, it is not easy to write because of the cold – seventy degrees below zero and nothing but the shelter of our tent – you know I have loved you, you know my thoughts must have constantly dwelt on you and – oh, dear me, you must know that quite the worst aspect of this situation is the thought that I shall not see you again. The inevitable must be faced – you urged me to be leader of this party and I know you felt it would be dangerous – I've taken my place throughout, haven't I? God bless you, my own darling, I shall try and write more later – I go on across the back pages . . .

[break]

Since writing the above we have got to within eleven miles of our depot with one hot meal and two days' cold food and we should have got through, but have been held for four days by a frightful storm – I think the best chance has gone, we have decided not to kill ourselves but to fight it to the last for that depot but in the fighting there is a painless end so don't worry. I have written letters on odd pages of this book – will you manage to get them sent? You see I am anxious for you and the boy's future – make the boy interested in natural history if you can, it is better than games – they encourage it at some schools – I know you will keep him out in the open air – try and make him believe in God, it is comforting. Oh my dear, my dear, what dreams I have had of his future and yet, oh my girl, I know you will face it stoically – your portrait and the boy's will be found in my breast pocket and the one in the little red Morocco case given by Lady Baxter. There is a piece of the Union Jack flag I put up at the South Pole in my private kit bag together with Amundsen's black flag and other trifles – give a small piece of the Union flag to the King and a small piece to Queen Alexandra and keep the rest, a poor trophy for you! – What lots and lots I could tell you of this journey. How much better it has been than lounging in comfort at home – what tales you would have for the boy but oh, what a price to pay – to forfeit the sight of your dear, dear face.

Scott finished the letter to his wife and, as quickly as his numb hands would allow, penned letters to Barrie and to the mothers of Bowers and Wilson before his stiff fingers gave out entirely. He hoped he had explained well enough how wonderful his two companions were. Are. Still alive, but barely. The end could not be far off now. They had decided, like Oates, that it would be a natural death.

With shaking hands, Scott lit the feeble spirit lamp they were cooking with, and scooped up a pannikin of snow from outside. It was still swirling white, as it had been for a week. Or was it more? He had to admit he was losing track of time in the cocoon. Still, it was bad enough outside that he wouldn't get his wish to simply die in his tracks. The tent would be their coffin.

'Tea anyone?'

The other two grunted from within their bags. He didn't tell them it would be the final one. The original plan had been for the two of them to strike out for fuel from the depot. Then, as the blizzard and Wilson's feet worsened, for Bowers to do it alone. On a fine day, he could cover twenty-two miles, the round trip, easily enough, particularly as he wouldn't be sledging. But the storm refused to abate. It taunted them in their little prison, laughing at each nibble of frozen pemmican or sip of insipid cocoa. Scott had put curry powder in with his pemmican and had only just stopped paying the price in indigestion and stomach cramps.

'Be along shortly.'

So the final scene would be played out in this shabby tent, rather than on the march. Not that he could walk anyway. Only a few days ago he had won The Best Feet In Tent award. Then two toes went, now all of them on the right had gone. The ankle had swollen, too. His foot rivalled Oates's bloated limb. Amputation was required. But he didn't fancy Bill sawing at it with a clasp knife. Not that Bill could really hold a knife now. His hands were gone. They were a sorry bunch, with Bowers the fittest in body, but quieter than ever, clutching his prayer book in his bag.

Eleven miles short. Such a pity. Could they have come through, as he suggested in his message to the British public, if they had not tended their sick? If Oates had walked out earlier rather than wait till it made no difference? Who could tell? The ways of providence were inscrutable. Now, all that remained was to choose the manner of passing on. Bill wanted them to have good clean, Christian deaths – Oates had effectively scuppered the idea of taking refuge in the pills – with no regrets.

Scott was denied that latter luxury. There was plenty for him to regret. Yet, he supposed, much to celebrate. It was up to him to tell the world about these men and their deeds and the manner of their deaths. To make King and country proud of them, causing the whole Empire to marvel at what Englishmen could do. He had started the diary for publication; now he was writing for posterity and Peter. He was already a ghost. As someone had said, they were as substantial as smoke on this continent. Just smoke on the ice. Who had said it? No matter.

As he waited for the ice for the last cup of tea to melt, he picked up his journal and pencil and scribbled a few lines. His hand was shaking, though, and his fingers ached with the effort. When he read it back, the page was barely legible. He put the pencil down. Pity. It really was too cold to go on.

* * *

The blizzard had gone now, blown out, although the biting cold remained. Scott had slipped away, not long after Bill Wilson had breathed his last. Despite the scabs and cracks on their skin, they looked at peace, the scowls and grimaces that had plagued their last hours on earth gone for ever. Now, there was only Birdie Bowers alive, his own appointment with the great passage over to the other side ticking down.

The times he had shared with the doctor often came back to him during those hours as he tried to ignore the famine clawing at his stomach. He found himself recalling that mad expedition to fetch the penguin eggs in the midst of winter. What had they been thinking? He remembered Cherry's fingers, like ripe plums, as he struggled to get the blubber stove going. Of the boy's disappointment when he broke some of the precious eggs, the goo dripping out of his mittens where he had stored them. The lost tent, the thought they might die in their bags, out in the open, the needle-cold temperatures, the rags of their clothing. Cherry begging Bill to give him morphia, to end it all, and the doctor refusing. Bill, like him, was a Christian and he was glad it hadn't come to that, then or now.

At least their deaths were as God clearly intended. He recalled Bill, at the end of the winter expedition, telling them he could not have hoped for two better companions. Cherry, tears in his eyes, saying the same thing. Poor Bill, and his poor, poor wife Oriana. Then there was Oates's mother, not to mention his own, Emily. And Taff, with Lois, and Norman, Muriel and Ralph. Kathleen and Peter, too. So many hearts yet to be broken.

Could he have spared at least one of those people? When the wind had dropped, Bill had told him that he, Bowers, could make it back to One Ton if he tried. Perhaps he could have. But with the wind in his face when he turned, he doubted if he could have made it back. How could he have abandoned his skipper? And to be the only man out of five to come back, the sole survivor? How would that seem? His place was here, with Scott and Wilson.

Besides, that discussion about him trying for One Ton had been hours ago, perhaps a day or more. The last of his once-formidable strength had almost ebbed. One Ton was beyond him. Birdie Bowers, though, had saved enough for one more task.

By the light of the last, guttering candle, Birdie had read the captain's final entry in his journal. He didn't agree with it all – it seemed cruel to blame poor Taff for any of this – but he couldn't alter it, not really. If he had the fingers he would have written in his own book that Scott was still puzzled and devastated by Taff's collapse; it was so unexpected, so untypical of the big Welshman.

Some would no doubt claim it was because Evans was a seaman, not an officer, perhaps, but that was piffle. Taff Evans, Lashly and Crean were a match for any man on the ice. If only he'd owned up about his cut hand, Bill Wilson might have helped. Too proud, he supposed. Like Oates. They were all too proud; Scott especially, but Birdie Bowers too. His own greed for the Pole had caused him to cast aside his concerns about the wisdom of four on skis and one not, and the division of supplies for five, not four. And the oil, the treacherous oil. He hoped God would forgive him for all his arrogance.

Apart from the suggestion that it was Taff's fault, Scott's was a fine document, one to stir the hearts of every Englishman. Briton, he should say. And he was gratified by the skipper's final appeal for the country to look after those left behind.

But to do its job, to give the Owner's words the power and passion they required, the document needed to be found properly. So he reached over and pulled the sleeping bag down, away from Scott's neck, and exposed his upper body so that he was mostly free of the reindeer sac. Then he pulled and heaved, sliding the dead body upwards, into a half-sitting position. He rested once he was satisfied, till the fire in his lungs and tubes subsided. Then, he carefully took the fallen pencil and slid it into Scott's cold grip. In the other hand, he placed the diary, glad there was still enough flexibility in the waxy fingers so that he appeared to be holding it. He pressed them together as hard as he dare.

Birdie leaned back and admired his work. Yes, it would do the job. Now, Robert Falcon Scott looked as though he had completed the final entry in his journal, that stirring Message to the Public, just before he expired. It was only fair. It had been his expedition, his success and, in the end, his glorious failure. The rest of them were just fellow travellers.

The effort to move the frozen, stiff limbs left him wheezing. Birdie Bowers was, for the first time in his life, drained of all power, an engine with no steam left in the boiler to drive it.

He leaned over and kissed the captain's ravaged cheek, did the same to Bill's forehead. Satisfied with the scene he had constructed, an exhausted Bowers pushed himself down into the bag, leaned against his superior officer's shoulder, and closed his eyes, certain he would wake up with his friends in paradise.

Epilogue

'To strive, to seek, to find, and not to yield'

Tennyson, *Ulysses*

Inscribed on the wooden cross that sits on Observation Hill as a memorial to the five. Chosen by Apsley Cherry-Garrard.

Sandwich, Kent, 1917

It was, in truth, far too blustery for a relaxing walk on the beach, but, after lunch, Kathleen Scott insisted they brave the winter winds. The intense, melancholic little boy that Peter had become stayed behind, painting a decoy duck a livid green. Gran put on his RFC great coat and a scarf given to him in New Zealand when he returned from the ice.

As they stepped outside, the air carried hints of rain. Kathleen sniffed the dampness. 'You know, I always wished I had been with Doodles when I heard the news about Con. I wanted to hug him so. Instead, I sat on a beach in Raratonga, in the drizzle.'

She had been at sea, en route to New Zealand via Tahiti. The message came by radio: 'Captain Scott and six others perished in blizzard after reaching South Pole, January eighteenth.' Not six, of course, as she later confirmed. She had needed all her self-control to carry on. They had assigned her an officer, who shadowed her in case she flung herself overboard. But she had Doodles to think about. Suicide was not an option, just as, in the end, it hadn't been for her husband.

'All those terrible images. I still get them sometimes, of the last few days hauling, broken in body and spirit. Those final ten days in the tent, the blizzard snapping at them. Men fading like wraiths. They don't come as much, thank God.'

527

Gran began to collect pebbles as they walked, looking for smooth, flat ones. It reminded him of yet another puzzle. 'I never understood why they carried on dragging the rocks,' he said, flinging a pebble into the grey sea. 'They were still there on the sledge when we found them.'

'I think because, having lost the Pole, they felt they had to come back with something of value,' suggested Kathleen.

Gran wasn't sure hauling thirty-five pounds of extra weight on those hideous last marches was worth the effort it must have cost them. But he supposed it was only a fraction of their total weight; and whether a sledge moved easily over the surface was more important than dead weight. The stones, with their coal seams and primitive tropical plants, would have pleased Scott and Wilson. That was some consolation.

He spun another pebble and watched it skim. 'Four times,' he announced. 'Not bad.'

'How did you get her to stop?' Kathleen asked.

'Mrs Oates?'

'Yes.'

'My Scandinavian charm?'

'That woman is immune to charm of any nationality, Trigger.'

He didn't mention his letter from Soldier or, indeed, the diary. They had discovered the journal when they had gone looking for his body. There was no sign of Titus, just his sleeping bag and the diary, abandoned by Scott when it was clear Oates wasn't coming back from that blizzard, during the three survivors' last desperate march to within eleven miles of One Ton. With no corpse, the relief party had erected a memorial to Oates, a note stuck to a cross commemorating a brave man.

Gran hadn't read the diary; he gave it to Atkinson to take care of, who eventually handed it to Teddy Evans. Gran often wondered if his story of a misjudged love affair was in there, the one Titus had outlined in that final, sad letter to him when he delivered the flag at Hut Point. How a young Titus Oates had become infatuated with Edie, a low-born Catholic girl who fell pregnant. How Mrs Oates had sent her off to Ireland to have the child and had paid the family for silence. While in the Inniskillings Oates had tried to trace Edie several times without success. Trigger didn't want to share that story with Lady Scott. There was no need; he had another explanation for Caroline's withdrawal from the field.

'I told her that Oates had asked me to ensure that your husband wasn't blamed.'

Kathleen Scott looked puzzled. 'Before he left, you mean? He knew they were going to fail? Even before they started the journey?'

Lady Scott clung to the belief, expressed by her husband, that Taff Evans and Oates, by faltering as they had, had helped contribute to the catastrophe. 'Not at all. He was sure they would make the Pole. Do you believe in dreams, Lady Scott?'

She started to laugh but realised the Norwegian was serious. 'In what way?'

'We spent a long time talking about dreams and premonitions that winter, waiting to go out and search the barrier for Scott and the others.' It had seemed interminable, those bleak months of darkness that prevented them launching the hunt for the polar party. There was also the question of Campbell's northern party, who had been marooned somewhere on the ice all winter. Who to look for first? Scott, who was surely dead, or Campbell, who might be alive but on his last legs?

The vote was unanimous, if riven with guilt at the choice. Find Scott.

They had finally begun a serious search on 29 October and found the bodies on 12 November. At the tent, before they collapsed it and made a cairn, Atkinson had read Scott's journal out loud and they had pieced together the terrible fate that had befallen the five.

'What exactly did you dream?' Kathleen prompted him. She had seen all too often how polar men seemed to drift away from reality, their gaze suddenly ill focused, their minds, and sometimes bodies, back on the ice.

'I dreamed Amundsen had made the Pole on the very day he did. I have witnesses. People I told.'

'Well, that could be coincidence. It was on your mind. And you are Norwegian. Perhaps it was wishful thinking.'

'Lady Scott! I did not wish my skipper to be beaten.'

The vehemence surprised her. 'No, of course not.' Even Nansen had been ambivalent about Amundsen's victory. For most Norwegians it was a tainted prize and Amundsen had not become the hero he had anticipated he would be. One of his crew, who had been denied a place in the final five, had even shot himself upon his return: Hjalmar Johansen, a great ice man by all accounts, who had saved Nansen's life in the North. Fridtjof had told her that Amundsen was already disillusioned, that the South Pole had not secured him the place in history he had imagined for himself, that perhaps posterity would judge the real victors to be the men who had died.

'Then you have to believe this, because I swear it is so. On the night of St Patrick's Day, I dreamed I met Titus. Out on the barrier, in a blizzard. He was all spent, in a bad way, with no boots on. I remembered that clearly. No boots. I held him in my arms. He told me it wasn't Captain Scott's fault, that it was damned bad luck, that is all. His head was in my lap when he died. He said he was looking forward to being warm again.' Again, he neglected to mention one salient fact: Trigger had been drunk on Tom Crean's beer when he dreamed this scene. There was no use in muddying the waters.

Kathleen Scott shook her head, not trusting her ears. 'Is that all he said?'

'Yes.' Although that wasn't quite true; in his dream Titus had talked about Edie at the end, wondering if she had given birth to a boy or a girl.

'And you believe this?'

'Yes.'

'That's why you were so distant when they found the bodies?'

'I suppose so. I had dreamed of Soldier alone in the snow, wandering around, lost, without his finnesko. On reading the journal of Captain Scott, I realised that was exactly how it happened.'

Kathleen thought this all superstitious nonsense. She did not give any credence to premonitions. 'Well, whatever the reason for

Mrs Oates stopping her demands for an inquiry and withdrawing her co-operation for the book, I am grateful to you, Tryggve.'

The wind was strengthening, threatening Lady Scott's hat, and they turned back for her cottage as a mixture of sea spray and drizzle was flung at them. 'There are days when I can't believe he has gone. I imagine him coming home, safe from the Pole, Peter running to greet him. How different life would have been.'

Perhaps, thought Gran. Or perhaps it would only have delayed the inevitable. The Captain Scott he knew would have volunteered for a warship as soon as the conflict broke out. He might still have died, one of the fourteen ships lost at Jutland, perhaps – Harry Pennell, master of the *Terra Nova* on her New Zealand voyages, had died there – or sunk by a submarine. Or he might have become a naval hero, he supposed, like Teddy Evans at Dover. There was no telling.

'You know, Lady Scott, I have talked to a lot of polar explorers in my time. Been there myself. There is something odd.'

'About what?'

'Your husband's diary.'

'Go on.' Her voice was as frosty as the ice cap itself.

'Those blizzards from the pole – katabatic winds, they call them – they never last ten days. Four, perhaps five.'

'You think he was lying?' she snapped.

'I don't know. I mean, there was a blizzard, of that I am sure. Cherry was trapped in one at the camp. But did it last to the very end? If Captain Scott couldn't go on, would Wilson and Bowers have left him?'

Kathleen Scott glared at him, suspecting a slight. 'What are you getting at?'

That the diary is not to be trusted. That nobody knows what happened in that tent. Did Scott really die last? Bowers was the stronger by far. Gran suspected he could have made One Ton if he had pressed on alone. But making it back to the tent, with a southerly in his face, would not have been so easy. And would he have abandoned his captain? No, not Birdie Bowers.

However, he could tell it was best not to dwell too much on

this with the widow. There was a version that she had chosen to believe and she would hate anyone who tried to disabuse her of it. He decided to backtrack. 'That, despite all the talk of dogs and horses, depots and man-hauling, in the end they really were unlucky. To have such an unusual storm pin them down. Ten days, that is bad luck in spades.'

'Oh. I see. Yes.'

He could see relief on her face and he felt some pity. She was going to have to live with those three dying men in their tent for the rest of her days. 'Blame the weather,' he said softly. 'Not the man.'

'I am sure you are right.'

Perhaps not right but, politically and emotionally, it was the correct interpretation. Personally, Gran thought they died of thirst; with no fuel to melt snow, dehydration would have taken them far faster than the lack of food. But it hardly mattered now. They had died, that was the one incontestable fact. 'You know, there are days when I can't believe we did what we did. Sailing to the bottom of the world and living down there for all that time. Or what those brave men achieved.'

'Brave?'

'Oh yes. Brave. When we found them Cherry said he didn't realise how much courage your husband had till that moment. He wasn't perfect.' Gran laughed, thinking of the times Scott had berated him for his imagined idleness, of his fury at Atch's foot or Teddy Evans's slackness. 'But we can't take that away from him.'

'A good death, you mean.'

Gran shook his head. 'No, Kathleen, a good life.'

She sniffed away a tear. When Lady Scott spoke, her voice was low and her gaze direct, as if, this time, she really wanted to hear the truth. 'In the end, wasn't it all just a terrible waste? Did they really achieve anything, Trigger?'

'Yes they did.' Gran stopped and fixed her, so Kathleen could be sure he wasn't being flippant or evasive. 'Amundsen won the Pole. But Scott, he achieved immortality.'

Appendix One

In the final days, Scott wrote letters to his widow (an edited version of which is used here), Wilson's and Bowers's mothers, J. M. Barrie, his own mother, and several others. There was also a general letter to the British people, which sought to explain – or offer excuses, depending on your perspective – the cause of the calamity that befell the expedition. It is undated.

Message to the Public

The causes of this disaster are not due to faulty organisation, but to misfortune in all risks which had to be undertaken.

1. The loss of pony transport in March 1911 obliged me to start later than I had intended, and obliged the limits of stuff transported to be narrowed.
2. The weather throughout the outward journey, and especially the long gale in 83 degrees S, stopped us.
3. The soft snow in the lower reaches of the glacier again reduced pace.

We fought every one of these untoward events with a will and conquered, but it cut into our provision reserve.

* * *

Every detail of our food supplies, clothing and depots made on the interior ice-sheet and over that long stretch of seven hundred miles to the Pole and back, worked out to perfection. The advance party would have returned to the glacier in fine form and with surplus of food, but for the astonishing failure of the man whom we had least expected to fail. Edgar Evans was thought the strongest man of the party.

The Beardmore Glacier is not difficult in fine weather but on our return we did not get a single completely fine day; this with a sick companion enormously increased our anxieties.

As I have said elsewhere, we got into frightfully rough ice and Edgar Evans received a concussion of the brain – he died a natural death, but left us a shaken party with the season unduly advanced.

But all the facts above enumerated were as nothing to the surprise, which awaited us on the barrier. I maintain that our arrangements for returning were quite adequate, and that no one in the world would have expected the temperatures and surfaces which we encountered at this time of year. On the summit in lat. 85/86 degrees we had -20, -30. On the barrier in lat. 82 degrees, ten thousand feet lower, we had -30 in the day, -47 at night pretty regularly, with continuous headwind during our day marches. It is clear that these circumstances come on very suddenly, and our wreck is certainly due to this sudden advent of severe weather, which does not seem to have any satisfactory cause. I do not think human beings ever came through such a month as we have come through, and we should have got through in spite of this weather but for the sickening of a second companion, Captain Oates, and a shortage of fuel in our depots for which I cannot account, and, finally, but for the storm which has fallen on us within eleven miles of the depot at which we hoped to secure our final supplies. Surely misfortune could scarcely have exceeded this last blow. We arrived within eleven miles of our old One Ton Camp with fuel for one last meal and food for two days. For four days we have been unable to leave the tent – the gale howling around us. We are weak, writing is difficult, but for my own sake I do not regret this journey, which has shown that Englishmen can endure hardships, help one another, and meet death with as great a fortitude as ever in the past. We took risks, we knew we took them; things have come out against us, and therefore we have no cause for complaint, but bow to the will of Providence, determined still to do our best to the last. But if we have been willing to give our lives to this enterprise, which is for the honour of our country, I appeal to our countrymen to see that those who depend on us are properly cared for.

Had we lived, I should have a tale to tell of the hardihood, endurance and the courage of my companions which would have stirred the heart of every Englishman. These rough notes and our dead bodies must tell the tale, but surely, surely, a great rich country like ours will see that those who are dependent on us are properly provided for.

R. Scott

Appendix Two

Afterwards . . .

There are those who claim Captain Scott was not a good judge of character. Yet the subsequent achievements of those involved in his expedition, some of whom are listed below, suggests he put together a remarkable group of men.

EDWARD 'ATCH' ATKINSON was the leader of the search party for Scott. He served as a surgeon commander in the First World War, picking up a Distinguished Service Order (DSO) and the Albert Medal. He was badly burned and partially blinded when his ship was torpedoed in Dover harbour (by his own side: it had caught fire and they thought the magazine might go up), earning his AM by tending the sick when badly injured himself. After a miserable few years following the death of his wife, he remarried but died suddenly on his way home from India in 1928 and was buried at sea.

VICTOR CAMPBELL was the man who kept the stranded six-man Northern Party together and alive and shepherded them home after appalling privations. A shy man, he let Raymond Priestley do most of the talking upon their return home. During the First World War, he fought as Commander of the Drake Battalion in Gallipoli and in the Dardanelles, where he received the DSO, in the Battle of Jutland and took part in the Zeebrugge raid on board HMS *Warwick* in 1918. Campbell served in the Dover Patrol and sank a U-boat by ramming it, for which he was awarded the bar to his DSO and later an OBE. He emigrated to Newfoundland in 1923 and died there in 1956.

APSLEY CHERRY-GARRARD served in the First World War but was invalided home. He died in 1959, still haunted by what would have happened had he moved beyond One Ton with the dogs. However, his true legacy is one of the finest works in polar literature because, with the encouragement of George Bernard Shaw, he wrote the classic *Worst Journey in the World* (1922), which looked at the winter expedition and Scott. He was very generous about Scott, although it is not a hagiography (he and Kathleen disagreed about his portrayal of Con). He later revised his opinion of Scott somewhat; he was also very critical of Teddy Evans. His later years were blighted with ill health and episodes of depression and an obsession with the expedition, although he did find solace in a happy marriage to a younger woman, Angela, and long sea voyages. Sara Wheeler's moving biography of him (see below) is well worth reading.

THOMAS CREAN was also awarded the Albert Medal. Crean was ready to serve in the RN, but was allowed to go on Shackleton's doomed *Endurance* expedition. It was Crean whom Shackleton took in the open boat when they rowed for seventeen days to get help for the men stranded on Elephant Island. In later life, he opened a pub in Annascaul called the South Pole Inn and died of a burst appendix in 1938, just shy of his sixty-first birthday. There is an excellent one-man play about him, called *Tom Crean, Antarctic Explorer* written and performed by Aidan Dooley.

FRANK DEBENHAM served in France and Greece as a major, till he was invalided out in 1916. The Australian founded the Scott Polar Research Institute in Cambridge and became a Professor of Geology at the university there. He taught navigation to cadets during the Second World War. Hugely popular with under-graduates, 'Deb' inspired new generations of polar explorers until his death in 1965.

EDWARD 'TEDDY' EVANS had a good war, being promoted to captain and earning the DSO in an action off Dover. In 1945, he was made a baron, becoming Lord Mountevans of the *Broke* and a full admiral the following year. He died in 1957. He is some-thing of a controversial figure, with several members of the party (Cherry and Wright) disliking him, although Oates got on well with him and he was certainly the life and soul of the wardroom. According to Sara Wheeler, when the expedition was deciding what to do about the legacy of Scott, Evans wanted to take out the mention of oil shortages from Scott's Message to the Public. Now why would he want to do that?

TRYGGVE GRAN survived the war as an air ace with seventeen credited kills. In fact, he claimed to have shot down Hermann Goering in 1917. They later became friends, which led Gran to some unfortunate political choices (allowing the Quisling govern-ment to issue commemorative stamps of one of his pioneering flights). Later on, he was rehabilitated and celebrated for his achievements. His polar diaries, when subsequently published, demonstrated a belief in premonitions and dreams. (He did dream that Amundsen reached the Pole on 14 December, although the letter Scott found was dated 16 December, and the Norwegians had already been in the vicinity for several days when it was written). He died in 1980, the last survivor of the expedition.

STOKER WILLIAM LASHLY was awarded the Albert Medal for his efforts in getting Teddy Evans back alive. He survived the sinking of his ship in the Dardanelles and served in the navy for the entire war. He died in 1940.

CECIL HENRY MEARES was the dog driver who felt under-used by Scott. He represents another 'if' in the story: what if he hadn't gone home on *Terra Nova*, and stayed to drive the dogs to One Ton, rather than the inexperienced Cherry? He served in the RFC and the newly formed RAF in the First World War, ending as a lieutenant colonel. He died in 1937, aged 60.

HARRY PENNELL, inevitably known as Penelope, was the navigator who took charge of *Terra Nova*, moving her back and forth to New Zealand. A man of incredible energy, he was very well liked by all, but especially by Bowers and Cherry. He served in the RN and was killed at the Battle of Jutland on 31 May 1916.

HERBERT PONTING. The photographer's story is a sad one. Ponco never felt he received the monies he deserved from the expedition and a series of failed investments and silly schemes (he created a line of soft-toy Adelie penguins called Poncos) left him very bitter. He died in 1935, at the age of 65, in relative poverty, but his Antarctic photographs remain a rich, astonishing achievement.

RAYMOND PRIESTLEY had served as a geologist on the *Nimrod* with Shackleton. In the First World War he served with the Royal Engineers on wireless communications, gaining a Military Cross. He became vice-chancellor of Melbourne and Birmingham universities and co-founded the Scott Polar Research Institute with Frank Debenham. He died in 1972.

KATHLEEN SCOTT created several memorials to her husband after his death. One is in Waterloo Place, London, and a second in Christchurch, New Zealand. The other is called Youth and stands outside the Scott Polar Research Institute in Cambridge. The model for this naked figure was A. W. Lawrence, brother of T. E., aka Lawrence of Arabia. She did have a one-sided infatuation with TEL, but, of course, it came to nothing. She married Edward Hilton Young, a politician, in 1922 and became Baroness Kennet when he was ennobled in 1935. She died in 1947. Her son Peter Scott served in the Royal Navy in the Second World War, winning the DSC (Distinguished Service

Cross) for bravery. He became a distinguished naturalist and ornithologist, creating the Slimbridge Wildfowl and Wetlands Trust. He died in 1989.

GEORGE 'SUNNY JIM' SIMPSON became director of the UK Meteorological Office (1920–38) and was president of the Royal Meteorological Society (1940–42). Scott described him as 'Admirable as a worker, admirable as a scientist and admirable as a lecturer'. He also laid the groundwork that, decades later, Susan Solomon would build upon to prove that Scott's really was 'The Coldest March'. Simpson said of Scott: 'He was the truest of scientists, a seeker of understanding and not of status.'

THOMAS GRIFFITH TAYLOR was London born but Australia raised. He became a distinguished (and often controversial, thanks to his views on population) professor of geography at the universities of Chicago and Toronto. He died in 1963, aged 73.

CHARLES 'SILAS' WRIGHT worked on wireless technology during the First World War and was awarded the OBE. We should be grateful that he wasn't chosen for the polar party, as he so badly wished, because he carried out important work on the development of radar prior to and during the Second World War. Sir Charles, as he became, returned to Canada after the war, then moved to California and served as a physicist in the US Antarctic Research Programme in 1960 and 1965. He died in 1975.

Appendix Three

Conversion of Celsius and Fahrenheit

Celsius	Fahrenheit
-100	-148
-50	-58
-40	-40
-30	-22
-20	-4
-10	14
0	32
5	41
10	50
15	59
20	68
25	77
30	86
35	95
40	104

Or to convert F to C, subtract thirty-two and multiply by five-ninths (i.e. multiply by five then divide by nine).

Author's Note

Death on the Ice is a novel, fiction based on fact. In order to keep the shape of the story, I have sometimes omitted or sidelined various incidents. One I regret is the story of the Northern Party under Victor Campbell. It was dropped off by *Terra Nova*, which later found it impossible to pick them up. The men's survival and gruelling march to safety is another example of incredible polar endurance by half-starved men. It's a story that deserves to be more widely known. Cherry, Wilson and Birdie, of course, had many more escapades on their Cape Crozier winter expedition than related here. See *The Worst Journey in the World* by Cherry, or Sara Wheeler's biography of the man for full details.

I have also moved a few dates (Ponting was attacked by the killer whales much later) but the majority of the episodes here are true. The entries in Scott's journals are more or less verbatim, but some of the letters from Oates to his mother and from Kathleen to Scott have been highly fictionalised. None can be relied upon as an exact replica of the original. This is a novel, after all. The letter from Amundsen to Nansen is based on a translation by Roland Huntford, although it is not an exact duplicate. The notice of the wedding for Captain Scott is extracted from an article in the *Daily Mirror*.

Many others have trodden these icy wastes before me and polar exploration has its own vast literature. I found the following books particularly useful and inspiring, however:

Cherry and *Terra Incognita*, both by Sara Wheeler. One is a biography of Apsley Cherry-Garrard, the other an account of her time in Antarctica, both first rate and highly recommended.

I Am Just Going Outside by Michael Smith. A very well-written, thoroughly researched biography of Captain Oates, with speculation about the child he may have fathered. Again, absolutely recommended. Michael Smith is also the author of *Tom Crean – Antarctic Survivor*, which tells far more about this remarkable man than is revealed here.

Captain Oates – Soldier and Explorer by Sue Limb and Patrick Cordingley. The first, excellent, biography of Oates, now re-issued. Details of the homecoming party were based on material here.

The Norwegian with Scott by Tryggve Gran. Gran's diaries, in which he talks about his dreams, especially the one of Amundsen reaching the Pole on the exact day he did so.

Scott and Amundsen by Roland Huntford. The controversial book that comprehensively debunked Scott, painting him as foolish and incompetent. It also suggests that Nansen and Kathleen had a full-blown affair and that Bowers may have died last. It contains brilliant original research on Amundsen, much of it translated from original Norwegian sources.

Captain Scott by Ranulf Fiennes. The case for the defence by one who has stood in his (snow) shoes.

Scott of the Antarctic by David Crane. A thorough, balanced overview of the life of Scott and the last expedition. The book faces up to Scott's mistakes, but also suggests why men were willing to follow him on to the ice.

Scott's Last Expedition, his journals edited by Max Jones. The complete version (they were edited for publication) with incisive comments by the editor.

The Last Great Quest: Captain Scott's Antarctic Sacrifice by Max Jones. The polar quest skilfully put into a larger context. Includes much fascinating detail on the aftermath and impact of the deaths.

The Coldest March by Susan Solomon. Painstaking research shows that Scott really did have bad luck with the weather.

The Worst Journey in the World by Apsley Cherry-Garrard. One of the Best Travel Books on the Planet.

A Great Task of Happiness by Louisa Young. Fascinating biography of Kathleen Scott by her granddaughter.

I May Be Some Time by Francis Spufford. Subtitled *Ice and the English Imagination*. Attempts to answer the question: why do they do it?

Hell with a Capital H by Katherine Lambert. Engrossing look at the Northern party, led by Campbell, who had their own epic struggle, which they survived.

The Voyage of the Discovery *Vols 1 & 2* by Captain Scott. The journal that upset Shackleton.

The Ice by Stephen J. Pyne. The science and history of Antarctica.

Nimrod by Beau Riffenburgh. Excellent and entertaining account of Shackleton's attempt on the Pole. Also the author of a very good book on Mawson (*Racing With Death*).

I would also like to thank the staff of the Scott Polar Research Institute in Cambridge, especially Heather Lane, Librarian and Keeper of Collections, and archivist Naomi Boneham. The SPRI holds a remarkable archive plus a museum with equipment from the expeditions and a collection of Scott's final letters on display. Well worth a visit (see www.spri.cam.ac.uk). Also worth seeing is Scott's *Discovery* which is now a museum, dry docked in Dundee (see www.rrdiscovery.com). There are excellent guided tours which, combined with the diminutive size of the ship, will only increase your admiration for the pluck and resilience of the polar explorers.

Oates's affair with Edie is fiction, although Michael White (see above), Oates's biographer, is convinced he did have a child in 1900. After his mother died, Oates's Antarctic diary was burned by his sister Violet on the instructions of Caroline. Violet disobeyed, at least partially, copying down key passages before destroying the bulk of it. We can only guess what else was in it.

There is a museum dedicated to Oates at Gilbert White's House in Selborne, Hampshire, that has many of his and the family's letters and artifacts. See www.gilbertwhiteshouse.org.uk. I would like to thank Oates's biographer Sue Limb (see bibliography above) for agreeing to read an early draft of the novel and for her suggestions. All the liberties taken with the story are mine, and mine alone.

I am particularly indebted to Louisa Young (Kathleen's grand-daughter) for also agreeing to meet with me and to read the book. She accepted that I was playing fast and loose with her family history with grace and understanding. I am also grateful to Roland Huntford for his help and advice. Equally, as always, the novel owes much to Martin Fletcher and to Jo Stansall at Headline and to David Miller and Susan d'Arcy. Thanks to them all.

The controversy about Scott and his methods continue. There are those who champion Shackleton or Amundsen at the expense of Scott, others who believe he has been maligned over recent years.

There is no doubt he made mistakes and then failed to learn from them (they knew about fuel-creep on the *Discovery* expedition, for example). The story is full of ifs: if he had had healthier horses, more secure cans for the fuel, more dogs, better weather. If Taff Evans hadn't kept his wound from the others, if Oates hadn't been chosen for the polar party or had declined. If Crean or Lashly had been the fifth man. If a sick Teddy Evans had remembered to relay the order that the dogs needed to go further south to Mt Hooper. If Cherry had pushed on; he was only two or three days' dog driving from the tent. This haunted him for the rest of his life. The list goes on and, I suspect, so will the arguments and discussions.

Robert Ryan
London, 2009

ROBERT RYAN

Empire of Sand

The First World War rages in Europe, but intelligence officer Thomas Edward Lawrence has been consigned to the Map Room at GHQ in Cairo. Yet, spurred on by personal tragedy, he is about to unlock a secret that will alter the course of history.

Lawrence is convinced that an Arab revolt is the only way to remove the Ottoman presence and achieve a free Arabia. But through his network of spies, alarming reports reach him of a tribal uprising against the British, orchestrated by infamous German agent Wilhelm Wassmuss. Hostages have been taken and the War Office in London immediately despatch government assassin Captain Harold Quinn to Cairo on a deadly mission.

With a shared purpose, Quinn and Lawrence begin the hazardous journey to the deserts of Persia. They soon discover that their German nemesis is an experienced master of stealth and deception. But has he finally met his match when he confronts the shrewd and resourceful tactician, Lawrence of Arabia?

Praise for *EMPIRE OF SAND*:

'Plenty of action, sharp dialogue and swift characterisation. The whole is intelligently structured so that this is absorbing and thoughtful as well as tense and exciting'
Daily Telegraph

978 0 7553 2926 7

headline
review

ROBERT RYAN

The Last Sunrise

1948: INDO-CHINA

Lee Crane is an American pilot flying transport planes
across South-East Asia for the highest bidder. He'll fly
anywhere, carry anything if the money is right. But his
experiences during World War Two still haunt him, and
when he meets a woman from the past, memories of a
time when his innocence was shattered threaten to
ground him.

1941: BURMA

Crane is a young and carefree pilot flying fighter planes
for the notorious Flying Tigers against the Japanese.
He's one of the best pilots in the air. But when he falls for
the charms of a beautiful Anglo-Indian girl, she has a
devastating effect on him. As the war ignites across the
region, Crane is separated from her, and, caught up in a
world of death and corruption, he desperately needs to
return to find his lover, no matter what the cost . . .

Praise for Robert Ryan:

'The flying scenes are brilliantly handled. Ryan's
research is impressive and his atmospheric portrayal of
wartime Burma gives the book the enjoyable feel of an
oriental reworking of *Casablanca*. Bold and successful'
The Sunday Times

'A superbly researched plot . . . and some truly gripping
aerial sequences . . . a ripping yarn of guts, gold and
lethal redheads. Buy it, but don't read it on an aeroplane'
Daily Express

978 0 7553 2190 2

headline
review

ROBERT RYAN

Dying Day

1948: Laura McGill, a beautiful woman in her mid-twenties, is waiting on a street corner in Piccadilly, London, a Cold .32 in her handbag. She is desperate to find out what happened to her sister Diana.

Both were Special Operations Executive (SOE) spies during World War Two. One night in 1944, Diana was flown into occupied France but never returned. Could she still be alive?

Despite attempts by the security services to stop her, Laura travels to Berlin to confront the man who sent her sister on her final mission. But she is about to get caught in the crossfire of a bloody turf war fought between the East and the West for control of the city.

Praise for Robert Ryan:

'The flying scenes are brilliantly handled. Ryan's research is impressive, and his atmospheric portrayal of wartime Burma gives the book the enjoyable feel of an oriental reworking of *Casablanca*' *The Sunday Times*

'Excellent, I cannot recommend it too highly. Robert Ryan writes elegantly and his prose is illuminated by provocative insights and descriptions' *Daily Telegraph*

978 0 7553 2923 6

headline
review

Now you can buy any of these other bestselling
Headline books from your bookshop
or *direct from the publisher*.

FREE P&P AND UK DELIVERY
(Overseas and Ireland £3.50 per book)

TO ORDER SIMPLY CALL THIS NUMBER

01235 400 414

or visit our website: www.headline.co.uk

Prices and availability subject to change without notice.